TO THE LADY BORN

A Medieval Romance

By Kathryn Le Veque

Printed by Dragonblade Publishing in the United States of America

Library of Congress Control Number 2014-019
ISBN 9781494947484

KATHRYN LE VEQUE NOVELS

The Fallen One (De Reyne Domination)
Fragments of Grace (House of St. Hever)
Lord of the Shadows
Queen of Lost Stars (House of St. Hever)

Time Travel Romance: (Saxon Lords of Hage)
The Crusader
Kingdom Come

Lords of Thunder: The de Shera Brotherhood Trilogy
The Thunder Lord
The Thunder Warrior
The Thunder Knight

<u>Contemporary Romance:</u>

Kathlyn Trent/Marcus Burton Series:
Valley of the Shadow
The Eden Factor
Canyon of the Sphinx

The Great Knights of de Moray:
Shield of Kronos

The American Heroes Series:
The Lucius Robe
Fires of Autumn
Evenshade
Sea of Dreams
Purgatory

Highland Warriors of Munro:
The Red Lion
Deep Into Darkness

The House of Ashbourne:
Upon a Midnight Dream

Other Contemporary Romance:
Lady of Heaven
Darkling, I Listen
In the Dreaming Hour

The House of D'Aurilliac:
Valiant Chaos

Sons of Poseidon:
The Immortal Sea

The House of De Nerra:
The Falls of Erith
Vestiges of Valor

<u>Multi-author Collections/Anthologies:</u>
Sirens of the Northern Seas (Viking romance)

The House of De Dere:
Of Love and Legend

<u>Note:</u> All Kathryn's novels are designed to be read as stand-alones, although many have cross-over characters or cross-over family groups. Novels that are grouped together have related characters or family groups.

Series are clearly marked. All series contain the same characters or family groups except the American Heroes Series, which is an anthology with unrelated characters.

There is NO particular chronological order for any of the novels because they can all be read as stand-alones, even the series.

For more information, find it in **A Reader's Guide to the Medieval World of Le Veque.**

TABLE OF CONTENTS

CHAPTER ONE

Hedingham Castle
January, Year of Our Lord 1388

H E WAS COMING.
She knew he was approaching and she knew why. Dear God, she knew and there was nothing she could do to stop him.

He'd been watching her for weeks with a lascivious look to his eye and at sup tonight, he couldn't take his eyes from her. His gaze had made her skin crawl, the dirty fingers of his mind reaching out to touch her. After the meal, he had ordered her to her room under guard and there was no way she could escape. He had her trapped. Heart pounding, tears threatening, it was a struggle not to panic. She knew he was coming for her.

God help me, she thought.

The halls of Hedingham Castle were sturdy and big, the corridors thick and smoky with the haze of greasy torches. The keep of the mighty de Vere family reflected the power of the family and the prominence. But tonight, it reflected the instability of the de Vere future. Troops from Bolingbroke filled the halls and grounds since Robert de Vere's flight to Ireland and to safety to avoid the barons closing in on him. But he left behind his sister, vulnerable to the enemy troops that now manned the battlements. Her punishment was now approaching.

The walls were so thick that she couldn't hear the voices of the guards in the hall. She couldn't hear when he approached, the garrison commander, her jailor, a man as vile as Lucifer and twice as ugly. As she sat huddled on a chair near the fire, fear eating holes in her, she was only aware that the man was upon her when the door rattled and jerked open. Old iron hardware squeaked as the garrison commander slithered into the room.

His brown eyes fixed on her and she met his gaze as bravely as she could. Her green eyes watched him, heart pounding in her ears, as he gave her a lewd grin and quietly closed the door. When he threw the bolt, she knew she was in trouble. Her palms began to sweat and it was a struggle not to scream. But she held her ground, courageously and foolishly, as he approached her. She could tell by the look in his eye that her life, as she had once known it, was over.

He was drunk. She could smell it on his breath from where she sat. When he ordered her to stand and remove her clothing, she refused. Unable to abide disobedience, the garrison commander grabbed her slender wrist and fractured the bones as he yanked her up from the chair and tossed her onto the bed. She tried to scramble off, to run, but she was a small woman against a large man and he didn't care how much he hurt her in the process. He grabbed an ankle and struck her on the side of the head to still her.

As he tore her undergarments to shreds and threw his big, smelly body on top of her, Amalie Leighton Rossington de Vere screamed at the top of her lungs, fighting with every ounce of strength she had to resist. But the garrison commander was too strong and too big; he quickly overwhelmed and trapped her, wedging himself between her supple legs and ramming himself into her virginal body. He grunted with pleasure as she screamed in pain.

The agony went on long into the night. When he wasn't raping her, he was beating her. By the time morning arrived, the garrison commander had raped his captive four times and beat her so badly that her right eye was swollen shut. When dawn arrived, he calmly replaced his clothing and left her chamber as if nothing was amiss. But clearly, a good deal was amiss. In his wake, he left blood and weeping.

A sympathetic guard, a very young man with sisters of his own, made sure the lady was tended and put to bed. When the garrison commander began to speak loudly of his conquest at the nooning meal, the sympathetic guard was sickened into action. Before the day was out, he sent a message to their liege, Henry of Bolingbroke.

Until a reply was received, he took the lady and hid her deep in the tunnels of Hedingham so the garrison commander could not abuse her again. The garrison commander roared and threatened, but no one would tell him where the lady was, mostly because no one knew but the young guard. He kept his mouth shut, praying for a swift reply from Bolingbroke.

Within a few weeks, his prayers were answered; the garrison commander was immediately recalled and another man assigned. All men knew and cheered the new commander, a knight of immense power and reputation, who was both feared and respected. Sir Weston de Royans was a man of supreme talent and strength, newly returned from the siege of Vilnius, a military action supported by Henry of Bolingbroke. Weston had led Henry's armies in their attempts to defend the Duchy of Vilnius, but the battle was still ongoing. It had been for years.

Now, Weston was coming to assume command of mighty Hedingham Castle, stronghold of the Earl of Oxford and the Duke of Ireland. It was no small assignment during this dark and volatile time.

But de Royans wasn't due to assume his position for more than a month, so the sympathetic guard spent the next forty-four days guarding the Lady Amalie against those who would resume where the banished garrison commander left off. Such were the orders of Bolingbroke, and the lady was allowed to heal from her ordeal physically. Mentally, it was another issue altogether.

For the occupants of the castle, including the Lady Amalie, the tides were about to turn with the appearance of Sir Weston de Royans.

CHAPTER TWO

H E WASN'T SIMPLY big; he was a colossal man among men, a Samson among average warriors, and was treated with all due respect. With his cropped blond hair, dark blue eyes and granite-square jaw, Weston de Royans was truly a sight to behold in a land of dark and colorless peasants. He was handsome, powerful, and intelligent, a devastating combination for the feminine palate.

It wasn't so much his size and physical strength that garnered respect from even the mightiest of men; it was also the way he handled himself, his well-spoken and calm manner, his wisdom when all else was chaos. He could pull a man's head off with his bare hands or gut with one stroke of his serrated-edged broadsword most impressively.

Quite simply, Weston was a man of brains as well as brawn. Henry of Bolingbroke had learned to depend heavily on him and had sent him to Hedingham Castle with the caveat that he could, and would, be recalled at any time. But until such time, Weston was needed at the volatile de Vere castle.

It was a cloudy day, threatening snow, as Weston and his column approached the massive de Vere bastion. The destriers were fatigued from a long day's ride across muddy and sometimes rained-soaked roads and the knights astride them were only marginally less fatigued. At the head of the group, Weston's dark blue eyes beheld Hedingham for the first time and his light brows, arched like a bird's wings, lifted.

"So this is Hedingham?" It was a rhetorical question. "I had heard it was a massive structure but surely that description did not do it justice."

His voice was deep, rippling up from his toes and vibrating through the massive muscles. Riding slightly behind him, a big knight with shoulder-length red hair replied.

"My uncle served the Earl of Oxford years ago," he said. "He said that Hedingham has great caverns beneath it."

"I have heard tale that it can hold out indefinitely during a siege." Still another knight, riding behind Weston, spoke up. He was muscular and bald. "I heard a story once that when King John laid siege to this place, they held out for months, eventually throwing fresh fish at John's army to prove that they were not starving."

Weston wriggled his eyebrows. "I would believe that."

The knight with the red hair spurred his charger up beside him. "What is the first order of business, my lord?"

Weston glanced at his second. Sir Heath de Lara came from an old and distinguished family. He was young and capable, trying to make a name for himself in troubled times.

"Gather the troops in the bailey," he said. "I will address them immediately and then we will observe Mass. Then find whoever has been in charge for the past month. I would meet with him privately."

"Sorrell was in charge," Heath replied. "I heard that he killed a de Vere relative and that was why Henry recalled him."

Weston cocked an eyebrow. "Sorrell has the self-control of a rabid dog," he muttered. "He should have never been left in charge of something this important."

"He has good family ties."

"His mother was a Bigod. A good family does not make the man."

Heath fell silent, glancing back to the big, bald knight behind him; the two exchanged glances, wondering what mess they were going to find in Sorrell's wake.

The man had always had a destructive and immoral reputation. Heath, and his counterpart, Sir John Sheffield, had as much tolerance for unscrupulous knights as their liege did. If de Royans had instilled one thing in them, it was the value of virtue in a world where not much of that seemed to exist. Chaste women and honest men were very important to de Royans because that was the code he lived by. Anything else was a lower life form and unworthy of his respect.

The two hundred man army passed through the small village that surrounded the castle. The road was muddy and uneven, and peasants scampered to get out of the way of the incoming army.

Being February, it was colder than usual. As the column passed through the town, snow flurries began to fall. They clung to Weston's blond eyelashes as he led his column through the muddy, dirty town and to the powerful castle on the north end of the village. He could see Hedingham's mighty keep rising four stories to the sky, a truly enormous structure made from pale stone.

Crossing the great iron and wood bridge that hovered above a ditch surrounding the castle, they were admitted through the gates and into the outer bailey beyond. The ground was frozen and the snow flurries were building up on the roofs of the outbuildings. The stables and all other structures were in the outer bailey except for the keep. The keep sat perched atop a giant motte surrounded by its own walls.

Weston took the army to the stables, dismounted, and sent his men about their duties. Eight days traveling in inclement weather had the men anxious to settle down and find some warmth. Weston paused for a moment as he gathered his bags from his charger, gazing up at the keep that was truly an impressive Norman structure.

Off to his left he could see a small lake surrounded by bushes and trees, suspecting that the pond was the fresh fish supply that John had been speaking of. As men and horses disbanded around him, he brushed the snow off his raised visor and began to walk.

He would eventually make his way into the keep but, at the moment, he wanted to see the size and details of his garrison. His analytical mind absorbed the size of the lower bailey, the capacity of the stables, and the outbuildings that housed the smithy and the tanner.

Weston digested the size of the keep, the slope of the motte and the strength of the walls. Nothing escaped his detailed examination as he made his way along the eastern edge of the outer bailey. To the right was the small lake and he headed in that direction to take a look.

The snow was beginning to fall harder now, sticking to the ground in a white dusting. Weston's massive boots made equally massive footprints as he moved through the brush that bordered the lake, gazing out over the half-frozen pond. He actually found it very peaceful and lush, this little lake, and he liked it a great deal. With the gray skies above and the white-dusted foliage, it was surreal and calm. He could imagine it in the summertime when the grass was green and the bugs danced along the surface. He wondered if he'd have the opportunity to see it.

Wiping the snow off his enormous shoulders, he was in the process of turning for the keep when something caught his attention. He could see a woman several yards away, dressed in a dark and heavy cloak that covered part of her face.

The woman was partially hidden by the snowy brush but he could see that she was of petite stature. She apparently didn't notice him because she didn't look up or give him any indication that she was aware of his presence. She was staring at the lake. Not interested beyond a cursory glance, he was turning to resume his path to the keep when the woman suddenly tossed off the woolen cloak.

Weston came to a halt as his gaze beheld the lady. The cloak had concealed a woman of unearthly beauty with long, silken blond hair to her buttocks and a body with full breasts and a slender torso beneath a simple linen surcoat. Once the woman's cloak came off, it was apparent that she was poorly dressed for the elements. Weston could see the outline of her torso and buttocks through the thin fabric; luscious features that caused him to move in for a closer look.

He moved to within several feet of her, stealthily, his dark blue gaze fixated on her. As delicious as her body was, it was her facial features that had his interest. He could see a pert little nose and rosebud lips set within a porcelain-like face. Even at this distance, he could see that she was an exquisite creature. As he paused amongst the trees and watched, captivated, the woman looked up to the sky, her eyes blinking rapidly as snow crystals fell against them. She seemed to look at the sky for quite some time, perhaps praying; he could not be sure. All he knew was that he had never seen such a beautiful woman.

He didn't even stop to think why she pulled off her cloak in this frigid weather. He was so focused on her lovely face that he was caught off guard when she plunged into the pond.

CHAPTER THREE

STARTLED, WESTON BURST through the brush as the woman's blond head went under the water. His first instinct was to go in after her but he knew, with his armor, he would sink straight to the bottom and drown.

He began shouting for his men as he yanked off his helm and tossed it to the ground, followed by his tunic. Pieces of plate armor began flying off and he broke several fastens in his attempt to quickly remove it. By the time he reached his hauberk, Heath was by his side and Weston bellowed at the man to pull on his mail. Heath, confused and concerned, did as he was told as Weston bent over at the waist and extended his arms. Heath pulled the mail coat off smoothly, leaving Weston clad in his heavy tunics, hose and boots.

Weston was still overdressed but couldn't waste more time removing the rest of his clothing. Time was passing and the lady's life was draining away the longer he delayed. As Heath watched in shock, Weston dove into the half-frozen pond and disappeared beneath the surface. John joined Heath at the water's edge, along with several men-at-arms, and they watched with apprehension as the ripples in the pond stilled and the surface began to smooth over. There was no sign of Weston and John turned to Heath, his round face full of horror.

"What happened?" he demanded. "Where is he?"

Heath, his brown eyes full of concern, pointed to the water. "Under there."

"Why?"

Heath shook his head. "I do not know." He pulled off his helmet when, seconds later, Weston had not reappeared. "He must need help."

Heath began to rip his tunic and plate armor off, falling over when he lost his balance in the process. John, unwilling to wait to disrobe, was already walking into the pond. He had no idea what had happened to Weston other than he was underwater and he was terrified that Weston was drowning. Before he could get too far, Heath grabbed him and yanked him back onto the snowy shore.

"No," he roared. "You fat ox, you'll sink to the bottom with all of that steel on your body. Think, you idiot!"

Anger added to the mix as John shoved at Heath, sending the man toppling over into the frigid water. Just as Heath righted himself and balled a fist to shove into John's face, Weston abruptly broke the surface of the water. But he wasn't alone.

"Take her!" he bellowed.

He was lifting a woman up in his enormous arms, keeping her head out of the water. Heath thrust himself forward, grabbing the lady from his liege as Weston struggled to move. His limbs were nearly frozen and he was having great difficulty moving his arms and legs. Heath, mired down in mud that had his boots wedged in, handed the lady off to John who managed to climb out of the lake with the limp lady in his arms.

"Blankets!" Weston roared as Heath reached out to help him. "Get blankets and wrap her up before she freezes to death."

The men-at-arms went on the run as John grabbed the nearest dry piece of clothing he could find, Heath's tunic, and struggled to wrap the lady up in it. His hands were freezing, too. Meanwhile, Heath pulled his half-frozen liege out of the pond.

Steam rose into the air from Weston's enormous body as he gave off heat against the frigid air temperature. He stumbled out of the pond and over to John, who had managed to wrap the woman up tightly in the heavy woolen tunic bearing the blue and yellow colors of Boling-broke. A couple of the men-at-arms suddenly burst through the snowy bramble; one had a giant horse blanket and the other one had a woolen tarp. Weston grabbed the horse blanket.

"Pick her up," he commanded John.

The knight obeyed, collecting the woman into his arms as Weston took the dusty horse blanket and wrapped the lady up in it. Nearly frozen himself, he didn't react when Heath tossed the woolen tarp over his shoulders; he was more concerned about the lady. Her face was gray, eyes closed, and he cocked an ear over her mouth to see if she was even breathing. After several long seconds, he could feel faint breath, hot and sweet, against his ear.

Exhausted, freezing, he began to stumble towards the keep with the lady in his arms.

"Go to the keep and tell them to fill a tub with warm water," he commanded his men, his blue lips quivering against the cold. "Find out if they know who she is."

Heath bolted towards the keep while John stayed with Weston, carrying the precious cargo towards the towering keep of Hedingham. They made quite a procession marching through the increasing snow, struggling along the slippery path up the motte before finally mounting the snowy, slippery, wooden staircase that led to the second floor level. It was the entry level and a blast of stale, heated air hit Weston in the face the moment he entered the door.

A cavernous hall opened up before him, two stories tall. Great Norman arches lined the hall as they supported a minstrel gallery on the second floor above. Weston charged into the room as servants began to rush towards him. Somewhere in the middle of it, Heath was shouting orders to the servants who were overwhelmed with what was happening. Two older women, both in tight wimples that nearly strangled them, pushed forward in the midst of the chaos.

"Lady Amalie!" one woman cried, reaching out to touch the pale, gray face. Feeling that it was like ice, she drew her hand back in shock. "She is dead!"

Weston pushed through them even though he had no idea where he was going. "She is not dead," he snapped. "I ordered a hot tub. Where is it?"

The other servant woman began pointing towards the alcove that housed the narrow spiral stairs. "This way, m'lord." She was practically jumping up and down as she attempted to lead the way. "Bring her this way."

Weston charged after the woman with Heath, John and two men-at-arms following him. The group entered the small, dark alcove and he followed the serving woman up the slippery, narrow steps, trying not to smack the unconscious lady's head on the wall in the process. With his bulk, stairs such as this were difficult enough without the added awkwardness of carrying a limp body.

It wasn't an easy trip. The third floor contained the minstrel gallery so they were forced to take the treacherous stairs to the fourth floor of the keep. They spilled out into a small corridor that had two doors; one immediately to the left and one further down the hall. The flighty servant indicated the far door and Weston proceeded in.

The room was spacious and warm, with a roaring fire in the hearth and furs on the bed and cold wood floor. It was a room that suggested the wealth of the de Veres, something not lost on Weston. He paused in the middle of the room as several servants hurriedly finished filling a big, copper tub near the hearth.

It was only partially filled with steaming water but Weston didn't want to wait. He lay the lady down on the big, fur-covered bed and began unwinding her from the horse blanket and tunic.

"Who is this?" he demanded from the serving women assisting him.

The younger of the pair, a woman with crinkled skin and missing teeth, spoke as she unwound the horse blanket from the lady's feet.

"The Lady Amalie de Vere," she told him. "She is the earl's sister."

Weston pulled the horse blanket free and tossed it back to one of his men-at-arms. His gaze moved to the unconscious woman's features, puzzlement registering on his face. She was absolutely exquisite, even gray and wet. Her face was sweet, with a gently pouting mouth and long-lashed eyes that were closed and still. As he continued to gaze at her, he felt something stir within his heart that he couldn't begin to describe – there was interest there, delight, and utter fascination. But there was also great confusion.

Not wanting to make a fool out of himself by staring at the woman, he pulled off the tunic with the help of the two women.

"She is nearly frozen," he said as he lifted her off the bed and turned for the heated tub. "She must be warmed immediately."

He laid her in the tub as servants continued to pour hot water into the mix. Weston was freezing, too, but at the moment he was more concerned with the lady. His knightly sense of chivalry was more important than his health at the moment but one of the two female servants, the plump one, brushed against him and noticed.

"M'lord." She had a hand on his muscular forearm. "You are nearly frozen yourself."

She began to shout commands to the men who were bringing buckets of water into the room, demanding warmed wine and blankets. Weston tried to wave her off but as he opened his mouth to do so, the lady in the water came alive.

Great gasps came forth and her eyes flew open. She began thrashing violently, as if trying to swim or save her life as the last thing she remembered, the icy grip of the lake, closed in around her. A hand flew up and caught Weston in the mouth, driving his teeth into his lip and bringing blood. Weston put his enormous hands on Amalie's shoulders and tried to steady her.

"You are safe, my lady," he said steadily, trying to break through her haze of fear. "You need not fear. You are safe."

Amalie gradually became lucid, realizing she was in her chamber with a few familiar faces. The haze was clearing yet her panic was not eased; there was so much fear and distress in her heart that nothing could soothe her. Adding to the fear was the square-jawed, enormous man hovering over her that she did not recognize. She began to fight viciously.

"Nay!" she cried, struggling to climb out of the tub. "Leave me alone!"

Weston had her in an iron grip. "Be at ease, my lady," he assured calmly. "No one will hurt you. You are safe."

Her panic was expelling itself in harsh little pants; it was as if she did not understand his words. Weston caught Heath's wide-eyed expression over the top of the lady's head and he jerked his head in the direction of the door, silently ordering the man to vacate. Heath took the hint and ushered the men-at-arms out as he went. The younger of the serving women slammed the door behind the unfamiliar knights, racing back to her position next to the tub as Amalie struggled to climb out.

"Ammy." She put her rough hands on Amalie's face, forcing her to look at her. "Look at me, lamb; you are safe, I promise you. This knight... he brought you here. He rescued you."

Amalie's green eyes were wide on the serving woman but at least she was calming. Weston was relieved. But his relief was short-lived as the woman suddenly began to weep.

"Nay," she breathed, her lovely face crumpling. "Nay... I ... I..."

She dissolved into distraught tears. By this time, she had stopped struggling and Weston removed his big hands from her shoulders when he was sure she wasn't going to bolt from the tub. He stood unsteadily, shaking because he was still soaking wet and nearly frozen, but his gaze never left Amalie and he had no idea why. As the plump servant tried in vain to comfort the lady, the other serving woman went to Weston and gently grabbed a cold elbow.

"Come and stand by the fire, m'lord," she encouraged. "You are nearly frozen. Come and be warmed."

He did as he was told but his eyes remained on the woman in the hot tub, weeping as if her heart was broken. His confusion grew.

"Who is she?"

The servant was trying to wring the water out of his sleeve. "The Lady Amalie de Vere," she said, realizing she wasn't doing any good with his wet clothing. "She is the earl's sister."

He had already been told that and was hoping for more information. Weston regarded the lady with a gentle gaze. He still wasn't sure what he was feeling at the moment because the lady was so overwhelmingly beautiful that he couldn't seem to feel anything other than complete fascination. The serving woman jolted him from his thoughts.

"May I take your wet clothing, m'lord?" she asked. "You must change into something dry before you catch your death of chill."

Weston was still gazing at the weeping lady as he pulled off his wet tunic with the automatic response of a child responding to his mother's command. He handed the woman the heavily-padded tunic, exposing his magnificent torso to the weak light of the room. He was brilliantly muscular with a thick neck and shoulders, enormously big arms and chest. His waist was narrow, disappearing beneath his leather breeches.

But the old serving woman didn't notice; she was more concerned with drying out the sopping tunic. There was a soft knock at the door and one of the male servants appeared with two cups of steaming wine in hand. The old serving woman took them from him and closed the door once more. She handed one of the cups to Weston, which he accepted gratefully.

"What is your name?" he asked the woman.

"Esma, m'lord," the women replied, then indicated her counterpart still kneeling by the tub comforting the sobbing lady. "My sister, Neilie."

Weston sipped the hot wine, still staring at the lady in the tub. "Why would Lady Amalie throw herself into the lake?"

Esma's wrinkled eyes widened with shock. "She... she threw herself into the lake?"

Weston nodded. "I watched her," he said frankly. "She removed her cloak and jumped in. Naturally, I went after her. I could not stand by and watch her drown."

Esma's astonished gaze moved to the lady in the tub. "'Tis not true," she gasped. "You must be mistaken, m'lord."

"I am never mistaken."

The servant didn't argue with him; his statement left no room for doubt. More troubling than that, she believed him. She blinked rapidly as if fighting back tears.

"God help her," she whispered. "My poor little lamb."

Weston looked at the woman. She seemed more saddened than shocked, not particularly surprised. She didn't give him much of an argument on what he had suggested regarding the lady's behavior. His analytical mind began to kick in.

"What do you know about this?" he asked her.

She looked at him, shocked. "I… I would know nothing, m'lord."

He didn't believe her for a minute. Now, she had his full attention. "My name is Sir Weston de Royans," he told her. "I am the new commander of Hedingham. In order for me to command effectively, I must know the truth of what has gone on before my arrival. Do you understand so far?"

Esma looked terrified. "Aye, m'lord."

"How long have you served de Vere?"

"Since before the lady was born, m'lord."

"How old is she?"

"Nineteen years, m'lord."

"Then you know everything that goes on at this place."

She nodded timidly, as if he were trying to trick her with his statement. "My sister and I assist the lady in her chatelaine duties."

"Then you will tell me why she threw herself into that lake."

Esma was torn. She eyed the now-sniffling lady in the tub, watching as her sister forced Amalie to sip at the warmed wine. She didn't want to divulge too much to this knight she did not know but, on the other hand, perhaps in doing so he would understand the fragility of Lady Amalie and treat her accordingly. The man had saved Amalie from a watery grave; perhaps that meant he was better than the last man that had held his position. Esma could only pray.

She moved closer to Weston, wringing her hands nervously. When she spoke, her tone was so soft he could barely hear her.

"I can only tell you what I know, m'lord," she whispered. "The last of Bolingbroke's commanders was a brutal man with no great love for the de Veres. He was personally offended by the earl's flight to Ireland to escape Bolingbroke's wrath and took his frustrations out on Lady Amalie."

Weston was studying the woman intently, seeing the pain ripple across her face as she spoke.

"What did he do?" he asked.

That brought tears to the old woman's eyes and she began wiping at her nose, dragging mucus across her cheek.

"He... he beat her severely one night," she whispered. "He broke her wrist and nearly killed her. After that, one of his men hid Amalie so the commander could not hurt her again. He also sent word to Bolingbroke of the man's actions. Until the commander was recalled by Bolingbroke, we spent weeks hiding Lady Amalie in caverns, holes and tunnels so the commander could not find her. She was living like an animal for weeks."

Weston's gaze moved to the beautiful creature in the tub, now calmly sipping her warmed wine. His gaze moved over her delicate features, the silken blond hair; knowing his predecessor as he did, he could only imagine what the man did to her. As he thought on that, disgust and fury such as he had never known began to surge through his big body.

With the heat of the fire upon him, he actually began to sweat from both the physical heat and the emotion he was feeling. The actions of unchivalrous knights always set his blood to boiling, fiends who hid behind their vows to mask vile actions. Men like that gave decent knights a bad name.

"That still does not explain why she threw herself into the lake," he said quietly. "My predecessor has been gone for weeks. Surely she feels safe now."

Esma looked at Weston with some surprise, wiping at her nose.

"Why should she?" she snapped softly, realizing too late who she was speaking to and demurring accordingly. "When we received word that Bolingbroke was sending a new commander to oversee Hedingham, you can imagine her fear. Perhaps… perhaps she is afraid you will do to her what the other one did."

It made perfect sense. He began to suspect why she had submerged herself in the lake and began to feel a good deal of sorrow as well as some revulsion. He downed the rest of his wine in one swallow and thrust the cup back at Esma.

"Go," he commanded softly. "Take your sister and go."

Startled, Esma began to feel the same desperation she had felt when the previous commander had made the same demand of her once. That was the worst day of her life. She was starting to think she had been too bold in speaking the truth to him; she did not know the man or anything about him. Perhaps she had offended him.

"Please, m'lord," she began to beg, tears in her eyes. "She cannot… you cannot… please do not hurt her. She cannot…"

Weston waved her off. "I will not harm her in any way," he said as he moved towards the tub. "You and your sister will go."

Esma was weeping softly as she scooted to the tub and pulled her sister to her feet. The old serving women clutched at each other, whispering between themselves as Esma pulled her sister to the door. It was apparent that the older woman did not want to leave but Esma forced her through the door. When the women vacated and Weston shut the door behind them, he returned his attention to the tub near the hearth.

His dark blue gaze fell on the back of a blond head, now drying in the heat of the room. Amalie hadn't moved a muscle. She sat in the big copper tub, still dressed in her thin linen surcoat, staring at the surface of the water.

Weston made his way to her, hesitantly, wondering what he was going to say. He was coming to realize that everything they had suspected about Sorrell was the truth and this woman was at the heart of it. Sorrell hadn't killed the de Vere relative as rumored but, as

Weston gazed at the face of the pale woman, he'd probably come close. Before he could speak, her soft voice filled the air.

"Did you fish me out of the pond?" she asked.

He was struck by the tone of her voice – smooth, silky and honey-like. In spite of the serious circumstances, he found it exceedingly delightful.

"Aye," he said quietly. "My name is Weston de Royans. I am the new garrison commander for Hedingham."

Amalie continued to stare at the surface of the tub, her green eyes, usually so beautiful and full of life, now dull with sorrow.

"You should not have done that," she murmured. "I will only do it again."

Weston's brow furrowed and he crouched beside the tub. He could only see her delicate profile as she stared at the water. She wouldn't look at him and he could feel her shrinking from his gaze. Not that he blamed her given her past experience with Bolingbroke men.

"Why?" he finally asked, baffled.

She lifted her face to look at him and Weston felt the physical impact as their eyes met. It was as if her great green eyes swallowed him up, holding him in a trance that he was unable to free himself from. All he could do was stare at her.

"Because I must," she said simply.

He was even more baffled, trying to figure out why she was so determined to harm herself. He should have, at the very least, been disgusted with her weakness. Given what Esma told him, however, and what he knew of Sorrell, he couldn't bring himself to lose respect for the woman. In fact, he felt strongly compelled to ease her mind.

"My lady," he said in his rich, deep voice. "I understand that you have not been treated kindly since your brother fled to Ireland and I will say now that it is a cowardly man who would leave his sister to the clemency of the enemy. But you must understand that I will not behave as my predecessor did. I have no intention of laying a hand on you. Under my command, you will be treated with respect. This I swear."

Amalie stared at him, emotions undulating behind the veil of the green eyes. It was almost as if she could not understand what he was telling her. But the glassy expression began to fade, the one so dull with sorrow, and he could see her lovely features twist with emotion. The great green eyes filled with tears again, spattering like raindrops against her porcelain cheeks.

"Please," she sobbed softly. "Please take your sword… please… will you not do me this one small mercy and end my torment?"

He stared at her, horrified by the suggestion. "I will not," he replied, standing to his considerable height. "Why would you ask such a thing?"

Her weeping grew stronger and she suddenly stood from the warm tub, water sloshing out onto the floor. Stumbling from the tub, she ended up on her knees at Weston's feet. She grabbed his leg, her forehead against his knee.

"Please," she begged him, weeping. "You are a knight. You are sworn to obedience. You must do as I ask."

He looked down upon her blond head, appalled and distressed by the request.

"I will not help you kill yourself." He reached down and grasped her arms. "Get up, now. You are simply overwrought. You need to rest."

He easily lifted her to her feet. She was weak, sobbing and wet, so for lack of a better action, he pulled her over to the fire to warm her up and dry her out. But she struggled against him, slugging at his hands, trying to push him away. Afraid she might try to throw herself in the fire, he tried to stay between her and the open flame.

When her behavior should have disgusted him, all he could feel was great concern. Whatever Sorrell did had seriously damaged the woman and his animosity towards the man increased.

As Amalie struggled and he continued to keep himself between her and the fire, he'd finally had enough. He couldn't stand here and scuffle with her all night. In a bold move, he put his enormous hands on both cheeks and forced her to look at him.

"My lady," Weston's tone was sincere, firm. "I understand you are afraid and I understand that in times past, you were treated with great disregard. But you must understand that this is no longer the case. I am here now and things will be different. You must not despair."

Amalie found herself gazing into a powerfully handsome face and eyes that were hard yet kind. It was an odd combination, one that, for a moment, stilled her raging despondency. Her tears inexplicably began to fade as their gazes locked. For the first time, they were able to get their first real look at each other without all of the snow, terror and chaos.

"Disregard?" she repeated, suddenly sounding very lucid. "Disregard would have been preferable. He used his fists on me as one would on an enemy. He cracked bones in my wrist. He hit me so hard in the face that my eye swelled shut. He did… unspeakable things. Is this what you call disregard, Sir Weston? For, quite clearly, it was more than that."

It was the first coherent statement he'd heard from her, one that had his disgust surging and his heart strangely twisting. She was well spoken and seemingly intelligent.

Weston had been a fully sworn knight at twenty years old and had seen many things in the thirteen years since. But what he was feeling as he gazed into the pale, beautiful face was something beyond compassion. He wasn't sure what it was yet but he knew it was different. Something in that pathetic little face moved him.

"Then I apologize for my misstatement," he said in a low voice. "Now that you have explained things, I do not consider what happened to you mere disregard. But I assure you that it will never happen again."

She held his gaze a moment longer before pulling away, firmly. He had no choice but to drop his hands from her face as she moved towards the fire again.

He bolted forward when she held her hands out against the flames to warm them, afraid she was going to try to jump into it. He still didn't trust her. Amalie saw the swift movement from the corner of her eye and it startled her. When she looked at him, he had his big arm between her torso and the fireplace. When their gazes met, he lifted a dark blond brow.

"Burning is a horrible death, my lady," he told her. "It is not swift or merciful. I would not recommend it."

She just looked at him, holding his gaze a moment, before looking away. "Then what would you recommend from a professional standpoint, of course?"

He couldn't tell if there was humor in that statement but one might have interpreted it that way. There was a funny little lilt to her tone. But he would not be lulled into a false sense of security with her manner, no matter how calm she seemed to be at the moment.

"I would not recommend anything for your purposes," he said. "The church frowns upon the taking of one's life no matter what the circumstances."

"What does the church know of my pain?"

"God knows of it; what God knows, the church knows. You must have faith."

As upset as she was, the knight's manner and words were making some impact. In spite of everything, he was settling her and she had no idea why. Perhaps, it was the fact that he had saved her from drowning herself. Or maybe it was because she saw something in his eyes that ensured honesty. Whatever it was, she could feel herself calming. But it did not erase her sense of hopelessness at her situation.

"Have faith in what?" she asked, her voice soft and hoarse. "I am a prisoner in my own home. When you leave, who is to say that the next commander will not resume where the other one left off? You cannot insure my safety for always."

He eyed her, the gentle slope of her torso as it descended into rounded buttocks, now outlined with the damp and clinging material. He'd never seen finer.

"I can swear to you, on my oath as a knight, that you will be safe from harm as long as I have breath in my body," he told her flatly. "No female under my protection will ever be mistreated, I swear it."

She turned to look at him. Now that she was regaining her senses, she had an opportunity to take a good look at him. It hadn't occurred to her until this moment that he was without clothing from the waist up. He was a tall man but it wasn't his height that was impressive; it was his sheer bulk. He had an enormous neck and shoulders, and his arms were the biggest she had ever seen. His chest was muscular and beautiful, his waist trim. But the sight made her heart race and she wasn't sure why. All she knew was that it made her uncomfortable.

"You will understand if I am dubious of your declaration," she said, moving away from him. "The last knight I came into contact with displayed less than chivalrous behavior."

He watched her move away, shivering even in the radiant heat of the blaze. He wasn't offended by her statement because he understood her point of view.

"Perhaps time will prove my trust, my lady," he said. "But until that time, I would ask one thing."

She glanced at him, now at a safe distance from his delicious, naked torso. "What would that be?"

"That you not make any more attempts to, shall we say, swim in a frozen pond."

She averted her gaze, looking back to the dancing flames. She seemed to get that glassy look again.

"My apologies to have troubled you," she said quietly.

He couldn't help but notice she hadn't given him a direct answer.

"You did not trouble me," he said. "But I have enough on my mind with a new command without the additional worry of the Lady of the Keep condemning herself to a watery grave."

She didn't say anything. He took a step towards her to make sure she heard him. "Lady Amalie?"

She looked up from the fire to notice he was much closer. Instinctively, she flinched and moved away from him. Her hands went up as if to protect herself.

"I will do my best not to cause you additional worry," she assured him quickly.

He could see the panic in her face and he stopped his advance.

"I have faith in the word of a lady," he replied, eyeing her a moment and realizing that she was still quite damp. He indicated her dress. "I will send your serving women in to help you change from those wet garments."

Amalie nodded briefly, watching him with her great green eyes as he collected his wet tunic from the stand near the hearth and proceeded to the door. Weston's eyes lingered on her a moment before quitting the room silently. Even after he was gone, she simply stood there, depression swamping her and her sense of desolation returning full-force. Whatever the knight said, she was sure he was lying. They all lied. They were all animals.

Amalie went to her dresser where, inside a lovely bejeweled chest, lay a delicate dirk that her mother had given her long ago. She collected the weapon, fingering it, feeling the sharp edge and wondering what it was going to feel like when it cut into her chest.

In her opinion, she had no choice. Better to take her life and end her torment than to bring a bastard into the world. That was one little element she had left out of her conversation with de Royans; she couldn't take the shame, more dishonor to be heaped upon the House of de Vere. That was something that men like Weston de Royans could never understand.

When Esma and Neilie came to the chamber several minutes later with food and more wine, Amalie was gone.

CHAPTER FOUR

THE ENORMOUS KEEP of Hedingham was in an uproar; men-at-arms were rounding up the servants and the knights were leading search parties of men, inspecting every nook and cranny. Every fireplace was searched and even the well. But Weston wasn't in the keep; when Esma and Neilie had roused the entire castle with their screams that the lady was missing, he had been in the great hall with his saddlebags, hunting for a dry tunic. Within the first few moments of the screaming, he returned to the pond.

It was an instinctive response. He charged out of the keep with only a dry tunic, breeches and boots on. The snow was coming down in great dumping heaps, piling up around the motte and on the slippery stone stairs that led down to the outer bailey.

He could hear the shouting in the keep as men called to one another in their search for the lady. As he nearly slipped on the last stone step and made his way into the lower bailey, he found that he was actually angry; angry at himself, angry at her for lying to him, angry at the inconvenience. But being a virtuous knight sworn to protect the weak and helpless, he was compelled to find her.

Weston's breath was hanging in the cold air in great foggy puffs as he made his way through the lower bailey towards the pond. The trees and brush surrounding it were now heavy with snowfall and he beat back the snowy branches as he made his way through. Snow ended up on his face, his arms, melting against his body heat and creating big wet stains on his tunic. Just as he neared the edge of the pond, something caught his eye.

It was the familiar figure of the lady, standing by the edge of the pond with her back to him. With all of the snow and weather, she hadn't heard Weston approach. He paused, inspecting her, seeing that she had a small dirk in her left hand but no other weapons that he could ascertain. Just as he finished his assessment, she brought the dirk up and pulled the sharp blade across the milky flesh of her right wrist.

Weston was jolted into action. He burst through the brush and grabbed her from behind by both wrists. Startled from completing her dastardly deed, Amalie screamed in fright, struggling fiercely against him. She was like a wild animal in his grasp, scratching at him and splashing droplets of blood from her cut wrist onto his forearm. As he tried to get the knife from her, she began kicking his legs and knees viciously.

"Nay!" she bellowed. "You will leave me alone! Go away and leave me alone!"

Weston managed to get the dirk from her, tossing it off into the half-frozen pond. That enabled him to get her in a viselike grip without fear of being stabbed. He boxed her up in his enormous arms, pinning her against his chest. He still had hold of her wrists, which meant they were twisted somewhat uncomfortably. But he didn't let go. His face was against the side of her head and he could feel her body tightly wound against him, still struggling with all of the power left in her small body.

"I will not let you kill yourself," he hissed. "Are you so foolish and weak that you believe killing yourself will end your torment? What awaits you in death is far worse than what ails you in life."

When the grunting and screaming died down, the sobs began to come. She was so close to him, tucked up against his chest with her head against his face. Amidst his anger and concern, he couldn't help but think how warm and supple she felt. Her hair, strands of blond so silken that they were as soft as feathers, was splayed on his arms and shoulders. He could smell the faint scent of violets.

It would have been a consuming and wonderful sensation had he not been so bloody furious. As she wept uncontrollably, he squeezed her in his iron grip.

"Do you hear me?" he was less hissing, more of a whisper now. "If you kill yourself, God will punish you for all eternity. Is that what you wish? To know eternal torment because of your weak soul?"

She suddenly came alive. Lifting her head, she butted him in the nose, causing him to see stars. But he kept his grip on her as she struggled to get a hand free to strike him. The wildcat was making a return.

"You know nothing," she spat. "You spout pious words yet you know nothing. Eternal damnation and eternal shame are my only choices; which would you choose, sir knight, or are you too pure to have ever been faced with such sorrow that it would tear away at your very soul?"

He hauled her up in his arms and turned around, beginning the trek back to the keep.

"At least I am not weak enough to try and kill myself," he said. "I have had enough of this behavior, my lady. If you cannot restrain yourself and deal with your demons accordingly, then I shall chain you to the walls of the vault until this madness passes. I will not have your blood on my hands."

She kicked at him, managing to make contact with his kneecap. Without his armor, Weston was vulnerable and he grunted in pain. Shifting his grip yet again, he turned her sideways so her feet were away from his vulnerable knees.

"If that is all you are concerned with, I absolve you," she grunted and twisted. "My actions are my own and you are not accountable."

"I am the commander of Hedingham which means I am, indeed, accountable no matter what you say. Your brother will believe I murdered you."

"My brother is an idiot," she snapped. "He is a self-centered fool and I hate him for leaving me to the mercy of barbarians."

He couldn't argue with her on that point; she was mostly correct.

But he wasn't finished with her yet.

"You will answer me," he commanded in a low, even tone as they began to cross the cold, snowy lower bailey. "I will have your word that you will not make any more attempts on your life or I will lock you in the vault and throw away the key. Is that in any way unclear?"

Amalie was beyond madness at that point; she was exhausted, freezing and wildly emotional. Her struggles increased.

"I do not hold to honor with any Bolingbroke bastard," she hissed. "I will make no such promises to you."

It was strong language, something that deeply displeased him. Instead of taking Amalie back up to her room at the top of Hedingham's towering keep, he trudged across the freezing bailey with her and to the enormous gatehouse which provided the link between the upper and lower baileys.

As Weston carried her across the snowy grounds, Amalie struggled and fought, eventually freeing one her hands and managing to slash him across the face. It was a brutal battle as he entered the gatehouse and was shown the stairs to the vault by a startled guard.

Weston managed to push his way down the narrow stairs with his struggling catch, entering the first of two open cells and, after much struggle, anchoring both of her wrists to heavy, rusty chains against the wall. But she still tried to kick him so he had the guard chain her ankles together. Only when she was completely contained did he take a look at her slit wrist; it was oozing but not life threatening. He ordered the guard to wrap the wrist and secure the lady for the night.

Weston stood back and watched as the guard carried out his command. The lady tried to scratch him, too, when he came close. When the wrist was finally bound with a strip of linen, the guard left the cell under orders to retrieve blankets for the lady's bed and to let Heath know that she had been found.

The guard passed off the torch to Weston, who stood near the open cell door with the heavily-smoking wood in his hand, watching the lady as she settled down out of pure exhaustion.

Amalie could see him from the corner of her eyes, standing there with the only source of heat and light in the vault and wondering what kind of lecture she was about to receive. It was her second attempt and he had caught her again so she was sure there would be some reprimand in that. He would never trust her again; that was for certain. He could have easily left her alone at this point but, for some reason, he lingered.

When he shifted on his big legs, she snapped at him out of pure fatigue. She couldn't take the silence any longer, waiting for the verbal lashing that was undoubtedly to come.

"Now you have chained me as a prize," she muttered. "Go and leave me alone. You need not worry over your reputation tonight, sir knight. I will not damage your good name."

Weston didn't say anything for a few moments. He just stood there. Then, she heard joints popping as he moved over to her, crouching a few feet away. She instinctively flinched when she realized he was close to her again, as if preparing for another go-around. But he didn't move towards her nor did he say a word; he just stared at her. Amalie avoided looking at him until she could no longer stand it.

When their eyes met, bright green against dark blue, she felt a jolt. She found herself studying his face purely out of curiosity, the square cut of his jaw and the dimples carved deep into each cheek. He had full lips and wide-set, murky blue eyes. He was, in truth, excruciatingly handsome if one liked that type. But Amalie would not accept or acknowledge an attraction of any sort, not to any man much less a Bolingbroke knight. After an eternity of staring at each other, she averted her gaze and closed her eyes.

"Do not sit there and stare at me," she whispered. "Go away and leave me alone."

Weston didn't abide by her wishes. He continued to stare at her, as if the sheer force of his gaze could cause him to understand such a woman. But he gleaned no such knowledge. Instead, his intense gaze succeeded in stimulating his interest. She was such an exquisite beauty, a woman of unnatural splendor. He tried to remember if he'd ever heard of Robert de Vere's angelic sister but he couldn't recall if he'd ever heard such a tale. It was a pity; a woman with this magnificence should have her name written in the stars.

"Why?" he finally asked.

He'd asked that question before but the answer had not satisfied him. Now, there had been a second attempt and he truly wanted to understand the motivation behind it. Instead of answering, Amalie simply shook her head faintly and a big tear rolled down one cheek.

Driven by curiosity, by increasing interest, Weston lowered himself to his buttocks on the cold and moldering floor.

"Lady Amalie," he began in his deep, sultry voice. "I realize that the past several weeks have been unstable to stay the least. I know your brother fled to Ireland like a coward, fearful of the barons who oppose the king he so deeply supports. I further realize that you have found yourself the victim of an unscrupulous knight. But I have heard tale of the Lady of Hedingham; what I heard was that she was a lady of magnificent beauty and strong character. Could it be that the rumors referred to you?"

It was a little lie but one that garnered a reaction. Amalie opened her eyes and turned to him, a dubious expression on her face.

"What have you heard about me?" she asked, almost in horror.

His expression was neutral. "Just what I told you. Surely this is not the same lady who has been attempting to end her life?"

She just stared at him before looking away again, closing her eyes. "You would not understand. I do not expect you to."

"I would like to know. I asked you once before but you evidently did not tell me the truth."

Amalie still refused to look at him but her manner turned harsh.

"Why do you wish to know?" she demanded softly. "You do not know me or care for my welfare. You certainly have no obligation to me other than to hold me captive because of my brother's actions. What in the world could you possibly gain by coming to know my mind?"

His brow furrowed. "Because I want to know why such a beautiful woman would think she has no alternative other than to end her life."

She eyed him, then. "Would you show such concern were I not beautiful?"

There was a sudden degree of uncertainty in his expression, as if her question had caught him off guard. "Aye."

She lifted an eyebrow at him. "You would? I wonder."

"Now you insult my integrity."

She sighed heavily and looked away again. "Let us speak plainly, Sir Weston," she said softly. "You have made it clear that your concern in my state has only to do with how you will be viewed by others should I manage to complete the deed. I am your responsibility and should harm befall me, you would be viewed as weak in your ability to protect me even from myself."

He had said that, it was true. But the more he gazed at her, the more it went beyond that simple explanation. He wasn't sure why, or how, only that he could feel it in his chest, something warm and fluid and nearly giddy. It was odd and he wasn't sure he liked it. The lady was, indeed, well-spoken and intelligent as well as beautiful. It was an alluring combination, one that made him forget how disgusting he found her weakness.

"It is true that I said that," he said quietly. "But surely you understand that I cannot simply let you end your life as you please. What kind of man would I be if I simply turned my back and let you drown in that lake?"

"A man who shows mercy."

"Mercy?" he repeated, trying not to raise his voice at the ridiculousness of her statement. "To let you kill yourself is merciful?"

She nodded, closing her eyes as tears coursed down her cheeks. "I am sorry to have troubled you; I truly am," she murmured. "You are involved in something that does not concern you and, for that, I am regretful. But you must let me do what I feel is necessary."

He was genuinely baffled, watching tears drip off her chin and suppressing the urge to wipe them away.

"Can you please tell me why you must do this?" He truly wanted to know. "It is my understanding that Sorrell severely abused you, but it was one time. It was not as if the abuse went on for weeks, day and night. I apologize if my words sound callous but, for an isolated incident in a lifetime that has surely known grace and peace, I fail to see why it is pushing you to the brink of suicide. Perhaps if I understood that, I could help you."

She looked at him with an expression of deep pain and deep indignity. "I have already asked you to help me but you would not do it."

He stiffened slightly. "I will not help you kill yourself."

"Then you cannot help."

Weston wasn't sure what more he could say. His compassion and concern for the woman was deepening. He continued to watch her as she silently wept, noting that her hands were beginning to turn white from being extended above her head and that the wound to her wrist wasn't bleeding badly at all.

He also noticed that she was shivering, something that was growing more pronounced by the moment. Her lips began quivering and turning blue with cold, and her face was unnaturally pale. Now in the icy box of the vault, the cold was seeping into her.

Eventually, she fell asleep out of sheer exhaustion. When the guard came back down the stairs, noisily, Weston rose to his feet and collected the blankets from the man, admonishing him to be quiet. The guard proceeded into the cell with a huge bale of musty hay and tossed it into the corner. Being winter, he brought what he could find as there was no fresh hay available.

As the guard quit the cell, his questioning gaze lingered on the still form of the lady. There was curiosity and some interest there. Weston caught the man's expression and he grabbed the guard by the neck.

"Do you know who I am?" he snarled.

The guard, wide-eyed, nodded. "De Royans, m'lord."

Weston glared at the man for a moment, silently implying his rank and power, before letting him go.

"You will spread the word that Lady Amalie is to remain untouched," he said. "Any infraction, no matter how small, will be lethally met. Is this clear?"

"It is, m'lord."

"Good. Send for some food. I am famished."

"Aye, m'lord."

The guard was gone and Weston turned his attention back to the sleeping prisoner. She looked so pathetic strung up with chains and he was beginning to feel caddish for putting her in such a position.

A gentle knight should have a better way to restrain the lady but all Weston could think of was brute strength. Lady Amalie was determined to harm herself and he was determined not to let her. It would reflect badly upon him. But maybe there was a small part of him that couldn't stand the thought of wasting all that beauty. She had been right – he might not have shown such regard had she not been so incredibly beautiful.

Weston crouched beside her as she slept uncomfortably. He could see that her hands were turning from white to an odd shade of gray and she was shivering uncontrollably. It was freezing in the vault but he didn't particularly notice; a body his size gave off a tremendous amount of heat.

He rose to his feet and made his way outside the cell to the keys hung on a big iron nail near the stairs. Collecting a key, he went back into the cell and very carefully unlocked one of the shackles on Amalie's wrist. He grabbed her arm before it could flop down, gently lowering it and supporting her limp body as he unlocked the other.

Surprisingly, she didn't awaken but he was expecting her to at any moment with the intention of putting his eye out. She remained limp as he gently scooped her up in his powerful arms and took her over to the pile of musty hay that was strewn with dirty blankets.

Weston lay her down upon the dusty blankets, studying her features now that she was at peace. It only served to reinforce his opinion that she was a magnificent beauty. Concern and knightly interest was beginning to transform into something deeper; he could feel it beginning to blossom. When it should have repulsed him, he found that he couldn't muster the strength to resist. He rather liked the feeling he had when he looked at her.

Taking a second dusty blanket, he realized it was very rough and a quick examination showed it to be a horse blanket. It smelled like mold. Making a face of disapproval, he checked the third and last blanket and saw that it was worse than the others. So he took what he had and gently draped it over her, carefully tucking it in around her slender body. He pulled it up over her ears, half-covering her face, hoping she would warm up and calm down now that she was asleep. Maybe the morning would bring a woman returned to her senses.

Weston sank down on his buttocks, hovering at the edge of the hay as he watched the lady sleep. All the while, his mind was whirling with thoughts and ideas on what he was going to do with her should she wake in the morning and resume her attempts to take her life. He honestly couldn't fathom what would drive the woman, or anyone for that matter, to such lengths.

Weston had spent his entire life in some manner of battle or warfare mode, in situations in which he was always attempting to protect his life. To willfully attempt to take one's own life had him troubled; it was against God's command and against the understood code of honor. It was the act of a coward.

Deep down, however, he understood suicide better than most although it was something he pretended didn't exist in his thoughts. Even when the soft river of memory began to flow through his mind, he angrily dammed the flow, unwilling to allow it to flood his mind. But flood it did – before he could stop the tide, he remembered his father, the strong and powerful knight who had taken his own life when Weston's mother had run off with Weston's own grandfather. It was a hideous black mark on the family honor, an honor that had meant a great deal to Weston's father. The man couldn't accept that his wife had left him for his own father.

Weston had been six years old at the time but he still remembered the shock of that dark and horrible night. To think of it again sickened him and he shook his head as if to shake off the terrible memories, struggling to dry up the river of memories. He didn't want to relive it.

Maybe that's why he was baffled by the lady's attempts to take her own life. He'd never understood that kind of torment, something that would drive one to destroy God's greatest gift. He couldn't tolerate weakness, not when he'd dealt with such family drama that he'd spent the past thirteen years struggling to rebuild the good de Royans name.

As he gazed at the shivering and sleeping lady, he knew he wasn't going to let this woman put a blemish on the reputation he'd worked so hard to achieve. He wouldn't let her damage the de Royans' name like his father and grandfather had.

As Weston pondered both the dilemma and his determination, he gradually came to realize that the lady was quivering violently in spite of the blankets. He rather hoped he would be able to leave her at some point and settle himself into Hedingham. But as he watched her shiver and shake, he knew he couldn't just leave her that way. The blankets weren't doing any good and he couldn't build a fire. So he used the next best thing; his substantial body heat.

It was all very practical and innocent. Carefully, he moved his enormous body next to the lady and silently lay down next to her. She was wrapped up in the horse blanket as he settled against her and carefully put his arms around her, pulling her against him.

He could feel her cold face through his tunic so he pulled her tighter, hoping to warm her somewhat. But what he didn't bank on was the fact that he liked the feel of her against him; burrowed in the blanket as she was, there was a significant barrier between their bodies so, in theory, he shouldn't have been able to even feel her. But he did. He wasn't sure how, but he did. And he liked it. Without realizing it, he pulled her closer.

It wasn't much of a movement but it was apparently enough. His pleasant thoughts of the beautiful lady were his last as Amalie opened her eyes and realized that he was holding her in a very intimate position.

Before Weston could draw another breath, Amalie howled with terror and her cold hands shot up through the blanket, emerging somewhere near her neck and catching him right in the face. Weston grunted as his head snapped back and stars burst before his eyes as the lady's fists made contact with his nose.

It was enough of a jolt that he lost his grip on her and she bolted from his arms. As he sat up, wiping the trickle of blood from his nose, he watched in astonishment as Amalie literally tried to climb the walls in her attempt to get away from him. But there was nowhere for her to go so he sat on the straw, watching her try to claw her way out of a stone wall, so much panic in her movements that it was truly an astonishing and horrible sight.

Weston didn't move to comfort her because she was like a wild animal and he knew that any attempts from him would only fuel her panic. So he sat back, silent and still as stone, until she exhausted herself.

Eventually, she crumpled into a corner in a heap of frantic breathing, and that was where she remained until she gradually fell into a fitful sleep. Or perhaps she passed out; Weston couldn't be sure. Either way, Weston didn't even try to cover her with the blanket. He was afraid it would set her off again. So he continued to sit there and watch her, shocked at her behavior. He'd never seen anything like it.

Well after midnight, he left the cell and locked her in, returning through the snowy bailey to the keep where he found Esma and Neilie sleeping in a small alcove in Amalie's dark, warm room. He woke the women, explained the situation, and sent them down to the vault with blankets and furs.

Weston wisely surmised that he was past the point of no return in his attempts to comfort Lady Amalie, so he sent familiar women to her aid. He was genuinely sorry that he'd not been able to ease the situation with Amalie; he sincerely would have liked to. Whatever was on the lady's mind, whatever she was going through, he was unable to make a difference.

But in the same breath, he wasn't about to give up. Perhaps, this was an opportunity to do for her what he couldn't do for his father. Perhaps, he could show her that taking her life was not the answer to her troubles. Perhaps, this was a battle he could win.

He had no idea the confrontation he was in for.

CHAPTER FIVE

H E WAS ALWAYS around.

Five days since Weston de Royans had taken command of Hedingham Castle, Amalie found that she couldn't draw a breath without the man being near to hear it.

Esma and Neilie were always with her, too. She was positive it was because de Royans had commanded it. Although she'd known the women since birth and they were always very conscientious, the lengths they were going to in making sure one or both of them was always by her side were too attentive to not be suspicious.

They were close enough to notice that she wasn't feeling well physically as well as mentally. As the days passed and her health declined, so did the desire to throw herself from the battlements. Amalie had always been a strong and practical woman and her behavior as of late had been uncharacteristic, borne from desperation more than anything else.

The truth was that she didn't want to die, not really. But the sentence she was facing as a result of that horrible night was becoming increasingly apparent, at least to her. More than anything, now she was simply feeling numb. Numb and sick.

The sixth day of de Royans' command, Amalie awoke late into the morning, having spent a restless night with vivid dreams. Burrowed deep in her warm, cozy bed, she opened her eyes to see that the room was fairly light, giving a hint of the late morning hour. It was quiet, bright and peaceful and she lay there a moment, settling her mind. It was like days of old, before the chaos of Bolingbroke. She almost felt happy again as the peace of the morning settled.

Rolling on to her side, she was immediately struck with a wave of nausea and suffered through a few dry heaves. The brief happiness she had felt only moments earlier was gone as reality washed it away. As she lay there, panting and struggling to overcome the nausea, Esma quietly entered the chamber with warm water and other implements in her hands. Amalie covered her face with a pillow so Esma wouldn't see her misery.

Esma saw her lady moving about and immediately set to helping her rise. As she chatted about the fact that the clouds had gone, leaving a bright, white, winter wonderland outside, she pulled back the oilcloth from the windows to allow fresh air and light into the room. Then she went to the wardrobe to select the lady's clothes for the day. It was all Amalie could do to sit up in bed without retching again as the old servant went about her duties and chatted.

Ignoring the woman as she began to pull out garments, Amalie made her way to one of the long lancet windows, gazing out over the brilliant white landscape. She drew in a few deep breaths, clearing her mind and fighting down the nausea. By this time, Esma had her garments and her toilette laid out, and Amalie sat down as she had a thousand times before as Esma prepared her for the day.

Dressed in a heavy, white, lamb's wool sheath and a heavy, soft crimson brocade surcoat, she was warm and fortified against the chill weather. Esma took her long, straight blond hair and brushed it vigorously, bringing out the natural shine and softness. From the nape of her neck, she braided a section of hair into a long rope and wrapped that around Amalie's head a couple of times, pulling her hair away from her face and creating a lovely halo of hair around her head.

Anchoring the braid behind both ears with small tortoise shell hair pins, she rosied-up Amalie's pale complexion by vigorously scrubbing her cheeks with warm water and finely crushed apricot seeds, an old family recipe. Amalie had porcelain skin, soft and smooth, now with a rosy scrubbed appearance. The end result was beautiful.

Depressed and ill-feeling though she might be, Amalie looked like an angel. The façade masked the turmoil beneath and it was the first time she'd allowed herself to be groomed in weeks. Whilst hiding out from Sorrell, she'd lived like an animal in dark rooms and tunnels. There hadn't been any semblance of civility.

With de Royans' appearance, there was no need to cower in the dark. He had promised safety and, since his arrival, he'd delivered. She was starting to emerge from the black and horrific state. But the gnawing fear still lingered.

"Do you feel like sitting in the solar today, m'lady?" Esma asked her as she put away the hair brush and comb in the enormous old wardrobe used by generations of de Vere women; it had carvings of angels scratched into the doors. "You have not worked on the gown you have been preparing for Lady Cecily's wedding. Would you like to work on that today?"

Amalie could tell by the tone of Esma's voice that she was trying to force her back into a sense of normalcy. She appreciated the attempt but was disinclined to show an enthusiastic response. Instead, she sighed faintly.

"I do not believe that shall be necessary," she said quietly. "I am quite sure that I am no longer to be invited to the nuptials. My brother's flight has left me a social outcast."

Esma tried not to agree, even if it was the truth. "But Lady Cecily has been your friend since you were both small girls," she insisted. "She has been adamant that you attend her wedding."

Amalie rose from the stool she had been perched on. "And her father is equally adamant that a disgraced de Vere be excluded." She put her hand on the woman's arm when she opened her mouth to protest. "Have no fear. I shall finish the embroidery on the dress and send it to Cece as my gift. Even if I cannot attend the wedding, I will still send her my love."

Esma smiled sadly, watching Amalie pace towards the lancet window again. "I'll take you down to the solar now, m'lady," she said in a tone that was, hopefully, encouraging Amalie to leave her chamber.

"Neilie and I will bring your meal to you."

Amalie waved her off. "Nay," she shook her head. "No food; not right now. I think... I think I might like to take a walk. The sun is shining and the land is wintery white. 'Tis quite lovely outside."

Esma murmured softly, "You always did like the snow, Ammy."

Amalie cast a glance at the woman, grinning weakly at the sound of her nickname that had been given to her at a young age. It made her feel safe and comforted in troubled times. It brought back memories of days when her life had been carefree and easy.

"Where is Owyn?" she asked. "He can escort me for my walk."

She spoke of the young soldier who had risked his life to protect her from Sorrell. He was the only man she trusted, de Royans included. But Esma shrugged her shoulders.

"I've not seen him in a few days, m'lady," she said. "But I will send someone to find him."

Amalie came away from the window. "Nay," she said pointedly. "You find him."

Esma was torn; de Royans had given her strict orders never to leave the lady alone. "Forgive me, m'lady," she suddenly rubbed at her knee. "My old knees have been paining me. It would be faster if I sent someone else to find Owyn."

Amalie wasn't fooled. She lifted her hand as if to ease the woman's mind. "Have no fear, Es," she said softly. "I will be fine. Please do as I ask."

"But..."

"Go," Amalie cut her off, adding softly, "please. I promise I will be safe and whole when you return."

Esma nearly refused again but thought better of it. She wasn't in the habit of doubting her mistress' word. So she nodded in resignation and quietly left the room. Her behavior was all an act. Once she cleared the door, she took the stairs in a panic. Finding Owyn wasn't her objective; finding de Royans was.

It was bright and chilly outside as she rushed through the half-frozen muddy lake of the lower bailey in her hunt for the commander. The old woman asked a couple of soldiers if they knew where de Royans was and they directed her to the small chapel near the outer wall. De Royans was known to pray daily and she did not want to interrupt him, but she felt that she must. She asked a soldier to enter the chapel and bring forth the commander. It wasn't long before de Royans appeared.

He emerged from the small, crescent-shaped chapel with two of his knights in tow. Dressed in a tunic, breeches and boots against the cold, he looked half-dressed and fairly out of place among the heavily-armored knights. Esma watched, twisting her hands nervously, as he sent his knights along their way and made his way down to her.

He was such a big man that the old woman shrank back as he approached. She was positive the ground shook when he walked as the mud sloshed under his enormous boots. Weston came upon her, concern on his face.

"Is something wrong?" he asked. "Who is with Lady Amalie?"

Esma looked as if she was about to cry. "She awoke in good spirits this morning, m'lord," the old woman told him. "She is dressed and says she wants to go for a walk. She sent me to find Owyn to escort her."

He digested her words. "I will therefore ask the question again; who is with her right now?"

Esma was guilty and anxious. "No one, m'lord," she said. "She sent me away. She would not let me send someone else for Owyn."

"You left her alone?"

"I did, m'lord. She forced me to."

Weston's jaw ticked as he brushed past the old woman on his way to the keep. By the time he got halfway across the bailey, he was running.

❧

ALONE FOR THE first time in days, Amalie felt some relief. She also felt a distinct sense of freedom. She returned to the lancet window for a few minutes, enjoying the limited view she had of the snowy landscape, before deciding she was feeling well enough, and brave enough, to venture from her chamber unescorted.

She didn't need to wait for the young soldier; she'd been traversing Hedingham's massive keep all her life and was rather disgusted to realize how fearful she was to maintain that familiarity. Gathering her cloak, a heavy, fur-lined garment with great slits cut out for her arms, she slipped it on as she quit the chamber.

Amalie mounted the narrow, spiral stairs that led to the roof of the keep. She shoved back the heavy door, dumping some snow onto her, but the hatch had apparently been cleared by the servants so it wasn't particularly heavy or dirty. As soon as she stepped out onto the wooden roof, she was hit by not only the brilliant sunshine, but also the brisk temperature. It was glorious.

Taking a deep breath, she felt contentment for the first time in weeks but the despondency that had caused her suicidal behavior was still there, still weighing heavy. Pulling her cloak tightly about her, she was comfortable as she stood in the cool sunshine, gazing out over the Essex countryside.

She lost track of time as she stood there, lost in thought, trying to reconcile the events of the past several weeks. Somehow it was easier to absorb everything in the brightness of the new day. She couldn't easily think of that horrible event or of the weeks that followed, but she could clearly think of the day Weston de Royans arrived and saved her twice from taking her own life.

She hadn't thought much about the man since that night in the vault other than when he was following her around although pretending that he wasn't. Her prevalent thought of the man was that he was, indeed, handsome with his blond comely looks and his big, muscular frame. But beyond that, she couldn't and wouldn't think of anything else. De Royans was here to execute his orders and nothing more.

"Lady Amalie?"

A soft, deep voice startled her from her thoughts and she turned to see de Royans standing behind her. In the brilliant sun, she had to take a second look at the man; she'd only seen him in the dark, or in the snow, or otherwise shadowed. She had to admit that her reaction was one of approval – he was dressed simply in breeches, heavy boots and tunic, and little more. Odd for most knights, he wasn't clad in layers of mail or protection. His dark blond hair was cropped close, glistening flecks of gold in the sunlight, and the dark blue eyes were intense. In truth, she'd never seen such a handsome man. He looked like a god.

"Sir Weston," she greeted, pulling her cloak more tightly about her in a subconscious move of self-preservation. "How my I help you?"

Weston was staring at her far more than he should have; groomed appropriately, she looked absolutely delicious. He'd been watching her for days, purely out of duty, but he had to admit he liked looking at her.

He'd been preoccupied with his tasks associated with commander of Hedingham. But as the days passed, he came to realize that he awoke every morning with Lady Amalie on his mind. That thought weighed more heavily as the days passed, and now, as he gazed at her in the brilliant new morning, he was starting to think he was insane – insane because this woman, this distraught, crazed woman, was starting to mean something more to him than a mere captive.

After a long pause, he answered her question. "Aye, my lady," he replied. "There is something you can do for me. You can escort me on a walk."

Amalie looked at him, her big green eyes absorbing his statement. When it occurred to her that Esma ran straight for de Royans and not Owyn as requested, she lifted an eyebrow.

"I am sure you are quite capable of walking by yourself," she told him. "I have requested another escort."

Weston just looked at her. Then, he chuckled softly, ironically, his big, white grin and dimpled cheeks causing Amalie's heart to leap strangely.

"My lady, I understand that you are more comfortable with Owyn.

But you must understand that the man has other duties that do not include you," he said. "Therefore, I would be honored if you would accompany me on my walk."

Amalie wasn't inclined to refuse him simply because the longer she looked at him, the more brutally handsome he became. It was a struggle to resist. More than that, there was something in his manner that amused her.

"You are most insistent," she said after a moment.

"I am."

"I would wager to say that young ladies do not often reject you."

His smile broadened. "I do not let them."

The corners of Amalie's mouth twitched and she bit her lip to keep from smiling at him; he was quite devilish about it. "Then you do not intend to allow me to refuse, either."

"That is correct, my lady."

He was still grinning broadly at her. As much as she didn't want to trust him, she found that she could not resist the charm he was intent to heap upon her. It seemed to come easily to him, as did the broad grin that spread effortlessly across his face. Without recourse, she finally shrugged.

"Very well," she told him. "You should know that I can walk for hours. I hope you can be derelict from your duties for so long."

He nodded, sweeping his arm gallantly towards the roof hatch. "As long as you require, my lady."

"I intend to walk into the town."

"Then I intend to go with you."

Her eyes lingered on him as she walked past him, as did his gaze on her. As she studied his strong, handsome face, he was studying the arch of her lovely eyebrows and the little dimple in her chin. She seemed to be in better spirits, which both pleased and relieved him. Weston was coming to hope that the dark night he had arrived had been an isolated incident, although something that dark and that horrific told him that it was not. Whatever she was feeling was still just below the surface.

In silence, they made their way out of the keep and down into the muddy, snow-piled lower bailey. As soon as they entered the bailey, Amalie saw the state of it and came to a stop, lifting her skirts and her cloak so the hem wouldn't become muddied. Weston sent a soldier to collect his mail and weapons, commanding the man to meet him at the gatehouse. Swiftly, he bent over and scooped petite Amalie up into his arms.

She was light, warm and soft, but Amalie's first reaction was one of panic. Weston could see it in her face, remembering the same look that fateful night in the vault. He hastened to reassure her.

"I am sure you do not want to soil your shoes or your garments, my lady," he told her quickly. "Please allow me to aid you through this mess."

Hesitantly, Amalie nodded, gripping his big shoulders for support as he trekked across the muck. She couldn't help but notice how powerful the man was and how strong and warm he felt against her. The sheer size of his neck, shoulders and biceps were astonishing, now heated and firm beneath her hands as he carried her across the bailey.

Amalie didn't want to like him or anything about him. But in the brief contact she'd had with him, it was clear that whatever charm or magic he held worked against her. Two sides of her brain, the self-protection side and the female, giddy side were colliding violently.

Weston held her until they reached the gatehouse. The entire time, he hadn't said a word and neither had she. Amalie kept her face averted, not wanting to look at the man who was so close to her. She could feel his warm breath on the side of her face, gentle and sweet.

Once at the gatehouse entry, which had been moderately protected against the snow, he carefully set her down on the moist earth. Still, they didn't look at each other; they pretended to find interest in everything else. Weston averted his gaze because he was afraid to set her off again while Amalie averted her gaze because she was confused at her reaction to his charisma. It was an odd, but not uncomfortable, mood.

But that mood was offset by the appearance of Weston's armor. The soldier that met them at the gatehouse with the man's protection was none other than Owyn. Young, completely smitten with Lady Amalie, he was tall, lanky and blond, and he smiled broadly at Amalie as he approached.

Weston couldn't help but notice that she smiled back and he felt a surprising stab of jealousy, which manifested itself into brusque movements as he took the armor from the young soldier. He resisted the urge to smash the man right in his face.

"Good morn to you, Owyn," Amalie greeted him.

"Good morn to you, my lady," the young soldier greeted, hardly keeping a rein on his thrill. "'Tis a fine day today."

"Aye, it is," Amalie spoke to him as two other soldiers, gatehouse sentries, began to help Weston with his mail coat. "I thought I might walk to town today. I asked if you could escort me but Sir Weston said you had other pressing duties."

Owyn looked to the big knight as the man straightened out the mail coat on his big frame. "My lord," he said with veiled eagerness. "I am scheduled for sentry duty on the north wall today but I am sure another can easily take my place. There is no need for you to disrupt your day escorting the lady to town."

Weston looked at the young man. He was moderately handsome and strong, obviously a brave man for what he had done to protect the lady from Sorrell. It was based on the respect he had for the young soldier's courage that he didn't bite the man's head off in his reply.

"You will not shirk your duties to another," he told him. "I will take the lady into town. You will return to your post."

Owyn's young face fell somewhat but he didn't argue the point. One did not resist the commands of de Royans and live to tell the tale. Everyone knew that; tales of de Royans' military prowess were legendary within military circles. The man was extremely likeable and extremely congenial given the proper circumstances, but once provoked or in battle mode, he was deadly. For a man his size, there was little else he could be; tales of de Royans tearing men's heads from their bodies with his bare hands were pervasive in knightly circles. Owyn, therefore, had a healthy respect for his new commander and would not dream of questioning an order.

"Of course, my lord," he replied, eyeing Amalie. "I only meant to offer should you have more important duties to attend to."

Weston pulled on his tunic. "Your offer is noted," he said as he straightened the tunic and reached for his sword. "Return to your post."

Disappointed, Owyn tried not to show it. He bowed respectfully to Amalie as he turned and retraced his steps back to the outer bailey. Amalie watched him go before turning to Weston.

"You lied to me," she said flatly.

Weston looked up from securing his scabbard, surprised. "When did I do this disgraceful thing, my lady?"

She faced him fully. "You told me that Owyn had other duties to attend to, which is why he could not escort me to town." She put her hands on his hips. "Clearly, he does not. Why did you lie to me?"

Weston stared at her, running a big hand through his cropped blond hair as he thought on his reply. "I did not lie to you, my lady," he said evenly. "Perhaps Owyn does not consider his scheduled duties important. I, in fact, do. He does, indeed, have duties to attend to. The moment he believes he does not is the moment I boot him from my service."

Her features turned hard. "You will not boot him from your service," she said firmly. "Owyn is a fine man."

"He is a soldier."

"He saved my life!"

"And for that, he will always have my respect." Weston realized he was close to having a battle on his hands and labored to ease the rising tide. "But you must understand that Owyn has his own duties to attend to and one of them does not include constant companion to the Lady of the Keep. What he did for you was strong and courageous, no doubt, and I intend to reward him in time. But the moment I arrived, you became my responsibility. Do you understand?"

"Why would you reward him for protecting me?" she wanted to know. "I am, theoretically, your enemy, de Royans. Why would you reward a man for siding with the enemy?"

He just stared at her, the dark blue eyes glimmering intensely. "Do I really have to answer that?"

"You do."

"Enemy or ally, what he did was remarkably brave and I reward bravery to the men under my command."

Amalie gazed steadily at him, a myriad of emotions running across her delicate features. She wasn't happy that Owyn was not allowed to accompany her; that was clear. But she also seemed pleased that de Royans intended to reward him. After a small eternity of uncomfortable silence, she finally averted her gaze and looked off towards the snowy countryside beyond.

"Come on, then," she grumbled, pulling her cloak more tightly around her. "Let us get on with it."

Weston's gaze lingered on her as she proceeded from the gatehouse and onto the frozen road beyond. It was muddy in patches, icy in others, and Amalie found herself dodging those areas as she moved down the road. Weston trudged on beside her, stomping through the mud and ice in his enormous, knee-high boots.

He kept looking at her from the corner of his eyes, wondering if he had been too harsh with her on the subject of Owyn. When he shouldn't have cared about her beyond his normal duties as commander of Hedingham, he realized he was concerned about building some manner of acquaintance with the woman and he would never be able to do that with Owyn always around.

She was already attached to the soldier, for good reason, and Weston found that threatening somehow. He had seen her face light up when she had seen Owyn, a smile so radiant that it outshined the sun. It was utterly beautiful. He was aware that he wanted to see that smile as well when she looked at him. He had no idea why, but he did.

Weston and Amalie had no more than a few exchanges between them and those exchanges had been unpleasant more than pleasant. It wasn't as if Weston knew her personally or deeply, so explaining his attraction to her was more of an instinct than anything else. He couldn't explain it any more than that.

"With the ground so saturated, perhaps it would be better if we returned to Hedingham for your palfrey," he suggested.

She leaped over a muddy puddle, took a couple of steps, and leaped over another. "No need," she said steadily. "I would rather walk."

He watched her dodge yet another puddle. "You are not walking," he pointed out. "You are leaping like a deer."

Skirts and cloak gathered up in both hands, she looked at him as he made leaping motions with his hand. He wriggled his eyebrows to punctuate it. She looked away, repressing the urge to grin at his expression. As irritated as she was with him, it didn't dull the man's charm as he wielded it like a sword against her. The more he would thrust, the weaker her parry.

"I am not leaping," she said as she skipped over a patch of snow.

"Aye, you are. It would be better to return for the horses."

She shook her head, gesturing on ahead. "We are nearly at the town as it is." She pointed out the obvious with a series of poorly-constructed buildings about fifty feet away. Then she looked at him. "Did you bring money?"

He lifted his eyebrows. "Money?" he repeated. "What for?"

"Because I want to buy things." She bit her lip, thinking now that she was going to punish him for being so insistent on escorting her. She would spend all of his money, which would assure that he would never insist on escorting her into town again. "As my escort, it is your duty to bring money. Surely you did not expect me to bring money."

He puckered his lips thoughtfully as he scratched his cheek. "I thought we were going to go walking in the meadows. I did not think I would need my purse for the deer and birds."

"You are a poor planner."

"How is that?"

"You should be prepared for anything."

He eyed her. "I am coming to see that is the truth with you around."

She couldn't help the grin that creased her lips as she leaped over another puddle. Weston saw it and he was enchanted. He wanted to keep the momentum going.

"What monumental purchase do you intend to make that I need to bring about an entire treasury?" he asked.

She shrugged coyly, eyes still on the road. "I am not sure yet."

"Diamond? Rubies?"

"I would not let you off so easily," she shot back. "Perhaps I wish to buy a small country. What will you do then since you are so poorly prepared?"

He was thrilled that she was responding to his attempts at humor. Rolling his eyes, he muttered as he looked away. "Sell you off to the highest bidder and let some other fool take his chances with your unreasonable demands."

She snorted. "You had the opportunity to pass me off to Owyn."

He grinned, meeting her eye. It was the first time they had openly smiled at one another, a bright moment in a week that had been full of desolation and darkness. He was having difficulty believing this was the same woman who had tried to take her life just a few days ago.

"I am sure Owyn would not refuse you," he said. "But whether or not he has the means to buy you anything you wish is another matter."

She lifted her eyebrows at him. "And you do?"

He shrugged. "Most knights are not poor, my lady," he said. "It costs a great deal of money to maintain this profession."

Given that her brother was an earl as well as a knight, she knew that. "Then your family is wealthy?"

He looked away, gazing across the snowy landscape. "Wealthy enough."

"Where are you from?"

"My family has lived at Netherghyll Castle in Yorkshire for over two hundred years," he told her. "My grandfather is Baron Cononley, Constable of North Yorkshire and the Northern Dales. He commands a large army."

"Will you inherit the title?"

"I will." The conversation had switched to him and he was suddenly very uncomfortable. He didn't want to speak of himself or his family, not in the least. "I suppose I should return to the castle and collect my purse if you truly wish to go on a purchasing offensive."

Subject successfully diverted, Amalie grinned, casting him a side-long glance. "No need," she said. "The merchants in town know me. They know they will be paid."

"Ah." Weston nodded. "I take it you have done this before."

She wriggled her well-shaped eyebrows. "Not me," she said. "My brother. He had his favorite merchants. There is a woman in town that makes sticky buns with cinnamon, honey and butter. They are decadent and my brother would often buy out her entire stock."

He wondered if mention of her brother would bring about bitter memories so he tried to stay away from any mention of him.

"Still," he said, "I should return to collect my purse."

She shook her head, leaped over another puddle, and slipped. He caught her before she could hit the ground. When she looked at him in apology, he merely shook his head at her.

"Fortunate for you that my reflexes are fast." He set her on her feet. "If you will not let me get the horses, will you at least let me carry you so that you will not fall?"

She straightened her cloak. "Absolutely not," she sniffed, looking around and realizing they were on the edge of the main avenue of the small village. The first thing that caught her eye was the stall with the cinnamon buns and she gathered her skirts with determination. "Come along, de Royans."

With a lifted eyebrow and a grin, he followed.

In spite of the big snow drifts and extremely muddy avenue, the street was crowded with vendors and customers. People were everywhere conducting business under crisp, sunny skies. Weston followed Amalie across the mud, watching her slide twice before regaining her balance.

He knew it was inevitable that she was going to end up on her arse at some point but he was helpless as long as she so willfully refused his assistance. He wished she wouldn't refuse him; he was thinking of any excuse he could come across to get her back into his arms. He hadn't been around her more than a half-hour and, already, he was succumbing to the attraction he felt for her. It was growing by the moment.

Weston could smell the cinnamon in the air as he approached the baker's stall. Amalie was already accepting one of the sticky-sweet buns from the woman, showing more joy than she had exhibited the entire time Weston had known her. She pulled off a piece and popped it in her mouth, groaning with delight as she chewed. Noticing de Royans standing next to her, she offered him the bun.

Weston waved her off. "No, thank you."

She only held up the bun higher, waving it in his face tauntingly. "You cannot resist."

Her humor was enchanting but he didn't crack. "Aye, I can."

"No, you cannot. Taste it and you will be enslaved to its delights forever."

He gave her a half-grin, then. "Then I most certainly will not taste it. I do not wish to be enslaved by a piece of food."

"Please?"

His grin grew. "Why is it so important that I taste it?"

She shrugged, without a good answer, and lowered the bun. But before she could take another bite, he suddenly grasped her wrist with surely the biggest gloved hand she had ever seen. It covered most of her forearm. He pulled her arm up until the bun met with his mouth. Their eyes met and Amalie watched as he took a big bite of the tasty treat.

Even when he began to chew, their gazes were still locked, an oddly fluid warmth beginning to flow between them. Amalie could feel herself getting sucked into the dark blue eyes, the excruciatingly handsome features, and, for a brief second, she allowed herself the weakness of giving in to whatever charm the man radiated. It was a truly delicious sensation.

Before she became too upswept in it, fear and disorientation swamped her and she yanked her hand away, averting her gaze nervously. Something about de Royans made her nervous and giddy at the same time and she had no idea how to gracefully deal with it.

Weston saw her reaction but he knew he hadn't imagined the warmth that had sparked between them just seconds earlier. It was inappropriate, wrong and undesirable, in any fashion, to imagine something more between the two of them. They were two different worlds and philosophies apart. But he was imagining it nonetheless.

"You are correct, my lady," he said in his deep, sweet voice. "I am now a slave to a piece of bread."

Even though she wasn't looking at him, she giggled. "As I have been for several years now." She turned away from the stall and, with the bun still in her hand, began to move down the avenue. "Do not feel so badly about it, de Royans. Good food has enslaved many a man."

He watched her lowered head, studying the fall of her hair and the shape of her head.

"Weston," he said quietly.

She came to a stop in the middle of the mucky road, turning to him curiously. "What did you say?"

His dark blue eyes glittered at her. "My name is Weston," he said quietly. "I would be honored if you call me by my name, my lady."

She stared at him, her features washing with confusion. He thought she looked frightened and he was fearful that he had overstepped himself. When she replied, it was carefully worded.

"Although I am flattered, I am not sure it is appropriate," she said quietly, some of the joy so recently acquired fading from her manner. "I have never heard of a jailor and captive becoming familiar on a first-name basis."

He lifted an eyebrow, approaching her with his hands coming to rest on his hips. "That is something else we must discuss," he said. "At no time have I called you a captive. I am not entirely sure where you received that impression."

Her brow furrowed. "My brother fled because the barons who oppose the king sentenced him to death for his support of Richard," she pointed out. "I did not flee with him and Bolingbroke confiscated Hedingham. What else am I if I am not a prisoner?"

Weston's dark blue eyes glittered at her. "A guest," he said quietly. "To me, you are a guest, my lady. Nothing more, nothing less."

"Can I leave if I wish it?"

He nodded. "I will not stop you. Do you have someplace else you wish to go?"

Amalie was surprised by his answer; she hadn't expected it in the least. "I... I suppose I could go to my mother."

"Where is your mother?"

"She has her own properties in east Essex. I have not seen her in years."

"Why not?"

She sighed faintly. "Because my mother does not acknowledge that she bore a daughter," she said, shrugging. "She has only ever acknowledged my brother as if he is an only child. I was sent to foster when I was three years old, returning to Hedingham two years ago. I am not entirely sure my brother wanted me here but he could not refuse my mother. She did not want me to live with her so she sent me to him. I am the child and sister that no one wants to be burdened with, apparently."

It seemed like a sad tale, Weston thought, but he didn't comment. He was coming to feel more and more pity for the woman who had not known much kindness in life. In a sense, he felt a kinship with her because their family ties were much the same; parents they did not bond with, general unhappiness, and then the added insult of an attack by a man who was supposed to show her respect based simply on the chivalric code. Weston's mood dampened, thinking of her story that seemed to grow darker by the moment.

Before he could reply, however, the sounds of horses and men suddenly distracted him and he turned to see several armed men on horseback escorting an expensive carriage.

And it was heading right for them.

CHAPTER SIX

THE SOLDIERS ESCORTING the carriage were well armed and clad in expensive tunics bearing colors of green and yellow. There was a well-dressed knight in the lead, snapping orders to the driver of the carriage to plot a smooth path through the road that was in impossible shape. The driver did his best but the carriage lurched and jerked through the mud.

Weston reached out to pull Amalie out of the road but she seemed distracted by the sight of the carriage. When she didn't move fast enough, he tugged on her arm and quickly moved her to the edge of the street. She fussed at him but he ignored her, more concerned with the heavily-armed men now making their way down the street.

Weston was armed but, for Amalie's sake, he didn't want to get into any manner of conflict. He wasn't sure, given her fragile mental state, that she would take it well. More than that, it would be just him against several armed men. As good as he was, the odds were not in his favor.

The big chargers splashed in the mud, causing Amalie to jump back to avoid being hit by the frigid goop. But she was waving at the carriage and a dark head suddenly popped out from one of the windows along with a gloved hand. Someone in the carriage was waving back.

"Amalie!" came a cry and the door suddenly jerked open. A dark-haired young woman appeared, smiling brightly. She waved again as she began to climb out of the cab that was still moving. "It has been too long, darling! I have missed you!"

Realizing that her driver was not stopping, the young woman snapped at him and the carriage came to an unsteady halt. The woman edged her way onto the muddied avenue and in Amalie's direction. She and Amalie came together near the edge of the road, hugging one another happily.

"What brings you to Hedingham?" Amalie asked. "You are far from your home."

The woman shrugged; she was rather plain in appearance, colorless in spite of the dark hair and light eyes. She was also rather tall for a woman, with gangly, long arms, and she wore expensive clothing. Given the new carriage and host of well-dressed soldiers, it was apparent that she came from money.

"'Tis not too far," she said. "Halstead is only a few miles to the south. I came into town to see Brigid."

Amalie knew exactly who she was speaking of. "Of course," she said. "I had forgotten. She is sewing your wedding dress, is she not? The woman sews beautiful garments."

The woman nodded eagerly. "She has been working on it diligently," she said. "I have come for some alterations. My wedding is the first of September, you know. You are coming, aren't you?"

For the first time, Amalie looked uncomfortable. She smiled, semi-nodded and semi-shrugged, as if unable or unwilling to make the commitment. "I would love nothing better, of course," she held her friend's hands tightly. "But... well, with what has happened with Robert, I am not sure that..."

The young woman cut her off. "Nonsense," she said firmly. "Even my father says it is rubbish; all of it. He says the only reason Bolingbroke took possession of Hedingham is because it is rich and powerful. Father says that all he wants is the riches and he is trying to kill your brother to get it, but Mother says that Father is jealous because he was not asked to occupy Hedingham. Bolingbroke is more powerful so he took the spoils."

Amalie's smile gradually morphed into something horrified as her friend chattered on. She knew that Weston was standing just a few feet away, hearing every terrible word that the woman was saying. So she did the only thing she could do; she turned to Weston to introduce her friend, mostly so Cecily would not say anything more that could be construed as a knock against Weston's loyalties.

"Sir Weston," she said politely, steadily. "This is the Lady Cecily Brundon. Her father is Lord Sudbury and Cecily is marrying Sir Michael Hollington, a knight under Thomas de Mowbray's command. Cece, this is Sir Weston de Royans, the current commander of Hedingham Castle and Bolingbroke's knight."

Cecily politely greeted Weston but the fact that she had been spouting off at the mouth did not go unnoticed. In fact, she seemed quite horrified by it as she clutched at her friend and tried desperately to change the subject away from the occupation of Hedingham. Her pale face was even paler as she and Amalie exchanged anxious glances.

"Surely Sir Weston will allow you to attend the wedding," she said to Amalie. "Perhaps... perhaps you can even come and stay with my husband and me for a time after we are married. I would love to have you as my guest."

Amalie knew she made the offer because Hedingham was occupied with men that did not view Amalie's brother in a favorable light. It was a hostile environment. Considering one of the subjects of her most recent conversation with Weston had been the fact that he did not consider her a prisoner, Amalie was emboldened by Cecily's offer. It brought about the fact that she was still invited to the wedding even after her brother's flight from England.

Still, she wasn't sure she wanted to attend, not after everything that had happened since that dark and fateful night. Her social standing was already damaged by her brother's behavior and she would become a social outcast completely once her condition was known.

Moreover, her child would be due around that time. Perhaps it was better not to enjoy the last remnants of a world she would eventually be exiled from. It would only remind her that she would never have a wedding, nor would she enjoy the benefits of a reputable husband. Her life, in many ways, was over even if the frozen pond hadn't ended it.

"Your offer is sweet," she said softly. "However, I fear that I will not be able to attend given… well, suffice it to say that it is better if I do not. My heart and prayers will be with you on your wonderful day, however. I wish you and Michael all of the happiness in the world."

Until this point, Weston had been standing strong and silent several feet away. Mostly, he had been watching Amalie and the way she moved, the way she spoke, the sensual pout of her lips on her amazing face. He'd been quite swept up in everything about her. He wasn't particularly offended when her friend lobbed insults against Bolingbroke but when she began to talk about the wedding, he could see a change come over Amalie. She went from radiant and happy to demure and, he thought, depressed. He didn't like the expression on her face at all. It reminded him of the night she…

"I will escort you to Lady Cecily's wedding, my lady," he interjected his offer before Cecily could respond. "It would be my pleasure."

Both Amalie and Cecily looked at him, each with distinctly different reactions. Cecily was thrilled while Amalie simply appeared more depressed.

"That is kind, Sir Weston," Amalie assured him quickly. "But it would not be appropriate."

He approached the ladies, his enormous arms folded across his chest and his focus on Amalie.

"Why not?" he wanted to know. "Lady Cecily has graciously extended the invitation. All young women love weddings and hope for one of their own someday. Why would you refuse to go?"

Amalie's composure fractured. Her mood was killed, her despondency swamping her like a black tide. She turned to Cecily and held the woman's hands tightly, kissing her on each cheek. When she pulled back, she forced a bright smile into the pale, colorless face.

"You will make a beautiful bride, sweetheart," she said hoarsely. "I love you very much. Please accept my apologies for not attending."

With that, she darted off before Cecily could respond. The woman watched her go with astonishment.

"Ammy!" she called after her, trying to follow but not wanting to get muddied. "Ammy, please come back! Please?"

Weston was already on the move, slogging across the muddy avenue as he followed Amalie's flight. She was several feet ahead of him, dodging big puddles. But in her haste, she ended up stepping in a couple and the mud splashed all the way up to her waist. He could see that her cloak was becoming one great muddy mess. He was nearly upon her when she suddenly stumbled and ended up on her knees in a puddle of muddy snow. Rather than jump up and continue, she simply hung her head and wept.

Weston came up behind her. Without even asking, he gently scooped her up under her arms and lifted her from the mud. Before Amalie could respond, or even fight him off, a heavily-laden wagon slipped in the muddy avenue behind them, careening into Weston. His big body took the brunt of the blow as both he and Amalie went down.

Amalie ended up face down in the mud, feeling Weston's substantial weight on top of her. She tried to get up but he wasn't moving very well. When he finally did roll off of her, his arms were wrapped around his torso as he struggled to his knees. Amalie could see that he was hurt and she forgot all about her sorrows and desperation. She gripped him by his big shoulders as if her small strength could steady him.

"Weston?" she gasped, greatly concerned. "Are you injured?"

He was smarting but trying not to show it. "A little," he grunted.

"Where?"

"My back and my ribs, I think."

By this time, the burly farmer who had been driving the wagon that had struck them came to see if they were okay. He could see the small lady trying to help the enormous knight and he rushed to the man's other side to help lift him. He helped Weston to his feet, listening to the man grunt.

"M'lord," he said anxiously. "I am sorry if I hurt ye. The horse slipped and the wagon followed. Are ye bad off?"

Weston knew it was an accident. He waved the man off, more concerned with his ability to make it back to the castle at this point.

"I have been worse," he replied, looking to Amalie covered in mud. "Are you all right?"

She nodded, her big green eyes wide with concern. "I am fine." She put her soft white hands on him, gently, as if to help him. "Let us return to the castle and have the surgeon examine you."

He tried to wave her off but couldn't quite summon the strength. The blow had been a hard one and his back and ribs on the right side of his body were killing him. Before he could reply, Amalie was calling to her friend across the street; Cecily hadn't left the scene yet.

Cecily's escort came rushing across the avenue with their big destriers, taking charge of Weston in an effort to get the man back to the castle. The last Weston saw of Amalie, she was climbing into the cab with her friend, which he thought was a far better place for her. He wasn't distressed by it in the least.

He couldn't mount a horse, so six men-at-arms walked him, however slowly, back to Hedingham as the lone knight escorted the carriage back up through the gates. By the time Weston reached the outer bailey, Heath and John were there to meet him. His brush with a runaway wagon had put the entire castle in an uproar as his men hastened to get him examined by the surgeon.

Weston resisted their attempts until he got inside the banqueting hall and saw Amalie there with Cecily, both ladies taking instructions from the castle surgeon. The wiry, old man, who had known Amalie since birth, was rattling off orders to the ladies and they were making all haste to fulfill them. As he watched, Amalie and Cecily flew into action.

When Heath and John pulled off his mail and tunic in a slow and painful process, Weston perched on the edge of the banqueting table while the surgeon examined him because it was more comfortable than sitting down. It kept some of the pressure off his sore ribs.

As the wiry man with the red beard poked and prodded, Amalie appeared at his side, holding a big bolt of tartan and taking a dagger to it. He watched curiously as she and Cecily ripped it up into great strips.

Those strips were then taken by the surgeon and wound around Weston's bruised ribs to keep them from moving around too much. Although the surgeon didn't feel any fractures, the fact remained that Weston was badly bruised and the tight wrapping would help.

When Weston should have been focused on his own injuries, he was more interested in watching Amalie. Through the entire incident, he noted that she was calm, in control, and precise in her movements. She dealt with the servants in a smooth, even tone and handled both the surgeon and Cecily with cool efficiency. The woman appeared as strong as a rock.

It was difficult to fathom that this was the same woman from only a few days ago, determined to end her life, and her efficient manner was something he found deeply attractive. More and more, he was growing increasingly interested in her to the point where he didn't care how inappropriate it was. He decided, at that moment, that he was going to make his interest known, but timing would be the key. He would have to be very careful how he went about it.

As Weston mentally schemed for Amalie, the old surgeon finally finished with the bindings and faced the big knight with his hands on his hips.

"Your pain shall be worse by tomorrow," he told him. "I would suggest that you rest for the remainder of the day. I will give you a potion to ease the pain and help you sleep."

Distracted from Amalie, Weston stood up from the edge of the table, grunting softly as he moved and putting his hand to his right side as if to hold in his guts. "No potion," he told him. "There is no need."

The old man just shook his head, his bearded jowls quivering. "I thought as much," he sniffed. "I never knew a knight who did not believe he was beyond my help."

Amalie was standing next to Weston, listening to the instructions. She turned her green-eyed gaze in his direction.

"Perhaps he is correct, Sir Weston," she said. "The day seems quiet enough and I am sure you have other men who can take your duties for you while you rest. Surely you can spare a few hours for your recuperation."

Weston looked at her, feeling himself relent with her soft words. But as he looked at her, he realized she was still muddy from where he had fallen on her and pushed her into the mud. His gaze was on the mud on her neck and shoulders as he spoke.

"I would not worry about me, my lady," he said. "But you, on the other hand, had an ox fall on you. Are you sure that you are well?"

She grinned at him, such a lovely gesture with a tiny dimple in her chin. "I am well," she reassured him. "But thank goodness for the soft mud or I might have been flattened."

Behind her, Cecily giggled. Weston lifted an eyebrow, amused, as both women chuckled. He nodded as if to concede the point.

"Kind words, my lady," he muttered.

She gave him an expression as if he had brought it all upon himself. "You called yourself an ox, de Royans, not I. I was simply agreeing with you."

He pursed his lips and shook his head at her, although he was both enchanted and amused by her humor. He turned away from the women and looked around for his tunic.

"Where is my clothing?" he asked to anyone who could answer him.

Heath and John were a few feet away. It was John who retrieved his woolen tunic from a bench near the great hearth. Heath sent a soldier for the mail coat, which had been whisked away by a squire when they had removed it from his battered body.

"Here is your tunic," Heath took it from John and handed it to Weston. "Your mail will be here shortly."

Amalie watched Weston's determination to return to duty and her humor faded. "The surgeon says you should rest, Sir Weston," she pointed out. "Perhaps you should listen to him."

Weston shook his head. "No need," he grunted as he lifted his arms to pull the tunic over his sculpted, and bound, torso. "I will heal with or without rest."

"Sir Weston." Cecily's pale face was open and anxious. "Will you not sit and take refreshment with us at least? Even that small respite might help and then you may go about your duties if you so choose."

Amalie looked at Cecily, her brow furrowing with some confusion as the woman asked de Royans to share what was considered a social event. In fact, Amalie hadn't even asked her friend to stay for refreshment, mostly because she didn't want to hear about the impending wedding. But Cecily's gaze was purely on Weston.

"Cece," she whispered. "You cannot ask that of him. He is the garrison commander."

Cecily ignored her, her hopeful face on Weston. "Please, Sir Weston? Perhaps you will tell us something of yourself. Since you serve Bolingbroke, it is possible that you and I know many of the same people."

Weston was flummoxed by the woman's invitation and his first instinct was to decline. But in the next breath, he realized that Amalie would be there. He wasn't about to pass up a chance to sit with her in conversation that would have nothing to do with suicide or horrors from the past. He knew she would steer clear of anything like that. It would be his chance to get to know the woman a little better in a perfectly proper setting.

"Very well," he said, moving to sit on the bench of the great banqueting hall's table. "If it would please you."

Cecily appeared thrilled while Amalie appeared resigned. Weston sat carefully on the bench, shifting until he found a comfortable position as Amalie sent one of the servants for food and wine. Both women sat across from Weston at the great table with Cecily taking charge of the conversation. Amalie stared at her lap.

"Do you know of my betrothed, Sir Weston?" Cecily began eagerly. "His name is Sir Michael Hollington, a knight under Thomas de Mowbray's command. Surely you have met him?"

Weston's gaze was mostly on Amalie but he forced himself to look at Cecily. "I am afraid I have not had the pleasure, my lady," he said.

"There are thousands of knights in England and I have not had the opportunity to meet every one of them."

It was a bit of a tribute to her ridiculous question but Cecily didn't catch on. It was becoming apparent that she was smitten with Weston's strong, blond good looks.

"A pity," she said. "He is an excellent knight; wealthy, too. My father has known him for years and was able to negotiate a contract with him when his wife died."

Weston glanced at her as a servant set a pewter cup of wine in front of him. "So you will be his second wife?"

Cecily nodded. "Michael's first wife bore him two daughters. He very much wants a son and paid my father handsomely for the privilege of marrying me."

Weston refrained from any outward reaction, although inside he was thinking on the desperation of a man who would buy another wife to bear him a son. In Weston's beliefs, a man married one woman for life, good or bad, sons or no sons, death or no death. He was fairly rigid in his thoughts on that matter. But instead of a reply to that regard, he merely lifted his cup.

"Then I wish you health and happiness in your marriage, my lady," he said. "May you bear many strong sons if it is God's will."

Cecily grinned happily, sipping at her own wine that a servant politely provided. Amalie collected her own cup and drank the toast, although her features were tight. She remained silent as Cecily continued the interrogation of Weston.

"And you, Sir Weston?" Cecily set her cup down and reached for some cheese. "Are you married?"

Weston shook his head. "I am not, my lady."

Cecily looked surprised. "Why not?" she wanted to know. "Surely you are much esteemed by Bolingbroke, which means you are wealthy and connected. Surely there is some young woman worthy of you."

Weston shouldn't have looked at Amalie as he replied, but he did. He wanted her to get the message. "There is, somewhere," he said, meeting her rather dubious green eyes. "When the time is right."

He watched Amalie flush a violent shade of red and look to her lap again as Cecily continued her onslaught.

"And your family, Sir Weston?" she asked. "Where are you from?"

"North Yorkshire," he replied, increasingly unwilling to carry on this line of conversation. "Netherghyll Castle is my family home."

"Will the castle become yours on the passing of your father?"

Weston looked at her, then, and his manner stiffened. "My father is already dead." He suddenly stood up from the bench. "If you will excuse me, ladies, I have duties to attend to."

Cecily's face fell as Amalie leaped up also. She was so red in the face that she was having difficulty looking anyone in the eye.

"Cece, I am sure you have many things to attend to." She gripped her friend by the elbow and was forcing her away from the table. "You must see Brigid right away. You do not want to keep her waiting."

Cecily looked rather confused that she was being led towards the entry of the banquet hall but the mention of her wedding dress got her moving in the right direction.

"Of course," she said, suddenly excited again. "Will you come with me to see her, Ammy?"

Amalie paused by the entry, not wanting to disappoint her friend but certainly not wanting to accompany her. She quickly thought of an excuse.

"Not today, sweetheart," she said. "I have not been feeling well lately and need to rest. But I thank you for your sweet offer."

"Are you sure?"

"Aye," Amalie hugged her. "You will be a beautiful bride, Cece."

"Please come to the wedding, Ammy. It will not be the same without you."

Amalie didn't want to commit. She smiled bravely and nodded somewhat, giving the woman the sense that she might, indeed, consider it. Cecily kissed her on the cheek and made her way through the forebuilding, down the stairs towards the outer bailey.

Amalie stood at the top of the steps and watched her until she dis-appeared from sight. Once the woman was gone, she turned to find Weston standing just a few feet away.

She gazed into his dark blue eyes, feeling the delicious liquid warmth spark between them again. But the warmth scared her still and she lowered her gaze, unwilling and unable to entertain it.

"I must go change from these muddy clothes, "she muttered, mov-ing past him. "I am glad you are not overly hurt, Sir Weston."

He watched her brush past him. "You will not call me Sir Weston," he told her as he watched her walk away. "Only Weston."

She paused, turning to look at him. "Weston," she corrected herself, her green eyes appearing uncertain, perhaps confused. "You… you may call me Amalie if you wish."

"Ammy," he said softly. "I have heard your servants and your friend call you that."

She smiled faintly, if not reluctantly. "That is what I called myself as a child because I could not pronounce Amalie. It has stayed with me, unfortunately."

He approached her with a smile on his face. "'Tis a sweet name. I should like to use it if it will not offend you."

She wasn't sure what she could say to him. The truth was that she would not be offended but she wasn't sure it was proper. She wasn't sure how the man's familiarity would be perceived by others. Still, she couldn't help herself from agreeing.

"It will not," she said quietly, eyeing him. "Are you sure that you are all right to go about your duties?"

He nodded, rubbing at the right side of his torso. "Well enough," he said. "It only hurts when I laugh."

"Coming from a man I have never seen laugh, you should be in fine shape."

He grinned. "That is the thanks you give me for saving you from a runaway wagon? You have a keen sense of gratitude, my lady."

She couldn't help but return his smirk. "I do not wish for you to think me ungrateful," she said. "Thank you for saving me from the runaway wagon."

He dipped his head gallantly. "I am your devoted servant, my lady."

He said it so dramatically that she giggled. But there was something more in his meaning, something deeper as she began to recall the history of their association. His small statement had brought that about and her smile faded as she gazed into his handsome face.

"You have proven that from the start," she said softly, her manner turning sincere. "I have not thanked you for the kindness and concern you showed me when you could have just as easily have disregarded me entirely. I am… grateful. Very grateful."

It was the first genuine thing she had ever said to him and his heart softened. He began to feel that liquid warmth flow again. As he gazed into her lovely eyes, he realized that her words, her manner, were giving him hope. Hope that there might be something more than polite acquaintance between them.

"I will always show you kindness and concern," he said quietly. "And I am your sworn servant for life."

"For life?" she repeated, a smile on her lips. "That is a bold declaration, Weston. Your future wife may have something to say about that. She may not appreciate the fact that you have made such a declaration to another woman."

He cocked an eyebrow, grinning as his dimples carved deep channels into his cheeks.

"I would not worry over that," he assured her, watching her shake her head in amusement at him. His smile faded. "I swore the night we met that I would always treat you with respect. I meant it."

Amalie was beginning to feel the warmth again, too. It flowed between them, binding them, filling them, until her heart was pounding loudly against her ribs. Weston's warm blue eyes had that effect on her and it was increasingly difficult to resist him.

"I appreciate that," she murmured. "More than you know."

The warmth was drowning them both. Weston just stared at her, unable to look away, feeling something deep in his chest that he could not describe.

"Will you please answer a question?" he begged softly.

"What question?"

He looked rather pained, his mouth working as he searched for the correct words. "When... when I look at you, I see such beauty and strength," he murmured. "I noticed it the night we first met and it grows stronger by the day. You have wit and compassion and honor; I have seen these things in you and it makes me increasingly troubled as to why a woman of your magnificence would try and take her own life. Can you please explain this to me? I truly wish to know because I am terrified that one of these days, I will not be there to save you from yourself. I feel as if I am living with an axe over my head, waiting for it to fall at any moment because I am still not certain you will not throw yourself from the battlements when I am not looking. It haunts me, my lady, in ways you cannot imagine."

Amalie was staring at him intently as he finished his sentence. "But why?" was all she could think to ask, earnestly, as if she were desperate to understand. "Why would you feel this way? I am nothing more than a captive, the sister of your enemy. Why would you feel this way about me?"

His dark blue eyes were unguarded. "Because I do," he said simply, but there was passion in his tone. "I do not know why I do, but I do. I cannot let anything happen to you and I need to know what is so horrible that you would feel the need to kill yourself. Do you not understand, Ammy? I would kill for you and I would die for you. I will protect you with everything that I am, always. But I cannot protect you from yourself and that sickens me. Will you not tell me why you would do this to yourself?"

She could hear his interest in her in his voice, his desire to have something more than a normal acquaintance with her, but her emotions were reeling. The most recent thoughts of a marriage she would never have suddenly weighed very heavily on her.

God, what she would have given for a marriage to Weston. But it began to occur to her that if he remained at Hedingham for any length of time, the truth of her condition would eventually become apparent to him. He would see it and lose all respect for her; she knew it. She could not let that happen. She couldn't stand to see his disgust for her in his eyes.

Tears began to fill her eyes, pain such as she had never known enveloping her. She felt as if she had been stabbed in the heart as the meaning of his declaration sank deep.

"Oh... Weston," she breathed. "Why on earth would you say such things to me?"

He tried not to look embarrassed or contrite, realizing that he had said everything he'd wanted to say to her without truly spitting it out directly. He could only answer her with the truth.

"Because my heart tells me to," he whispered. "I cannot explain it more than that."

Instead of turning and running from him, she acted on impulse. Moving to the man, she put her soft hands on his face and, very gently, kissed him on his left cheek.

Amalie dropped her hands and moved away from him quickly. The action was like the blink of an eye; quickly there, quickly gone, but the heat, the desire, had been unmistakable. Weston stared at her in astonishment as Amalie forced a tremulous smile.

"You are very kind and very sweet, Weston," she whispered. "I swear that you do not have to worry about me any longer. What happened on the night you arrived... I was momentarily insane. I cannot tell you more than that but it will not happen again. I swear it. You needn't worry over me any longer."

Before he could say a word, she fled to the spiral stairs that led up to her chamber. Weston stood there, heart pounding, feeling her kiss on his cheek as the greatest single gift he had ever received. It had been soft, sweet, delicious. Had she not moved so quickly, he knew he would have taken her in his arms and kissed her deeply. He realized his hands ached to touch her, his arms to hold her. But she had fled swiftly, leaving him speechless and thrilled.

He wiped his fingers across the spot she had kissed, bringing them to his mouth and brushing his lips against them, wondering if he could taste her. He could.

Weston did not follow her when she fled. Amalie was a delicate creature emotionally and he knew she would not take it well if he followed her. She needed to be alone, to unwind herself, to breathe again after the emotional day she'd had. But he knew for a fact that he would have those spiral stairs closely watched for any sign of her.

He sent a servant to find Esma.

CHAPTER SEVEN

WESTON WAS STANDING on the outer wall of Hedingham, watching the activity in the bailey below. It was a truly massive place that could house an enormous army. So far, he had six hundred men from Bolingbroke to command plus the two hundred personal retainers he had brought with him. With an eight hundred man army at his disposal, it was an impressive sight.

When he hadn't been focused on Amalie since his arrival, he'd been surveying Hedingham and inspecting the troops. Since he was a man who liked strict order, the first thing he did was create an armory in the northwest tower of the outer wall because there seemed to be no central armory at Hedingham.

The second item on his agenda was to build a troop house to hold the bulk of the army which was, as of now, sleeping in any dry place they could find. Most of them loaded up in the banquet hall and in the galleries while a few of them found lodgings in one of the smaller outbuildings that was, for the moment, vacant.

Weston knew that it wasn't a prime time of year to be building but he also knew it would give the men something to do. So he and his knights began to organize the men into groups; there were those that would collect rock and stone, those that would shape it, and those that would build. They had started their ambitious project yesterday and he was pleased to see that things were falling into place.

His plan was to put the building against the western wall near the north tower and he stood now, gazing down on the men who were clearing away the foundation for the building. Heath was particularly good at building and he watched the red-haired knight down in the middle of the action, directing the men to clear away and compact a foundation that would, when finished, house close to five hundred men on two levels. He planned to incorporate a second story into it. It would be a big building that would take up a good portion of the lower bailey but, fortunately, the lower bailey was enormous and had room to spare.

It was enough to keep his time occupied. But he kept looking up to the enormous keep, imagining Amalie within the walls. Their last conversation still had him reeling; her soft kiss on his cheek, the sheer beauty of the woman. He'd caught glimpses of her humor, her wit, and it had him enamored just like everything else about her.

Weston could sense a tremendous amount of strength behind the lovely façade and it was something he wanted to get to know much, much better. The only reason he hadn't flatly informed her of his interest was because she was still so emotionally fragile. He was afraid it would somehow upset her. So he had resorted to kind words and innuendos instead. At least he hadn't driven her off. Not yet, anyway.

As he stood upon the battlements with his enormous arms crossed, watching the activity below, John mounted the ladder from the bailey and came to stand next to him. The big, bald knight made some small talk with him, shouted a few heckles down to Heath, before turning his full focus to his liege.

"How are your ribs?" he asked.

Weston twisted his torso gingerly. "Sore," he said. "I will not wear this damnable wrap beyond today. The only reason I allowed the surgeon to wrap me was because Lady Amalie seemed so distressed about my injury. It was to ease her more than me."

John's gaze drifted from Weston's torso to his face. He'd been spending a lot of time with Lady Amalie; they all knew it. She was a beautiful little thing so no one particularly blamed him, but rumors had already started about his interest in her, something that John doubted Weston was aware of. He'd been so singularly focused on the lady that there hadn't been time for much else. His activity on the battlement right now was a rarity.

"She has been through a great deal, no doubt," John commented. "Who knew that Sorrell was capable of such atrocities?"

Weston nodded faintly, watching Heath as the man surveyed off another section of digging. "If I ever see that man again, I intend to have serious words with him," he said. "To beat a woman, any woman, is a travesty."

John lifted his eyebrows. He, too, was watching Heath below. "It was not simply the beatings but the humiliation as well," he said. "To announce to the entire castle of his conquest is purely despicable. It wasn't as if he raped a lowly serving wench. He was speaking of a well-bred lady and should have kept his mouth shut. The man is no better than a dog."

Weston was still gazing at Heath but as John's words sank in, he lifted his head, struggling to process the words as if someone had spoken a foreign tongue to him. He didn't quite comprehend at first. His gaze was fixed on the keep as he blinked, digesting the words, coming to understand them. Then, he looked at John.

"What did you say?" his voice sounded strangely confused.

John met his gaze. "I said that Sorrell was a dog. If I see that man again, I will..."

Weston cut him off, brutally, smacking him in the chest with an enormous fist. "Nay," he growled, suddenly sounding quite lucid and dark. "Before that; what did you say about raping a serving wench?"

John wasn't following him. He spoke as if it were something they both already knew. "I said that it wasn't as if Sorrell raped a serving wench and boasted about it," he said. "He abused the earl's sister and then announced it to the entire castle. What kind of man would do that?"

Weston was staring at him with a stone-like expression, so tightly coiled that any small movement would crack him.

"Where did you hear this?" he finally asked.

John heard the tone, studied the body language, and began to realize that Weston must not have heard the rumors. The man had been so busy with Lady Amalie that he'd not spent much time with the men, at least not enough to hear what they knew about Sorrell. Most of Weston's company had been kept with the lady or his knights, not the troops that had been here during Sorrell's tenure. There was some fear in John's expression as he replied.

"I heard it from some of Sorrell's men," he said steadily. "Were… were you not told this, West?"

The hand that had so sharply thumped him now grabbed at the collar of his tunic. "Told what?"

"That Sorrell raped Lady Amalie," John said quietly. "The night he nearly beat her to death, he went about announcing his conquest of the lady for all to hear. I suppose it was his way of punishing Robert de Vere by brutalizing the sister. If you'd only speak to some of the men, they can confirm this. Sorrell told everyone who would listen that he raped the lady and was damned proud of it."

Weston just stared at him, a strange, slack-jawed expression coming to his face. It was clear he was shocked, but the truth was that he was beyond shocked. He was in a world of outrage and astonishment, so much so that he could hardly contain it. He couldn't believe what he was being told but, in the same breath, it explained everything Amalie had been unable to tell him. She had admitted to being beaten, of course, but rape was an entirely different issue.

It was no wonder the woman had been trying to kill herself. The most precious thing she held of value had been brutally taken from her, shame beyond measure heaped upon her as a foolish commander had boasted of his deed. The thought of Sorrell brutalizing that petite, beautiful woman nearly had Weston exploding; his ability to contain himself grew weaker by the moment.

"What else do you know?" he growled.

John didn't back away although he wanted to. "Nothing more to that regard," he said honestly. "But I have heard some of the men say that you are following the same path that Sorrell did."

"What does that mean?"

"That you are showing the same interest in her that he did right before he raped her."

Weston let go of John's tunic in a sharp gesture, stunned. His dark blue eyes were wide. "Are they truly saying that?"

John nodded. "They are," he replied. "But they do not know you the way I do. They do not know that you are virtuous and chivalrous. I know you would never brutalize the lady and have told them so."

Weston looked away, horrified. His hands formed enormous fists which he braced against the parapet, hanging his head as he digested what he had been told. It was difficult to consume everything at once but his most prevalent thought was of Amalie. He felt ill when he imagined her going through such fear and torture. She was a tiny scrap of a woman against a fairly large man. He was sure she had fought for all she was worth; he had seen it that night in the vault, the panic she had exhibited when she had awoken in the straw and realized Weston was next to her. Now, it all made sense.

Knowing she was compromised, his interest in her should have died at that very moment. For any other woman, it would have. Chastity in a woman was the most important thing to him, more important than money or titles or connections. But as repulsed as he should have been, he found that he couldn't bring himself to feel it. All he wanted to do was pull Amalie into his arms and swear to her that it didn't matter. The problem was that he didn't know if he truly could. His moral code told him one thing while his heart told him another.

He left the battlements without another word and made his way to the outer bailey, marching through the muddy rivers caused by melting snow. The keep loomed ahead and he looked up at the soaring walls against the blue expanse of sky. He had to see Amalie. He wasn't sure what he was going to say to her but he knew he had to see her. His head, his heart, felt as if they were about to explode but he maintained his composure, struggling as he entered the inner bailey and made his way into the keep.

It was still and quiet as he made his way into the keep through the enormous forebuilding and took the stairs up to the great hall. A few servants were going about their tasks, two of them seated before the great hearth and stripping great bough of rushes from two huge branches. He could smell the pine. He continued up the spiral stairs until he reached the fourth floor where Amalie's chamber was. Moving down the dark corridor to her door, he knocked softly.

His second rap pushed the door open slightly; it had not been locked. Curious, he pushed the door open further and was met with Esma and Neilie. Esma had garments in her hand and Neilie was sweeping near the hearth. When they saw Weston, they froze like frightened animals.

Weston noted their expressions as he moved into the room. The first thing he noticed was that Amalie was not there. He looked at Esma.

"Where is Lady Amalie?" he asked.

Esma swallowed. "She is not here, m'lord."

His brow furrowed. He didn't like the sound of that. "Where is she?"

Esma glanced nervously at her sister before taking a deep and steadying breath. "She told me to give you a message, m'lord."

"Message?" Weston repeated, increasingly concerned. "Esma, where did she go? You know that you are not to leave her alone."

Esma nodded quickly. "I know, m'lord," she said. "She is not alone."

"Then were in the hell is she?"

"The nuns are with her."

He was thoroughly perplexed. But rather than explode, he held up a calming hand. If he yelled, he would frighten the women and he'd never get anywhere that way. He took a deep breath to steady himself.

"Start from the beginning," he said patiently. "What is Lady Amalie's message to me and where is she?"

Esma clutched the few garments she had in her hands against her chest like a shield, as if to protect herself from de Royans' anger.

"She said to tell you that she is very grateful for your kindness but she will no longer be a burden to you or to Bolingbroke." The old servant had tears in her eyes. "She has gone to live with the nuns."

Weston wasn't much clearer than he was before. "Where?"

"In town," Esma told him. "There is a nunnery that was started by Lady Amalie's ancestor. The Benedictines live there."

He stared at the woman as it was all becoming clearer now. "She has gone to the nunnery?"

"Aye, m'lord."

His expression moved into a scowl. "She *what*?" he boomed, watching the women leap with fear. "Why in the hell did you not tell me sooner? Did she go alone?"

By now, Neilie had joined her sister as they both cowered from de Royans' wrath. "She did not go alone, m'lord," Esma said, her voice quivering. "Owyn escorted her."

Weston was losing a handle on his anger. "Owyn again," he growled. "Did she send for him to escort her?"

Esma nodded, the tears starting to fall. "She did," she replied. "She knew you would not escort her if she asked you, so she asked Owyn to take her."

"That is not true," he pointed out hotly. "She asked Owyn to escort her because she knew I would refuse to let her go at all."

"That is possible, m'lord."

Weston was furious, which wasn't a normal state for him. His emotions were involved, making him less in control of himself and more volatile. His first reaction was to find Owyn and beat him to a pulp. But he knew in the same breath that Amalie had ordered the young man to do it and he would not have refused her. But knowing that did not ease his anger.

"How long ago?" he asked, struggling with his composure.

Esma thought a moment, wiping at her cheeks. "An hour, perhaps more."

"I did not see her leave."

"She knows every way in and out of Hedingham, even the secret ways."

His jaw ticked. "Where is this nunnery?"

"Not far; it is to the north of town. You cannot miss it."

Weston's jaw was ticking furiously, feeling foolish that he'd not seen her leave no matter if she knew secret ways or not. It was his job to know everything. He felt like a failure. Compounding that was the fact that Owyn had escorted her. The soldier was supposed to be loyal to him but it had been clear, since before his time at Hedingham, that Owyn was loyal to the lady.

Weston knew he was going to go and retrieve her. It was just a matter of convincing her to leave the convent before he was forced to burn it down. As he pondered that predicament, he caught sight of Esma and Neilie from the corner of his eye. He turned to look at them.

"I will ask you a question and I require total truth," he said to both of them. "To evade my question or lie to me will incur serious consequences. Is that clear?"

The women nodded fearfully and he continued. "Esma," he looked at the serving woman. "You told me the night I arrived that Sorrell had abused Lady Amalie severely. You said that he broke her wrist and nearly killed her."

Esma nodded. "That is true, m'lord, all of it. Ask any of the soldiers, for they will tell you…"

Weston cut her off. "I know it is the truth," he said. "But what you did not tell me was that Sorrell raped her. Is this true?"

Esma and Neilie looked as if they were about to become ill. Neilie broke down in tears, weeping into her apron as Esma struggled not to succumb to tears as well.

"Several times, m'lord," Esma finally whispered, tears streaming down her cheeks. "He hurt her very badly."

By this time, Weston's mercurial fury had abated, leaving nausea and sorrow in its wake. It was confirmation of the rumor from people who would know the truth. He gazed at the women, understanding how hard it must have been for them to stand by helplessly while all of it went on. The depth and breadth of what the occupants of Hedingham endured during Sorrell's tenure was still revealing itself to him in all its horror. It must have been hell.

"Why did you not tell me that?" he asked hoarsely.

Esma wiped at her eyes. "We did not know you, m'lord," she murmured. "It was enough to tell you that she was abused. I did not want more shame to be heaped upon her by telling you that the commander had stolen her innocence."

"Is that why she tried to kill herself?"

Esma closed her eyes and nodded; she couldn't even reply. Weston sighed faintly, his eyes trailing to the bed where the deed undoubtedly happened. In his mind's eye, he could see sweet, little Amalie fighting off a drunken knight to no avail. The pain she must have felt, the shame, was immeasurable. He closed his eyes to the horror of it, turning away from the bed.

"So she has committed herself to a convent because she was raped," he muttered, looking up to the heavens as if to beg for wisdom. "Dear God, is it really true?"

Esma, unsure if it was a rhetorical question, answered him. "It is, m'lord," she said. "She is compromised. She knows she will never be a marriageable prospect now that she has been ruined. Perhaps it was Bolingbroke's plan all along. Perhaps he ordered his commander to do it to punish the earl for fleeing England like a coward. Perhaps he..."

She froze when she remembered who she was talking to. Weston, pale and drawn, turned to look at her, unmoved by her words. He was more focused on the fact that the servant mentioned that Amalie was no longer a marriageable prospect.

"Her friend, Cecily, was here earlier," he said. "The woman was spouting off about her wedding and I could tell that Amalie was upset by it. Cecily invited her to the wedding but Amalie refused to go. Is that why? Because she feels she is no longer a marriageable prospect?"

Esma nodded faintly. "More than likely, m'lord."

Weston just stood there, finally shaking his head and quitting the chamber. Esma and Neilie watched him go, hearing his footsteps disappear down the staircase before turning to each other with varied degrees of anxiety.

Without another word between them, they went back to their tasks in a mechanical, repetitious fashion, cleaning the chamber of a woman who would never return.

CHAPTER EIGHT

THE MOTHER ABBESS was not surprised to see Amalie de Vere within the walls of the Benedictine nunnery founded by her ancestor, Alberic de Vere, shortly after the invasion of William the Conqueror. She had seen Amalie many times over the years, as she was the patroness of the convent along with her brother, the current Earl of Oxford.

Mother Mary Ruth had been at the convent for most of her seventy years, quite an old lady by any standards, and remembered three generations of the de Vere family. Upon seeing Lady Amalie, she greeted her warmly. She was thrilled at the lady's visit. But she was not prepared for the lady's request.

The tiny Mother Abbess had to repeat the request to make sure she had understood correctly. "You... you wish to join the nunnery?"

Amalie was standing in the spartanly furnished entry of the convent with her satchel at her feet. Dressed in a sturdy, brown woolen surcoat, a soft eggshell colored shift and the heavy, fur-lined cloak that Esma and Neilie had cleaned of the mud, she looked determined.

"I do, Mother Mary Ruth," she said decisively. "I would make a good nun. I am not afraid of hard work or difficult conditions. I understand it would be much different from the life I have been living at Hedingham but I truly feel that this is where I need to be."

The Mother Abbess gently took Amalie's hand. She held Amalie's warm digits in her tiny, cold palm. It was apparent that she was shocked by the nature of the request.

"Lady Amalie," she said evenly. "I have known you since birth, my child. You and your brother have been great patrons of our convent. You have been both generous and attentive. But never, at any time, did you mention your desire to assume a life entirely devoted to God. Why, may I ask, have you made this decision?"

Amalie knew that question would come sooner or later; she wasn't so sure she was prepared for it sooner. She hadn't had time to think up a truly believable lie. But after what had happened with Weston earlier in the day, she had reacted more on impulse than on a carefully planned idea. She was terrified of Weston's advance, terrified of the potential of her own feelings for the man, and terrified of what would happen when the truth became known.

As she tried to think of something reasonable to tell the Mother Abbess, all that came forth were frightened, embarrassed tears.

The Mother Abbess could see the distress in the young woman. She took Amalie by the hand to a small room off the entry. There was a chair, a table and little else, and she gently pushed Amalie down onto the chair. As she sent another nun for some wine, the elderly abbess returned her attention to the distraught young lady in the chair.

Like everyone else in Hedingham, she had heard of the young earl's flight to Ireland when a price was put on his head by opponents of the king. She had also heard rumors for years that the young earl was, in fact, more than a supporter of the king. Words like "lover" had often come in to play where the rumors were concerned. It was a terrible reputation for the man, even more terrible for his sister.

Lady Amalie had always been a genuinely beautiful and good girl, kind and generous, where her brother could be a monster. When the earl fled and left Amalie to the mercy of his enemies, there were whispers of panic and sorrow about the town on behalf of the young woman. Bolingbroke's men still occupied the castle, which was why, the Mother Abbess suspected, Lady Amalie had come. She wondered what had taken the girl so long to seek sanctuary.

The wine came and the Mother Abbess forced Amalie to take a few sips of the tart, red wine. As Amalie began to calm, she looked at the

Mother Abbess apologetically.

"I am sorry for my lack of composure," she said quietly. "I am afraid these days have been difficult ones."

The Mother Abbess put a gnarled hand on her shoulder. "I understand, child," she said softly. "Please tell me why you feel the need to join the Benedictine order."

Amalie sniffled, wiping delicately at her nose. "Surely you have heard that Bolingbroke now inhabits my family's home."

"I have."

"I must get away from them."

"Then we shall give you sanctuary. You need not join us in order for the convent to provide you with protection."

Amalie looked at her, wide-eyed and relieved. "Is this true?" she wiped at her nose again. "I... I did not know that."

The Mother Abbess smiled warmly. "If that is your wish, then we would be happy to care for you. All of the armies in the entire world, including Bolingbroke's, cannot breach this place. You are safe here."

Amalie wiped a shaky hand over her face. "I do not know what to say," she said. "Gratitude is not enough. I was so fearful that I would have nowhere else to go."

The Mother Abbess held her hand. "Of course you do," she said. "We are happy to have you."

Amalie looked up at the woman, knowing that she needed to be completely truthful with the woman so she would know what she was dealing with. It would be unfair to keep such important information from the woman. The tears began to return.

"Thank you," she whispered. "But... but there is more to it than mere sanctuary."

"More? What more?"

Amalie took a deep breath, nauseous that she would be forced to put into words her painful shame. Speaking it would be reliving it and she tried not to let her nerves and emotions swamp her as she summoned the strength to speak. Her body was quivering with tension as she spoke.

"After my brother fled, Hedingham was confiscated by the Earl of Derby, Henry of Bolingbroke." She was speaking so softly that it was difficult to hear her. "Henry sent a battalion of men to occupy the castle, including a commander who was purely evil. I was able to avoid him for a good length of time but, unfortunately, he started showing interest in me. Horrible, vile interest. One night, he became drunk and... he came to my room for carnal purposes. When I refused, he beat me so horribly that he cracked my wrist. I fought him as best I could but he was too strong. When the beating was over, he... I was unable to fight back, you see, so he... he took me by force."

The Mother Abbess was gazing at her with wide eyes, pity and horror overwhelming her. As Amalie struggled not to dissolve into tears again, the old woman sank to her knees next to her, holding her hand tightly. There was a great deal of pity in her expression.

"My sweet, dear girl," she whispered. "I am so sorry for you."

Amalie half-shrugged, half-nodded as if to accept her condolences, but she wasn't finished with her story yet.

"The beatings went on well into the night," she murmured, tears beginning to stream down her face again. "After every beating, he would take me again, more brutally than before. By morning, I was nearly dead from being abused as the commander left my chamber and went about the castle bragging of his conquest. I was saved from further abuse by a young soldier who hid me away from the commander so he could not find me to repeat his evil deeds. My servants and I lived in the stables, in tunnels, and in other parts of the castle so he could not find me. But our prayers were eventually answered and the commander was sent away."

The Mother Abbess held her hands, caressing them gently. "God is merciful," she whispered. "But you should have come to me immediately. Why didn't you?"

Amalie shrugged, sniffling. "I do not know," she said honestly. "Hedingham is my home, I suppose. I would not let anyone chase me from it."

The Mother Abbess' old eyes were sharp. "Yet something has," she whispered knowingly. "A brutal man could not do it. What has sent you to me now?"

Amalie lifted her gaze, thinking of Weston, of the truth she had hidden from everyone until now. She found she could hardly keep it to herself any longer, the horrible truth that ate at her like a cancer. She struggled to keep her composure together as she spoke those fateful words.

"That night of horror took root," she whispered, closing her eyes tightly when she could no longer meet the woman's gaze. "I carry his child."

The Mother Abbess didn't openly react but, inside, she hurt deeply for the beautiful young women. The admission had been like a dagger to her soul, sharp and painful. She suddenly felt very protective of Amalie, a fierce lioness of virtue when others would seek to harm her. She put an old hand on Amalie's lowered head, reassuring and warm. She could think of nothing else to do that would be of any comfort.

"Not to worry, Ammy." Then she did something out of character; she kissed the top of the blond head to comfort the lady so desperately in need of it. "We shall take care of you. You needn't worry in the least."

Amalie's face was streaming with tears. She still couldn't bring herself to look the woman in the eye. "But... but what of the baby?" she wept.

Mother Mary Ruth stood up stiffly; her old knees weren't as spry as they used to be. She could see that she had a job ahead of her, a task of great care. Generations of the de Veres had taken care of her order. Now it was time for her to take care of the de Veres.

"We shall worry over him when the time comes," she said firmly. "For now, I will have you rest until supper. Will you do this?"

Amalie nodded but she was still sobbing softly. The Mother Abbess gently pulled her to her feet, holding her hands tightly. If the old woman was shaken by the news, she didn't let on, at least to Amalie. Right now, she deduced that the woman needed someone to show some strength for her, not weigh her down with more tears. She led her towards the door and opened it.

"Come along," she said gently, motioning to a nun down the corridor to come to her. "Sister Teresita will take you to rest now. I will see you at supper."

Amalie let the nun lead her away, deep into the bowels of the old Benedictine nunnery that had stood for centuries. The Mother Abbess stood there long after Amalie had disappeared into the darkness, her thoughts wandering to the horrible deeds committed against the young woman. It was a tragedy in a world that was full of tragedy. She struggled not to let the depression of the events get to her. Turning on her heel, she went about her business.

Lady Amalie would fit well with them, she was sure of it. And Mary Ruth would personally kill the next Bolingbroke bastard who set foot at the nunnery. There was nothing as dangerous as an avenging angel.

CHAPTER NINE

May 1388

"A MMY?" SISTER TERESITA stuck her head inside the hot, smoky kitchen. "He is here again."

Amalie looked up from the carrots she was preparing for the evening meal. She was flushed rosy from the heat, a heavy kerchief on her head keeping her blond hair back from her face and scratchy garments of rough wool covered her tender body. She wiped the sweat from her forehead with the back of her hand, knowing what Sister Teresita meant without much explanation.

"De Royans?" she asked the obvious.

Sister Teresita nodded. "He has come bearing gifts again." The woman came into the kitchen, eyeing the young woman who had become her friend over the past few months. "He says he is not leaving until he sees you."

A brief flash of pain crossed Amalie's features before she turned back to her carrots, washing the dirt from them in the bucket of fresh water she had just brought in from the well.

"He always says that," she said. "Tell him that I am busy."

"I always tell him you are busy. He always comes back." Sister Teresita put a small, rough hand on Amalie's forearm. "Why will you not see him? He seems so sad when you send him away."

Amalie looked at the young nun, an unattractive woman with big moles on her face. But she had a heart of gold and had become a dear and gentle friend. After a moment, she shrugged.

"I have nothing to say to him," she said, moving the carrots from the bucket into a bowl. "He will forget about me soon enough."

Sister Teresita smiled sadly, patted Amalie's hand, and left the kitchen. Amalie thought a moment on Weston. He had come daily to the convent since the day she had committed herself. He always came with gifts, always asking to see her, and she always sent him away. She didn't want to, but she knew she had to. As much as it hurt her heart, it was the right thing to do. She didn't want the man to see her humiliation.

She rubbed at her growing belly, the pregnancy quite evident at four months. She looked as if she had a small pumpkin under her skirts. The child was very active and she would lie still at night, feeling it roll around in her belly. There were times when it brought her great joy and other times when she felt so shameful that she wished she could die. But she was beyond the temporary madness of suicide. Now, she was determined to have the child considering it was the only child she would ever have. With no husband, it was guaranteed. Her life, as she saw it, was over before it began.

She wasn't particularly miserable at the convent but she wasn't particularly happy, either. She deliberately stayed away from town and avoided any manner of news that came from the castle. Her focus was on the convent, her duties, and the impending child. So she pushed thoughts of de Royans from her mind and collected her big, reed basket.

The garden to the rear of the nunnery was sprouting with spring vegetables. There were several particularly large cucumbers she had wanted to collect earlier but her basket had been full of carrots. Donning a woolen cloak that was heavy and wet at the bottom, she proceeded out into the cool spring day.

The garden was big and plentiful, and all of the nuns worked it at one time or another. Amalie spent a good deal of time here because it kept her constantly busy and she needed to feel occupied. Leisure time brought about thoughts of great depression and anxiety so she tried to always be busy.

Thoughts of Weston were heavy in her mind and heart at all times; the fact that he showed up daily to speak with her only deepened her sense of sorrow. She would never forget about the man if he kept coming around. On the other hand, she didn't want to forget him at all. It made for a difficult dilemma.

Wandering out into the damp plants which had just had a dousing of seasonal rain, she knelt beside the cucumbers and began to separate them from the vines. It was dirty work and her fingers were cold with the wet earth, but she didn't particularly mind. She rather liked gardening. Grasping a cucumber, she took a small knife and cut it free of the plant.

Cutting the second cucumber, she heard footsteps approach and she didn't bother to look up. Thinking it was Sister Teresita, she spoke.

"Sister?" she said. "Can you please help cut some cucumbers off of this vine? They are fairly ripe and I am afraid they will rot with all of the rain we have been having."

She was indicating the plant in back of her. When she didn't receive a reply, she turned to look at the nun. But the only thing she saw was enormous boots standing a few feet away. Startled, she lifted her eyes to see Weston gazing down at her.

Their eyes met and the spark, dormant for these past few months, ignited with a fury. Having no idea what to say to the man, she simply sat there, apprehensive and fearful that he was going to give her an earful for sending him away day after day. He had been persistent and she had been cruel.

She waited for the boom as the painful seconds ticked away and neither of them said a word, but Weston merely smiled when he realized she wasn't going to jump up and run away.

"Greetings, my lady," he said in his soft, rich voice. "I was just leaving the nunnery and thought I might check the back door just in case you happened to be around. I see that my instincts were correct."

The sound of his deep, beautiful voice almost brought tears to her eyes. It had been so long since she had heard it. She sighed faintly, resigned at his appearance and unwilling to fight it further, though she should have been. She should have run for her life.

"So you have found me," she said softly, her gaze lingering on him. "You are looking well, Weston."

His smile broadened. "And you are more beautiful than I had remembered," he said, keeping his manner even and steady, although it was difficult. He wanted to explode at her. "Are you well?"

"Verily."

"That is good to know. I have been very worried."

"Why? You knew I was here. You must assume that I am well taken care of."

Weston shifted on his big legs. He was in full armor this day, looking every inch the imposing Bolingbroke knight. But his face, feature for feature, was calm and more handsome than she remembered. He was so big and blond and beautiful. The more she looked at the man, the more she felt herself softening.

"I had to see for myself," he said quietly.

"And so you have. Is there anything else you wish to know?"

"Are you happy here?"

He was straight to the point. She nodded, looking back to her cucumbers. "The nuns are very kind to me."

He suddenly crouched down to bring himself more to her level. His dark blue eyes drank in her face, every lovely line and every gentle slope. He could hardly believe he was looking at her after all of these months; he'd spent ninety-one days being disappointed daily when the nunnery turned him away in his attempts to visit Amalie, and every day he would return to the castle knowing he would try again the next day. She was the last thing he thought of at night and the first thing he thought of in the morning.

"I have come daily to see you but you have sent me away," he said quietly. "I always hoped that one of these days you would agree to see me."

She looked up from her cucumber. "I hope you will be satisfied now that you know I am well."

"I am." He watched her fiddle with the cucumber. "I just wish you had not left in the first place."

"I was not going to stay at Hedingham with a host of Bolingbroke soldiers around me."

"I understand," he said quietly. "But I swore to protect you. I wish you had trusted my word."

"I did trust it," she replied, fussing with the cucumber out of nervousness. "But I felt that it was best for me to come to the nunnery. I am assured safety and protection here, for always, with no more knights to attack me."

He watched her put the cucumber in her basket. The silence between them grew heavy as she fidgeted nervously and he groped for the proper words. He didn't want to upset her or frighten her, but there was much to say to her. Three months of longing had seen to that.

"Amalie, I must say something," he finally said, watching her look up at him with her beautiful green eyes. He met her gaze, praying he wouldn't send her running back into the nunnery with what he was about to say. "I know what happened with Sorrell. I know what he did to you."

She stared at him and he could see her cheeks reddening. "I told you what he did."

He shook his head. "You did not tell me everything." His voice was a whisper. "I know about the rape. I know it was because of the rape that you tried to kill yourself. So many times I asked you why and you would not tell me, but now I know. I just wanted to say how sorry I am that he did that. I am so sorry you had to go through that horrible ordeal."

By this time, her eyes were beginning to water. As he watched, she turned away from him and broke down into soft sobs. Weston knew he had to say everything he needed to say, and say it quickly, before he lost her completely. He was afraid she would run back into the nunnery and he would never see her again.

"What I am trying to say is that it does not matter to me that you are compromised," he said quickly, softly. "I know you believe yourself an undesirable marriage prospect and that is why you committed yourself to the nunnery, but I am here to tell you that I would be deeply honored if you would accept my proposal of marriage. I could think of no greater privilege than to become your husband, Ammy. Perhaps the lure of working in the garden and wearing woolen underwear is a greater attraction to you, but I pray that you will at least consider marriage to me as an alternative."

She was looking at him by now, astonishment on her face. But the tears were still flowing, dripping off her chin, as her green eyes fixed on him, holding him captive within their vibrant gaze. After a small eternity of staring at him, she simply shook her head in bafflement.

"Oh... Weston," she breathed. "Why would you do this?"

He shrugged, feeling somewhat uncomfortable. But now was the time for truth. "Because I cannot forget about you no matter how hard I try," he whispered. "Your spirit and your beauty have marked me and I know in my heart that I cannot go on without you. Committing yourself to this convent has crushed me, Ammy. I have come every day to ask you to marry me and every day you have sent me away. I love your courage, your humor, your kindness and your compassion. You are a rare woman and I would never find another like you if I lived to be one hundred. I know that you do not love me but, perhaps, you will in time. I only ask for that opportunity. Please do not send me away again."

She sat frozen as he finished his sentence. He didn't think her eyes could get any bigger, her expression any more shocked, but it did.

"You... you *love* me?" she gasped.

He nodded without hesitation. "I do."

He watched a myriad of emotions run across her face, from shock to disbelief to joy. He was particularly focused on the joy and thought, perhaps, that there might be a chance. But she suddenly closed her eyes and put her dirty hands to her ears.

"Nay," she shook her head violently. "Do not say such things. You will regret it."

His brow furrowed, concerned. "I will never regret it, not ever."

She began to sob loudly. "Aye, you will. Go away, Weston. Go away and never come back."

He wasn't about to leave; he reached out and grasped her arm to steady her. "I will not go away and I will never regret loving you. Why do you say such things?"

She was growing louder and more animated. Yanking her arm from his grasp, she tossed the cucumber basket aside and rose to her knees. Weston watched, shocked, as she pulled tight her apron and surcoat around her torso to display her gently swollen belly.

"Because of this," she wept painfully. "Weston, I did not try to kill myself because the commander raped me. I tried to kill myself because of the child he implanted in my womb. The worst night of my life resulted in a baby and I was determined to die rather than live with the shame. But you stopped me; again and again, you stopped me without truly knowing how it was affecting my life. When my attempts at suicide failed, I did the only thing I could do; I committed myself to the nunnery. You wanted to know everything, Weston. Now you know and now you will leave and never look back."

Weston stared at her, at her swollen midsection, and he had never felt more sickened in his life. He didn't know what to say; he just stared at her. Amalie gazed steadily at him, her sobs fading as she looked into his astonished, horrified expression.

"But there is more," she sniffled, sobs fading as a great and awful pain took hold in her heart. "You have confessed your thoughts and I will confess mine. Weston, I committed myself to the convent because I knew I was falling in love with you, too, and I knew there was no chance for a future between us. You are a strong and virtuous knight, and you must have a bride that reflects that. I do not reflect that. Thanks to a drunken knight, my life has been ruined. I would not ruin yours as well."

Weston abruptly stood up and turned away, his mind reeling. He knew he loved her; God help him, he knew it. But there was a great portion of him that was sickened and shamed by what had happened to her, the deeply religious side that was rigid and unbending when it came to issues of morality. But the compassionate side of him, the side that loved her deeply, knew that it was not her fault. What happened to her had been completely beyond her control. Amalie was still pure and innocent in his eyes in spite of her condition. He simply couldn't bring himself to condemn her.

"It does not matter," he finally muttered, sighing deeply and turning to look at her. "What happened to you was not your fault. You did not invite the man to rape and beat you; it was completely beyond your control. I will not condemn you for something that was not your fault."

Amalie stood up, stiffly, her expression laced with anguish. "Please go, Weston. The longer you stay here, the more difficult it will be for both of us."

He shook his head. "I am not going anywhere," he said. "I am going to take you from this place and we are going to be married."

Amalie's eyes widened. "But..." she struggled to summon the words. "But you cannot."

"Why?"

"Because everyone will think the child is yours and that is not fair to you. It is a shame you should not bear."

He shook his head again, making his way over to her slowly with a pensive expression on his face. Finally, he stopped in front of her, the dark blue eyes full of warmth and compassion.

"I am unconcerned about that," he murmured. "I should only be so fortunate for men to think that we loved each other enough to demonstrate that love, married or not. I have spent my entire life running from shame, Ammy. I grew up with it, so much so that I have spent the majority of my knighthood proving that I was more pious, moral and chivalrous than anyone else around me. I thought the only way to do that was to pray more than anyone else, fight harder for the church than anyone else, and condemn those who were weak or foolish. But you… you have changed all of that. I do not care if men believe we have sinned before marriage because you and I know the truth. I love you, Ammy. That will never change, no matter what."

Her tears were gone now, being replaced by something so warm, so hopeful, she couldn't dare bring herself to believe it. Timidly, she reached out to him and he caught her dirty hand, bringing it to his lips for a tender kiss. He didn't care that her fingers were covered with dirt; he kissed them anyway. His blue eyes blazed as he gazed down at her.

"What shame have you been running from?" she asked softly.

He sighed faintly, her hand still against his mouth. "You have revealed your great secret so I suppose it only fair that I reveal mine," he murmured. "I was six years of age when my mother began an illicit affair with my father's father. My father, so humiliated by the fact that his wife left him for his own father, took his life. I found my father's body, impaled upon his sword. My younger brother, who was five years old at the time, helped me remove the sword from our father's body and then we went to my mother to tell her what had happened. Instead of being distraught, she smiled. I will never forget the look on her face. And then she married my grandfather and they have been married ever since."

Amalie's eyes widened with shock. "Oh, Weston," she breathed. "What a terrible story. I am so deeply sorry for you."

He shrugged it off. "It is of no matter any longer," he said. "In a sense, it made me who I am. I live cleaner than most knights and I believe that God has a hand in all things. He teaches us what is right, what is wrong, and leads us to do what He feels is best."

She regarded him as he still held her hand to his mouth; she could feel his hot breath from his nostrils on her skin.

"Did He lead you to me?" she asked softly.

Weston nodded without hesitation. "He knew that you needed me. And I suppose, in a sense, He knew I needed you; I fell in love with a woman that, under normal circumstances, I would have condemned.

Perhaps... perhaps God's lesson to me in all of this is that compassion is sometimes the greater glory. Even now, I feel no distress in raising another man's child as my own. All I know is that when I look at you, all I can feel is love and joy. Surely there can be no wrong in that."

She smiled at him, hesitantly. "And all I know is that I have felt nothing but pain and humiliation since that horrible January day," she said quietly. "I believed my life to be over; I truly did. Now... now I feel overwhelmed with hope. I still cannot believe you feel as you do."

He returned her smile, moving closer to take her in his arms. For the first time, he relished the sensation of her against him, knowing she was agreeable to his advances. He gazed down into her lovely face, feeling so overwhelmingly joyful that it was in danger of exploding out of every pore in his body. Their relationship was now beyond commander and chatelaine; everything he had hoped for and dreamed about was coming to fruition.

"Then you are agreeable to marrying me?" he asked.

She still appeared hesitant. "I am still not sure it would be..."

He cut her off with a gentle squeeze. "Please, Ammy. Do not break my heart."

A gentle smile broke through as she gazed up at him. "I would not knowingly do such a thing," she murmured. "If you are sure that marriage is what you want, then I am agreeable."

He leaned forward, closing his eyes and kissing her forehead reverently. The gesture was sweet and delicious, and Amalie began to tear up again. She collapsed forward against him, cheek against his broad chest, struggling to stave off the tears. His strength enveloping her was a delicious sensation.

"This seems like a dream," she whispered, feeling his powerful arms wrap around her. "I never dared to hope that you would feel for me as I feel for you."

He kissed the top of her head. "I want to make you happy, Ammy. It is my greatest desire."

She lifted her head from his chest, gazing up at him with her green eyes. "You are a sweet and compassionate man," she whispered. "I will always do my best to be worthy of you."

He smiled at her. But more than that, he was seized with an overwhelming urge to kiss her. Gently, his lips slanted over hers in their first kiss, something so sweet and warm that it brought waves of excitement and contentment. But within the first few seconds, Weston knew that he must taste more of her and he pulled her more tightly against him, his tongue licking at her lips until she opened wider and invited him in.

He tasted her deeply, knowing she was better than he ever imagined she could be. He'd finally found what he'd been searching for his entire life; love, life, happiness in the most unexpected of circumstances. It was heaven.

Amalie clung to him, experiencing the newness of her first true kiss and very quickly realizing that she liked it. The drunken soldier had never kissed her; his mouth had been in other places. So the experience of Weston's soft lips against hers was truly something amazing. Even as he became more aggressive and plundered her tender mouth with his tongue, gently yet passionately, she wasn't the least bit intimidated. In fact, she learned quickly and was soon matching him suckle for suckle.

Weston put a reluctant end to it when he grasped her face gently, suckled her lower lip, and then kissed both cheeks before pulling back to look at her. His handsome face was lined with joy.

"As much as I could stand here and kiss you all day, I am not entirely sure that this is appropriate given that we are standing in the garden of a nunnery," he murmured, kissing her lips once more before dropping his hands from her face. "Let us collect your belongings and return to Hedingham."

She watched him, her kiss-swollen lips within her rather serious face. "Are you truly sure about this, Weston?" she asked softly. "I would not blame you if you changed your mind."

He took her hand in his enormous gauntlet. "I will never change my mind. I am more worried about you changing yours."

She smiled weakly. "I will not change my mind."

"Then we have nothing to worry over."

She shook her head, still rather dazed by the situation. When she attempted to reclaim her basket with the spilled cucumbers, Weston retrieved it for her and carried it in to the nunnery. He didn't want her to exert herself any more than necessary, already the protective husband.

He found that the Mother Abbess had been more difficult to convince that his intentions were true than Amalie had been. The old woman was very protective of her young charge and Weston spent the rest of the afternoon stressing to the woman that he loved Amalie and would provide a good home to both her and the baby. Only with the greatest reluctance, and with Amalie's approval, did the Mother Abbess finally relinquish her charge with the condition that a priest be sent for to perform the ceremony right away. A rider was sent to St. Andrew's Church in Halstead for a priest.

It was close to midnight by the time Weston and Amalie return to Hedingham as husband and wife.

CHAPTER TEN

H EATH AND JOHN were on the battlements of Hedingham when Weston de Royans and his new wife approached astride Weston's big, blond charger.

They admitted the commander and greeted the lady, who was clad in a rough woolen cloak as Weston lifted her down from the horse. They had all known that she had committed herself to the nunnery because of the rape, and not one of them blamed her, so it was a distinct surprise to see her return with de Royans after all of these months. They also knew that Weston had gone to the nunnery every day to see her but had always been turned away.

The gossips had been spinning rumors fast and furious that de Royans was in love with the woman and she had spurned his advances. The rumors had spread from the castle to the town and the peasants would actually turn out to see de Royans ride to the nunnery astride his massive warhorse, only to be sent away when the lady would not see him.

It had become something of a sad love story and the talk of the town, which was ironic considering Weston had finally claimed the lady and returned her to the castle under the dead of night. No one in town had been awake to witness it but there was little doubt the news would spread like wildfire come the morning.

Heath greeted the lady kindly, trying not to appear too surprised, and unstrapped her satchel from the horse's saddle, handing it to her with a respectful smile. Weston removed his weapons from the saddle, turning the beast over to a sleepy groom as he faced his men.

"You were gone a long time," Heath commented. "We were about to send out a search party."

Weston lifted an eyebrow at him. "You knew where I was."

Heath's grin broadened. "We thought that perhaps the nuns had their fill of seeing you day after day and had finally taken you hostage."

Amalie giggled as Weston shook his head in disapproval.

"Dolt," he growled, although it was good natured. "As if I could not fight off a gang of nuns."

"The brides of Christ are frightening, West."

Weston fought off a grin, indicating Amalie standing next to him. "As you can see, I finally brought the lady home," he said. "But I married her before I did. Meet the Lady Amalie de Vere de Royans."

The smiles vanished from Heath and John's faces as they stared at Amalie in shock. After an odd, uncertain silence, Heath was the first one to react.

"Congratulations, Lady de Royans," he said, eyeing Weston. "I hope you know what you have gotten yourself in to."

He meant it in jest. Amalie smiled timidly at Weston. "I am not entirely sure but it is too late now," she said, looking at Heath. "I do hope you will tell me anything that you feel I need to know."

Heath's smile was back but Weston cut him off, putting an enormous arm around Amalie's shoulders and leading her in the direction of the keep.

"He will keep his mouth shut if he values his life." He cast Heath a long look. "Secure the posts for the night. I will sleep in the keep tonight."

Heath and John nodded, watching the pair fade off into the darkness of the upper bailey. It was shocking news and a swift announcement. Weston wasn't wasting any time with the young lady he had just rescued from the nunnery. When the couple was out of sight, and earshot, John turned to Heath.

"He *married* her?" he hissed. "God's Beard, what possessed the man to do that?"

Heath shrugged. "You know he is in love with her," he pointed out. "What did you expect when he was going to the nunnery every day, trying to catch a glimpse of her? Did you not think he was serious about her?"

John just shook his head, baffled. "But… Sorrell took the woman. He used her. What does West want with Sorrell's leavings?"

"He must not look at it that way."

"How else could he look at it? She is soiled."

Heath's expression grew serious. "I would not say that if I were you. Keep it to yourself. If West is in love with the woman, then he will likely take your head off for it."

John put his hands up in supplication. "I realize that," he said. "But the Weston we know would have never looked twice at an unchaste woman. Has the man changed before our eyes and we did not realize it?"

Heath simply lifted his shoulders and began heading off towards the gatehouse. "Men in love are known to do strange things," he said. "It would be best if you kept your thoughts to yourself on this subject."

John nodded in agreement, watching the red-haired knight move off in the darkness. He had duties he had to attend to as well, going about them with his mind lingering on his liege and the woman he married. Maybe Heath was right; maybe love did do strange things to men. But he couldn't imagine the pious and moral man he knew as his liege having changed so much that he would marry a compromised woman.

It was an appalling prospect.

☙

ESMA AND NEILIE wept when Amalie roused them from their beds in the alcove of her bedchamber. The old serving women hugged and kissed her, so very glad to see their young lady. When Amalie told them that she and Sir Weston had been married, the women had wept harder.

The purpose of waking the women from their beds was not to announce the marriage; it was to get them out of the chamber. Under no circumstances was Weston going to allow the servants to sleep in the chamber he shared with his wife, tonight of all nights, so he carefully suggested to Amalie that the women might be comfortable in another chamber.

Amalie had no idea what he meant until it gradually began to dawn on her that the bridegroom might like to have his bride alone on their wedding night. She eventually chased Esma and Neilie from the chamber and bolted the door behind them, but by the time she turned to face Weston, she was quivering with fear.

The fire in the hearth popped now and again as the two of them silently faced one another. Weston wasn't oblivious to the fact that she was nervous, probably more than a normal bride would be given the circumstances, but he tried to keep his manner calm and comforting, hoping that would ease her.

He began to remove his tunic, his mail, piece by piece as Amalie remained by the door. When he shirked off his mail coat and realized she was still standing there, shielded by the shadows of the room, he put his mail coat on a chair near the hearth and held out a hand to her.

"Are you going to stand there all night?" he asked softly. "Come in and make yourself comfortable."

Amalie took a few steps away from the door, her green eyes wide with fear. Weston didn't even realize how terrified she was until she came into the light of the glowing hearth and he read the panic on her features. He reached out a hand, gently cupping her beautiful face.

"I swear there is nothing to fear, my angel," he murmured. "I will not make you do anything you are uncomfortable with, I swear it."

She gazed up at him, smiling gratefully, but he could see that her eyes were starting to water. Then she removed the heavy woolen cloak that had concealed her condition from everyone, tossing it onto the floor. Slowly, she began to untie the bib-apron that was layered over the rough woolen surcoat.

"I know you will not," she whispered. "You have always proven yourself to be sweet and gentle. But my last memory of a man in this room was not a pleasant one. Even as I stand here, my heart is thumping and fear grips me, yet I know that what I share with you tonight will be completely different from my only experience with such a thing. I... I am so ashamed."

She hung her head and he could see fat tears running down her cheek. He moved to her, gently, cupping her face with his two enormous hands and forcing her to look at him.

"We do not have to do anything you are uncomfortable with," he reiterated, kissing the end of her nose. "It would be best if we simply go to sleep and deal with the rest of this when the time is right. Is that acceptable?"

She looked up at him, his extraordinarily handsome face, and the kindness of his blue eyes. The man was trying so hard to make things well for her; he'd been doing it since nearly the moment they had met. He was always going out of his way to make things easy for her when all she did was make them difficult. She put her hands on his, feeling his firm, warm flesh beneath her fingers.

"Nay," she shook her head after a moment. "It is not acceptable. This is our wedding night and it is my right to come to know my husband as a wife should. I cannot live with silly fears for the rest of my life." She suddenly pushed up against him, her hands moving down his enormous forearms, gripping at him. Her eyes were fixed on his full, smooth lips. "I would ask a favor of you, West."

He couldn't take his eyes off her luscious face, feeling her soft and supple body against him. "Anything, my angel."

"Would you...?" she paused, swallowed, and started again. "All I have ever known of the ways of men is horrible brutality but I know it is not always this way. Even as I stand here with you, I am almost paralyzed by fear and I do not want to be, not with you. Would... would you show me what intimacy between a man and a woman is truly meant to be like, as to erase these horrible memories?"

He stroked her cheeks with his thumbs. "It would be my pleasure," he said softly. "Unless you have any objections, may I take the lead?"

She nodded her head, hesitantly, and his smile broadened. Dropping his hands from her face, he turned her around and deftly untied the apron she was fumbling with. He began to talk as he undressed her.

"You and I spent a great deal of time together before you went to the nunnery," he said as he pulled the apron over her head. "I hope you have not forgotten about everything we talked about."

She watched the apron end up on top of the old cloak as he went to work on the fastens of her surcoat.

"We did not speak on anything truly significant during that time." She thought about it. "I remember that you are a very poor planner and complain if you have to spend the slightest amount of money on me."

Weston rolled his eyes. "And you, madam, are a slave to a sticky bun. If I were baker, I could rule your world."

She laughed, pulling her hair over one shoulder as he finished with the fastens on the surcoat.

"You already rule my world," she said softly, glancing over her shoulder at him. "I am not the least bit sorry, either."

He smiled at her, pulling away the top of her surcoat and realizing her soft skin was now exposed. He leaned down, delicately kissing the top of her shoulder.

"Neither am I."

The laughter faded and Amalie closed her eyes as Weston slid the surcoat off her body. It landed at her feet, leaving her clad in only her shift, as he came up behind her and very carefully wrapped his big arms around her.

She kept her eyes closed, head bowed, as his mouth moved to the tender nape of her neck, kissing her softly as his big arms hugged her carefully. It wasn't long before his hands moved to belly, feeling the gentle rise of it through the linen shift. He rubbed his hands over her stomach, acquainting himself with her, as his lips feasted on her neck.

It was thrilling, erotic and pivotal. Weston was already so consumed by the woman that he could hardly think straight and he struggled not to let his excitement veer out of control. With his considerable power, he didn't want his lust to overtake him enough so that she was frightened by his onslaught. So far, he'd set a slow pace of discovery and she was responding in kind. He was determined to keep her calm as he explored her blossoming body.

He took her over by the fire and sat her down on the warm furs in front of the hearth. He pulled off his tunic, revealing his spectacular, muscular shape as he knelt down in front of her. With them both on their knees, they faced one another. Weston studied her beauty in the firelight, swearing that he had never seen anything so beautiful. He could hardly believe she belonged to him. After several long moments of pause, he reached out and began to unlace the front of the shift.

Amalie watched his fingers, closing her eyes as he moved forward and kissed her cheek, her neck, as the lacings opened wider. He was so gentle about it that she felt no fear when he lifted the shift over her head, leaving her naked. Weston didn't stare at her or make her feel self-conscious. His lips returned to her neck, her shoulders, gently grasping her hands and kissing them when she lifted her arms to cover her bare breasts.

"You are so beautiful," he breathed, his mouth on her collarbone.

Amalie genuinely felt no fear, only excitement that made her heart race and her breath come in harsh, little pants. Weston still had hold of her hands and somehow managed to pull her down onto the furs. Before she realized it, she was on her back gazing up at him. It was then that he paused to take a good look at her.

She had magnificent breasts, swollen and round with pregnancy, and a beautiful shape to her hips. Her legs were slender and lovely, and her belly tight and rounded within the cradle of her pelvis. Weston began to kiss her neck and shoulders again as he unfastened his breeches.

By the time he reached her cleavage, he had slipped out of the leather pants entirely and tossed them aside. Completely nude, he lay down beside her on the furs, the light of the fire illuminating their bodies as his big hands moved very gently over her. One hand was behind her head as the other began to roam.

Her belly, slightly rounded, drew his lust. He'd never been with a pregnant woman before and wasn't hard pressed to admit he found it wildly arousing. He couldn't even think that the child wasn't his; it didn't matter. It was part of Amalie and Amalie was part of him.

When he was finished kissing her cleavage, he moved down to her belly and began to gently kiss it, acquainting himself with both her body and the child she carried. His free hand began to move to her silken thighs, becoming acquainted with the feel of her skin. She had such beautiful skin. But the moment his hand moved to her pelvis near the dark junction of curls, he felt Amalie stiffen up beneath him.

Startled, he lifted his head to see her laying there with her eyes tightly shut, tears streaming down her temples. He lifted himself up, looming over her in the firelight.

"What is wrong, my angel?" he whispered, concerned. "Have I hurt you somehow?"

She opened her eyes and burst out sobbing, as if she had been holding it back for days. "Nay," she wept. "'Tis that... only that the only person who has ever touched me there... God, it hurt so badly. I am so frightened."

He gathered her up against him, their naked flesh touching for the first time, and held her tightly. She was unbelievably soft and warm, and he could feel her swollen belly against his abdomen. He'd never felt closer to anyone than he did to Amalie at this moment; it went beyond the physical. He felt as if their hearts were somehow intertwined. His lips were by her ear as she wept softly against him.

"I am sorry," he murmured, kissing her ear, her cheek. "I told you I would not make you do anything you were uncomfortable with. I meant it."

She shook her head. "Nay," she struggled to overcome her weeping. "I do not want you to stop. You promised you would show me what it was supposed to be like, Weston. I will hold you to that."

He gazed into her wet green eyes, dubious. "Are you sure?"

She nodded, trying so hard to be brave. She swallowed the remainder of her tears. "Aye. Please do not stop."

He held her hand as he returned to her pelvic region, stroking her growing belly, feeling her soft skin beneath his touch. He moved lower, feeling the soft mat of curls against his fingertips and feeling Amalie start as their hands drifted over her dark thatch. But that was as far as she was willing to go and she pulled her hand away, wrapping her arms around his neck and holding him down to her. Weston held her body against him with one arm as his hand began to roam more freely now.

He began to kiss her mouth, his kisses gentle and passionate, as his hand became bolder and began to finger her mons Venus. He began to stroke her, gently, whispering sweet words when she tensed until she gradually relaxed again.

His stroking grew bolder and he encouraged her to part her legs so they weren't so tightly clamped together. With sweet words, gentle kisses and touches, he was able to convince her to part her legs fairly wide, enough so that he had unencumbered access. As he slanted his lips over hers, hungrily, he gently inserted a finger into her warm, wet folds.

Amalie whimpered with fear but he maintained his calm demeanor, talking her through her fear until she relaxed under him again. He stroked in and out of her a few times, mimicking the lovemaking they would soon be doing, and she gradually began to respond to him. He inserted two fingers into her, and then three, listening to her gasp softly at the sensual invasion. She was very wet and he knew that her body was ready to accept his. But it was her mind he was still worried about.

He shifted, turning her away from him so she was facing the fire. He wedged himself against her, his enormous arousal pushing at her buttocks. He'd never been with a pregnant woman before and until he could safely navigate making love to her face to face, he thought it best to enter her from behind. He didn't want to squash the child. As Amalie lay on her side, her arm upstretched around his neck, Weston came in from another angle, his mouth to her neck as a hand moved to her breasts.

This time, she didn't start when he touched her. Weston gently fondled her breasts, listening to her gasp softly and thinking she sounded much like a kitten purring. The same hand then moved to her right leg, lifting it slightly to allow him to enter her. Her soft mat of curls was damp with moisture as he inserted a finger into her again just to make sure she was ready for him. When she didn't jump at his touch, he put his heavily-aroused member against her threshold and gently thrust.

The most she did was groan softly as he slid into her, nearly half his long length on the first try. With his mouth to her neck and his hand on her belly, he gently thrust again, sliding into her tight walls until he was completely seated. Amalie closed her eyes, surrendering to him, feeling nothing of the terror she had known before and all of the passion that Weston had intended. She wasn't frightened anymore, of anything.

Weston was unbelievably aroused as he thrust into her, one big arm holding her against him while the other roamed between her breasts and belly. As their passion grew and his thrusts increased, he moved to hold her right leg up by the knee, allowing him the freedom to wedge his big body between her legs from the rear.

It had been so long since Weston had last been with a woman that he could feel his climax rapidly approaching, but he didn't want to take it without her taking her pleasure also. He wrapped her right leg around his hip, backwards, and his hand moved to the dark curls that were drenched with moisture from their bodies.

He fondled her woman's center, feeling the hard little nub of pleasure buried deep within her slick folds. As he rubbed her, Amalie suddenly stiffened and he could feel her throbbing walls around his arousal, pulling at him, demanding his seed. Another few thrusts and he answered her, spilling deep into her body, feeling wave after wave of pleasure wash over him.

Even after it was over, he continued thrust into her, gently, feeling his arousal die but not wanting to relinquish this bliss, not even for a moment. But he eventually slowed to a halt, very carefully taking her leg and removing it from his hip. His big arms were wrapped around her as he kissed her neck, her shoulders, gently.

"Are you all right?" he whispered.

Amalie's eyes slowly opened and she stared into the fire, thinking on his words. His question brought so many thoughts and feelings to mind that it was difficult to grasp just one.

"Sweet Jesus, West," she murmured. "It… it is difficult to comprehend."

He kissed her ear. "Why, my angel?"

Her eyes began to water. "Because," she whispered, the tears falling. "I did not know… I did not realize it could be like this. I have been living in such fear and now… now, I can hardly believe the beauty of it."

He hugged her gently. "Then I have accomplished what you asked me to do. I have made you understand that the union of a man and a woman is meant to be joyful."

She simply nodded, sniffling away her emotions, and he swept her into his arms and carried her to the bed. Esma and Neilie had kept clothes on her bed for the past four months, knowing that Weston went to the nunnery daily to try to convince her to return and expecting that, one day, she would, indeed, return with him. He buried her under the heavy coverlet, climbing in next to her and wrapping his big body around her.

He took her twice more than night, relishing each touch, each kiss, warming her to his touch and loving her reaction. From a woman who had only known the brutality of lovemaking, she responded admirably. Every time became better than the last.

Weston finally figured out how to make love to a pregnant woman face to face.

CHAPTER ELEVEN

August

BEING THAT IT had been a surprisingly cool summer, it hadn't been too difficult for Amalie to conceal her condition. Esma and Neilie found out, of course, and for a week thereafter, they burst into tears every time they looked at her. But Amalie was no longer fearful, no longer facing an uncertain future.

The summer had gone by with nary a bump and Weston had managed to dissolve her fears with his love, support and reassurance. The frightened, timid woman was blossoming into a stronger version of her former self, the woman who existed before Sorrell nearly took the life from her. It had been an amazing transformation, something Weston was completely responsible for.

The freezing cold rain of March and April had turned into a cooler than usual summer. Now that Amalie had returned to Hedingham, she settled back into her normal duties as chatelaine as Weston took charge of the garrison. The months following their wedding were normal months with normal activities, and every night there was a big meal in the banqueting hall full of life and laughter and wine. Since the weather was still cool, Amalie had been able to mask her growing belly with cloaks and aprons, and felt comfortable attending these public meals.

She'd had the opportunity to come to know Heath and John a little better, men who had served Weston for years and men who were deeply devoted to him. She found Heath to be very kind and the more congenial of the two, while John seemed easily volatile and tended to yell at the men a good deal. Still, it was a good group and life at

Hedingham was good for the first time in many months.

On a cloudy morning in late August, Weston rose before sunrise to go about his duties as Amalie slept warm and cozy past dawn. She rose to a stoked fire but the room was still cold, and she hissed and hopped around as Esma and Neilie brought around hot water to aid her in her toilette.

Wrapped in a heavy robe, she sat on a stool as her servants helped her wash her hands and face, grumbling because her back hurt as the women finished with her toilette. Everything went smooth until they helped her into a heavy surcoat of emerald brocade. Even though it was a roomy garment, it would no longer accommodate Amalie's growing belly. The servants tried repeatedly to secure it without making it look awkward, but to no avail. So they tried four other garments that were the roomiest ones Amalie had, but none of them fit her any longer. At nearly eight months pregnant, she had finally outgrown her wardrobe. When Amalie realized this, she burst into tears and climbed back into bed. Esma went for Weston.

He had come all the way from the gatehouse where he had been speaking with two knights passing through to Ipswich from London. Men like this always brought news and it was important that Weston stay abreast of both rumors and truths. But Esma's whispered words had him excusing himself from the huddle of knights and making his way back to the keep in the misting rain. It was coming down heavier by the time he entered the forebuilding of the keep.

Entering the warm, fragrant chamber he shared with Amalie, he could see her sitting in their bed with a pillow hugged up against her body. She turned when she heard the door open, seeing Weston's wet face smiling back at her. The sight of him had her bursting into tears and he removed his helm, setting it near the hearth as he made his way to her.

"What is the matter, my love?" he asked gently, pulling off his enormous leather gloves. "Why are you crying?"

She sounded so pathetic and dramatic that it was an effort for him not to laugh at her when she spoke.

"Nothing fits," she sobbed, slapping angrily at the bed. "I have grown as fat as a cow."

He bit his lip to fight off the grin at her big, pouty tears. "That is not true," he told her flatly. "You are beautiful and luscious."

"But my clothes no longer fit," she frowned tearfully. "Nothing fits. I cannot go out in public any longer."

He couldn't help but grin, then. He was wet and didn't want to get any water on her, but he sat on the edge of the bed anyway.

"Is that what is troubling you?" he reached out, tucking a stray piece of blond hair behind her ear. "No worries, my angel. We will go into town and find that seamstress – what is her name?"

"Brigid," she told him, unhappily wiping at the tears on her cheeks.

"Brigid," he repeated. "We will commission the woman to make you new clothes."

She eyed him, though the tears were fading as his words brought her comfort. "Are you sure?" she sniffed. "I am almost eight months pregnant. Any garments she makes for me will not be useful after the child is born."

"It is of no consequence. You must have clothes to wear."

She was still reluctant, but just for a moment. "Very well," she said. "Will you at least bring your purse this time so you can pay her? I know how you hate to spend money."

He lifted an eyebrow at her, though he was pleased that she was at least no longer weeping. "Cheeky wench," he pretended to scowl. "I have no issue with spending money for a worthy cause."

Tears gone, she smiled at him. "I am a worthy cause."

"Indeed, you are." He took her hand and kissed it. "This is an opportune time to increase your wardrobe. You will need something to wear to Cecily's wedding."

Her smile vanished. "I am not going. I told you that."

Weston knew this was a sore subject with her and he scratched at his neck, thinking of the words that would not send her off into fits.

"Cecily has sent several missives reminding you of the date. It is, in fact, in just a few days. Will you disappoint her?"

The frown was returning to her face. "I do not want to," she admitted. "But I cannot go… not like this."

He sighed patiently. "My angel, I know how you feel," he said softly. "But I truly feel that it would be good for you to attend. You know as well as I do that…"

She tossed back the covers angrily. "I am not going, Weston," she insisted. "Everyone will see that I am with child and they will whisper wicked things behind my back. I will be ashamed. Why do you want me to expose myself to that?"

He remained calm, watching her as she climbed out of bed. "Are you ashamed of me?"

She paused in her ranting, stopping to look at him. "Of course not," she insisted softly. Then she looked to her blossoming belly, rubbing at it. "But this… I can no longer hide this, Weston. Everyone will believe… they will talk…"

"They already talk and you know it," he said. "Should you hide here until the babe is born? Should you let tongues wag and create wild stories that are not true or should we face this issue head-on and let everyone know the truth?"

Her brow furrowed with confusion, perhaps disbelief. "The *truth*?" she repeated. "You would tell everyone the truth?"

He stood up and faced her. "The truth is that we are married, deliriously happy, and expecting our first child." He went to her and put his enormous hands on her shoulders, reassuringly. "I am not ashamed of your belly and everyone will believe it is my child. If I am not ashamed, you should not be, either. Be proud that you have a wonderful life with a man who loves you deeply. Not even your silly friend Cecily can make that claim."

His words were sweet and reassuring but she still wasn't convinced. "But if they have heard the rumors of the attack, then they might suspect that…"

He cut her off. "I am the father. Even if they speculate otherwise, they will never know for sure. You are my wife and the child in your belly is ours. You have no cause to be ashamed. If we are to have any chance of restoring an honorable reputation to the House of de Vere, then you must believe that. We must hold our heads high."

She gave up arguing with him about it, mostly because he made sense. She watched his handsome face for a moment, speculating on his feelings, his motivation.

"Honor means a great deal to you, doesn't it?" she asked softly.

"Next to you, it means everything." He stood up from the bed. "Think of our children, Ammy. The de Vere name has been damaged by your brother's actions. And now with the rumors that surround you, it has sustained another hit. It's important that we face these issues and show people that we are proud and unafraid. It is important to rebuild what has been damaged. Does that make any sense?"

She nodded faintly. "It does," she admitted softly. "But I am still afraid."

"I know. But you needn't fear with me by your side; I will protect you, always."

She gave up and went to him, moving to hug him but realized he was still wet from the August mist. She giggled as he held her at arm's length, kissing her on the nose, the lips. Her green eyes glimmered adoringly at him.

"I am truly fortunate to have you." She patted his cheek. Then her grin grew hopeful. "Can we go to Brigid right now?"

He shook his head. "The weather is wet," he told her. "I will bring the woman to you. I do not want you out in the elements."

She stood on her toes, kissing him again and accompanying him to the door as he collected his gloves and his helm. Even after he left, her thoughts and heart were still warm on him, thinking on this man who had been able to see past the shame and darkness that surrounded her. She reflected on her life, thinking she must have done something terribly good at some point in order for God to have rewarded her with a man as amazing as Weston.

She thanked God daily for her blessings.

CB

CECILY'S FAMILY HAD an expansive fortified manse in the town of Sudbury, about three miles to the east of Hedingham Castle. Brundon Manor had been built by Cecily's grandfather, Sir Albert Brundon, who had prospered as a sheep farmer, and the family owned nearly the entire town. They were very wealthy and very political. Many people of political importance would be at the wedding and as the party from Hedingham made their way to the fortified gates of the manse, Amalie was feeling more and more anxiety. Even if Weston was convinced that this was the right thing to do, she was still apprehensive.

Apprehensive or not, her angelic looks masked her angst. The seamstress in the village, the same one who had made Cecily's wedding gown, had constructed a beautiful confection of gold brocade and satin with a waistline that gathered underneath her breasts so the emphasis was completely off her big belly.

It was, in fact, difficult to see her belly at all for all of the layers of billowing fabric. More than that, the neckline was off the shoulder, drawing the eye to the delicious swell of her breasts, something that Weston found utterly arousing. He was positive she would outshine every woman at the wedding, including the bride, and he wasn't the least bit sorry about it. He was so proud he could burst.

He rode astride his big, blond charger next to the cab carrying his wife. Heath and John rode behind him, absolutely thrilled to be at a wedding where there would be many unattached young ladies and copious amounts of alcohol. Young bucks that they were, women and alcohol pleased them immensely. Ten men-at-arms rode in strategic placement around the carriage while young Owyn drove the cab.

Weston wasn't completely thrilled with his wife's savior driving the carriage but Heath had selected the man for the detail, not entirely aware of who he was until Weston mentioned it. But Weston let it go, realizing he wasn't threatened by the soldier any longer no matter what the young man felt for Amalie. Since their marriage, Owyn had made a point of staying away, something that Weston had been grateful for.

Perhaps the man stayed away only out of fear, but Weston was grateful nonetheless. Amalie had never asked where the soldier was and Weston had never offered. That bright smile he had once seen given to Owyn those months ago was now reserved for him alone.

On this day towards the end of September, the sky above was brilliant blue. Weston glanced up, watching the breeze push cotton-puff clouds across the sky, watching ravens soar on the drafts. He felt happy and proud to be here. When the guards at the gate admitted the party from Hedingham through the entrance, Weston rode at the head of the delegation as they approached the main house.

It was a long road, rocky but fairly well kept, lined with statues of saints. It was rather ostentatious and more than once he cast Heath and John humorous glances. There were valets, servants and grooms everywhere to attend to Cecily's guests, men dressed in fine silks especially for the occasion. Heath and John kept looking around for the women.

When they reached the entry to the manse, Weston dismounted his charger and strapped the muzzle on the beast so the grooms could handle him and not get their arms bitten off. When one of the valets moved to open the cab door, Weston barked at the man, who immediately backed off. Weston wanted the privilege of opening the door himself, which he did and extended his hand to his wife.

Amalie put her small hand in his, stepping out of the cab and looking resplendent in her golden gown. She smiled up at her husband, seeing reassurance and pride in his features. The dress and matching cloak billowed out behind her and the valets scrambled to keep it out of the mud. Weston led her up the stone steps with the regal air of a queen, taking her hand and tucking it possessively into the crook of his elbow just before they reached the great and ornate door.

More valets greeted them at the door to collect the lady's cloak.

Weston unfastened the ties around her neck, handing the enormous cloak over to the servants as he took his wife by the hand and proceeded into the great entry hall beyond.

Amalie was a little uncomfortable leaving the cloak behind because it was one more layer of clothing to hide her growing stomach, but Weston kissed her hand, softly reassuring her that she did not need the cloak. She looked like a goddess with her flowing, golden gown that quite cleverly disguised her belly and he was as puffed up as a peacock. As they moved into the great hall, they ran headlong into the crème de la crème of Suffolk and Essex society.

The wedding was planned in the great formal gardens to the rear of the manse, unusual given that weddings were almost always held in churches. The weather was cooperating and beneath the bright blue sky, blooming flowers were daring to show their faces. Roses and camellias bloomed in colors of pink, yellow and white, while great stalks of purple foxgloves reached for the sky. The great entry of Brundon ran the width of the house with its swept wood floors and oak-paneled walls, and Amalie could see the garden as she and Weston navigated deeper into the room.

Weston didn't know the nobles of Essex and Sussex like Amalie did so he didn't feel the apprehension that she did as she faced her peers. There was a massive table laden with flowers and food against the wall while servants passed around fine wine in cut crystal chalices.

As Weston took a chalice for both himself and Amalie, passing a cup to his wife, he couldn't help but notice that no expense had been spared for the wedding; the monstrous room was full of flowers and finery, smelling of fresh rushes and smoked meat. It was truly a sight and he began to feel bad that he and Amalie had been married without fanfare or luxury. He had fairly forced her into a dull wedding in a nunnery. He tried not to feel too guilty as he took his wife to the food table.

"Look at all of this food," he muttered, collecting a pewter plate handed to him by a hovering servant girl. "What would you like to sample, my angel?"

Amalie looked over the table, smelling and visually inspecting all of the wonderful foods. There was a roast swan with the feathers replaced to make it look like a living bird again, peacock that was dressed with boiled fruits, different types of fish in spiced milk, rice with grapes, almond milk puddings with rose petals, an almond subtlety that was shaped to look like Brundon Manor down to little flags flying from the battlements, plus a variety of cakes and honeyed sweets. It was truly a display of wealth and luxury.

Amalie went along the table, tasting everything before she would allow it on her plate. Fortunately, the nausea that had plagued her for the first few months had vanished, leaving her constantly ravenous. Weston simply held the plate and dished up the food she wanted while Heath and John, dressed in their knightly best tunics bearing Bolingbroke's colors, followed behind. The knights ripped legs off peacocks and dug their fingers into the chicken dishes until Amalie admonished them on their manners. Contrite, they tried to be less beastly about it as they licked their fingers and devoured the meats.

"Lady Amalie," came a rather loud and pompous female voice. "What a surprise to see you here, my dear." Amalie heard the voice, a piece of chicken halfway to her mouth, and turned to the source. On the approach was a round, well-dressed woman with her pale blond daughter in tow. The round woman was rather plain looking but it was apparent she was wearing every jewel she owned. She was covered in them. Her quiet daughter was lovely in a pale sort of way, smiling and waving at Amalie when their eyes met. Amalie put the chicken back on the plate and smiled weakly at the pair.

"Lady Ovington, you are looking well." She indicated Weston. "I do not believe you have met my husband, Sir Weston de Royans."

Lady Ovington's hawk-like eyes zeroed in on Weston; he could feel her calculating stare. "Sir Weston," she sounded rather imperious, as if she were sizing him up. She pointed to her daughter. "My daughter, the Lady Laurel."

Weston nodded politely. "My ladies, it is a pleasure."

Lady Ovington's old and shrewd gaze drifted over Weston a moment as she put her hand on Amalie's arm. "My dear, he is quite attractive, is he not?" she commented. "We had not heard that you were married, Amalie. Were we not invited?"

It was a bold question and Weston already didn't like the woman. He looked at Amalie, wondering how she was going to deal with this type of question. It probably wouldn't be the last time she heard it today. But Amalie merely smiled, a forced attempt, and replied politely.

"Had we been married at the castle, you would have most certainly been invited," she said evenly. "However, we were not. Weston is the garrison commander for Hedingham."

Lady Ovington's fuzzy brow furrowed. "Garrison commander?" she repeated, looking to Laurel. "Had we heard about this? I seem to recall hearing something about a garrison commander and Lady Amalie..."

Laurel, a truly good and gentle girl, cut her mother off. "I believe we did hear of a wedding, Mother," she said, her nervous eyes moving to Amalie. "You were married at Bolingbroke, were you not?"

It was a lie to throw her mother off the scent. Amalie could see what Laurel was doing and she appreciated the help. Lady Ovington was one of the worst gossips in the shire.

Amalie nodded quickly. "My husband comes from a very old and distinguished family," she told the pair. "His grandfather is Baron Cononley, Constable of North Yorkshire and the Northern Dales. Weston will inherit the title."

That seemed to impress the old snoop somewhat. But it was evident that she wasn't finished yet. She clutched Amalie's arm companionably.

"And your brother?" she asked leadingly. "We heard such awful things about him, Amalie. I pray they were not true."

Amalie's smile tightened. "What did you hear?"

Lady Ovington lowered her voice. "That he fled to Ireland in disgrace," she said, clucking softly. "I am so sorry for you, my dear. To have such ties with the king and now... well, now your castle belongs to

Bolingbroke and the de Vere name is no longer favored. I am very sorry for you."

Amalie had about all she could take. She pulled her arm away from the probing old gossip and wrapped her hands around Weston's forearm.

"No need," she said evenly. "Weston and I are very happy and all is well. I would not worry if I were you."

Lady Ovington looked surprised. "But… my dear," she began to feign distress. "You do not need to pretend…"

Amalie turned her back on her. "Good day, Lady Ovington," she said crisply. "Come along, Weston. We have better things to do."

It was a direct insult against Lady Ovington, who stood there with her mouth gaping as Amalie and Weston walked away. Weston took his wife's lead, his free hand over hers as it clutched his elbow. When they were at the opposite side of the table, well away from the Ovingtons, he collected another small crystal glass of wine for Amalie. She took it gratefully and downed it all in one swallow. He smiled.

"Excellent, Lady de Royans," he said softly. "You had no problem handling that old cow."

She eyed him, licking her lips of the sweet wine. "She is one of the worst," she hissed. "If any rumors get started, they will come from her."

"Then let us lose ourselves in this crowd," he said. "Surely there are nicer people to speak with."

"There are."

"Then let us find them."

They did. Amalie ran into several people she knew right away; the mayor of Hedingham was in attendance, a round man with bad teeth who greeted her fondly. Weston had already met the man, months ago on one of his daily trips to the nunnery when Amalie was still in residence. They were also greeted by the mayor's daughter, a young lady who had just crossed the threshold into womanhood, a pretty girl with long, red hair that Amalie knew well.

When Heath and John pressed their attentions on the young woman, whom they had also met during their months at the castle, Amalie shooed them away. In her opinion, the mayor's daughter was much too young for either of them; at thirteen years of age, she was still a child. Dejected, the knights found sport elsewhere.

While Amalie chatted away with an old widowed noblewoman by the name of Lady Henny, Weston went back over to the food table to retrieve some edibles. Amalie had left her plate on the table when she had departed from Lady Ovington, so Weston reclaimed the plate and piled fresh food upon it. He took it back over to his wife, who was speaking quite companionably to old Lady Henny. The old woman had her by the hands, speaking to her of something trivial. Then she laughed at her own story. Amalie was laughing with her and Weston took a moment just to watch his wife. She was such a glorious creature to watch. His heart softened at the sight of her, smiling as Lady Henny suddenly grabbed Amalie by the arm and peered flirtatiously up at him.

"Dearest Amalie, your husband is quite comely," she said as if it were some great secret. "I do believe he is more handsome than my dear Edward."

Amalie winked at Weston as she answered. "Weston is quite comely, that is true," she agreed. "I do believe I shall keep him."

"You do not want to give him up? I shall pay a handsome price for a handsome man."

Amalie laughed. "Nay," she assured her. "He belongs to me and I do not wish to relinquish him."

Lady Henny giggled like a girl; it was really quite funny to watch. "Pity," she sighed. "Perhaps if you grow weary of him, you will let me know."

"You would be in for a very long wait."

Lady Henny laughed again, putting her arms around Amalie to hug her but her left arm brushed against Amalie's firm belly. The old woman's laughter faded and her eyes bulged as she put a warm, gnarled hand on Amalie's rounded stomach.

"My goodness," Lady Henny gasped as she felt the warm firmness beneath the material. "I did not know you were with child, my dear."

Amalie's smile vanished. "Aye," she began to stammer, suddenly very uncomfortable. "It is not something I wish to…"

Lady Henny put two hands on Amalie's belly, interrupting her. "I can feel the child," she announced. "Why have I not heard of this before?"

Amalie tried to discreetly pull away from the woman, grasping one of the old hands so it would not probe her any longer. "We do not wish to announce the child yet. Please do not…"

The old lady pretended not to hear her. "This is such a wonderful blessing, Amalie," she insisted. "Surely you should like to shout this to the world."

The old woman opened her mouth in an apparent attempt to make such an announcement but Amalie grabbed the old arms, forcing her to quiet, forcing the old woman to look at her. There were tears in Amalie's eyes as she spoke.

"Please keep this to yourself," she begged in a whisper. "I do not wish to announce it yet. The pregnancy has… has not been good and I do not even know if I will be able to carry this child to term. Please keep this to yourself and tell no one until I make the announcement. Do you understand me?"

The old woman's expression slackened as Amalie's words began to sink in. She could see that Amalie was verging on tears and she threw her arms around her, kissing her cheeks.

"I will not tell a soul," she whispered reassuringly. "I swear it. I am sorry to have upset you so. But if you need me, do not hesitate to send word. I shall be at your side quickly."

Amalie forced a smile, wiping at the tears that were starting to flow. Weston stood by, watching the old woman comfort her, until finally reaching out to take his wife's hand. He had been close to taking the old woman's head off until Amalie had convinced the old bird to shut her mouth. Still, he was struggling with his anger towards the old woman for upsetting Amalie so, but he pushed it aside in order to comfort his wife.

"Come along, Ammy," he said softly. "It looks as if they are about to begin the ceremony."

Lady Henny clutched Amalie's arm from the other side. "She must have a chair, Sir Weston. She cannot stand in her condition."

Weston nodded to agree but Amalie shook her head firmly. "Not if I am the only one sitting," she declared. "I do not want to be the only one sitting."

Lady Henny patted her hand. "'Tis all right, my dear," she said. "You do not have to sit if you do not want to."

Weston was thinking seriously on chasing the old woman away. Although she seemed genuine, he didn't know her and was, therefore, wary of her intentions. Amalie seemed to be comfortable with her, however, so he allowed the woman to remain. She was matronly and caring, a manner that Amalie responded to.

As they made their way through the crowd that was gradually filtering out into the brilliant garden beyond, Amalie noticed that Cecily's betrothed was already outside. She pointed him out to Lady Henny.

"Look," she said. "There is Sir Michael Hollington, Cecily's intended. He is a knight for Thomas de Mowbray."

Weston glanced over at the man they were pointing at and his brow furrowed. "That man?" he clarified.

Amalie nodded. "Do you know him?"

Weston's dark blue gaze settled on the man, inspecting him at a distance. He was much older than Cecily and his once-muscular body had gone to fat. In fact, he was very old and very fat, and Weston recalled that Cecily had told them he had been married before. From the looks of him, he could have been married several times before. After a moment, he simply shook his head.

"Nay," he said. "I do not. But... she is truly marrying him?"

Amalie looked curiously at him. "Why do you ask that way?"

"What way?"

"As if you disapprove."

Weston shrugged his shoulders. "It is not my place to approve or disapprove," he said, directing the ladies over to a less crowded area of the gardens. "But he does seem rather old."

Amalie wriggled her eyebrows. "Cecily is not exactly young, either," she admitted. "She is twenty-four years old."

Weston hissed. "No wonder her father agreed to the marriage," he whispered. "He was afraid he was going to be burdened with a spinster daughter."

Amalie slapped at his arm to shush him as Lady Henny giggled. "'Tis true, Sir Weston," she agreed, lowering her voice as she reached across Amalie and put her gnarled hand on his big wrist. "Cecily is the eldest of two of the homeliest daughters you will ever see. I fear that if Lucifer himself made an offer of marriage to one or both of them, their father would have gladly accepted."

As Weston grinned and Lady Henny snickered, Amalie shushed them both. "Deplorable behavior for a wedding," she scolded, although she was smiling. "Enough, both of you, or I shall find more suitable company."

Weston shook his head. "Not to worry, Lady Henny," he said. "She cannot leave us. I am holding her too tightly."

Lady Henny giggled gleefully. Amalie, too, was grinning as they found a spot that was less crowded amongst the guests. The flowers were blooming and it was a truly lovely setting. But she was having difficulty seeing the groom's balding head and she suddenly looked around, curiously.

"Why, do you suppose," she wondered aloud, "did they choose to wed in the garden and not the church? It did not occur to me before this moment that Cecily is not being wed at St. Andrew's Church in town."

Lady Henny patted her on the hand. "Because she cannot," she said. "Did you not hear of the scandal?"

Amalie shook her head and turned to her. "What scandal?"

Lady Henny wasn't shy about sharing what she knew, which is why

Amalie had asked the woman to please keep the secret about the pregnancy. She knew that Lady Henny liked to talk, a silly old woman with a heart of gold.

"I have heard that Lady Cecily succumbed to one of Bolingbroke's knights," she whispered as if it were the deepest, darkest secret in the world. "Several months ago, in fact. Surely you already know this story; the knight was stationed at Hedingham."

Amalie shook her head, her brow furrowing with curiosity. "I have not heard anything. Who is the knight?"

Lady Henny clucked sadly. "Bolingbroke has kept you bottled up because of your brother, poor dear. I am surprised you have been let out for this wedding."

"That is not difficult considering my husband is the garrison commander." Amalie struggled not to snap. "What happened with Cecily and the knight?"

Lady Henny was dramatic in her recitation. "It would seem that a knight named Sorra was traveling to Hedingham and stopped for the night in Sudbury," she whispered. "Lady Cecily somehow met this knight and a torrid affair ensued. It was quite clear that the knight compromised the lady, which is why her father gladly took the offer from Sir Michael for her hand. Sir Michael may not be a young or handsome man, but he is willing to overlook Cecily's indiscretions. He needed a wife and Cecily needed a husband."

Amalie could feel the blood drain from her face. "She… she never said anything to me about a love affair."

Lady Henny shook her head. "According to my servants, who are very reliable, it was no love affair. It was lusty and breathless. Our Lady Cecily is a naughty girl, indeed, and the priests of St. Andrew's would not allow her to be married in the church."

Amalie just stared at the old woman, the color gone from her face. She could feel Weston's grip on her tighten.

"You said this knight's name was Sorra?" he asked, his deep voice quiet.

Lady Henny nodded briskly. "Do you know of him? He was said to be Bolingbroke's man stationed at Hedingham."

Sorra, Amalie thought. *Sorrell.* She suddenly felt woozy, gripping Weston as her knees went weak.

"I think I am going to be sick," Amalie whispered tightly to Weston. "Please… get me out of here."

Weston was calm; shocked, but calm. He put his arm around his wife's shoulders, waving off Lady Henny when the woman tried to pursue.

Quietly, quickly, he escorted Amalie from the garden as the last of the guests were filling it up. He took her into the great entry hall, looking for the first empty and available room where they could have some privacy. A small but richly-garbed room immediately off the entry suited their purposes and he took her inside, closing the door just as she started to gasp.

"Breathe, my angel, just breathe," he said softly, steadily. "Get hold of yourself."

She was trying to calm down but she couldn't quite master it. "Poor…" she gasped, weeping. "Poor Cecily. He must have… before he came to Hedingham, he must have… but she never said anything to me about it. That beastly man had his way with Cecily before he came to Hedingham and… what he did to me…"

Weston pulled her into his embrace as she grew hysterical. His mouth was by her ear.

"Perhaps he did," he whispered, trying desperately to calm her. "It makes sense now why Cecily is marrying a man with one foot in the grave and grown children. She could do no better. But you, on the other hand, have a husband who loves you deeply and is accepting your child as his own. Do not worry about Sorrell's actions in the past. You cannot change them and nothing he does should be shocking to you. But have no doubt that someday, at the time of my choosing, I will find Sorrell and I will make him pay. For everything he did to you, every pain and every humiliation, know that I will make him pay a thousand times over. The man will wish he had never been born."

By this time, she had stopped gasping and was gazing up at him with tears on her cheeks. His words touched her deeply; he'd meant to comfort her and he had. But she was still upset.

"How fortunate I am to have you," she whispered. "I thank God every day that He has brought you to me."

He smiled faintly. "I do the same."

She watched him kiss her hand, succeeding in calming her with his tender manner and strong words. But she was still shaken, the cold grip of a bad memory struggling to pull her back into the depths of despair again.

"Please," she begged softly. "I just want to go home."

He touched her cheek, kissing it. "I know," he said softly. "But I do not think we can pull Heath and John away from the unpledged ladies. They are like foxes in the hen house and I will not leave them here. They would wreak terrible havoc and I would be to blame."

It was a bit of humor in a tense moment. Amalie smiled weakly and he smiled in return, touching her cheek again.

"Then we will stay?" he asked softly.

She nodded reluctantly. "As you say."

He kissed her forehead and turned her for the door. "That is my good angel," he whispered, opening the door for her. "Let us watch your friend marry Methuselah."

She hissed at him to shush him and he laughed low in his throat, taking her hand and tucking it into the crook of his elbow as he led her out to the sunny garden, now full of people.

As the September day remained clear of rain, Cecily was married to her knight by a priest her father had paid a tremendous sum to. It had been the only way the man would do it given the circumstances. But it was a joyous day full of food and laughter. And when the ceremony was over, a wedding feast ensued that went all night and well into the morning.

Amalie, however, was exhausted before the festivities were even in full swing. She had stood through the entire ceremony, conducted like a Catholic mass in the open, so there were plenty of ups and downs. Weston would help her rise and help her back to her knees at the proper time. But she remained as long as she could in an upright position, finally seated at one of the feasting tables and eating nearly everything Weston would put in front of her.

They sat together, mostly just the two of them, watching the dancing and revelry, laughing at Heath and John as they preyed on the single women in the room. Heath ended up with Lady Laurel Ovington later in the evening and that was where he stayed, entranced by the pale beauty with the kind eyes. John, however, remained the hunter, getting quite drunk and happy with the mayor's young daughter, so much so that Amalie sent Weston over to the pair to break it up.

Weston didn't like to get involved in his knight's affairs but he understood his wife's discomfort with a knight being so aggressive towards a very young lady. When Amalie asked him how he would feel if John was paying such attention to their daughter, Weston immediately went on the offensive. Amalie watched him from a distance as he pulled John aside and whispered a few words to him, grinning as she watched John's reaction. The man wasn't happy in the least and nearly threw a fit as Weston pulled him away by the neck.

As she sat there and observed, she began to realize that the soreness in her back that she had been experiencing all day was now manifesting itself into fairly regularly cramping that stretched around to her belly and radiated down her thighs. She was becoming aware that the pains were growing worse at regular intervals.

Although she had never had a baby before, she wasn't entirely naïve; it began to occur to her what the pains were and as she realized that she was in labor, she felt stabs of fear and excitement. When Weston returned to her several minutes later with a pewter chalice of ale in his hand, she simply smiled at him as he sat down beside her. He returned the gesture.

"You have ruined John's life, just so you are aware," he told her.

She lifted an eyebrow. "Me? What did I do?"

"You have separated him from the only woman he has ever loved."

She made a face at him. "Pah," she sniffed. "He will not even remember her name in the morning."

Weston snorted into his cup, taking a healthy swallow of the ale. He noticed that Amalie was simply sitting there, watching the room, and he collected her hand and kissed it.

"Can I get you something else, my love?" he asked. "I am sure there is at least one dish on that table you have not yet tasted."

She pursed her lips wryly. "You needn't be so smug about it," she scolded. "There is not one bottle of wine or ale around this place that you have missed out on."

He laughed and kissed her cheek, hugging her as he did so. He was fairly liquored up at this point but not terribly so; just enough so that he was laughing at nearly everything that went on. Amalie put her hand up, patting his cheek as he nuzzled her neck and kissed her chin. He was being quite affectionate with her in public, something he didn't normally do, but the alcohol had that effect on him. Amalie was enjoying it.

"West," she began casually.

"Aye, my love?" he responded softly, kissing her ear.

"I think we should return home soon."

"Why? Are you not enjoying yourself?"

"I am," she said. "But I do not wish for our child to be born at Brundon."

He kissed her ear again, her cheek, and then suddenly froze. He pulled back to look at her, his dark blue eyes wide with astonishment.

"What do you mean?" he whispered fearfully.

She was smiling. "I mean that I believe the baby is coming."

"The baby is coming?" he repeated.

She saw the instant fear in his eyes and she laughed, patting him on the cheek. "Not to worry, sweetheart," she said. "All is well. But I do think we should return home soon just to be safe."

Weston was on his feet, suddenly looking very sober. "Are you in pain?"

"Not much. But it is growing worse."

That was all he needed to hear. Weston whisked her out of the great hall with little noise or fanfare, collecting Heath as he went and informing the man of the issue at hand.

Heath swung into action, collecting John from the great hall, Owyn and the ten men-at-arms from the kitchen area, and forming the escort party for Weston and Amalie in record time. In the dead of night, but with a full moon to guide them, they made it back to Hedingham in under an hour.

Weston was holding his beautiful new daughter by morning.

CHAPTER TWELVE

September 1392

THE KITCHEN OF HEDINGHAM was on the ground floor of the keep, a big room that served as both storage and cooking area. Heat traveled upward and, consequently, the floor above it was always fairly warm. On this warm September day, the kitchen was fairly steamy as the cook, a fat woman with wild red hair and limited teeth, made a fruit compote of apples, pears, honey and cinnamon. Heat was steaming up from the big pot into the floors above it.

Amalie stood next to the woman, supervising the process and making sure the women didn't overcook the fruit. She had two toddlers who wouldn't eat it if it was cooked to a brown mush, so she hovered over the woman and watched her stir, making sure there were no brown spots on the fruit until she was satisfied. As the cook continued to stir, Amalie made her way out of the kitchen and up to the first floor of the keep.

The room smelled heavily of rushes and smoke. There was a blockage in the chimney and three male servants were attempting to unblock it. She watched them for a moment and, determining there was nothing she could do to assist or encourage, she made her way towards the entry. As she neared the door that opened into the forebuilding, she was met by Esma.

The serving woman had garments in her hands of some sort, holding them up to show Amalie and nearly hitting her in the nose with them. As Esma apologized, Amalie stood back with a grin.

"I nearly lost an eye," she teased the woman, trying to get a look at what had her so rattled. "What do you have?"

Esma was obviously upset. "This," she held up a tiny pair of breeches. "They are too small for him, my lady. He is a big boy now and these breeches are far too small. I must either extend the legs or make him new ones."

Amalie waved her off. "Make him a new pair," she said. "'Tis nothing to get upset over."

Esma nodded. "Aye, it is," she insisted. "If the lord sees these breeches on the boy, he'll become upset about it. He does not like the baby ill-dressed."

Amalie just shook her head. "The baby will not be ill-dressed," she scolded softly. "He is the best dressed two-year-old boy in all of Essex, I would wager, and the most spoiled. In fact, both children are terribly spoiled. Do you know where my husband has taken them?"

Esma shook her head. "Nay," she replied. "The last I saw, he was heading towards the stables."

Amalie sighed and moved for the door. "That is because Aubria very much wants a pony," she said. "I must stop him before he makes any foolish promises I will not let him keep."

Taking the steps from the keep, Amalie emerged into the warm and unseasonably dry September sunshine. Dressed in a pale blue shift and darker blue surcoat, she looked serene and lovely. As the years had passed, Amalie had only grown more beautiful, something that matched the wise and generous soul beneath. She and Weston had become great benefactors in Essex, generous to the nunnery, the poor and to the churches in the surrounding communities. Slowly but surely, they had rebuilt the prestige of Hedingham and the de Vere name, something that was important to them both.

Especially with two children, who would benefit from the legacy set forth by their parents. It was important to both Amalie and Weston that the children be left a strong reputation. Amalie moved through the outer bailey, greeted by John overhead on the walls, pointing towards the stables when she asked if he had seen her husband. Just as she passed the big troop house that her husband had built a few years ago, the stables came into view and she could immediately see Weston and her two children in the stable yard.

Weston was standing with a tow-headed toddler in his arms while a small girl at his feet was being shown a black and white pony. As Amalie approached, an old stable groom held the pony by his halter, leading it around in a couple of small circles for the little girl's approval. Amalie could see her daughter jumping up and down with excitement and her lips twisted wryly, knowing she was going to have a fight on her hands when she denied her daughter the pony.

Weston caught movement from the corner of his eye, turning to see that Amalie was nearly upon them. He smiled at her, drinking in her radiant beauty. He swore that every day saw his love for her deepen, so enchanted by the glorious creature he had married.

"Greetings, my angel," he said sweetly.

Amalie smiled at him; it was difficult to be cross when he was so sweet and handsome. "Greetings," she replied. "What are you doing?"

It was an obvious question, to which Weston wriggled his eyebrows. When the baby saw his mother, he whined and extended his arms to her. Amalie took her son from his father, kissing his blond little head as he snuggled up against her.

Weston moved away from his wife and son, crouching down beside his daughter. "Aubria is inspecting a pony," he said, casting his wife a long look. "What do you think about him, Mummy?"

Amalie rolled her eyes at him but smiled when her daughter turned to look at her. Aubria Maud de Vere de Royans was surely the most beautiful child to have ever walked the earth. With her big brown eyes, long blond hair and her mother's delicate features, she looked like an angel. She was sweet, bright and very persuasive, characteristics that had Weston deeply in love with the child. She belonged to him regardless of the fact that he had not fathered her and he spoiled her accordingly.

"I think he is a beautiful pony," Amalie said the only thing she could say as her daughter beamed up at her. "Are you happy, sweet-heart?"

Aubria nodded so vigorously that her blond hair flopped down over her eyes. "Dada says I am old enough to ride him."

Amalie smiled weakly. "He did?" She motioned to her daughter. "Pet the pony, sweetheart, while I speak with Dada."

Aubria happily did as she was told as Amalie's smile faded and she crooked a finger at her husband. Weston caught the look, kissed his daughter on the head, and stood up. He went over to his wife, looking like a scolded dog, knowing she was displeased. They moved a few feet away from Aubria so the conversation would not be heard by little ears.

"You know how I feel about this, West," Amalie half-whispered, half-hissed. "She is too young for a pony."

Weston did the only thing he could do. He put his big arms around both her and the baby, trying to soothe the savage beastie.

"She is *not* too young," he countered softly. "I promise she will only ride it when I am with her, or even Heath or John. She will never ride alone, I swear it. She has to learn to ride sooner or later, Ammy. You cannot keep her a baby forever."

Before Amalie could reply, the baby in her arms rubbed his eyes and began to fuss. She tucked her son's head down onto her shoulder and began to rock him before refocusing on her husband.

"I do not like it," she said simply. "If she were to fall and get hurt, I do not know what I would do."

Weston kissed her forehead, then kissed his sleepy son on his soft little cheek. "Nor do I," he said. "But we cannot keep the children in a cage until they grow up simply because we are fearful for their safety. Children must grow and learn; this is just one of those times. Aubria will be fine and, soon enough, Colton will have his own pony as well."

Amalie rolled her eyes, gently rocking two-year-old Colton Mars-ton de Vere de Royans; two years younger than his sister, he was the spitting image of his father. Named for his grandfather, and carrying the de Royans traditional name ending in "ton", he was also extremely strong willed and stubborn. Amalie knew what that meant should his sister get a pony.

"If Aubria gets a pony, Colton will want one," she pointed out. "He wants everything she has and I do not want a two-year-old boy riding a pony."

Weston smiled at her, at his sleepy son. "He has to learn to ride some time. There is nothing wrong in starting him young."

Amalie didn't want to argue with him. She had made her wants known and they would have to reconcile this at some point very soon when the children were not around. For now, she wanted to bring the children inside and feed them. It was nearing noon and they would be hungry.

"We will discuss this later," she said. "I am going to take the children inside and feed them."

Weston pulled her close, kissing her sweetly until Colton grunted and put his baby hand on his father's face to push him away from his mother. The baby was territorial, irritable and sleepy, a bad combination. Weston laughed softly at his son, grabbing the little hand and kissing it.

"You cannot have her all to yourself, little man," he teased the boy gently. "She belongs to me."

Colton growled at him again but he was grinning. He laughed and fussed when Weston nibbled on his fat, little fingers and pretended to eat his arm. As Amalie turned for the keep with the grumpy child in her arms, Weston returned to his daughter, who was still petting the black and white pony.

About the time he coaxed her away from the animal and picked her up, he could hear commotion near the gatehouse. With his daughter nestled in his enormous arms, he made his way across the outer bailey, following his wife who was several feet ahead of him. Just as he neared the bridge to the inner bailey, a shout from Heath stopped him.

He could see the red-haired knight jogging towards him, mail jingling. Amalie continued on as Weston came to a halt and waited. Heath came upon him, his gaze fixed on Weston.

"Your brother is here, West," he said.

Weston's eyebrows rose. "Sutton?" he looked surprised. "Where is he?"

Heath pointed to the gatehouse. "He is at the gatehouse speaking with John."

Weston veered away from the keep and headed towards the gatehouse. He was excited to see the brother he hadn't seen in almost five years, a man who also served Bolingbroke and had been in Lithuania doing battle for the Duchy of Vilnius for the past several years. Not only was he excited to see him, but he also wanted Sutton to meet his family. That, more than anything, excited him.

Weston arrived at the dusty gatehouse to find his brother off his mount and laughing uproariously with John. But Sutton de Royans' attention was diverted by the appearance of his older brother and, for a moment, his handsome face slackened in surprise. Weston kept walking until he was within arm's reach. He threw a big arm around his younger brother, hugging him fiercely and attempting not to smash his daughter in the process.

"Sutton," he pulled back to look his brother in the eye; the man was a couple of inches taller than him with the same dark blue eyes, big body and good looks. He smiled broadly. "When did you return from Vilnius?"

Sutton returned his brother's grin. "A few months ago," he told him, his gaze then moving between his brother and the beautiful, blond child in his arms. "I spent some time at Bolingbroke Castle before returning to Netherghyll. I have just come from there. We must speak, West."

Weston could tell by the tone of his brother's voice that something was amiss. In fact, he knew his brother wouldn't be here if something significant hadn't happened, which concerned him.

He nodded. "Of course," he said. "But how did you find me?"

"Henry told me," Sutton replied. "He said you had been the garrison commander of Hedingham since Robert de Vere's flight to Ireland."

Weston shrugged. "Almost since that time, indeed." He could see that his brother was looking at Aubria and he turned to look at her, too. "Much has happened in those years. I would like for you to meet your niece, the Lady Aubria de Royans. Aubria, this is your Uncle Sutton."

Sutton was studying the little girl carefully, finally holding out a hand to her in greeting. "I thought you were an angel, my lady," he said as she put her small hand timidly in his. "Or perhaps you are a lovely spirit. Do you have wings to fly with?"

Sutton could be a charmer. Aubria grinned. "No," she said. "You are silly."

Sutton grinned, bringing her little hand to his lips for a fatherly kiss. "I do not believe you," he teased her. "You are much too lovely to not be an angel. Did God send you here, perhaps? Are you magic?"

Aubria giggled, yanking her hand from his grasp and bringing it to her lips, shyly. When she started to bite her nails, a nervous habit, Weston gently grasped the hand and pulled it away from her mouth. Then he turned around, motioning for his brother to follow.

"I am anxious for you to meet my wife," he said. "She is in the keep with our son."

Sutton wriggled his eyebrows. "It is a lot to absorb," he admitted as he walked behind Weston. "I return from a jaunt overseas to find my brother married and with children."

Weston patted Aubria's little leg affectionately. "Life has never been better," he said. "We are very happy here."

Sutton studied the little girl in his brother's arms as they made their way to the bridge that crossed over into the inner bailey. "Your wife is the sister of the earl?"

Weston looked at him. "She is," he replied. "Who told you?"

"Bolingbroke," Sutton answered. "He also told me something of her history."

Weston was fairly certain what he meant but he didn't want to get in to anything in front of Aubria so he changed the subject.

"Why have you come?" he asked. "Surely it was not simply to visit me."

Sutton was back to grinning. "And why not? Can I not visit my own brother?"

"You never have before."

"True. But, then again, you and I have always been together up until the past few years. I have never had to go anywhere to visit you."

"So why are you here?"

Sutton sobered, suddenly serious. "I came to deliver some news. Grandfather passed away nearly a month ago." He paused as they set foot on the bridge, turning to look at his brother, noting how the man appeared older, wiser. "You are now Baron Cononley, Constable of North Yorkshire and the Northern Dales. Congratulations."

Weston stared at him, digesting the information. He didn't say anything as he resumed walking. Sutton followed.

"And what of her?" Weston asked softly.

Sutton glanced at him. "You mean Mother?" he shrugged, looking up at the massive keep that loomed before them. "She is well and sends her affections. She will be thrilled to know she has grandchildren."

Weston's jaw ticked faintly. "That may be," he growled, "but she will never meet them."

Sutton scratched his head, feeling the rise of the old argument. Weston had never forgiven their mother for her treatment of their father, blaming the woman for the man's suicide. He'd hardly spoken to her in thirty years. Sutton had been a little more forgiving for the sake of family unity, but Weston had disowned both his mother and his grandfather. It put Sutton in an awkward position.

"Netherghyll Castle is now yours," he told him quietly. "She lives there. What are you going to do; throw the woman out of the only home she has ever known before you will take possession?"

Weston's tick was growing worse. "She can rot for all I care."

Sutton grimaced. "West," he hissed reprovingly. "She is our mother, for God's sake. If for no other reason than that, you must show some respect."

Weston didn't say anything more. If the conversation continued, his voice was going to get louder and he didn't want to frighten Aubria. By the time they reached the keep, he set the little girl gently to her feet so she could take the stairs into the entry by herself. She didn't like any help up the stairs. Weston and Sutton followed her slowly until they reached the top and Aubria sprinted off, calling for her mother. They could hear Amalie's faint reply.

"My wife's name is Amalie," Weston told his brother as they mounted the steps up to the banquet hall. "I am not sure what Henry told you, but I will tell you that regardless of the woman's past or family relations, I love her with all of my heart and she is the most beautiful, accomplished and sweet woman on the face of this earth. I would kill for her a thousand times over so be aware of that when speaking with her. If you bring up anything unpleasant that you might have heard or if you upset her in any way, know that my wrath shall be swift. Is that clear?"

Sutton looked at him with an expression between boredom and fear. "Give me the benefit of the doubt, will you?" he fired back softly. "She is your wife and my sister. I would not dream of offending or hurting her. But answer one question before I meet her."

"What?"

"Is it true that she was pregnant when you married her?"

"Did Bolingbroke tell you that, too?"

"Nay. I heard it from others."

"It is true."

"Was the child yours?"

"No."

They paused at the top of the spiral stairs. The banqueting hall was beyond and they could hear a woman's voice intermingled with those of the children.

"Was she really raped by Sorrell?" Sutton appeared perplexed, almost pained.

Weston lifted an eyebrow. "That is old news."

"Perhaps it is, but some of Henry's men, who were here four years ago when Bolingbroke confiscated the castle, were more than free in telling me about it."

Weston merely nodded faintly. "Old rumors. Old and painful. She does not deserve it."

"Then the little girl…"

"Is my daughter."

Sutton didn't say anymore; he didn't have to. He knew the truth, puzzled by his stubborn and pious brother's marriage to a compromised woman. The Weston he had known his entire life would have spit upon such a trollop. He was so rigid in his thinking when it came to things like morality and chivalry that there was no gray area, no forgiveness or compassion. But this new Weston, the man who was married with children, was not the same man he had known. Things were puzzling, indeed.

Weston and Sutton entered the enormous banqueting hall, spying a woman and two small children at the head of the banqueting table. Servants rushed around, bringing food to the table as the men approached.

Amalie looked up from her attempts to feed her finicky son, her green eyes falling on a tall, blond knight beside her husband. Weston went to her and kissed her on the cheek as he faced Sutton.

"Amalie," he said. "I would like for you to meet my brother, Sutton de Royans. He has newly arrived today by surprise. Sutton, this is my wife, Amalie, and our son, Colton."

Surprised, Amalie smiled brightly at the good-looking knight who faintly resembled her husband. He wasn't as handsome, in her opinion, but he was taller and had a good deal of the same muscular build.

"Sutton," she went to him, holding out her hand to greet him. "It is a pleasure to finally meet you. Weston has spoken fondly of you and I was hoping to have the chance to know you someday."

Sutton could see, in that instant, what had his brother so captivated; the woman was positively magnificent. With her big green eyes, delicately arched brows and sweet smile, she was one of the most beautiful women he had ever seen. He took her hand chivalrously, bringing it to his lips.

"I had no idea I had a sister until just a few moments ago," he replied. "My brother is an extremely fortunate man."

Amalie's grin broadened as she looked to her husband. "I can see he is your brother," she said. "He is a smooth-tongued devil just like you are."

Weston laughed softly. "He learned everything he knows from me."

"I would not be surprised."

Sutton, grinning, let go of her hand because his brother reached out to snatch it from him. Good naturedly, the men took a seat at the table as Amalie returned her attention to her picky son, who was tired and grumpy and did not want to eat. Weston and Sutton watched her with the children a moment, her gentle manner and sweet features, before Sutton resumed their earlier conversation.

"I was not present when Grandfather passed away," he said. "I received word at Bolingbroke."

Weston was watching his wife as she tried to coerce Colton into drinking some cow's milk. "Did she send you word?" he asked.

Sutton shook his head. "You can say her name, you know."

Weston tore his gaze away from his family and gave his brother a stony expression. Sutton lifted an eyebrow when he saw the reaction, realizing his brother wasn't going to refer to their mother in any other manner.

"Aye," Sutton said after a moment. "Mother sent word to me. She knew that you would probably burn any missive she sent to you, so she asked me to deliver the news personally."

"That was wise."

Sutton shook his head, regretful of his brother's attitude even after all of these years. It didn't surprise him but he was hoping that time might have eased it. But rather than argue with his brother about it, he simply continued the conversation.

"I was able to attend Grandfather's funeral," he said. "We buried him at the church of St. John the Evangelist."

Weston nodded, thinking of the man he resembled a great deal. Although he had disowned the man long ago, he still felt a pang of sorrow at his passing. But the sensation confused him, feeling sorrow for a man he had sworn to hate, so he ignored it.

"I know the church well," he smiled weakly. "Remember how you and I used to run about the churchyard and play games? The priests would throw rocks at us to make us go away."

Sutton laughed softly. "One of them hit you in the forehead once; do you recall? Instead of running away, you ran at the priests and threw rocks at them. You hit one of them right between the eyes."

As the men laughed at the memories, Amalie was listening. "Weston, you didn't," she scolded softly, fighting off a smirk. "How old were you?"

Weston shrugged. "Four or five years old, I think," he looked at his brother. "The priests went and told father what we did. Do you remember? When we told him our side of the story, he threw rocks at the priests, too."

They burst out laughing as Amalie grinned; memories of Marston de Royans brought good feelings. It had been a long time since Weston and Sutton had reminisced about their father and the recollections were fond ones. As they continued to laugh about the rock throwing incident, a serving wench brought out ale and food. Starving, Sutton dug in with gusto.

Meanwhile, Colton, tired and frustrated, started howling as his mother tried to feed him more bread. Amalie picked the baby up and called for Esma, who met her at the base of the stairs to collect the little boy. Esma cooed to Colton as she took him up to his nap. Free of the weepy child, Amalie returned to the great hall.

She plopped down next to Aubria as the little girl chewed on her cheese. Collecting her own bread and cheese, she took a healthy bite as she focused on her husband.

"Am I to understand that your grandfather has passed on, West?" she asked.

Weston and Sutton had moved on to the next subject, the fact that Henry of Bolingbroke had taken another quest to Lithuania to fight for the Duchy of Vilnius once again, but turned their attention to her when she spoke. Weston nodded without enthusiasm.

"So I have been told," he said.

When he didn't elaborate, Sutton stepped in. "He is now Baron Cononley, Constable of North Yorkshire and the Yorkshire Dales. Your husband has inherited a great legacy and a great fortune, Lady de Royans."

Amalie didn't react other than to keep her gaze fixed on Weston. "Does this mean we will be moving to Yorkshire?"

Weston shrugged, averting his gaze. He hadn't thought on what they would do. Perhaps he didn't want to. They were happy at Hedingham and he didn't want to disrupt that peace. On the other hand, he had a responsibility to fulfill his legacy.

"I am not sure what it means," he said quietly. "We will discuss that at a later time. Right now, I simply want to speak with my brother, whom I've not seen in a few years."

Amalie sensed his confusion, his disquiet. But she was feeling some confusion herself and would not be put off. "But you are the garrison commander of Hedingham," she said. "And the castle is my home. I am not entirely sure I am happy about leaving."

Weston wasn't particularly pleased that she hadn't respected his wishes not to discuss it. "I would not worry," he said, eyeing her. "It is not your concern."

She frowned. "Not my concern?" she repeated. "Of course it is my concern. Hedingham is my home."

He looked pointedly at her. "And Netherghyll is mine," he said, inferring by his tone that she needed to keep quiet for the moment.

"Either way, we will do what I feel is best. I will not discuss it with you right now."

Amalie could see that he was growing agitated on the subject and his words were harsh. Stung, she shut her mouth and turned her attention to her daughter.

Aubria was finished with her meal, crumbs on her face, and Amalie brushed them off and lifted the little girl from the bench and put her to the floor. But instead of accompanying her mother up the stairs to naptime, Aubria dashed to her father. Weston lifted the little girl up and sat her on his thigh, smiling at her when she grinned up at him with a sweet, little smile that was the mirror image of her mother's.

Amalie wasn't in any mood to deal with a disobedient daughter. She went to her husband and lifted the child up from his lap, listening to Aubria scream as she was carried from the banqueting hall. Weston watched them go.

"She may remain with me if she wishes," he told Amalie.

Amalie didn't look at him as she carted the weeping child from the room. "She needs her nap."

Weston watched her disappear into the stairwell, suspecting he had hurt his wife's feelings with his curt replies. He could feel it in her body language, in the way she spoke to him.

The truth was that anything that had to do with his grandfather or mother usually had him barking, even to those he loved. It was a subject they kept buried because it was something he never wanted to discuss. As much as he wanted to speak with his brother, he needed to soothe his wife first. But more than that, they needed to discuss their future. He shouldn't have snapped at her.

Remorseful, he turned to his brother, smiling weakly. "Sit and enjoy your food." He stood up from the table. "I shall return shortly."

Sutton was well into the meal and waved him off, mouth full. "I will be here when you return."

Weston quit the banqueting hall and disappeared up the spiral stairs. Sutton watched him go, knowing what turmoil the man must be feeling at the latest news. But he also knew that, no matter what, Weston would fulfill his destiny. As Sutton delved into a big piece of fatty pork, he hoped that Weston's wife wasn't going to make that decision difficult.

CHAPTER THIRTEEN

WESTON FOUND AMALIE in the master's chamber, in bed with both of the children. Unfortunately, both Weston and Amalie had taken to sleeping with the children when they were infants, which made their bed rather crowded now that the children were growing older. They were increasingly able to transition the children to their own beds at night, or rather Amalie was mostly able to, because Weston was rather soft about it. When Aubria produced a pouty lip, his resolve would evaporate so, more often than not, Mother had to put the children in their own beds.

Which was why he was surprised to find all three of them piled into the big master's bed. But he knew it was indicative of her mood, of the uncertain future and stirrings she had heard in the banquet hall with the sudden appearance of Sutton, so she clustered the children in the bed with her where she felt comforted. He quietly entered the room, shutting the door softly behind him. He tried to be quiet as he went to the edge of the bed to see if all three of them were sleeping.

Amalie's green eyes greeted him, gazing up at him in the dim light. He smiled faintly and, with extreme care, began to remove his armor. Pieces ended up near the door and the mail coat ended up tossed over a frame, usually used to dry clothing on. Sitting in a chair to remove his boots, he very carefully climbed into bed next to Amalie.

His enormous arms went around Amalie and Aubria, his big hand on Colton as the little boy slept like the dead. When he had his family in his arms, all was right with the world. He nestled his face into the back of Amalie's blond head, smelling the faint scent of violets intermingled with her delicious musky smell, a scent all her own. He inhaled deeply.

"I am sorry if I was short with you," he whispered into the back of her head. "I did not mean to be. But the appearance of my brother and the news he bears has left me somewhat rattled."

Amalie could feel his enormous body against her, warm and powerful. True, she had been upset, but she couldn't remain angry with the man for long. She sighed, whispering in the dim light.

"You told me you did not wish to discuss it," she murmured. "I suppose I should have listened."

He kissed the back of her head. "I should not have snapped," he whispered. "We can discuss it now if you wish."

She nodded and he climbed out of the bed carefully, pulling her up. With a lingering glance at the sleeping toddlers, they slipped from the room and silently closed the door.

The children's chamber was next to theirs and they went inside. It was cluttered with neat piles of clothes thanks to Esma and Neilie, and the two little beds were covered with fluffy furs and linen coverlets. Toys littered the floor, little wooden carts and poppets made from rags.

"It never occurred to me that we would ever leave Hedingham, although I suppose it should have." Amalie turned to look at him. "This is the only home I have ever known. I had hoped our children would grow up here."

He watched her reach down and pick up a toy, pensively moving to put it on their daughter's bed.

"I understand," he said quietly. "But with my grandfather's passing, all of his titles and lands become mine. They should have been my father's."

She looked up at him as he spoke the last sentence; there was something sad to his manner, contemplative, as he leaned against the windowsill. His dark blue gaze embraced the Essex landscape beyond as she watched him, seeing the depression in his manner. She was coming to realize that it was time for truth between them.

"West," she said softly. "I have never once asked you about your father or mother or that mess involving your grandfather. You spoke of it once, years ago, and we never discussed it again. But I think you need to tell me everything so I understand the dynamics of your family. All I know is that you hate your mother and, other than your brother, there is no one in your family that you are close to."

Arms folded across his massive chest, he turned to look at her. "There is really not much more to tell," he said. "My mother fell in love with my grandfather and left my father for the man. My father killed himself as a result."

"But surely there is more to it than that."

He shrugged. "Perhaps there is, but it does not matter to me," he said. "All I know is that my mother's actions drove my father to suicide."

She watched him, his tense body language, as she carefully chose her words. "May I speak freely on this subject, sweetheart?"

He cocked his head. "Of course you can. Say what is on your mind."

She smiled timidly, formulating her thoughts. "I do not want to offend you because I certainly do not know exactly what happened between your mother and father, but we both know that my situation was dire when you met me. Is that a fair statement?"

He wasn't quite following her but he nodded. "I would say so."

"Yet you did not judge me," she said softly, coming towards him. "You knew the situation, as horrible as it was, and you accepted me and loved me in spite of everything because the truth of the matter was far more complex than the public perception."

"What are you driving at?"

She stopped when she came to him, reaching out a soft hand to rest on his big forearm. "All I am saying is that your perception of what happened between your parents and your grandfather was from a child of five or six years old," she said softly, gently. "The truth of it, the complexity of it, could have been much, much different. I am not saying anyone is innocent and I am certainly not saying that it is not as bad as you have perceived. Did you ever, as an adult, ask your mother what truly happened?"

He was torn between defiance and some remorse. "Nay," he said. "There was no reason to. My father is dead because of her."

Amalie pressed herself against him and he unwound his arms from across his chest, putting his left one around her shoulders.

"Was your father a wise and reasonable man?" she asked.

"Of course he was."

"Did your mother put the sword in his hand and force him to fall on it?"

He unwound his arm from her and moved away. "She may as well have," he insisted. "It is her fault."

Amalie could see he was growing agitated again. "Sweetheart, I am not trying to upset you," she insisted. "All I am saying is that there is probably more to the story than a six-year-old child was told. As you did not judge me harshly even in my dire situation, perhaps you should give your own mother that benefit as well. You told me once that you thought perhaps God had expressed to you that compassion was the greater glory; does that hold true for everyone or just me?"

He had been pacing away from her, suddenly turning to her with a taut and angry expression. His big hands worked and his jaw flexed. She could tell he was gearing up for a harsh retort but he bit his tongue, unwilling to be cruel when she was only trying to help. Besides, she was so soft and sweet and beautiful that it would have been like lashing out at a helpless kitten. He simply couldn't do it.

"You are my heart and soul, Ammy," he said softly. "But I cannot extend that same compassion to my mother. After all of these years, the hatred is deeply ingrained. I do not know if I can undo what years of anger have done."

She went to him, wrapping her arms around his neck and hugging him tightly. Weston clung to her, feeling her soft body against his, drawing strength from her.

"I am not asking you to undo anything," she whispered, kissing him on the cheek. "I am simply asking questions to better understand what has happened. And if we must go and live at Netherghyll Castle, then I look forward to it. It is where you were born and is therefore my home as much as Hedingham is."

He smiled weakly at her, kissing her soft mouth. "I am a baron now, after all."

Her smile grew. "Of course you are, sweetheart," she said encouragingly. "And you must live at your seat. Aubria and Colton will know many wonderful years there. And so will the next child."

He cocked his head. "If we have any more," he said thoughtfully. "I am already the most blessed man on earth. One or two more children would only add to that bliss."

She smiled and kissed him again. "If we go to Netherghyll, let us leave while the weather is still good. I do not wish to travel with a large belly and two small children."

It took him a moment to realize that she had been telling him that another child was on the way. His eyes widened. "We... we are expecting a child again?"

She laughed softly at his reaction. "It is still early, but I believe so. I have not been wrong yet."

His shock grew. "And you are only telling me this now?"

She shook her head helplessly. "I have only come to suspect in the past day or so," she said, putting a hand on his cheek, something that always, without fail, calmed the man. "I am telling you of my suspicions as soon as I have them. I pray we have another strong son, like Colton, in the exact image of his father."

He wrapped her up in his enormous arms, hugging her tightly. "And I pray that you come through unscathed," he whispered, kissing the side of her head. "Although you and I have had two children together, it still scares the wits from me to watch you go through such pain."

She smiled warmly, pulling back to look at his strong face. "If I am not afraid, you should not be either. We have such intelligent and beautiful children."

The shock and apprehension were fading from Weston's face, being replaced by unadulterated joy. He hugged her again, picking her up off the floor and spinning her around a couple of times. He listened to her squeal, laughing with her. When he set her down, he kissed her happily, lovingly.

"My life is already so wonderful," he murmured. "I cannot imagine that it would become more magnificent than it already is but I see that I am wrong. Every day with you, Ammy… every day is a treasure."

She kissed him softly. "I love you, West," she murmured, then fixed him in the eye. "I am looking forward to going to Netherghyll, only…"

"Only what?"

She shrugged, trying not to dampen the moment. "What will become of Hedingham if we leave?"

He shook his head. "Nothing will happen to it," he said. "It will remain here, strong and secure."

Thoughts of her brother came to mind, thinking of the time he would return from exile to claim his castle. He was, after all, a favored of the king and as everyone knew, men fell out of and in to favor all of the time. It was the way of things.

She didn't say anything about her brother because the subject of him was much like the subject of Weston's mother; it was best not to discuss it. For four years, they stayed away from the subject of their respective families altogether and had never regretted it.

"So," she said as she moved away from him and bent down to pick up yet another toy, pretending to occupy herself. "When will we leave for Netherghyll?"

He shrugged. "I am not sure," he said. "I must speak with my brother and find out what I can about my grandfather's passing and the state of his properties."

She picked up a few more toys, her arms now full of them. "Will Sutton go with us?"

Weston nodded firmly. "Absolutely," he said. "I am looking forward to serving with my brother again. He will be my right hand, the commander for my troops."

"How many troops does your grandfather have?"

Weston could see that she was busy cleaning up the floor so he moved for the door, eager to get back to his brother. Things were right between them again and he was relieved; not that they could ever stay upset with each other for long. They were too rational to let arguments or misunderstandings get out of hand.

"Usually around a thousand men," he said. "That is something I must speak with my brother about."

She waved him off as she deposited her armfuls of toys onto Aubria's bed. "Go on, then," she said. "I will see you later."

He paused by the door, watching her blond head as she straightened up. "Ammy?"

She paused, looking up at him. "Aye?"

He smiled affectionately at her. "I love you, my angel."

She returned his smile. "I love you, also."

He flashed a brilliant grin at her and slipped through the door, leaving Amalie grinning in the wake of his departure. She felt like the most fortunate women in the world and she thanked God yet again for her husband, the new Baron Cononley.

❆

WESTON HAD JUST made it down to the great hall when a soldier suddenly burst in through the entry, moving right to him. Weston paused, halfway to the banqueting table where his brother still sat, as the soldier came upon him. They had a few exchanged words and then the soldier quickly ran out the way he had come. Weston looked at Sutton and motioned to him.

"Come with me," he said to his brother. "We have apparently received a royal messenger."

Sutton, feeling stuffed and lethargic from his meal, nonetheless bolted up from the bench.

"A royal messenger?" he repeated, confused. "Why would the king be sending you a missive?"

Weston shrugged as his brother joined him and they made their way to the forebuilding of the entry.

"I would not know," he replied. "I have lived here for four years, in the castle of a man who is the king's lover, and the king has never even acknowledged the fact that Bolingbroke has acquired Hedingham. I am, therefore, curious."

They trotted down the stairs to the upper bailey. "Do you suppose the king is demanding you vacate the castle?"

"I suppose we shall find out."

"What will you do?"

"I was leaving, anyway."

The corner of Sutton's mouth twitched. "When do we leave for Netherghyll?"

They emerged into the bright September day and headed for the gatehouse as Weston wriggled his eyebrows wryly. "Ahead of the king's troops, who are probably heading in our direction as we speak."

Sutton laughed softly as they crossed the bridge and continued into the lower bailey, which was busy at this hour. Peasants brought supplies, the blacksmith was shoeing an unhappy horse, and several dogs ran about and barked at people. It was the usual chaos on any given day. The gatehouse was already in view and they could see several soldiers milling about as they approached. As they drew near, Heath broke away from the group and jogged towards them, his mail and armor jingling.

"A messenger from Richard, West," he said, flipping his long red hair out of his eyes. "I kept the man at the gatehouse. I did not know how comfortable you wished to make him so I held him there."

Weston nodded as he continued towards the gatehouse with his brother, now with Heath in tow.

"A royal messenger?" he repeated.

"Aye."

"Did the man say what his message was?"

Heath shook his head. "Nay," he replied. "He said it was a message for Lady Amalie de Vere."

Weston passed a glance at Heath, at his brother, wondering what message the king could possibly be sending to Amalie. As he reached the great stone gatehouse, the soldiers cleared away and the royal messenger came into view.

It was a knight in fine armor, a big man, young, with hazel eyes and a handsome face. He stood by the portcullis, relaxed and seemingly unconcerned with all of the Bolingbroke men milling around him. Weston walked up to him without delay.

"I am Sir Weston de Royans, Baron Cononley." He used his title for the first time, feeling the satisfaction of it. "I am the garrison commander for Hedingham. I understand you have a missive for the Lady Amalie."

The knight nodded. "I am Sir Range de Winter, my lord," he introduced himself. "I come from the king directly with a message for the lady. Is she available that I might deliver it personally?"

"I am Lady Amalie's husband," Weston told him. "She is occupied with our children at the moment. You may deliver your missive to me and I will ensure that she receives it."

The knight didn't argue or question. He simply nodded, passing a glance at the soldiers surrounding them.

"Then perhaps I may deliver the message to you in a less traveled area," he said. "It is rather sensitive in nature."

Weston nodded, once, and motioned the knight to follow. De Winter followed him, a big man with long legs. Heath and Sutton also followed at a distance, their curious eyes on de Winter. The four of them made their way towards the keep. But as they crossed the bridge to the upper bailey, Weston suddenly came to a halt and turned to de Winter.

"I do not wish to go to the keep where my wife is," he told him. "No one can hear your missive here. You will tell me what message the king has sent to my wife."

De Winter spoke without hesitation. "The king wishes to inform the Lady Amalie de Vere that her brother, Robert, was killed in a hunting accident," he said. "The Duke of Ireland's body is due to arrive in London sometime next week and the king thought that his sister would like to attend his funeral."

Weston struggled not to show his surprise. "A hunting accident?" he repeated. "Where did it happen?"

"In Leuven, my lord," de Winter replied. "He was hunting wild boar and was gored."

Weston stared at the man a moment before finally shaking his head, turning away as he absorbed the information. "So he was in France?" he muttered, more to himself than to anyone else. "We thought he was in Ireland."

De Winter continued with his missive. "There is more, my lord," he went on. "Aubrey de Vere has been granted the title Earl of Oxford by the king and Hedingham has been restored to the de Veres. Lord Aubrey will be arriving next month to take charge of Hedingham. If Bolingbroke does not surrender peacefully, the king has assured the Earl of Oxford the support of crown troops in his quest to regain the castle."

Weston turned to look at him, piecing together what he'd been told. He couldn't decide if he was insulted by the king's threat of military action or not. Maybe he was even relieved by it because now there would be no choice for Amalie but to go to Netherghyll. In an odd way, his path had been set in stone now. His new life was about to begin and he wasn't the least bit sorry. Already, Hedingham seemed like a distant memory.

"So the king's chamberlain and uncle to Robert and Amalie, having fallen out of royal favor with Robert's behavior, is now suddenly back in the king's graces and granted the earldom of Oxford, including Hedingham Castle." He took a few steps towards de Winter, closing in on the big knight. "And you are here to tell me that if I do not vacate my troops from Hedingham, then the king and de Vere will lay siege to

Hedingham to regain it?"

"That is the gist of it, my lord."

"Does Bolingbroke know?"

"This I would not know, my lord."

Weston studied the man a moment before turning away, digesting the surprising information. This day had been full of surprises all the way around.

"He probably does not know," Weston muttered to himself as his dark blue gaze lingered on the great pond of Hedingham. "He has returned to Vilnius and would, therefore, not have received the news yet. But it would be my assumption that he will relinquish the property rather than risk a battle at this point. Things have been peaceful for the most part for the past few years and a battle for a holding would only cause problems for Bolingbroke."

De Winter stood there, watching de Royans, feeling the stare from the knights behind him. He wasn't afraid; he knew he wasn't in any danger. But he was not insensitive to the political and family dealings going on; there was an abundance of it.

"I have been requested by the king to receive Lady Amalie's answer, my lord," he said.

West looked at him. "Answer to what?"

"If the lady will be attending her brother's funeral and also if Bolingbroke intends to relinquish Hedingham without bloodshed."

Weston didn't have to think on his answer; he already knew what it would be. "My wife will not be attending the funeral of the man who fled England like a coward and left her to the mercy of the enemy," he said flatly. "As for the surrender of Hedingham, tell the king that Aubrey de Vere can have it. I will pull Bolingbroke's troops out of here before the week is out."

It was less of a battle than de Winter had expected. He was, frankly, astonished that Bolingbroke's garrison commander gave up without a fight. Saluting smartly, he turned on his heel and returned to the gatehouse. As the man's bootfalls faded off down the road, Heath approached Weston as Sutton watched de Lara walk away. Heath's manner was timid.

"What do we do now?" he asked quietly.

Weston lifted his eyebrows. "You heard the man," he said dryly. "We must vacate the premises. Send word immediately to Bolingbroke of our intentions. The man has returned to Vilnius to fight for the Duchy there so I do not expect him to receive the news in a timely manner; still, it must be sent. You will tell Henry that I am ordering all Bolingbroke troops returned to Bolingbroke Castle and Hedingham surrendered to Aubrey de Vere on the orders of the king. In a separate missive, I will be informing Henry of Bolingbroke that I am resigning my post effective immediately in order to assume my rightful position as Baron Cononley. Heath, you will be returning with the troops to the Bolingbroke Castle. I will take John with me to Netherghyll."

Heath looked as if the man had just struck him. "I have to return to Bolingbroke?" he repeated. "Why me? Why not send John?"

Weston put a hand on Heath's shoulder; he could see the man was upset by the directives. "You did not let me finish," he assured him. "After you have returned Henry's men to Bolingbroke, you will proceed to Netherghyll to serve at my side. You are an excellent knight, Heath. I would not be without you."

The sun shone again in Heath's expression as he smiled and bolted off, intent to carry out Weston's instructions. When the redheaded knight left, Weston turned to Sutton. His brother was grinning at him.

"It has been an eventful day for you," he observed. "But, as with all things, the mighty Weston de Royans does not crumble. The bigger the burden, the stronger he becomes."

Weston smirked. "Eventful day, indeed," he said, motioning the man with him as he headed back towards the outer bailey where most of the soldiers were. "It will be a minor issue to clear out of Hedingham and return Henry's troops. The bigger issue will be packing my wife, my children, and the entire household. It will be a massive undertaking."

Sutton's smile faded as they entered the heart of the big lower bailey. "You told the king's messenger that your wife will not be attending her brother's funeral," he said. "Will that be her decision as well? She may wish to go."

Weston shook his head. "She will not, believe me," he said. "Her brother... well, suffice it to say that she has no great love for the man. Every bad thing that has happened to her has been a direct result of his actions. The man was vile and despicable and I would be lying if I said his death brought me sorrow."

Sutton suddenly grabbed him by the arm, forcing Weston to look at him. There was much bafflement on Sutton's face as he spoke.

"West, I have to ask this," he said, his voice low and hissing. "You are not the same brother I have known since birth. The man I knew was rigid in his beliefs of right and wrong, of good and evil. I arrived today to find out that you not only married a woman who had been compromised by another man, but you are raising her child as your own. The brother I have known would have spit upon such a trollop before taking any interest in her. What on earth has changed you?"

Weston's dark blue eyes glittered. "My wife is not a trollop and if I ever hear you refer to her as one again, I will kill you. Is that clear?"

Sutton put up his hands in supplication. "A figure of speech, West. I was not intending to insult her."

Weston would not forgive so easily on a subject so close to his heart. If his brother said it, he was thinking it, and that upset him greatly. "Yet you did," he growled. "I will not hear that come out of your mouth again."

Sutton took a step back, his hands up in a sincere show of apology. "I did not mean to," he insisted. "I was only making a point. I simply wanted to know why you have changed so much. It is truly puzzling."

Weston knew it was a legitimate question, something no one who knew him before he met Amalie had dared to ask of him. But Sutton was asking and he was expecting an answer. Weston didn't want to answer him, mostly because any answer would make him sound like a hypocrite, but he respected his brother enough that he reluctantly responded.

Forcing himself to cool, he raked his hand through his cropped blond hair, thinking on how he would respond. He was careful in his reply.

"People change, I suppose," he said quietly, averting his gaze. He didn't want to look into his brother's probing eyes. "'Tis true that my life has been devoted to piety, chivalry and honesty. 'Tis also true that I viewed unchaste women as great sinners. That still has not changed. But Amalie… she was different from the moment I met her, I suppose. Everything that happened to her was not her fault. She was the victim of an unscrupulous knight and a weakling brother. I never blamed her for what happened to her and loved her regardless. She does not deserve the stigma that has been held over her head, the whispers of shame that have followed her. She is a good and true woman and I will kill anyone that says otherwise. If that is the explanation you seek, then you know the truth of it."

Sutton nodded faintly, absorbing the information, inevitably thinking about their mother. If Weston was capable of accepting a soiled woman as his wife, then perhaps he was capable of forgiving the woman who gave birth to him. Sutton was encouraged.

"Good enough." He clapped his brother on the shoulder, a twinkle to his blue eyes. "I am glad you have some humanity in you now. It was rather difficult living up to your perfect standards all these years."

Weston grinned in spite of himself. "My standards are still perfect."

Sutton laughed softly and, together, the two of them continued to the courtyard where the troops were beginning to assemble thanks to the shouts of Heath and John. Weston would address the men and inform them of their future directives. Then, he planned to head to the keep to inform his wife of the latest news.

From this point on, their lives were going to change.

CHAPTER FOURTEEN

SEATED IN THE CARRIAGE that had once belonged to her mother, Amalie was struggling not to retch with the rolling motion. In the two weeks since they had left Hedingham, any movement at all set her stomach to lurching. That, coupled with traveling with two very small children, had her absolutely miserable. She couldn't focus on herself because the children needed her, so it had been a huge struggle to overcome her misery in favor of the children.

Weston hadn't been insensitive to the fact; he had watched her health deteriorate for days since leaving Hedingham. He had two hundred men, five wagons and three knights with him, a large brigade that traveled northward from Essex en route to Yorkshire.

They had two hundred miles to cover before their arrival to Netherghyll, something he was increasingly excited about. But Amalie's early pregnancy misery dampened his enthusiasm as he grew increasingly concerned for her health. The constant travel was making her symptoms worse.

The news of her brother's death had been lingering with Amalie since their departure from Hedingham, but not because she was grieved by it. There was almost seven years in age difference between them and they had never been particularly close. Robert had been involved in court intrigue and rumors that he was the lover of the king had plagued the entire family for years. To Amalie, he was a distant acquaintance who happened to be her brother and nothing more. She didn't feel the animosity or anger towards him that Weston did. She simply didn't care one way or the other, in spite of everything, and when Weston informed the king that she would not be attending her brother's funeral, she agreed with his decision. She was eager to put all of that ugliness behind her and move forward with her life.

The first week and a half, they passed through Essex, Cambridgeshire and Lincolnshire. The weather had cooperated and the travel had been fairly pleasant. But Amalie had been positively green in the carriage, so much so that on this day as the caravan passed into South Yorkshire, Weston finally took the children from his wife and gave them over to Neilie and Esma, riding in one of the big provision wagons driven by Owyn. Weston kept the young man in his troops purely out of respect for the fact he had once saved Amalie's life, and Owyn had assimilated himself as one of Weston's loyal men. He was no longer the smitten soldier; he was now a de Royans warrior.

Weston put Sutton up on point and rode next to the wagon carrying his children to better protect them. But as the day passed, Aubria wanted to ride with him, a definite no-no as far as his wife was concerned because she didn't like the children around the excitable chargers. But Weston relented and allowed the little girl to sit in front of him. He could only hope that Amalie was asleep and unaware that he was breaking her rules.

Seeing his sister riding with their father, Colton began to scream because he wanted to ride on the warhorse, too, prompting Weston to recall Sutton from the head of the column and send John to replace him. Sutton took his nephew, a blond-headed little boy who acted quite a bit like Sutton had as a youngster, and rode carefully with him for a mile or so. He was scared to death that he was going to drop the child somehow. But Colton wasn't satisfied riding slowly so Sutton began to trot with him, then canter, until finally he was riding like the wind up and down the column to a chorus of Colton's delighted screams.

Weston watched the antics, grinning. Even the men-at-arms were grinning. Aubria was a much less demanding audience, sitting on her father's armored legs, satisfied with the slower pace so long as she had her poppet with her. Sucking her thumb and holding her baby, she eventually drifted off to sleep.

But trouble was coming. It wasn't long before Amalie stuck her head out of the cab, roused by her son's cries, to see what was going on. Weston saw her head and tried to get his brother's attention, but Sutton was having too much fun spinning his warhorse in circles and listening to Colton's uncontrollable giggles.

By the time Sutton realized he was being hailed, Amalie had seen the goings-on and was furious. She shouted to the soldier driving the cab and he came to a halt. Sick, exhausted, she climbed out of the cab as the entire column came to a stop.

Knowing he was in a good deal of trouble, Weston spurred his charger to where she was now standing in the dusty road. He smiled sweetly at her as he approached.

"Hello, my angel," he said softly. "What can...?"

She cut him off with a hand gesture that looked like a guillotine falling. "What is your brother doing with Colton?" she demanded, pointing to the pair. "I cannot believe you would allow him to be so reckless with my baby."

Her sickness was affecting her mood, now a frightening thing that could burst in all directions if he wasn't careful. He kept his voice calm and soft.

"Do you not trust me enough that I know when Colton is in danger?" he asked patiently. "My brother is quite competent and careful. He is simply entertaining his nephew while Mother sleeps. I see nothing wrong with it."

She just growled at him, having no answer to that. Stomping her foot angrily, she burst into tears as she turned back for the cab. Weston watched her climb in with a heavy heart, hissing softly as he bade the carriage driver to remain still for a moment. Then he spurred his charger back to the wagons, handing over his dozing daughter to Esma. He swiftly returned to the carriage and dismounted.

Weston went to the window of the cab, his enormous head filling it up as his gaze fell on his miserable wife.

"I am sorry, my love," he reached in and tried to grasp a hand. "I did not mean to upset you. Sutton and I were merely entertaining the children so you could rest. If I thought my brother had been reckless with the boy, I surely would have stopped him."

Amalie sobbed into her handkerchief. "He is just a baby," she wept. "You cannot be so rough with him. What if the horse falls? What if he is thrown? What would I do without my Colton?"

Weston sighed, feeling like a lout. He finally managed to grasp her hand and squeeze it gently.

"Would you feel better if you rode with me awhile?" he asked gently. "I know the rocking of the carriage makes you ill. Why not ride with me and get some fresh air?"

Kerchief to her mouth and nose, she reluctantly nodded. Weston opened the cab door and helped her out. Gently, he lifted her onto his charger and then mounted behind her. With a wave of his big arm, he directed the column forward once again.

It was much better riding with Weston on his horse, which had a surprisingly smooth gait. Amalie leaned back against him, her tears fading and her stomach settling somewhat. Over to her right, Sutton had taken up with Colton again and was now jogging around, turning wide circles in the grass, and Colton was yelling with delight. He was holding on for dear life, bouncing up and down in his uncle's strong grip.

Both Amalie and Weston turned to watch Sutton entertain the boy, who was absolutely thrilled. It was hard to be angry when Colton was having so much fun. He kept turning his big, beaming smile up to his uncle, demanding that he go faster. He kept saying "up, up" and kicking his feet, not exactly precise communication but Sutton knew what he meant. Sutton looked to Weston, who merely shrugged and looked to Amalie. Unwilling to dampen her son's enthusiasm in spite of her fears, Amalie simply waved them on.

The Sutton and Colton Show went on the rest of the afternoon. Amalie had calmed riding with her husband on his great warhorse, feeling better than she had in days. She eventually fell asleep against him and he moved himself to the middle of the column, protected by the surrounding soldiers since he was compromised with a sleeping woman on his lap. He didn't expect any trouble with a column this size but he wanted to be safe.

Just after sundown, he called a halt and they set up camp. While he left Amalie and the children inside the cab, Weston made sure their lodgings were set up and a warm fire was burning in the portable bronze furnace. Neilie and Esma fixed the beds, which were piles of rushes covered by furs and coverlets. The soldiers set up a blazing bonfire and roasted a three-point buck over it. The smells of roasting venison filled the night, usually a delicious smell but now something that made Amalie gag.

It was a cool night, quiet and peaceful, as Amalie sat with Weston, Sutton and the children for their evening meal. Colton was now quite attached to his new best friend and ate off of Sutton's trencher.

Aubria, very much her father's child, sat next to Weston as he gently fed her pieces of well-cooked venison. Amalie picked at her meal, struggling to swallow her bread and cheese, having absolutely no appetite for meat. She watched her children with the two big knights, thinking Colton's infatuation with Sutton to be rather sweet.

Sutton seemed like a calm, considerate man, much like her husband. She had spent a small amount of time with him and had come to know him somewhat, but her morning sickness had prevented too much contact. She was sleeping or miserable a good deal of the time.

Watching Sutton with Colton, his gentle manner, warmed Amalie to the man. He seemed genuinely affectionate towards the little boy, who was growing tired and becoming a handful for his uncle. Finally, Amalie put her plate aside.

"Sutton," she said as she extended her arms in Colton's direction. "I will take him to bed now. Thank you for entertaining him today."

Colton saw his mother coming and began to howl. Sutton picked him up and handed the kicking child over to Amalie, who put her hands on his ankles to still the kicking feet.

"My pleasure, Lady de Royans," Sutton said, his eyes twinkling. "He is an intelligent, strong lad."

"Please, call me Amalie," she smiled wearily at him. "And he is a handful. You can admit it."

Sutton grinned. "He reminds me a good deal of his father."

Weston, drawn into the conversation, looked up from feeding his daughter. "That is not true," he countered. "He is exactly like you were, Sutton; brilliant and wild."

Sutton just grinned, watching Amalie calmly, firmly, instruct her son to stop kicking. Feet stilled, Colton began to cry, exhausted from his busy day, and Amalie rocked him gently.

"I am going to put him to bed," she told Weston. "Please bring Aubria when she is finished eating."

Weston nodded. "I will, my angel."

She disappeared into the big tent, leaving Sutton and Weston with Aubria. The little girl had been eating steadily but finally slowed down, exhausted and full. When she began rubbing her eyes, Weston picked her up and carried her to the tent as well. Sutton sat alone by the fire for several minutes before Weston and Amalie reappeared without the children. Weston had his wife by the hand as he led her back over to the fire.

"You should really lie down, my angel," he was saying as she sat next to Sutton. "You are exhausted and we have a full day ahead of us tomorrow."

Amalie waved him off, accepting the cup of wine that Sutton poured for her. "I would simply like some time with my husband, without screaming children. Is that too much to ask?"

Weston grinned as Sutton suddenly stood up. "Perhaps I should leave," he teased. "I have a feeling the soldiers would rather have my company."

Amalie waved him down. "Sit," she commanded softly. "I have not had much of a chance to speak with you over the past few weeks. I should like to come to know my brother."

Sutton sat back down, grinning, and reclaimed his cup. He took a gulp of the tart, sweet wine. "What would you like to know?"

"Are you married?"

Sutton shook his head as Weston snickered. "I am not," he said. "But not for lack of trying."

Amalie lifted an eyebrow. "Do tell the story," she said. "I cannot imagine a handsome and strong man like you having difficulties with women."

Sutton shrugged, eyeing his brother, who continued to snort. "Well," he said reluctantly. "I only just met her when I returned for Grandfather's funeral. Her father is Lord Clifford of Skipton Castle."

Amalie smiled. "Is that so?" She warmed to the conversation as Weston stretched out behind her, his big torso against her back. "What is her name?"

Sutton sighed faintly, as men usually do when recalling a beautiful woman. "Paget," he said. "The Lady Paget Clifford."

Amalie's smile grew; she could see that he had a dreamy-eyed expression. "What does she look like?" she asked.

Sutton shrugged, looking to her cup. "The most beautiful woman I have ever seen besides you," he glanced up, winking at his grinning brother. "She has long brown hair and the most beautiful brown eyes. She looks like a goddess."

Amalie sipped at her wine. "Have you spoken to her?" she asked. "Does she know of your interest?"

He half-nodded, half-shrugged. "I have spoken with her on a few occasions," he said. "The last time I saw her was when I was heading out of town to go to Hedingham. She was shopping in town and I spoke with her briefly until her father chased me away."

Before Amalie could reply, Weston entered the conversation. "You must be persistent, Sutton," he advised. "You must go after what you want. If I had not gone after Amalie, she would still be at the nunnery and I would be a very lonely man."

Sutton's eyebrows lifted as his gaze moved between Weston and Amalie. "The nunnery?" he repeated, surprised. "Do you mean to tell me that you violated the sanctity of a nunnery to capture your bride?"

As Amalie giggled, Weston shook his head. "I did not capture her."

Amalie leaned towards him. "You did, in a manner of speaking."

He looked at her, bordering on mock outrage. "I did no such thing."

"You tracked me like a hound."

"Never did I track you; follow you, aye. Track you, no."

"You practically tied me up and carried me away."

His eyebrows flew up. "Is that so?" he huffed. "You ungrateful wench. The next nunnery we come across, I shall dump you off and leave you there."

Amalie laughed heartily, looking at Sutton. "Your brother came to the nunnery every day for three months, demanding to speak with me," she told him. "I sent him away every time until one day, he grew wise and came to the rear of the nunnery where the garden was. He found me there and has been my shadow ever since. I believe the point he is making is that if you truly want Lady Paget, then you should not give up."

Sutton thought on that a moment, watching Amalie and Weston grin at each other as if enjoying some private joke between them. He wanted that, too. The more time he spent with his brother and his family, the more he realized he wanted the same thing for himself. He finished what was left in his cup and set it down.

"There is a tournament scheduled in Keighley on the first day of November," he said. "I am thinking on competing. Perhaps she will be there and perhaps I can ask for her favor then."

"The first of November?" Amalie blinked thoughtfully. "That is only two weeks away."

"Thirteen days," Weston said as he sat up from where he had been stretched out next to his wife. "Perhaps I will compete also. It has been a long time since I have gone to sport against my brother."

Amalie's brow furrowed as she looked at him. "I do not think I like this idea," she said. "Tournaments are dangerous."

Weston put his hands on her shoulders, kissing her cheek as he winked at his brother. "They are not dangerous to me," he said. "Just everyone else who gets in my way."

Sutton snorted, rising wearily to his feet when he saw that Weston was doing the same and pulling Amalie along with him. The hour was growing late and they had a big day ahead of them on the morrow.

"Not to worry, Amalie," Sutton said. "Weston is invincible on the tournament circuit. There is not a man in England that can beat him, except perhaps me."

"We shall see, little brother," Weston said, guiding his wife towards their tent. "We shall see."

Sutton merely grinned as he dipped his head in farewell towards Amalie, disappearing off into the darkness. Weston gently pulled her into their tent, closing the flap. The soft glow of the fire outside lit the interior of the tent, illuminating the shadowed features of the children as they slept.

Weston lay down on their pallet, pulling Amalie down with him when she was finished checking on the children. Bundled up against her husband's broad chest, she slept the sleep of the dead, dreaming of blond-haired boys, lovely lord's daughters, and a distant tournament field.

Morning came with a loud clap of thunder and a vicious storm.

CHAPTER FIFTEEN

AMALIE'S FIRST GLIMPSE of Netherghyll Castle had her very curious about it. On the rise in the distance, she could hardly see it through the rain. But as the column drew closer, the details of the dark and expansive structure gradually became clearer.

The thunder rolled overhead and the rain came down in sheets as they approached. Amalie's attention was on the great, dark gray walls of Netherghyll, encircling the top of an entire hill like the embrace of a great, iron chain. There was a narrow road that led up the slick and muddy hill to the castle and nothing more than a massive, iron portcullis that opened wide at a hole in the wall to admit them.

The wall was at least twenty feet high, an impenetrable shield, and the iron portcullis was a colossal thing that would hold steady if God himself tried to breach it. As the carriage passed into the massively expansive bailey of Netherghyll, Amalie's gaze fell on the enormous keep.

It wasn't a keep liked Hedingham, a singular massive block reaching for the sky. Netherghyll's keep was more like a complex of buildings nestled right in the middle of the bailey. Amalie could see at least three buildings pieced together with a central courtyard in the middle of them that had a lovely garden laid out in it.

The building farthest to the west looked like an enormous hall with a pitched roof while the building attached to it on the east side was taller, about three stories, built heavy and squat. The building attached to the east side of that building, forming the third side of the cluster, was two stories, long and thick-looking. She could see small windows in the squatty keep and the long, thick building. All in all, it was an enormous complex that was now her home.

Beside her, Aubria had awoken from her nap and was standing up, peering from the carriage door window just as her mother was. Amalie smiled at her daughter, hugging the child gently as they both observed their new surroundings of muddy ground and rain-soaked buildings.

The column came to a halt and Amalie could hear Weston bellowing orders in the distance. Men began to move about and John, astride his big warhorse, suddenly bolted by, spraying mud as he went. The commotion was enough to wake Colton, who rose with a wail and began rubbing his eyes.

Amalie picked her son up and cradled him on her lap, comforting him as the little boy fully awoke. Sounds of the column disbanding were all around them and Amalie was increasingly eager to get out of the cab. She was tired of travel, slightly nauseous, and eager to explore her new home. But she waited patiently until Weston suddenly appeared at the door and the children squealed at the sight of him.

Weston yanked the door open, kissing his daughter on the cheek as he lifted her into his enormous arms. The rain was misting by now and Amalie shook her head as Aubria's blond hair began growing damp.

"Put her back in the cab, West," she admonished. "She will get wet out there."

He held out his hand to her. "We are going inside." He took her hand and helped her maneuver out of the cab with Colton in her arms. "The hall is warm and dry, and there should be plenty of food. Are you hungry?"

She wriggled her eyebrows at him. "Yes and no."

He grinned and kissed her hand as they began to move towards the hall. The mist wasn't too bad but the black mud was awful. Amalie tried to keep her skirts up with Colton in her arms, trying not to slip in the bog.

"I would sell my soul for a hot bath right now," she muttered.

He smiled at her, taking her elbow to help her and Colton through the muck. "No need," he said. "We can provide one without such sacrifices."

Amalie glanced up at the pitched-roof hall they were heading towards; it was big and dark-stoned with a heavily-thatched roof at a sharp angle. The structure looked austere, cold and serious, as tall as two stories with a long, block-like shape. At the roof peak was a corbel carved like a gargoyle's face, something rather eerie.

"So this is where you grew up?" she asked.

He nodded, looking around, reacquainting himself with his boyhood home. He felt a sense of comfort to be here but he also felt a strong sense of dread as memories of his father's suicide swamped him. Before they could close in on him completely, he focused on answering his wife.

"Until I was seven years old," he replied, trying to mask his unease. "I was born here."

She held on to Colton with two hands as Weston helped collect her skirt. "When were you here last?" she asked.

He helped her up onto the steps that led to the great hall, freeing her from the dark mud.

"I went to foster when I was seven," he said. "I spent my early years at Pembroke Castle before my master moved to Bolingbroke Castle. I was knighted at twenty years of age, whereupon I swore fealty to Bolingbroke. I have returned home twice during all that time, both times because of Sutton."

Amalie looked up at him. "Why? What happened to Sutton?"

Weston shook his head faintly. "Once because he had been badly wounded in a skirmish and it was feared that he was not going to survive, and the second time because he got into trouble with my grandfather and I had to intervene. I will say no more about that incident, so do not ask."

Amalie fought off a grin because he was wriggling his eyebrows as he spoke. She suspected it was something very naughty more than something very evil. Sutton was not the evil type. So she simply nodded her head as he pushed open the massive wood and iron doors to the great hall. A blast of warm, smoky air hit her in the face as she and Colton entered, followed closely by Weston and Aubria.

The hall was vast and long, with an enormous hearth on the western wall that was taller than Weston. Huge plumes of smoke billowed from it, wafting up to the ceiling. There was a giant banqueting table in the center of the room, full of food and pitchers of wine. There was also a woman standing next to the table, rather small, with a tight wimple and well-made clothes. The woman was a distance away so Amalie couldn't see much of her features, but she suspected who the woman was. As Amalie stood uncertainly, inspecting the room and waiting for direction from her husband, Sutton came in behind them and shut the door.

Sutton went straight for the woman standing near the table, reaching out to embrace her. Amalie turned to look at her husband, silently asking for direction, but the expression on his face was one she had never seen before. His eyes were on the woman in Sutton's embrace, but his features were hard and edgy. His jaw ticked faintly. She wasn't sure what to say to him as Aubria interrupted the silence.

The little blond girl put her hands on Weston's mailed cheeks, patting him gently.

"Dada?" she said in her sweet, little voice. "I'm hungry."

Weston tore his gaze off the woman in the distance and looked at his daughter. "We shall get you something to eat, my angel." He kissed her cheek, his eyes moving back to Sutton and the woman in his arms. He put his arm around Amalie's shoulders to move her forward. "Come along."

Amalie followed Weston to the great table in the center of the hall, all the while watching Sutton interact with the small, tightly-wimpled woman. As Weston and Amalie came to the table, Sutton caught sight of them. He smiled broadly at his brother and his family.

"Look at Weston's children, Mother," he ran a gloved hand across Colton's white-blond head. "This is Master Colton de Royans and that beautiful young lady is the Lady Aubria. Are these not the most beautiful children you have ever seen?"

Amalie watched apprehensively as the woman's eyes filled with a lake of tears. She clasped her hands tightly against her breast as if fearful to let herself go, wanting to embrace her grandchildren but not knowing how her eldest son would react. She was a small woman with deep blue eyes and Amalie could see the resemblance between the woman and her sons. She seemed so small and frail, her features fine and angelic. Amalie couldn't imagine what this tiny, delicate woman did to ever offend Weston so much that the man never wanted to speak to her again.

"Aye," she breathed. "They are the most beautiful children I have ever seen. I am so happy to meet them."

By this time, everyone was looking to Weston, who continued to stand like stone. Amalie would never dream of going against her husband, but she was coming to feel uncomfortable at his stony, brooding stance. More than that, he hadn't even introduced her, which she thought very rude. She waited a few seconds for him to say something, anything. When he didn't, she could no longer keep silent.

"My lady," she greeted Weston's mother. "I am Weston's wife, the Lady Amalie de Vere de Royans. I am happy to meet you."

Weston's mother fixed on her, blinking back a tide of tears. "Lady Amalie," she repeated as if it were the most beautiful name in the world. "I am so glad you have come. I am the Lady Elizabeth de Royans. I... I did not know that Weston had married."

Amalie was starting to feel the least bit perturbed at the way her husband had treated his mother although she kept reminding herself that he had his reasons. Deep-seated family reasons that she would not dispute. Still, since Weston wasn't speaking, she took the lead. She didn't know what else to do.

"We were married four years ago last May," she said. "We have lived at Hedingham, my family's home, since then. Have you ever been to Essex, my lady?"

Lady Elizabeth was struggling; that much was evident. Amalie naturally felt very sorry for the woman.

"I have not," Elizabeth said, trying very hard to blink back her tears. "I have spent most of my time in Yorkshire, although I visited London as a young girl. I think I should like to go back some day."

As Amalie warmed to the conversation, Colton suddenly started kicking his feet. "*Hungry!*" he growled. "Mama, bread!"

Elizabeth laughed with delight at the child, looking to Amalie. "Please," she indicated the table, heavy with food. "Sit and eat. There is plenty of bread for Colton."

Amalie didn't even look at Weston as she pushed past him, setting Colton down on one of the carved wooden chairs. Then she turned to take Aubria from him, but he waved her off silently and sat the girl down next to her brother.

Sutton plopped down next to Colton and tore apart a loaf of bread, handing the boy the soft, white middle as Aubria reached for a hunk of yellow cheese. Colton, reunited with his best pal Sutton, chewed happily. As Elizabeth timidly moved up beside Sutton to better inspect her grandchildren, Amalie turned to Weston.

"Aren't you going to say anything to her?" she whispered. "You are making this extremely uncomfortable."

Weston's jaw ticked as he looked at her. He couldn't even reply, mostly because he wasn't sure what to say. He was deeply torn with the old memories, the old hatred, flooding him. Finally, he just shook his head and pulled off his helm, setting it on the table as he took a seat on the other side of Aubria.

Amalie watched him, understanding his manner but not agreeing with it. She could see what a difficult time he was having in spite of his stony demeanor. With Sutton feeding Colton, she moved to her husband and gently pulled back his mail hood, revealing his damp, cropped blond hair. She put her hands on his enormous shoulders, kissing him on the temple as he reached up and clasped her hand. He squeezed it tightly.

"Has the rain been merciless, Lady Elizabeth?" Amalie asked politely. "The land seems very wet."

Elizabeth looked up from Colton, smiling. "This time of year it is always very wet," she replied. "The snows will come soon enough and we will have more than our share. Last winter was particularly difficult. In fact, that was when my husband fell ill and…"

She suddenly trailed off, almost choking on her words, realizing she had brought up the crux of all of the problems between her and Weston. They hadn't been there five minutes and already she had brought up the subject of Heston de Royans. Her eyes widened as she looked at Weston, who was focused on the wine in his hand. He showed no reaction as he silently gulped his wine and Elizabeth refocused nervously on Amalie.

"Well," she shifted subjects quickly. "It was quite a bad winter so I can only hope that this winter is not so bad."

Amalie smiled, gesturing to the great hall around them. "Even so, Netherghyll's hall is quite warm and lovely. We should be able to weather the elements quite nicely in here."

It was small talk, something to try and break the horrendous tension filling the room. Weston sat silently next to Aubria, drinking his wine and gazing off into the room as if remembering happier times within the old walls. Amalie wasn't sure what more she could say, struggling to think of something else they could lightly converse on. But before she could think on something, Elizabeth unwittingly asked a question that only made the tension grow worse.

"Please," she begged softly, "tell me how you and Weston met?"

Amalie's warm expression faded, wondering how to tactfully and carefully explain that particular event. Before she could reply, Weston suddenly came to life and looked at his mother.

"That is a conversation for another time," he snapped in a low, steady voice. "Right now, I would like to settle my family into their chambers and my wife requires a hot bath. I would assume my wife and I are occupying the master's chambers?"

He sounded so cold; Amalie had never heard that tone from him, ever. She looked startled as Elizabeth seemed to quiver, shocked that her eldest son was actually addressing her. But she recovered quickly.

"The servants are clearing my things from the master's chambers right now," she assured him. "We can put the children in your former chamber, Weston. Sutton, you will occupy your former chamber as well."

Weston abruptly stood up. "You can clear out your possessions at another time," he said brusquely. "My wife requires a bath and she will not wait."

Elizabeth looked stricken as Amalie put her hand on Weston's enormous forearm. "I can wait, West," she said softly, steadily. "I am sure the servants are moving as fast as they can in removing your mother's possessions. I am sure it will not be much longer."

Weston just stared at her. Then, he walked away. Amalie watched him go, watching his tense body language as he quit the hall. She was rather surprised he had left but she knew it was because he couldn't adequately deal with what he was feeling at the moment. She turned to Elizabeth and Sutton.

"Would you mind tending the children?" she asked. "I must… speak with my husband for a moment."

Sutton already had Colton on his lap, feeding the kid off his own trencher, while Aubria stood up on her chair, pulling dried pieces of fruit off a platter and stuffing them into her mouth.

"Of course." Elizabeth quickly moved beside Aubria so the little girl wouldn't fall off the chair. "It would be my greatest pleasure to come to know my grandchildren. Thank you so much for asking."

Amalie smiled weakly in response as she moved to Aubria. "Sweetheart, this lady is Dada's mother," she said softly. "She is your grandmother. Can you introduce yourself?"

Aubria looked at Elizabeth with her big, brown eyes. Her mouth was full as she spoke. "Aubria Maud de Vere de Royans."

She ran her words together, coupled by the full mouth, which made her barely understandable. Pieces of dried fruit were flying out all over the place. But Elizabeth laughed softly in delight, sweetly hugging the child now that Weston wasn't around.

"It is a pleasure, lovely Aubria," she said softly. "May I sit and eat with you?"

Aubria nodded and returned to her fruit. Amalie took it as her cue to leave so she pulled her cloak about her body tightly and followed the path her husband had taken out of the hall.

It was oppressively misty and gray outside, and their column had mostly disbanded. She looked around the massive expanse of the bailey, finally spying her husband several yards away speaking with John.

Gathering her skirts, she braved the black mud again as she made her way towards him. John saw her coming first and pointed her out to Weston, who immediately headed in her direction. He met her halfway across the enormous, swampy ward.

"What are you doing out here?" he asked, taking her arm and trying to turn her around for the hall. "Where are the children?"

"I left them with your brother," she said. "I must speak with you."

"Later." He was still trying to turn her around. "You must go back inside. It is much too wet for you."

She stopped him from pushing her around. "Nay, Weston. I must speak with you *now*," she said firmly. "I realize that you harbor no great love for your mother, but what you did in there was shameful. You could have at least been civil."

He looked at her, his face hard. "You will not tell me how to behave with my mother. It is not your business."

Her eyebrows lifted. "Not my business?" she repeated, struggling not to snap. "Then tell me how you would have me behave? Am I to ignore and hate her, too, because you do? Am I to pretend the woman does not exist and be ungracious? Please tell me now so there are no misunderstandings in the future. If you would prefer I treat her as a ghost, then I will. But like it or not, we are all going to be living here together for quite some time and I do not want to ignore the woman who gave birth to you. That fact alone garners my respect."

His jaw ticked as he listened, eventually averting his gaze because he could not look her in the eye. As she waited expectantly, he struggled with an answer. Finally, he swooped down and lifted her into his arms. Then he began to march off towards the hall complex.

"Where are we going?" she asked, arms around his neck.

His dark blue eyes were fixed on the buildings ahead. "To a private place."

Amalie didn't say another word. Weston marched through the muck with her in his arms, bypassing the hall and crossing the garden that was lodged between the three buildings in the center of the bailey. He made his way to the long, two-story building on the far east side of the complex and entered through a heavy iron and wood door, one that was rather short for his height so he had to bend down to enter.

Once inside, a narrow, cold and dark corridor embraced them and Weston set her down, quietly closing the door. He took her hand, leading her down the hallway until they came to a small flight of stone stairs that doubled back on itself to the floor above.

They mounted the stairs to the second floor and into a corridor that had more light in it from long lancet windows that were cut into the wall almost to the ceiling. Weston took her to the end of the hall and opened another small wood and iron door, emerging into a small room with a cold, dark hearth in one corner.

Amalie looked around; it appeared as if the room hadn't been used in years. It was dusty and bare, and soot turned the wall around the hearth black. She looked curiously at her husband as he quietly shut the door.

"What is this room?" she asked.

Weston wearily pulled off his helm, peeling back the hauberk and scratching at his scalp. "It was my father's solar," he said, looking around. "I spent many happy hours in this room with him."

She regarded him carefully. "Is this where he killed himself?"

Weston sighed heavily, meeting her gaze. "Aye."

She sighed also, feeling his pain, and went to put her arms around him. He was wet and covered with armor, but it didn't matter. He wrapped her up in his arms, his forehead against hers, drawing strength from their love and bond. She was the one element in the world that kept him together, body and soul.

"I am so sorry, sweetheart," she murmured. "I know this place must bring back dreadful memories. I wish I could help ease them."

He kissed her forehead. "I appreciate that," he said. "And as for my mother, I do not expect you to ignore her. Your behavior with her was perfectly acceptable and I am untroubled by it. But as for me... well, I haven't seen the woman in years. Right now, I am dealing with the resurgence of bad feelings and memories. Perhaps, in time, they will fade. But right now, I am doing the best I can."

She patted his cheek, kissing him. "I know you are," she soothed. "I do not mean to be short with you but you must understand that I am in an awkward position. I would never dream of offending you or going against your wishes, yet I have met the woman who gave birth to you and am understandably respectful of that. I am in the middle of a battle that I cannot win or aid in. It is strange to say the least."

He kissed her gently, rocking her in his big arms. "I know," he murmured. "And for that, I am sorry. But you are sweet and gracious and endearing to everyone and I do not expect that to change with my mother. She will fall in love with you as I have."

Amalie wrapped her arms around his neck, hugging him tightly. "Everything will be all right," she whispered. "Perhaps, with time, there will be some civility towards your mother."

"I would not bank on it."

She pulled back to look at him. "Perhaps not," she said. "But would you at least do something for me, please?"

"Anything."

She knew he would, too, if she asked. For his sake, she felt that she should ask.

"When the time is right," she said carefully, "and you are feeling enough at ease, will you please ask your mother why she did what she did? Why she left your father for your grandfather? Your only knowledge of the event is from a six-year-old child's perspective. As an adult, I would encourage you to gain an adult's perspective. That way, if you continue to hate the woman until you die, you will at least base it upon the answers received as a grown man and not an impressionable child. Please, West? I do not like seeing you in such turmoil. Maybe knowing the truth would ease you."

His first instinct was to refuse her. But gazing into her green eyes, he was reluctant to admit that she had a point. He simply pulled her against him, his massive hand on the back of her head as his arms wrapped tightly around her.

"I cannot make any promises," he murmured. "But... I will think on it."

She hugged him tightly. "That is all I can ask for," she said. "Until that time, if it ever comes, would you at least try to be civil? I do not want the children to see how you behave with your mother and behave towards her in the same fashion. I do not want them to think it would be acceptable behavior towards me someday, either."

She had a point. Aubria and Colton were extremely impressionable and he didn't want his own feelings and actions clouding their young minds. After a moment, he nodded.

"What I feel towards my mother is my burden alone," he said. "I do not expect my entire family to take up arms on my behalf. Your concern is noted and I will do what I can to amend accordingly."

She smiled. "Thank you, sweetheart. You are a kind and compassionate man."

He kissed the side of her head, pulling back to kiss her mouth. It was the first time he had been truly alone with her in a couple of weeks and his kisses grew hungry, amorous.

Amalie clung to him, responding to his desire, knowing that an onslaught like this usually led to passionate lovemaking, something that was usually a daily event with them but something they'd not had the privacy for since they had left Hedingham. But they were both bundled up against the weather and Weston was in full armor, so he reluctantly backed off, smiling at her as he gave her a final, lingering kiss.

"Let us return to the hall and retrieve the children," he said softly. "I am sure our chambers are prepared by now. I would like for you to lie down and rest and I know the children will be tired as well."

She nodded, licking her lips and still tasting him upon them as he led her from the small, dark chamber. But as she walked from the room, she swore she could feel the ghost of Marston de Royans lingering behind her. She wasn't sure why, but she thought she could. *Odd*, she thought. She wasn't hard pressed to admit the chamber gave her an eerie feeling.

CHAPTER SIXTEEN

WESTON COULDN'T WAIT any longer. He'd already dressed in his heavy linen breeches, his leather breeches over those, a heavy tunic and a thick leather vest over that. He'd even lingered over pulling his boots on, but he could no longer delay as he waited for Amalie. He was expected in the armory to finish dressing in his heavy armor, something he would need for the day ahead.

On the first of November, the day of Keighley's tournament had arrived. Weston had entered to compete against a field of some of the best knights the north of England had to offer.

But dampening his excitement was the fact that Amalie was feeling horrendous. It was early morning and she couldn't even move in their bed without heaving. She wanted to go to the tournament so badly that she was driven to tears by the fact that she felt so awful.

Weston busied himself in their enormous chamber, pretending to fiddle with this or fuss with that, when what he was really doing was waiting for her to sit up in bed and announce she was going to get dressed. But so far, he hadn't seen any improvement.

When he was finished with the boots and there was nothing more he could do, he finally rose from the chair he had been seated upon and made his way to the bed, gazing down at his wife. She lay on her back with an arm over her eyes, as pale as the linens she lay upon. He sighed heavily, resting his enormous hands on his hips.

"I must go and don my armor, my angel," he told her. "Will you be all right?"

She nodded, but even the mere motion of that caused her to retch.

The problem was that there was nothing in her stomach to come up, so the action was painful. Lying sweaty and spent on the linens, she rolled onto her side with her hand over her mouth as she heaved, while Weston put a comforting hand on her shoulder. He hated seeing her so ill.

"Oh... Ammy," he bent over and kissed her pasty cheek. "You cannot go anywhere today. You must stay here."

She burst into tears, so very close to the surface. "I do not want you to go without me."

"Then I will not go," he assured her. "I will stay here with you."

She opened her eyes, great green things in her ashen face, and looked up at him. "But you must go," she insisted. "You are the new Baron Cononley. You must show your power and skill to your subjects. It is important."

He pursed his lips and lowered himself onto the bed beside her. "It is more important to take care of my wife," he told her. "If you stay here, then I will stay here."

She wiped at her eyes. "But... but the children have been looking forward to it," she said sadly. "Colton wants to see all of the knights. He will be so disappointed."

Weston smiled faintly. "I know," he said. "Sutton has him so worked up about it that all he talks about is swords. He calls them 'surds'."

That brought a smile to Amalie's pale lips. "I know," she whispered, giggling weakly. "And the chargers are not horses; they are 'he-he'."

Weston laughed softly, kissing her hand. "He is such a joy," he said. "Every day is a day of discovery with him. I feel as if I have been reborn through the eyes of my two-year-old son; everything is so wonderful and new."

Amalie's smile lingered. "For Sutton, too," she murmured. "I swear Sutton spends more time with him than you do, if such a thing is possible. He makes your brother long for a son of his own."

Weston nodded thoughtfully. "Which is why he is already dressed for the tournament today," he said. "Remember that the lovely Lady Paget Clifford will be there. I do not believe that Sutton will take 'no' for an answer this time."

Amalie sighed. "I was hoping to introduce myself and, perhaps, put in a good word for your brother."

Weston could see that she was growing distressed again over not attending so he hastened to keep the mood light.

"Here is what we will do, my angel." He kissed her forehead and stood up. "I will send some bread up to you. You can eat that, can you not? It will settle your stomach as I go to the armory and finish dressing. By the time I am dressed and all of our gear is packed into the wagons, you should be feeling better and dressed yourself. I will return for you then."

She looked at him dubiously. "I will try," she agreed. "You know I will."

"I know." He winked at her and turned for the door. "I will make sure that Esma and Neilie have the children up and dressed."

Amalie waved him off and closed her eyes, hearing the door shut softly. Her mind wandered to the children, now up and getting dressed, excited for the day's events. Then she thought of her proud and strong husband as he prepared for his first tournament in six years.

Amalie wasn't particularly thrilled that he hadn't competed in a while because she was fearful that, perhaps, his skills were not up to par, but Weston didn't seem concerned about it. He was more excited than any of them, excited to show his power and talent off to his new subjects. He intended to show all of North Yorkshire what the new baron was capable of.

The past two weeks at Netherghyll had been peaceful for the most part as Amalie and the children became familiar with their new surroundings. Weston and Elizabeth had stayed clear of one another; from the moment all of her possessions were moved into her new quarters in the long, two-story building attached to the keep, Elizabeth had been something of a recluse.

Every night, Weston and Amalie would sup with the children and Sutton, with no sign of Elizabeth. Weston never said a word about it but Amalie suspected Sutton wasn't particularly pleased with his brother's disregard for their mother; it was becoming increasingly apparent.

For the first week, Amalie thought it was probably more of a blessing that the woman hadn't shown her face. It made for peace amongst everyone as Weston settled in as Baron Cononley and as Amalie settled in as Lady of the Keep. But as the second week of their residence progressed, Amalie was coming to feel bad that Weston's mother had made herself a prisoner in her own home. So twice she had tried to visit Elizabeth and twice Elizabeth had sent her away, claiming illness. Amalie was fairly certain the woman wasn't sick. She would have to be clever in her approach since Elizabeth was deliberately being reclusive. Amalie was foolish, she knew, in having grand dreams of Weston eventually forgiving his mother so they could be one big happy family, but they were her dreams nonetheless.

Amalie lay in bed on this bright November morning, thoughts of Elizabeth de Royans on her mind, as Esma entered with a tray of food and drink. Amalie tried not to retch at the sight of it and lay in bed, eating bread, for several minutes while Esma went about cleaning up the chamber. They all knew Amalie was pregnant again and, as with her previous two, she tended to be quite sick at the onset, so Esma was very conscious of that. She urged Amalie to sit up after a while, hoping that the bread had settled everything down.

Fortunately, it had. Amalie was feeling much better, enough so that she was even able to eat some of the porridge and honey on the tray. There were pieces of apples, cut up, and she ate those as well.

Feeling well enough to get dressed, she bathed quickly in warmed rosewater that Esma brought her, scrubbed her face, brushed her teeth with a soft reed brush, and donned a lamb's wool sheath so soft that it was like feathers. Over that, Esma dressed her in a radiant scarlet surcoat that went brilliantly with her coloring. Esma also styled her hair in a fashionable braid that draped over one shoulder, into which she wove ribbons of scarlet and gold. A golden belt embraced her hips and sturdy golden slippers were on her feet. All in all, she looked spectacular considering she still wasn't feeling completely herself. But Amalie was determined to attend the tournament.

As soon as Amalie opened the door to her chamber, she ran headlong into Neilie escorting Aubria and Colton down the stairs. The children saw their mother and ran to her, and Amalie ended up carrying Colton down the narrow spiral stairs of the keep. Esma and Neilie fussed at her for doing so, as Weston had done several times also, but she waved them off, kissing her son and hugging him happily. He was with Weston or Sutton so often that she felt she didn't get to see him nearly enough.

Once they reached the keep entry, Aubria began asking for her father and Colton squirmed to be set down. Esma and Neilie had their hands full with the family's items that they would take with them to the tournament field; extra clothing for the children, toys and other possessions like blankets.

Amalie waved them onward to the party that was collecting in the bailey, grabbing both of her children by the hands and preparing to take them outside herself. But as she took the stairs that led from the entry down into the courtyard with the bailey beyond, the squat, sturdy two-story building off to the left caught her attention. She gazed up at it, knowing that Lady Elizabeth had two rooms with windows that faced out over the bailey. In fact, she swore she could see the woman looking down at them.

That gave Amalie an idea. Instead of heading out to the bailey where her husband was undoubtedly tying up the loose ends before they headed off to Keighley, Amalie took the children into the two-story building where Lady Elizabeth was lodged.

It was dark, cool and musty inside as Amalie led the children up the stairs and directed them to Lady Elizabeth's elaborate door. On the occasions that Amalie had come to see the woman and was subsequently sent away, she had been alone. Now, she wasn't alone. She had brought the magic keys that would open the woman's door. She planted Aubria and Colton in front of the door and told them to knock.

Aubria did, loudly. Colton saw what his sister was doing and he began to knock loudly, too. Being the more verbal of the two, he began to yell as well. Amalie fought off a smile, watching her children practically beat the door down and having no doubt that it would have the desired effect. She didn't have long to wait.

The children hadn't been pounding a minute when they all heard the bolt thrown. In short order, the door hesitantly creaked open. But Colton threw his weight behind a shove that pushed it wide open, charging into the room as if he belonged there. Aubria followed.

Amalie came to stand in the doorway, watching her bold, young son face his grandmother and demand "eets". Lady Elizabeth, pale and tightly wimpled, tried very hard to understand him.

"He is asking for sweets," Amalie said softly. "He believes it is his right to have sweets from everyone."

Elizabeth looked at Amalie, grinning, before turning back to Colton. "Is it sweets you want, young man?" As Colton nodded vigorously, she looked rather concerned. "I am afraid I do not have any sweets for you. But… I do believe I have something you might like. Will you come with me?"

She was holding out her hand to him. Colton took it boldly. When he realized she was walking to the adjoining chamber, he took the lead and practically yanked the woman into the room.

Amalie could hear them in the chamber, Lady Elizabeth's soft, gentle voice and a squawk from her son now and again. She took a step inside the door, looking around at the lavishly-appointed chamber; rich wall tapestries and plates decorated the walls and hearth. Aubria was making herself quite at home, nosing around Lady Elizabeth's fine table and touching the blown glass pieces. Amalie saw what she was doing and hissed at her, calling her off. Aubria turned her big brown eyes to her mother, quite innocently, and continued doing just as she pleased.

Amalie lifted an eyebrow at her disobedient daughter and entered the room, taking the little girl's hand and pulling her away from the table with its fine treasures. As the two of them stood patiently just inside the doorway, Elizabeth and Colton emerged from the adjoining chamber and Amalie could see immediately that her son had a small sword in his hand. It was about a foot long, very dull steel, with a rather elaborate hilt for such a toy.

Colton swung the sword around happily and Amalie realized that, very shortly, she was going to have a serious fight on her hands when she took it away from him. Before she had the opportunity, Elizabeth spoke.

"I pray you are not offended that I have given Colton this sword." She looked at Amalie. "It belonged to Weston as a child and I have always kept it safe, hoping that I would be able to give it to Weston's son someday."

That brief explanation removed all willpower from Amalie; certainly she could not take it from Colton now. Although she wasn't thrilled with him having a small sword, she moved forward to her son and pretended to show interest in it.

"That is a fine weapon, Colt." She held out her hand. "May I see it?"

Colton let her touch it but he wouldn't let go of the hilt. Amalie ran her fingers over the cold steel, seeing that it was, indeed, very dull and somewhat thick. He probably couldn't hurt himself with it if he tried. Feeling slightly better, though still not completely convinced, she turned to Elizabeth.

"It was very kind of you to give it to him," she said. "If Weston approves, then he may keep it."

Elizabeth smiled timidly and Amalie shifted the focus from Colton and his new sword to the true purpose of their visit.

"In fact, Weston and Sutton are competing in the tournament at Keighley today," she went on. "We would like very much for you to join us."

Elizabeth's smile faded and she looked surprised. "Join you?" she repeated. "I… I do not know, my lady. Surely Weston wishes only for his wife and children to attend. I would be of no value to him, I am sure."

Amalie cut her off. "Ridiculous," she snapped softly. "Please come with us. Weston and Sutton usually help me mind the children but they will be occupied. I could use your assistance, especially with Colton. He is a rather lively child."

Elizabeth looked to Colton, now slashing through the air with his mighty sword. It was evident that she was torn as she watched the tow-headed little boy pretend to be a knight, much as her young sons had done those years ago. Her reluctance grew until, unable to hold back any longer, she turned to Amalie.

"I would like nothing better than to come with you to Keighley, my lady," she said softly. "But let us be plain; Weston has no use for me and I am sure he would not want me at the event. Although your offer is gracious, I must decline."

Amalie gazed steadily at the woman, realizing the taboo of discussing the subject had been broken. As Aubria went back over to the table with the blown glass figures and Colton leapt about with his sword, doing battle against unseen enemies, Amalie went to the small, blond woman with the dark blue eyes.

"I understand that you are attempting to abide by Weston's wishes given his behavior towards you," she lowered her voice. "He has explained to me, from his perspective, what his relationship is with you. But as I explained to Weston, what happened was a very long time ago and he only remembers the event from the eyes of a devastated six year old. I would like to understand what it was that made my husband turn against you, if only so I will not continue to force you two together if it is sincerely not appropriate. As Weston's wife, I seem to be caught in the middle and I would like to understand what, exactly, I am in the middle of. Would you be so kind as to explain what happened those years ago so that I may understand?"

Elizabeth looked at her fearfully for a moment. But then, her expression began to flicker with sorrow, with recollection, and finally with resignation. She watched the children, including Aubria as the little girl picked up one of the precious glass pieces, before finally returning her attention to Amalie.

"I would like to," she murmured. "But I am afraid that Weston will become angry if I do."

"He will not become angry because I will not tell him."

Elizabeth looked rather surprised by that. "Why would you not tell him?"

"Why should I? If you want him to know, you will tell him your-self."

Elizabeth sighed, hesitation on her delicate features. "It was a long time ago, my lady."

Amalie could see that the woman was torn. "I realize that," she said softly. "I also realize that you do not know me. Although I am Weston's wife, you do not know me at all. Perhaps you do not trust me with such family secrets and, to that regard, I understand. I am not so sure I would tell a stranger my deepest secrets, either. But I love your son with all of my heart and soul. He is the most remarkable, kind, considerate and generous man in the world. I would kill or die for him. And you are his mother, the woman that has given birth to him, and I am inherently respectful of you for that reason alone. You seem kind and sweet, and I would like for my children to come to know and love you. But I cannot truly allow that until I know what has happened that would make Weston so angry towards you. He has told me his version of the story. Will you not tell me yours?"

Elizabeth gazed steadily at her, realizing that her initial impression of Amalie had been correct; she was beautiful, kind and intelligent. Sutton had extolled the virtues of Weston's wife to her but she did not truly believe him until now. Anyone who would love her son so much instinctively had her trust and admiration. She dare not hope for more than that, but something in Amalie's manner gave Elizabeth comfort.

"What would you like to know?" Elizabeth asked softly.

Amalie regarded her carefully. "The truth," she replied. "What happened between you, Weston's father and Weston's grandfather?"

Elizabeth lifted her eyebrows and averted her gaze, moving for one of the two finely-covered chairs in the room. As Colton leapt and slashed and ended up knocking over a small shovel used for the fireplace, Elizabeth suddenly seemed very old and very tired. She watched the little boy pick up the shovel and resume his fighting.

"Weston does not truly know all of it," she murmured. "You were correct when you said that he remembers everything from a six-year-old child's perspective. He was too young to tell the truth."

Amalie sat down in the chair opposite Elizabeth. "Did you ever try?"

Elizabeth shook her head, looking at the hands in her lap. "Nay," she replied. "He was too upset over his father's death and his grandfather thought it would be best to send him to foster to help him forget. But the problem was that Weston went away before I was able to speak to him about it and he ended up blaming me for everything. I have never been able to convince him otherwise."

"Then tell me the truth. I want to understand."

Elizabeth looked up from her hands. "The truth is rather shocking."

Amalie lifted an eyebrow. "Not any more shocking than what Weston has already told me."

Elizabeth shrugged and looked to her hands again. "I was the only child of Hugh de Busli of Laughton Castle," she said softly. "My ancestors arrived with William the Conqueror and my family history is distinguished. When I was in my youth, my father and I would visit Heston de Royans, as my father and Heston had served together under Henry the Third."

Amalie interrupted softly. "Heston?"

Elizabeth nodded, smiling faintly. "Marston's father and Weston's grandfather."

Amalie shook her head. "I understand that all of the de Royans men share names with the 'ton' ending. Before Colton was born, Weston and I spent hours reviewing names that would follow that tradition. He would not consider anything else."

Elizabeth laughed softly. "Well I know it," she sobered. "There is a long line of de Royans men that bear that tradition; there was Newton, Eshton, Preston and so on. You will see this on Weston's written patins of lineage that he presents at the tournament today."

Amalie chuckled, rolling her eyes. "I hope we do not have too many sons," she said. "We will run out of names. But forgive me; I interrupted you. Please continue."

Elizabeth nodded, thinking on where to resume her story as Colton suddenly found something else of interest near the hearth and began chopping at it with his sword. Aubria was still fingering the glass figures.

"As I said, my father and Heston had served together under King Henry," she went on. "Although I did not know it at the time, my father and Heston were in negotiations to wed me to Marston. Heston was not too terribly old at the time. I was around seventeen years of age when I first met him and he had seen forty-three years. He had been long widowed; Marston's mother had died giving birth to Marston. I remember thinking that Heston was very kind and very handsome, but not much beyond that. Marston was in London at that time, serving in the king's ranks. When my father and Heston reached a contract between Marston and me, I was left behind at Netherghyll to await Marston's return from London."

Amalie regarded her for a moment. "Your father left you alone without a chaperone?"

Elizabeth nodded. "It was quite proper, I assure you," she said. "For all intents and purposes, I was Marston's wife, so it was quite acceptable. Heston and I spent a great deal of time together, waiting for Marston to return from London so that we could be wed. But the more time we spent together, the more we began to realize that we had feelings for each other. Heston was a wonderful and generous man. In fact, the way you described Weston is the same way I would describe

Heston. I was horrified, of course, when I realize I had fallen in love with the man, more horrified and thrilled when he told me he loved me in return. We spent three blissful months together until Marston returned from London, and then…"

Amalie could see where the story was leading, or so she thought. She was compassionate in her reply. "And then you had to marry him."

Elizabeth nodded, smiling weakly. "I had no choice," she whispered. "It broke my heart to have to marry the brash young knight, whom I did not know at all. Heston stood stoically throughout the ceremony but his heart was breaking as well. But we had no choice in the matter; either of us. That night, Marston became drunk and… well, suffice it to say that the consummation was not as I had hoped. Marston was not the man his father was. He was rash, loud and powerful, but had little concept of compassion or feeling. He hurt me that night and Heston could do nothing about it except hold me and cry. It was devastating for us both."

Amalie gazed at the woman, feeling more sadness and pity than she had ever felt in her life. She also felt a kindred spirit in Elizabeth, a woman brutalized on her wedding night. Reaching out, she put her hand on Elizabeth's tender wrist.

"I am so sorry," she murmured. "But how did Marston's death come about?"

Elizabeth seemed to grow more nervous. "Early on, it was clear that Marston wanted nothing to do with me," she whispered. "Other than our wedding night, he made no effort to accomplish his husbandly duties. He would be gone for weeks at a time, returning for brief periods in between. I began to hear rumors of his mistresses and of de Royans bastards. Of course, Heston and I were deeply in love so I did not particularly care about Marston's behavior. He was not a wicked man; he simply did not want a wife. I received all of the love and attention I could ever want from Heston. But then I became pregnant and everything changed."

It took Amalie a moment to realize what she was saying. Slowly, her eyebrows lifted. "Then Marston is not...?"

Elizabeth shook her head. "Nay," she murmured. "Heston is Weston's father."

Amalie tried not to appear too shocked. "And Sutton?"

"Heston's also."

Amalie took a deep breath, absorbing the information. "And Weston does not know?"

"He never gave me the opportunity to tell him. Sutton does not know, either."

Amalie averted her gaze, digesting the news and struggling not to judge the woman or openly react. "You said everything changed once you became pregnant," she said. "What happened?"

Elizabeth wriggled her eyebrows and looked back to her hands. "Marston found out, of course," she said. "I would not tell him who the father was and he beat me almost to death before Heston was able to intervene. Heston almost killed his son but I stopped him. After that, Marston became a bitter drunk. He would drink himself into oblivion daily and beat the servants habitually. He would ride out into the countryside and we heard stories of him raping women and burning homes. Heston kept me safely protected or Marston would have surely beaten me as well, maybe worse. This went on for months until Weston was born. And then... when Weston was born, something in Marston changed again. He gazed at the baby, retreated to his solar, and we barely saw him anymore after that. He spent his days drinking and sleeping."

Amalie was coming to think she had gotten more than she had bargained for with the story. It was absolutely tragic, on so many levels. Elizabeth finally looked up from her hands, fixing her gaze on Amalie.

"Sutton was born a little more than a year after Weston," she said softly. "Marston would come out of his solar on occasion and, as the years progressed, he seemed to lose his hostility. He clearly adored Weston and Sutton, like an older brother would. The boys adored him in return. He stopped drinking and seemed ready to assume the mantle of an honorable man. But he wanted the one thing from me that I could not give him; respect and obedience. I was deeply in love with Heston and he, with me. Even though we were not married, he was my husband in my heart and spirit and body. I would not leave Heston to assume a life with Marston. So one day, Marston went into his solar and fell upon his sword. It was Weston and Sutton who found him there, dead."

Amalie knew that part of the story and it was a horrible tale. She could only stare at the woman, shaking her head with sorrow. "Weston said that when he told you of Marston's death that you smiled," she whispered. "He has never forgotten that."

Elizabeth cocked her head faintly. "I do not believe I smiled," she said thoughtfully. "In truth, I do not know what my reaction was other than to think that years of torment, for both Marston and me, were over. Marston was not, nor had he ever been, a happy man. But I was very sorry that Weston had to be the one to find Marston's body."

"Perhaps you should tell him that one day," Amalie said, squeezing Elizabeth's wrist. "If nothing else, tell him that. He needs to hear it."

Elizabeth nodded somewhat hesitantly, timidly putting her free hand over Amalie's hand that clutched her wrist. Amalie smiled at her.

"Please come with us to Keighley," she begged softly. "I want you to come."

Before Elizabeth could reply, Colton suddenly threw himself on his mother's lap, whining for sweets. Aubria, distracted from the glass, also came over to her mother and tried to climb up in her lap as well. They were demanding attention, which wasn't unusual, but this time they had cut Elizabeth's reply short.

Amalie was in the process of explaining to the children that their behavior was rude when Weston appeared in the doorway.

CHAPTER SEVENTEEN

THE CHILDREN SQUEALED when they saw their father and rushed to him. Weston was weighed down in full battle armor, complete with weapons slung about his body, and he couldn't pick up both children simply because of the bulk and sharp edges. But he did manage to collect Aubria, his dark blue eyes blazing at his wife.

"What are you doing in here?" he demanded. "You were supposed to come to the bailey."

Amalie stood up from the chair, disturbed by his sharp tone. "The children and I came to visit your mother," she replied steadily. "I have asked her to come with us to the tournament."

Weston just stared at her as Aubria tried to get his attention and Colton whined at his feet.

"That is not your decision to make," he told her. "Come with me now."

Amalie grew defensive. But in that defensiveness was defiance. "Gladly," she snapped, turning to Elizabeth. "Will you gather your cloak and attend us, Lady Elizabeth?"

Elizabeth looked startled and terrified. Her gaze moved between Weston's enraged features and Amalie's lovely face. Before she could reply, Weston barked again.

"If she is coming, then Sutton can bring her," he grasped Colton's little hand, noticing the sword in it. His features slackened. "What is that?"

Amalie moved towards him. "It was your sword when you were a child," she said, somewhat softer. "Your mother gave it to him. She has been saving it all this time."

Weston stared at the sword, his jaw ticking furiously. When Colton lifted it to show him, it was all he could do to fake a smile at his son. But he couldn't say anything about it, not when the little toy brought back so many painful and wonderful memories. He used to fight his father with the toy for hours on end, Marston always pretending to let him win. He could still see Marston going through exaggerated death throes before falling in the dirt. The longer he stared at the dulled blade, the more powerful the emotions became until he finally looked away.

"Come along," he said. "We must leave."

He was out in the hall but Amalie wasn't following; she was standing in the doorway. "But what about your mother?" she wanted to know. "Weston, I would like for her to come. Please?"

He paused to look at her, Colton in one hand and Aubria up in his arms. His jaw was still ticking.

"Not today," he snapped softly.

"Why?"

"Because I said so."

"Please, Weston. Do not be unreasonable. There is no reason why she cannot…"

"If you keep arguing, I will leave you behind as well."

Amalie's fury soared. Outraged, the extreme emotion surged her nausea again and she marched up on him, pulling Aubria from his arms. Snatching Colton's little hand, she glared furiously at her husband before leading the children down the flight of stairs. Weston's gaze lingered on her a moment before following. He didn't give his mother, standing in the doorway of her chamber, as much as a hind glance.

Amalie took the children outside. But instead of heading towards the caravan now poised for departure in the bailey, she entered the keep. She began calling for Neilie, as the woman was older and did not travel well, and was therefore not attending the tournament. By the time Amalie hit the third floor of the keep, Neilie appeared and took the children from her.

With the children tended, Amalie continued to the fourth floor chamber she shared with Weston and slammed the door, throwing the bolt. Then she promptly went to the basin and proceeded to vomit up all of her breakfast.

Sick and heaving, she heard someone try the door latch. She knew it was Weston but she continued to heave until there was nothing left in her stomach. She could hear Weston knocking on the other side of the door.

"Go away, Weston," she shouted, miserable and sick. "Go to your tournament and leave me alone. You are mean and insensitive and… and… cruel!"

She was still bent over the basin when the door suddenly exploded. Weston came barreling through, crashing through the splintered wood and iron; he had kicked the door so hard that pieces of wood had literally flown all over the room. Momentum carried him to the other side of the chamber before he could regain his balance.

One of the pieces from the flying door struck Amalie in the hand. She gasped as she pulled out the knife-sharp shard. Blood began to stream immediately.

Weston saw the blood right away, ripping off his helm and tossing it to the bed as he made his way to his wife. But his gesture had terrified Amalie and she tried to get up and run away from him, but ended up stumbling. Cowering, she began to weep loudly as blood streamed down her arm.

Weston came to a halt when he saw how frightened she was. His fury instantly abated and he put his hands to his face, wiping at it, struggling to compose himself.

"Ammy, I am sorry," he said softly. "I did not mean to injure you. Let me see your hand."

Amalie yanked it away from him as he tried to grab it. "Why… why…" she sobbed. "Why did you do that?"

He looked back at the remains of the door, realizing he had burst in like a madman. But he had been angry and disoriented and hadn't thought on his actions. His jaw ticked heavily as he reached down to grasp her, pulling her up off the floor even as she wept and struggled.

"I am sorry," he repeated. "I... I let my anger get the better of me. I should not have and I am sorry."

He led her over to the bed but she was still trying to pull away from him. "Why did you do that?" she sobbed angrily. "What if I was standing by the door? You would have killed me!"

He was coming to feel very foolish, very disturbed. "I knew you were not standing by the door," he told her. "I could hear you retching."

She finally managed to pull away from him, stumbling onto the bed and holding up her bloodied arm up as if to defend herself from him. "I have never seen you do that."

He sighed heavily, laboring for calm. All he could do was shake his head. "I do not like being locked away from you," was all he could say. "I will never be kept from you, not ever."

"You frightened me."

He could see that; her bloody arm was still up and she was leaning away from him in fear. Now he was coming to feel overwhelming pain.

"Do you truly need to be frightened of me, Ammy?" he asked softly. "Have I ever hurt you? Have I ever threatened to hurt you?"

She shook her head and the arm came down. Then she fell on the bed, sobbing into the coverlet. Weston stood over her with his fists resting on his hips, feeling like the biggest lout in the world. He did the only thing he could do; he lowered himself to his knees and took the non-bloody hand into his massive glove.

"I cannot apologize enough for frightening you," he murmured, kissing the fingers. "I explained my reasons, weak as they are. Please know that I am deeply sorry. I would sooner throw myself on my sword than hurt you in any way."

She lay there and wept and he finally stood up, going to the basin and collecting a linen cloth that they used to dry their hands with. He went back to the bed, wearily, and began to wipe the blood off her hand. By the time he started to wrap it, she had stopped weeping and was gazing up at him with red-rimmed eyes. He kissed her hand as he wrapped it.

"You told me that you were going to leave me behind," she sniffled. "Would you really?"

He puckered his lips contritely. "Nay," he admitted. "I was angry."

"But why? What did I do?"

"You did not come out to the bailey. I had to hunt you down. And then you pressed me about inviting my mother and it angered me."

She was quiet as she watched him finish off the wrapping. "Do you realize that every time I come within close proximity of your mother, you bark at me as if you hate me as well?"

He didn't say anything; he continued to hold her hand, staring at it, and she sat up. Her free hand went to his face, stroking his cheek tenderly.

"You told me that you were not disturbed with my contact with your mother but it is clear that you are," she said softly. "We never have harsh words but with the introduction of your mother, now we have. I do not like it."

He grunted. "Nor do I," he agreed. "I do not know why I behave that way. I know you do not mean harm. It has nothing to do with you. Every time I see my mother, I feel such rage. That is all I have ever known with her."

Amalie gazed at him, thinking of the revelations his mother had told her. She began to seriously doubt if he would ever ask his mother the truth of what had happened all of those years ago. And she was fairly certain that if he ever found out she had withheld information she had learned in her talk with Lady Elizabeth from him, it might damage the trust between them. Although Amalie had promised Elizabeth she would not tell Weston, she didn't think, in good conscience, that she could keep such monumental information from him. He had a right to know.

"But that is not all you have ever known with me," she murmured, wrapping her arms around his neck. He responded by enfolding her in his warm embrace, his face in the crook of her neck. "Please do not speak so harshly to me when I have done nothing to deserve it."

He nodded, his lips against her collarbone. "I will not do it again, I swear it," he murmured. "I am so sorry, Ammy. Please forgive me. I did not mean to upset you so."

She hugged him tightly, ignoring the poking of the armor. "You are forgiven." She kissed his cheek. "But I have something I must tell you. I must be honest."

His face was still pressed into the crook of her neck. "What about?"

She sighed nervously. "Do you trust me, West?"

He didn't say anything for a moment. Then, he pulled back to look at her as if confused by the query. "What manner of question is that?"

"Please answer me."

"Of course I do. I would trust you with my life."

She put her hands on his cheeks, gazing into his amazing and handsome face. "Given the dynamics of your family and your feelings towards your mother, I had a serious conversation with her," she said softly. "I did it because I love you, West, and I am greatly concerned with your attitude towards her. I do not want you to be on edge for the rest of your life, living in the same keep with a woman that you hate. It is not good for you, or for us. You see what that hatred does even to you and me. So I asked her to tell me the truth of what happened and she did. Will you hear me explain it to you?"

He looked at her, feeling the familiar anger rise, struggling to keep his composure by reminding himself that Amalie only asked out of love and concern. Truth be told, he wasn't entirely angry about it. He suspected she would sooner or later. He couldn't think of a good reply so he simply kissed her and released her from his enormous embrace, rising to his feet.

"Perhaps someday," he said quietly. "But not today. I have a tournament to focus on and I do not want to be distracted."

She nodded. "I understand," she murmured, climbing off the bed to stand next to him and unwrapping the careful wrap around her hand in the meantime. "But will you allow me to say one thing about it?"

"If you must."

She grasped a huge glove, gazing up into his dark blue eyes. "Then I will say only this; you do not know the entire story and until you do, I would ask that you show at least some measure of consideration towards your mother. Please, West. It is important."

"I do not know if I can."

"Can you do it for me? It would make me very happy."

He sighed heavily and tried to avert his gaze but she would not let him. She pressed herself against him and put her hands on his face, forcing him to look at her.

"Please, West," she begged softly. "I know it is difficult. I know you do not want to. But I would not ask if I did not feel strongly about it. I want you to show the woman the same consideration you would show any other noble-bred lady. Be polite; that is all I ask."

He gazed down at her, a mixture of uncertainty and refusal on his face. But she smiled at him and he could not resist. He nodded his head, once, but it was enough. Amalie put her arms around his neck and pulled him down to her level, kissing him on the cheeks sweetly.

"Thank you," she murmured. "I love you very much."

He returned her kisses. "And I love you," he whispered. "Now, can we go?"

She grinned, releasing him as he went over to the bed and collected his helm. She watched him put it on his head and adjust it.

"Will you do something else for me?" she asked softly.

He glanced at her as he straightened out the helm. "What is it?"

"Ask your mother to come with us. I fear she will not come if I ask her. She knows that you do not want her to attend so the invitation must come from you."

He paused, gazing at her as he geared up for an argument. But he didn't get very far; the expression on her face softened him, weakened him, and he knew it would be of no use to argue or refuse. It would only upset her and he didn't want to see her upset. He'd already upset her enough. So he nodded in resignation.

"Very well," he grunted.

She pointed at the shattered door. "Go now," she instructed steadily. "Ask her politely, please. The children and I will meet you in the bailey."

He looked at her, realizing she was ordering him about. He made one last stab at controlling the situation. "I would rather collect the children and you go collect my mother."

She fought off a grin at his last stand. "Nay," she replied, shaking her head firmly. "Go and retrieve your mother. I will see you in the ward."

He sighed heavily but did as he was told. Amalie watched him quit the room, shoving aside the bigger pieces of the broken door so she wouldn't hurt herself on them. As his bootfalls faded down the steps, she collected a small comb and smoothed out her hair where it had been mussed. After a final glance, and a check of the wound on her hand that was now sealed up and no longer bleeding, she quit the room in search of her children.

CHAPTER EIGHTEEN

WESTON REALIZED BY the time he reached the block that housed his mother's chambers that he was considering going back on his word to Amalie. He just couldn't fight thirty-one years of ingrained hatred. But it seemed so important to Amalie that he make the effort. So he was doing this purely for his wife's sake. His feelings did not come in to play. What he did, he did for her and her alone.

But with every footstep that drew closer to Elizabeth's chambers, he could feel himself harden. As his bootfalls echoed against the stone step that led to the second floor, that steely, morose and stiff demeanor he had when he was around his mother began to overtake him.

Torn between giving in to the comfort of his usual behavior and his inherent desire to please his wife, he suddenly realized that he was standing at his mother's door. He lifted a hand to knock, let it drop as he pondered what he was going to say, and then finally lifted his gloved hand a second time and pounded. He had to force himself.

He took a step back as the bolt on the door was thrown, and still another step back when the door cautiously opened. Elizabeth's timid features gazed out from the crack in the door and, realizing that Weston was in the hall, she opened the door wide. Her guarded yet earnest gaze met him.

"Greetings, Weston," she said with a mixture of pleasure and fear. "I am honored by your visit. How may I be of service?"

He just looked at her. His first reaction was to continue his hateful ways and he had to remind himself again that he was here on his wife's errand. No more, no less.

"My wife wishes for you to come to Keighley," he said without emotion. "If you will please gather your things, we are prepared to depart."

Elizabeth looked as if he had just given her a direct order. She rushed back into her chamber, looking rather disoriented as she went for her cloak but realized it wasn't the one she wanted, so she scooted into her second chamber and emerged seconds later with a heavy blue cloak slung across an arm.

In a rush, she went for her small ladies' bag that held things like her coinage and a comb, but she ended knocking it off the peg and into the small glass figurines that Aubria had loved so well. The figurines scattered, some shattering on the floor. Horrified, Elizabeth tossed her cloak aside and quickly began picking up the pieces, setting the broken shards back on the table with trembling fingers.

Weston stood in the doorway, watching her pick up the glass with shaking hands. It was clear that she was rattled, now having broken some of her pretty and expensive things. With a faint sigh, he entered the room and took a knee beside her, picking up a couple of the broken figurines and setting them back on the table. Shocked, Elizabeth looked at her son with surprise and gratefulness.

"Thank you, Weston," she said, feeling much distress at the glass all over the floor. But she stood up, not wanting to cause any further delay, and swiftly moved to retrieve her cloak. "I was hoping to give some of those glass pieces to Aubria. She seems to like them so."

Weston could see that the woman was struggling with her heavy cloak, making nervous chatter, absolutely terrified of her enormous son and his attitude towards her. If he thought on it, he felt rather bad for causing her such distress but there was a greater part of him that resisted any sentiment towards the woman whatsoever.

I want you to show the woman the same consideration you would show any other noble-bred lady. He could hear Amalie's words rattling around in his head and, with another sigh, one of resignation, he went to his mother and took the cloak from her. Shaking it out so the creases would smooth, he placed it on his mother's slender shoulders.

For the second time in as many minutes, Elizabeth looked startled by his actions, even more startled when he politely fastened the front ties of the cloak. Weston didn't meet her eyes until he finished tying off the ends and when he looked at her, a strange thing happened.

Suddenly, he was four years old again, sitting on his mother's lap, enjoying her warm hugs and gentle voice. He had visions of her feeding him cakes with raisins and nuts, and singing softly to him when he was ill with fever. Staring into her deep blue eyes, he remembered how much he had loved her. If he thought hard on it, he still loved her. She was his mother. But he was still deeply, deeply hurt and confused. It created a massive conflict within him.

He dropped his hands from her neck, went to her open chamber door, and slammed it shut. The entire building rattled with the force of the door shutting as Weston emitted something of a frustrated roar. Terrified, Elizabeth moved away from him, stumbling against the wall as she watched him pace in circles like a caged animal. The helm came off, clattering to the floor, as he wandered around, working his enormous hands and grumbling to himself. He finally kicked at the door and rammed an enormous fist into a table next to the door. The table collapsed and Elizabeth shrieked, fearful that he was going to kill her where she stood. She gasped and trembled, watching her son pace.

Finally, Weston settled himself unsteadily into the nearest chair. He just sat there, twitching and grinding his jaw. When he finally looked up at his mother, his eyes were filled with turmoil.

"Why?" he finally hissed. "Why were you so happy when my father killed himself?"

Elizabeth stared at him with wide eyes, struggling to keep her composure. It was the first time in thirty-one years that Weston had addressed her regarding Marston's death. In fact, it was nearly the first time in all those years he had addressed her at all. She took his question extremely seriously.

"I was not happy when Marston killed himself, Weston," she said quietly.

His features tightened. "Do not lie to me," he hissed. "I saw your expression. You smiled when I told you what he had done."

Elizabeth struggled to stay calm. "I do not believe that I did," she insisted softly. "In shock, people can do a great many things that they do not remember. But believe me when I tell you that I was not happy for your father's death, not at all. It was a shattering and terrible blow. My biggest regret is that you and Sutton happened across his body first. If I could have protected you from that blow, please believe that I would have."

Weston's tight features eased somewhat, but not entirely. He was still boiling over with emotion. He averted his gaze, running his hand through his cropped blond hair, fighting to discern just one thought out of the hundreds that were rolling through his mind.

"You shamed him," he finally muttered. "You shamed him by carrying on with his father. How could you do such a thing? Explain this to me so that I understand."

Elizabeth, oddly, was calming quite a bit. She had dreamed of this day for years, the day when Weston would ask her what truly happened and she would have the opportunity to vindicate herself. She had planned what she would say. But now, given her earlier conversation with Amalie, she changed her tactics. She wanted to explain it to her son in terms he could understand. She knew she would only have one chance to do it and she wanted to do it right.

"I would be happy to and I thank you for giving me the opportunity," she said softly. "But before I explain, may I ask you a question?"

He rolled his eyes, his jaw ticking. Then he waved a careless hand at her. "If you must."

Elizabeth chose her words carefully. "Your wife is a gracious and lovely woman," she said quietly. "I am so happy you have met her. It is obvious that she loves you a great deal. Surely you must love her as well; I can see it plainly."

He just sat there, grinding his jaw, realizing her question was more of a statement of fact. He lifted his eyebrows at her.

"Are you asking me if I love my wife?"

"I am."

He ground his teeth so hard that he ended up biting his lip. "I do not see where that is any of your affair."

"Please," Elizabeth begged softly. "I am trying to explain things to you and it would help if I could present you with something relatable."

His brow furrowed. "Relatable?"

"Do you love your wife?"

He nearly exploded but managed, somehow, to dig deep and keep his calm. "I do," he said through clenched teeth. "I love her more than anything on this earth. Why do you ask?"

Elizabeth drew in a long, thoughtful breath and planted herself on a small stool near the table with the shattered glass figures. She gazed at her son imploringly.

"Please do me the courtesy of hearing me out before passing judgment," she said softly. "If, at the end of my explanation, you decide that you still must hate me, then I will not protest. In fact, I will leave Netherghyll and you will never hear from me again. Is that fair?"

He looked at her, some confusion on his face. He wanted to agree with her but couldn't quite bring himself to do it. "Go on."

Elizabeth quickly thought of the best way to explain what she must because she could tell that Weston did not have the patience for anything long or drawn out. She had to be concise and to the point or else she would lose his attention. She squared her shoulders and began.

"Do you remember my father, Weston? Your grandfather, Hugh de Busli?" she asked softly.

Weston nodded faintly but he did not speak. He was looking at her almost as earnestly as she was looking at him and Elizabeth continued.

"My father and Marston's father, Heston, both served King Henry and were great friends," she explained quietly. "My father brought me to Netherghyll to enter into a contract of marriage between Heston's son, Marston, and me. When the terms of the contract were settled, I remained behind at Netherghyll to wait for Marston's return from London where he was serving the king. If you recall, Heston had long been widowed. Heston was kind, compassionate, humorous and generous. It was just the two of us waiting for Marston's return and as the days passed and I came to know Heston, I also came to realize that I loved him. It was not a difficult thing to do. And Heston, having been a very lonely man for quite some time, fell in love with me as well. He simply couldn't help it."

By this time, Weston wasn't looking quite so belligerent. In fact, he looked rather sympathetic. "So it started back then."

Elizabeth nodded. "It did," she admitted. "But it was all quite proper, I assure you. Heston did not compromise me. He was desperately torn, of course, loving the woman meant for his son, but sometimes, the heart is stronger than the mind. There are emotions that one simply cannot overcome no matter how right or wrong they are."

Weston understood, and was reasonably sympathetic, but he would not let on, at least not yet. "What happened when my father returned to marry you?" he asked quietly.

Elizabeth smiled sadly. "How would you feel if you had to watch Amalie marry another man? That is what Heston suffered through. Your father returned from London simply because he had been ordered to; he had no use for a wife. He did not want me. But he was forced to marry me so he did, as Heston stood by and watched, knowing that his son did not want to marry. Do you have any idea of the pain Heston must have endured?"

By this time, Weston was feeling much more compassion and far less frustration. He could feel his fury abating but it was still a struggle; it had been something he'd held on to most of his life. It was difficult to let go. But in truth, because he loved his wife so, he understood exactly what his mother was saying. He was starting to see the situation from an entirely different angle At that point, his hard stance started to slip away.

"So my grandfather watched the woman he loved marry his son," he clarified quietly.

Elizabeth nodded faintly. "He remained stoic and calm throughout the ceremony," she said softly as she reflected back on the painful memories. "He played the part of the proud father at the wedding feast as Marston drank himself into oblivion. When it came time to consummate the marriage, Heston had to practically carry Marston to our wedding bed because he was so drunk. And he left me with his drunken son, who was so angry that he had been forced to marry that he beat me soundly on our wedding night. He was quite… brutal."

Weston stared at her, seeing a huge parallel between his mother and Amalie. Their first intimate experience with men had been a harsh, cruel thing. But as the shock of his parents' marriage began to settle, as reality loomed, he could feel more turmoil within him.

"My father was not a brutal man," he insisted. "I have many fond memories of him. Never once did I fear him and never once was he cruel."

Elizabeth nodded patiently. "Marston was not, by nature, a brutal man," she agreed. "But it was different when he was drinking. He became someone else, someone horrible. And he was extremely resistant to being married and took his drunken frustrations out on me. The next morning, he awoke sober with no memory of what he had done other than a battered wife, and went on about his business as if nothing had happened. Heston, however, found me bruised and bleeding, tended me, and wept over what had happened. It was terrible for us both. But he could do nothing more. He could not avenge me. I was another man's wife."

Weston gazed steadily at his mother, absorbing her explanation, reconciling himself to it. It was information he had never heard before, shocking and deeply troubling. He kept seeing Amalie after Sorrell got through with her, bruised and bleeding, with no one other than servants to tend her. It tore his guts out to think on it. His jaw began to tick as he averted his gaze, unsure if he wanted to hear the rest of it. But he had come this far; he had to see it through.

"Continue, please," he asked quietly.

Elizabeth took herself back to those days of anguish, sorrow and hope. "After that night, it was apparent that Marston wanted nothing to do with me," she said softly. "I was a wife in name only. He made no attempt to carry out his husbandly duties. He returned to London immediately after the wedding where he continued his tasks as a knight to the king and where he also kept many mistresses. Being married was not going to stop him from continuing his rutting ways. I began to hear rumors, of course, but there was nothing I could do about them. I was told that your father has at least three bastards, although I never saw the children personally. Heston did, however. He paid sums of money to support the children on Marston's behalf."

Weston's gaze was guarded, laced with sorrow as he looked at her again. He was coming to see that, from her perspective, Marston de Royans wasn't perhaps such a great and noble man after all. It was a sickening realization.

"What happened between you and my grandfather during this time?" he asked quietly.

Elizabeth shrugged faintly, looking to her hands. "Heston and I were deeply in love so I did not particularly care about Marston's behavior," she said honestly. "Marston was not an evil man, Weston; he simply did not want a wife. But Heston did. So Heston and I continued on at Netherghyll, loving each other deeply and being very happy together. A year and a half after Marston and I were married, you were born."

Weston's guarded gaze washed with shock. He stared at his mother, wide-eyed, rising from the chair with his jaw hanging slack. The realization of her words slammed into him until he could hardly keep his balance.

"But you said…" he regrouped and started again. "You said that my father left for London after you were married. How can he be…?"

"Because Heston is your father, Weston," she said softly, watching the anguish roil through his enormous body. "Marston is not."

Weston was so shocked he could hardly speak. He stared at the woman, his eyes wide with astonishment.

"My... my grandfather is, in reality, my father?" he repeated, his tone a hoarse whisper.

Elizabeth nodded. "He is Sutton's father as well," she said quietly. "No matter what you think of me or Heston, please know that you were conceived in love. Heston and I loved each other very much and we loved you as well. That is more than can be said for any child Marston fathered, or any child that he and I might have had together. If you love your wife as you say you do, then surely you can understand that love is greater than contracts or perception or shame. Love is the strongest thing of all."

Weston stared at her. He struggled to accept the truth but, in the same breath, he understood what she meant completely. He had loved Amalie so much that he had married her even though she had been pregnant with another man's child. He could see his mother and grandfather, or more correctly, his father loving each other in spite of the complicated situation.

He couldn't even imagine the strength Heston had that allowed him to remain composed when the woman he loved married another man. It was a terrible story yet one that was oddly inspirational. He began to feel weak and ill as the sorrow pent up from all those years of hatred began to drain out of him. He began to feel so incredibly sorry for his mother and what she had been through. If even half of what she told him was true, it was a sorrowful tale, indeed.

Weston turned and walked away; he could no longer look at Elizabeth's pale and lovely features. He put his hands on his face, wiping the sweat off his upper lip as if to wipe away the turmoil he was feeling. But there was still one thing he had to know.

"Marston knew that Sutton and I were not his sons," he finally said, his voice weak and deep. "How did he react?"

Elizabeth sighed. "Strangely enough, it seemed to settle him down a great deal," she said honestly. "He returned from London and remained, barricading himself in his chamber and drinking his days away. It appeared he wasn't sure what to do or how to react. He could see how much Heston and I loved one another and he told Heston once that he wished he had been a better man. When you and Sutton grew older, Marston would emerge from his chamber and play with you. Do you remember? That little sword I gave Colton?"

Weston nodded, turning to look at his mother with tears in his eyes. The memories were too much for him to take.

"I remember," he whispered. "He used to let me win. He would fall on the ground and writhe around dramatically."

Elizabeth saw the tears in his eyes and she stood up, making her way towards him.

"He loved you, Weston," she whispered. "He loved Sutton, too. I think... I think looking at you two made him think of the life he had lived and the things he had done wrong. I think he was trying to make up for the evils he had committed against me, against our marriage, by being a friend to you and your brother. But Marston was a man in great turmoil and the drink only made it worse. He was a man in utter pain, always, of a life gone wrong by his wrong choices."

Weston blinked and tears streamed down his face. "Why did you not help him?"

She put a small hand on his enormous arm, feeling the bulk and power of her son within her grip.

"How?" she asked softly. "By assuming my role as his wife? Heston was my husband in spite of the fact that we were not legally married. We were as much married in our hearts as any legally married couple; more perhaps. I would not leave Heston, the only man I had ever loved, not even for the man legally my husband. Perhaps it is selfish, but I would not do it. And Marston never asked. I think he knew as well as I did that he was incapable of being a good husband. He had far too many demons working against him to accomplish this."

Weston looked at his mother, tears dripping off his chin. "You will tell me honestly," he whispered, "what drove the man to kill himself."

Elizabeth shrugged, her hand gently caressing his big arm.

"I do not know," she replied. "But I do know that he was very drunk when he threw himself upon his sword. Drink always turned him into something terrible and unrecognizable. Perhaps all of his demons finally caught up with him and he could find no other way to end his anguish. I remember when you told me what he had done. I remember thinking that Marston was finally free. Finally without pain or anguish. For Marston, the pain was over and he was finally free from whatever horrors plagued him during his time on earth. In that respect, I was happy for him."

Weston's dark blue gaze grew intense. "Perhaps you do not re-member smiling when I told you of his death, but I will swear to the day I die that you did."

She averted her gaze as she remembered that particularly dark day. "If I did, it was only because I was happy that he was finally free. It certainly was not because I was glad for his death."

Weston didn't say anything more. The entire conversation had been more than he could absorb and as much as he wanted to linger on it, digest it, his family was waiting for him in the bailey and he had a tournament to attend. Muddled, he moved away from his mother and picked up his helm, plopping it on his head.

Then he turned to her, observing the very small woman he resem-bled a great deal. He just stared at her a moment, unable to voice what he was thinking. In truth, he didn't know what he was thinking. But he did know one thing; Amalie had been right. Perhaps he had been wrong all along.

Silently, he held his elbow out to his mother. Elizabeth stared at the armored appendage for a moment before carefully, and very gratefully, slipping her hand into the crook. Without another word between them, Weston led his mother down to the bailey.

CHAPTER NINETEEN

T HE WEATHER WAS mild this late in the fall, the air cool but not too
cold, and the sky was cluttered with puffy white clouds.

Weston and Sutton rode at the head of the column from Netherghyll along with thirty men-at-arms spread out from the front to the
rear. The carriage, driven by Owyn and containing Amalie, Elizabeth,
Esma and the children, was well-protected tucked in the middle of the
group while Heath and John, bellowing for the men to keep pace, rode
to the rear.

Horses snorted, men coughed, and mud lined the sides of the road
from the unseasonably heavy rains that had plagued the region.

The standards of Baron Cononley snapped in the light breeze as the
column of men and horses advanced towards the town of Keighley. It
was the first time Weston had ridden under his hereditary banners and
it was a fulfilling experience. He kept glancing up at the bright blue,
silver and white banners with the silhouette of a great fanged beast on
them. The men-at-arms wore the Cononley tunics of blue and white,
announcing to the world of Baron Cononley's presence. The knights,
however, did not wear their colors yet; that would come on the
tournament field.

The seven mile trip from Netherghyll had been an easy and pleasant
ride so far. Sutton made small talk as they crossed the miles, a cover for
the curiosity that was consuming him.

When he had seen Weston arrive in the bailey with their mother on
his arm, he had been seized with the urge to know why his brother was
suddenly so polite towards Elizabeth. He'd spent the past five miles

chatting about anything that came to mind when what he really wanted to do was ask a thousand questions that might garner him a punch in the face. So he bided his time, thinking he was very clever when he slipped in a well-timed comment.

"I noticed that you and Mother seem more companionable," he said, glancing over at his brother. "That pleases me a great deal, West."

Weston wouldn't look at him. He'd spent the past five miles knowing this subject would come up and trying to think of a way to avoid it. But he knew he couldn't. He'd also spent the past five miles embroiled in more inner turmoil than he had ever known, dwelling on the revelations his mother unloaded on him and trying to figure out how, exactly, he felt about all of it. He still didn't know.

"You and my wife, I am sure," he grunted.

Sutton lifted an eyebrow. "Why? Has she forced you into making peace with Mother?"

Weston gave him an intolerant look. "There is no one on this earth strong enough to convince me to do something that I do not want to do, not even my wife."

Sutton snorted. "You are a fool, West."

Weston's eyebrows flew up in outrage. "A fool?"

Sutton didn't back down. "Aye," he insisted as if daring his brother to throw a punch at him. "You are a fool if you believe any part of that statement. You forget, Brother, that I have spent the past several weeks with you and your wife. I have seen how much control she has over you. If she wanted the moon, you would figure out a way to give it to her."

Weston growled and made faces at his brother, finally lifting his big shoulders and looking away. "There is no crime in wanting to make her happy."

Sutton was back to grinning. "Nay, there is not," he agreed. "Truth be told, if she was my wife, I would behave in the exact same fashion. I envy you, Brother. You are one of the most fortunate men I have ever known. You have a beautiful wife, a strong family, a son to carry on your name. I want what you have."

Weston turned to look at him, the angry posturing gone from his features. "You will," he assured him quietly. "That is why we are traveling to Keighley, is it not? We must ensnare your lovely Lady Paget."

Sutton laughed softly, looking rather hopeful. "That is my intent."

Weston wriggled his eyebrows. "Have no fear," he assured him. "I will turn Amalie loose on the woman and she will belong to you by sundown. My wife is very persuasive."

"I am coming to see that," Sutton agreed. "The woman must work magic if she has you in her spell."

Weston just grinned, his gaze moving over the green landscape as they moved south through the gently rolling hills. Thoughts of his wife began to turn into thoughts of his mother and their conversation. The smile faded from his lips.

"You spent more time with Grandfather than I ever did," he said in a complete change of subject. "What is your opinion of the man?"

Sutton looked at him, wondering at the sharp shift in focus and the motivation behind the question. But he answered.

"He was wise and generous," he said, reflecting back on the broad, blond man who had raised him. "He was easy to laugh and liked to play jokes on me. But he was also a fierce fighter. I remember several years ago when I was newly returned from fostering at Pembroke, there were rumors of a marauding band of Scots plaguing the area. They struck at a few of Grandfather's holdings and I rode out with him to fight the Scots. The man was absolutely fearsome in battle, West, much like you are. In fact, you and Grandfather are so similar in so many ways that it is uncanny. I loved and admired him a great deal."

Weston listened to his brother, feeling strained and remorseful all of a sudden by the fact that the man he had always known to be his grandfather was, in fact, his father. He intended to tell Sutton when the time was right but he wasn't quite sure how. To Sutton, he was sure, it would be far less of a shock. Sutton adored the man.

"Other than very early childhood, I never knew him well," Weston muttered. "I really only saw him three times in my adult life; once at my knighting ceremony, once when you were gravely injured, and then that time when you…"

Sutton cut him off. "We do not speak of that incident," he said flatly. "It would be better if you blocked that out of your mind."

Weston fought off a grin. "She *was* rather…"

"Enough or I will run you through."

Weston broke down in soft laughter. "It would make a good story to tell Lady Paget."

Sutton rolled his eyes as he unsheathed his broadsword. He raised it threateningly at his brother. "I swear by all that is holy, if you mention one word of that to her, I shall shove this sword so far down your gullet that…"

By this time, Weston was roaring with laughter, reining his charger out of his brother's furious path. "I will not tell her," Weston assured his brother as he dodged the man. "My lips are sealed."

Sutton still had the broadsword leveled at him. "Have you told anyone else?"

"Nay."

"Not even your wife?"

"Nay. I swear it."

With a final glare, Sutton sheathed the sword. "Well and good for you," he said, glancing up at the angle of the sun. "We should be seeing Keighley shortly. Do you want me to announce our arrival to the marshals or do you want to do it personally?"

"You do it," Weston said, still snickering about his brother and the incident that he was not permitted to speak of. "I need to settle my wife and children first. Amalie is not feeling well."

"The pregnancy?"

Weston nodded his head with regret. "Poor woman. She is miserable."

Sutton fell silent, his thoughts moving from his brother's wife to the tournament ahead and the lovely Lady Paget. But thinking on a woman he very much wanted to know had him thinking of falling in love again, which brought him back to his brother's question about their grandfather. It started him pondering the path of that subject again.

"Why did you ask me about Grandfather?" he asked.

Weston glanced at his brother. "Curiosity, I suppose," he said, though that wasn't entirely true. "Mother and I had a conversation earlier today."

Sutton looked at him, surprised. "Truly? What about?"

Weston sighed and averted his gaze, studying the surrounding lush and green landscape as he spoke. "Many things," he said. "Mostly, we discussed our father."

Sutton was truly stunned; he hardly dared to hope. "And?"

Weston shrugged. "And there is a good deal more we must discuss at a later time," he told him. "But I wanted you to know that I am… trying. I am trying to overcome everything I ever believed about her."

Sutton's handsome face lit with a smile. "I cannot tell you how happy I am to hear that, West," he said sincerely. "Truly, I am thrilled and grateful."

Weston merely grunted and Sutton didn't push. It was a huge step in the right direction as far as Sutton was concerned. As they crested the hill, the berg of Keighley suddenly spread out below them, dotting across the green fields with businesses and homes.

Smoke trailed into the sky from dozens of chimneys as people went about their business on the roads and in the fields. People were everywhere, especially with the tournament circuit in town. As Weston and Sutton paused, inspecting the sight before them and determining the best path to the tournament field on the opposite side of town, they could suddenly hear screaming back in the carriage.

It caught both their attentions, but it wasn't so much screaming as it was Colton yelling at the top of his lungs. Spurring the chargers back along the column, they came upon the cab to find Colton struggling to climb out of the window. The boy was howling as Amalie tried to pull him back inside without bumping his head on the rim of the window.

"Colton," Weston leaned over and addressed his son. "What are you doing, lad?"

"He wants to ride with Sutton," Amalie replied from inside the carriage, sounding impatient and weary. "West, can you please pull him out? He is kicking me in the face."

Weston leaned over and pulled his son from the window. But Colton wasn't satisfied. He held his arms out to his mother and chanted frantically.

"Surd!" he demanded. "Surd, Mama!"

Amalie extended the small toy sword to the boy, who took it happily. But he continued to whine until he was handed over to Sutton, who gleefully took his nephew and cantered off with him. Weston watched his brother a moment before returning his attention to Amalie.

She looked pale and exhausted from having just done battle with a two year old, and he was immediately sympathetic.

"Are you not feeling well again, my angel?" he asked.

She shook her head wearily. "Nay," she sighed. "Your mother suggests that licorice root will help. Do you suppose we can find some in town?"

He nodded firmly. "I will send Heath at this very moment to procure some." He sought out Heath with a piercing whistle, waving the man forward before returning his attention to his wife. "We have arrived at the town so it should be another half-hour before we reach the tournament field. Can you last that long?"

She nodded. "I shall have to."

He gave her a wink and headed back to the front of the column, commanding the men to move forward at a quickened pace. Heath joined him at the head of the group and he sent the man along his way with orders to procure licorice root.

The party of Baron Cononley made its way down the hill and into the outskirts of the busy, bustling town. Weston thought he might skirt the edge of the berg, the path of least resistance, on his way to the tournament field. But as he entered the very busy village, he decided to make his presence known and parade down the main avenue. It was his first show as Constable of North Yorkshire and the Northern Dales and he realized that he wanted to announce himself.

Already, people were staring and pointing at him and he felt extremely proud to be at the head of his own delegation. His standards waved in the stiff breeze and four powerful knights on big, hairy chargers supported his ranks. There was much to be proud over. As he entered the main hub of the town, however, he realized that he wasn't the only one announcing himself.

His puffed-up pride took a dousing when he realized that there were at least three parties ahead of him as they made their way towards the enormous tournament field. They were well dressed and well supported, just as he was. He and Sutton spied the crimson and gold of the Earl of Billingham far on ahead, followed by the green and white of Baron Bradford, and finally the yellow and red of the baronetcy of Rochdale. Big houses had come to compete this day and Weston knew they were in good company.

As they entered the main bulk of the city, Sutton tried to turn Colton back over to his mother but the boy screamed as if he were being murdered. Reluctantly, Amalie allowed her son to continue riding with his uncle, something that made the lad extremely happy and kept the peace. The child thought he was a real knight, swinging his toy sword around and smacking his uncle with it a couple of times. Sutton had to stay sharp to avoid losing an eye.

People were turning out in clusters to see the fine carriages and knights move through the dusty main avenue; children lined the streets, eager to see the knights, while whores crawled out of their hovels to catch the eye of the men to ensure they had business for the duration of the tournament.

Weston and Sutton rode through the streets on their big chargers, eyeing the children, the great parties in front of them, and the situation in general. Weston kept an eye out for Heath returning with the much-

KATHRYN LE VEQUE

needed licorice root while Sutton pointed and explained the sights to Colton.

The party slowed down when they came to a crossroads near the tournament field, mostly because the parties in front of them were backed up as stewards recorded their arrival and then directed them to an area where they could camp. There were great clusters of smiths plying their trades, conducting business in the middle of the road. There were also vendors setting up, including a man with a little monkey. Colton saw the monkey and he began to scream.

The screaming brought his mother's attention. Amalie's head popped out of the cab at the sound of her son. "West?" she called. "What is Colton's trouble?"

Weston watched his screaming son. The lad was pointing at the man with the monkey and Weston reined his charger back near the carriage.

"He wants that little beast, I believe." He indicated the white-bearded monkey several feet away. "See it over there? The little monkey?"

Amalie's gaze fell on the little creature as Colton nearly came apart. His screaming filled the air and was attracting attention. Frustrated and sick, she jerked open the door of the cab and stepped down into the street below. Weston made an attempt to offer his assistance but she pushed past his big, blond charger and made her way to Sutton. As Colton screamed and kicked, she held up her arms.

"Give him to me, Sutton," she instructed.

Sutton obediently handed down the boy, all kicking feet and screaming mouth. Amalie was stern with the boy.

"Colton," she said firmly. "You will cease this behavior at once. If you continue to scream, I will not let you see the monkey. Do you understand?"

Colton stopped instantly, looking at his mother with his big, dark blue eyes. He looked so much like his father that it was frightening at times. Then he began to cry, laying his head on her shoulder as if she had just broken his heart. Amalie rocked him gently as she walked over to the man with the monkey.

The man was older, clad in strange and colorful clothing that was not from England, and very eager to show off his little pet. He had trained the little beast to do tricks for the few coins it would bring. Amalie held her suddenly-shy son on her hip, his head on her shoulder as she pointed to the monkey.

"Look, Colton," she said, pointing. "He is smiling at you."

The little monkey flashed his big-toothed monkey smile, removing his tiny little hat. As the old man prompted him, the monkey inched over towards Colton, who quickly forgot his tears and his sudden shyness. He was very interested as the monkey approached. Amalie held out a hand to the little creature, who grabbed on to her fingers much to Colton's delight. Then Colton wanted to pet the monkey, who grabbed on to his little fingers as well. Colton laughed happily and the monkey, frightened, scooted back to its master.

It was noisy, smelly and dusty. Traffic was so backed up that they were virtually at a standstill on the busy avenue, but Weston didn't mind; he was enjoying watching his wife and son play with the monkey. Aubria, who had been asleep in her grandmother's arms inside the cab, had awoken and was now being helped out of the carriage by Elizabeth.

Weston watched as his mother took Aubria protectively in-hand and escorted her over to where her brother was playing with the monkey. After a minute or so of laughing at the monkey, now doing tricks on its master's arm, Aubria predictably turned to her father.

"Dada?" she pointed at the monkey. "Can I please have him?"

Weston wasn't any good at denying his daughter whatever her little heart desired. But the expression on Amalie's face naturally cautioned him.

"I do not think so, my angel," he said. "He must stay with his master."

Aubria's lovely little features molded into a pout. "But I *love* him, Dada," she insisted. "Can I please have him?"

With a heavy sigh, Weston climbed off the charger. This wasn't an argument he was going to win on the back of a horse. As he made his way to his daughter and tried to explain to her why she couldn't have the monkey, Sutton sat atop his destrier and grinned. Between Colton screaming for the monkey and Aubria's unhappy tears, Weston had his hands full and Sutton thought it was all great fun.

He was having a good time at his brother's expense until he looked over his shoulder at the traffic backing up on the crossroads and caught sight of the Clifford banners back in the pack. He flew into panic mode and bailed off his charger.

"She is here," he hissed at Amalie and Weston. He jabbed a gloved finger at the traffic backing up towards the east. "Those are her father's banners."

Amalie was particularly interested as she turned to gain a better look. But that took Colton away from his monkey so she handed the boy over to Weston, who was crouched down next to his sobbing daughter. Leaving Weston with two weeping children, Amalie and Sutton moved towards the edge of the avenue where there was a better vantage point.

"See?" Sutton pointed to the green and yellow Clifford banners. "Right there; that is her father's party. The green and yellow standards."

Amalie spied the rather large group. From what she could see, there was no carriage or wagon, but she could see at least two small palfreys among the warhorses. They were difficult to make out with all of the people and clutter in the way.

"Were you formally introduced to her, Sutton?" she asked.

He nodded his head. "Aye," he said. "At Grandfather's funeral. But her father would not let me speak with her beyond the short introduction."

Amalie's gaze was on the party in the distance. In truth, they were not too far away but there were gangs of people and horses between them.

"Does your mother know Lord Clifford?" she asked.

Sutton nodded. "She does. He and my grandfather were friends."

Amalie pondered that information for a moment before turning on her heel and making her way back to Weston. He was still crouched on the ground with Aubria in one big arm and Colton in the other. The little monkey was on the ground in front of them, doing somersaults, and the children were laughing loudly as their tears were forgotten. As Amalie approached, Weston stood up to meet her but she wasn't focused on him. She was focused on Lady Elizabeth.

"My lady?" she reached out, taking Elizabeth's hand gently. "I have need of you."

Elizabeth had been standing next to Weston, watching her joyful grandchildren with a big smile on her face. But seeing that Amalie had need of her prompted the woman into action and she willingly went along. As Amalie and Elizabeth began to walk away, Sutton followed. But Amalie stopped him.

"You stay with Weston and mind the children," she told him. "Your mother and I shall return shortly."

Baffled, Sutton watched the women head off towards the traffic in the crossroads. He could see that they were in deep conversation, looking towards the Clifford banners and gesturing. Weston, curious, stood beside his brother and watched as his wife and mother made their way through groups of people and horses, heading off towards several parked parties on the road to the east. They weren't very far away, certainly not far enough away that Weston could not get to them immediately if necessary, so he let them go. But his features were folded into a frown.

"Where are they going?" he demanded.

Sutton had a good idea. "I believe they are going to greet Lord Clifford and his lovely daughter."

Weston pursed his lips wryly and shook his head, turning around when he heard his daughter squeal to see that she was now holding the monkey in her arms. Colton was jumping up and down beside her and laughing. Weston's wry expression turned into a smile at the sight.

"If Ammy has anything to say about this, you shall be a betrothed man by sunset," he said as he moved back to his delighted children. "I would be prepared to enter into negotiations if I were you."

Sutton stood and watched his mother and sister-in-law as they approached the Clifford party and he clearly saw when Lord Clifford climbed off his horse and bowed gallantly before them. He could see Amalie talking, gesturing with her pretty hands, and soon enough, Paget appeared on one of the palfreys from back in the column. The young woman was dressed in bright blue, a stunning color, as she climbed off her palfrey and joined the conversation.

Sutton's heart was doing strange things as he watched the scene. Paget was more beautiful than he remembered and it was all he could do to keep from running over to the woman and announcing himself. But he kept his cool, watching and waiting for Amalie to do her magic. *You shall be a betrothed man by sunset.*

He sincerely hoped so.

CHAPTER TWENTY

THE LADY PAGET GLORIANA CLIFFORD was the exquisite beauty that Sutton had described. A small woman with brown eyes, silky brown hair and a big, beautiful smile, Amalie liked her right away. She had a silly giggle that suited her and was quick to laugh.

Within the first few minutes of meeting her, Amalie knew she had made a friend simply by the way she and Paget were easily able to communicate. The young woman was very friendly and seemingly quite bright. But also within the first few minutes of meeting, a bit of bad news was delivered.

Lord Clifford was apparently intending to enter into marriage negotiations with one of the barons who would be attending the tournament and had brought his daughter along so that the prospective groom could get a look at her. Paget didn't seem particularly happy but she wouldn't go against her father. Still, Amalie could sense that the woman remembered Sutton from their brief meeting. She could see the interest in the woman's eyes when they spoke of him.

So Amalie went on the offensive and threw all of her family's power behind her pitch on Sutton's behalf. A few well-placed names, including the fact that her brother had been the Duke of Ireland, and Lord Clifford suddenly seemed very interested in Sutton de Royans.

The de Veres were very well known in England, with a huge foothold in Ireland, and much more prestigious than a mere baron. Amalie made sure that Lord Clifford understood their importance. She didn't know if Sutton had any property and a glance at Elizabeth showed the woman to be negatively shaking her head when the subject came up, so

Amalie assured Lord Clifford that Sutton de Royans was not only related to the powerful de Veres but that he was also due to inherit titles and property that would make him a very wealthy man. No mere baron could compete with the massive barony of Ulster, which Amalie would inherit from her mother. Somehow in the conversation, it ended up belonging to Sutton.

As she told Lord Clifford about the rich lands of Ulster that Sutton would rule over, she wasn't at all upset that she had just handed over her inheritance. She had Weston and her children, and they had a wonderful life together. Nothing could make her life any sweeter than it was and especially not an Irish baronetcy that had historically been a troubled land. But the rich lands would be perfect for Sutton and Paget, embarking on a new life and establishing their own family. At least, she hoped so. She could see that Lord Clifford agreed.

Extracting a promise from Lord Clifford that would allow Paget and Sutton to spend some time together during the tournament, Amalie waved farewell to Paget as Lord Clifford's party moved off into the vast area that was designated as an encampment site for tournament participants.

In fact, most of the traffic was starting to thin out so Amalie and Elizabeth made their way back to the de Royans party which now waited patiently for them as others moved past. Amalie couldn't wait to tell Sutton the good news. But as the women crossed the last few feet towards their party, a charge of warhorses nearly ran them down.

Amalie had to jump out of the way to avoid being run over by three bachelor knights heading towards the tournament grounds. They pulled to a halt at the last minute as Amalie picked herself up off the ground, chastising her on her carelessness until they got a good look at her beauty. Then, their tone changed dramatically and as one young knight tried desperately to woo her, Weston marched up and yanked the man off his charger.

Amalie shrieked with fright as Weston pounded the hapless fool with his huge fists. His friends saw that their comrade was being beaten by an enormous knight so they jumped off their chargers and went to assist, but Sutton and John intercepted them and a nasty fight ensued. Soon, the men-at-arms got involved and, shortly, a brutal street brawl spread throughout the avenue, spilling into different competing houses as men began to throw punches simply because punches had been thrown at them.

Amalie and Elizabeth raced to the carriage to get out of the line of fire. Amalie opened the door and ushered Elizabeth in but she didn't follow. As Elizabeth sat down and fearfully pulled the children onto her lap, Amalie peered around the side of the carriage to see what was going on.

Weston had apparently knocked out the knight who had nearly run her over, as the man lay motionless in the street, and was now pulling Sutton and John away from brutalizing a pair of young knights. As Amalie watched, Heath suddenly appeared in the melee and began banging men on their helms with the butt of his sword, sending them crashing to the ground. He was having great fun with it, all of this as he held a sack of licorice root in his left hand.

It was chaotic and messy. The fight began breaking up as men, dazed and beaten, wandered back to where they belonged, including the thirty men-at-arms who had accompanied the de Royans party from Netherghyll. Weston and Sutton suddenly emerged from the disbanding group, laughing and joking with each other as if they had just come from a party.

There wasn't a mark on either of them. Amalie stood near the carriage, her mouth hanging open at the sight. She had no idea why they were so happy when men were scattered all over the road as a result of their fists. Weston went to her, pulled her to him and kissed her soundly on the mouth.

"Are you all right, my angel?" he asked.

She looked back at him with some shock. "I am fine. Are you...?"

He cut her off. "You did not hurt yourself when you fell?"

She shook her head. "Not at all," she replied. "Certainly not enough for you to beat that knight senseless."

Weston just shrugged and turned her back for the carriage. "Get in," he told her. "We are moving on to the encampment area so we can set up the tents."

Amalie watched Sutton mount his charger and move off towards the tournament arena. "Where is he going?" she wanted to know.

Weston shut the cab door behind her. "To deliver our patins," he told her. "He shall return shortly."

"Good." Amalie regarded her husband for a moment, a knowing expression on her face. "I have much to tell him."

Weston lifted an eyebrow with interest. "Truly? What is that?"

She smirked victoriously. "Lord Clifford will allow him to speak to Lady Paget," she said, excitement in her tone. "But... well, I had to lie a bit to accomplish this."

He grinned. "What in the world could you lie about?"

"I said that Sutton would inherit title and property."

Weston shook his head. "Then Lord Clifford is in for a big disappointment. We must hurry and marry Sutton to Lady Paget before her father finds out."

Amalie began to look less excited and more hesitant. "But it is not entirely a lie, West."

"Aye, it is. Sutton has no inheritance."

"But I do," she said softly. "I will gift my inheritance to Sutton and he and Lady Paget can live happy and wealthy."

Weston cocked his head. "What inheritance is that?"

She shrugged, averting her gaze somewhat. "You have your great inheritance, West, so I saw no harm in gifting Sutton with mine," she said softly, looking to him again. "It makes no difference to me but to Sutton, it will be a great deal."

"You still have not told me what inheritance. In fact, I did not even know you had one. You never told me."

"You never asked," she said, a twinkle in her eye. "I thought I was prize enough."

His grin returned. "Of course you are. But I would still like to know what I am giving up."

She laughed softly. "I have inherited the barony of Ulster through my mother's Irish holdings," she told him. "It is a large holding to the north of Ireland with fairly rich lands. I will gift it to Sutton. The hereditary title is Baron Tirone."

Weston stared at her a moment before lifting his eyebrows in surprise. "Ulster?" he repeated. "And you are just telling me this now?"

"It never came up."

Now his brow was furrowed. "I am not entirely sure I want to give this up."

She pursed her lips impatiently. "Your brother has nothing, West. You have everything. Are you truly so selfish?"

He wasn't entirely serious about not wanting to give up her inheritance but he made a good show at it. "I may want to have a piece of it."

"Then we shall negotiate that when I gift Sutton with the property so that he may marry Lady Paget."

The truth was that he was very pleased and deeply touched with Amalie's generosity and he knew Sutton would be positively thrilled. It was an amazing gesture of graciousness on Amalie's part and he reached into the cab, taking her hand and bringing it to his lips. He smiled at her as their eyes met.

"I already have the best part of it," he murmured.

She grinned at him. "What is that?"

"I have the heiress."

She laughed softly as he kissed her hand one last time and turned for his charger. Amalie's heart swelled with pride and love as she watched him mount his charger and, soon, the carriage began to lurch forward. Onward they went into the vast area that was designated for the competitors' encampment.

ℭ

THE TENTS WERE old, having belonged to his grandfather, but were in exceptionally good shape for their age; Weston simply had not had the time to get new ones made. The beautiful colors of blue and silver glistened weakly in the sun from the three massive tents that comprised Baron Cononley's encampment and Weston was very proud of his brilliant display.

After settling in at the competitors' encampment and setting up beneath a massive oak tree, several stewards came around to announce that there was to be a meeting of all competitors at sundown. Sutton still hadn't returned from delivering their patins so Weston spent his time inspecting his joust equipment before submitting to his squire and a smithy as they tried to fix the broken link on his breastplate that had snapped on the trip from Netherghyll.

It was early afternoon as Weston stood in the largest tent as they worked on his armor. As he stood with his arms lifted, his focus was on Amalie and the children a few feet away. Amalie was trying to fix a small tear in Colton's little breeches but the boy didn't want to cooperate.

In fact, the boy was throwing himself down on the ground in a fit as Aubria tugged at her mother's sleeve and whined about being hungry. Amalie was very patient with the pair, telling her daughter to wait a moment as she struggled with Colton. But Aubria grew frustrated and weepy, turning to stomp away from her mother but getting her legs swept out from under her by her thrashing brother. Aubria fell down on Colton's face and both children began screaming.

Weston broke from his still stance, moving to sweep Aubria up off her of her brother and chase away her tears. He kissed her and hugged her, and she was happy. Amalie finished with the small stitch in her son's breeches and she pulled him to his feet, gently soothing his tears. Colton felt that his nose was irreparably damaged by his sister's fall but Amalie assured her son that his nose was fine. She finally picked him up, her hand on his little head as she kissed his cheek sweetly. Just as she moved over to where Weston was standing, Sutton suddenly entered the tent.

Amalie glanced at her brother-in-law but didn't give him a second thought as she took Aubria from her father. Sutton, however, was intensely fixed on his brother. He didn't even respond when Colton began crying for him.

"I need a word with you," he said to Weston. "Now. Outside."

Weston looked at the man, catching something in his tone but not particularly concerned with it. He moved past his wife and children, patting Colton on the head as he went. He followed Sutton outside into the cool afternoon.

Sutton pulled him several feet away from the tent before stopping. Weston fussed with the strap that the squire had just fixed as he came to a halt beneath a big, gnarled oak.

"What is …?" Weston began.

Sutton cut him off before he could even get the question out of his mouth. "Sorrell is here," he said.

Weston stopped fussing with the strap and looked at his brother, his dark blue eyes widening. "What?" he hissed. "Did you see him?"

Sutton nodded, looking rather ill. "I did." He blew out his cheeks heavily. "Remember I told you that I had heard that he had been sent north? The rumors were correct. He was sent to Billingham. He is here with a contingent of knights from Billingham Castle."

"Billingham is an ally of Bolingbroke."

"Exactly."

Weston stared at him. Sutton watched, concerned, as the color seemed to drain out of his brother's face. Weston held Sutton's gaze for several long and painful moments before turning away to compose himself. He dragged his hand over his face, laboring with every breath to maintain his control.

"Sweet Jesus," he hissed. "Is it really possible?"

Sutton nodded. "I thought you should know. I came as soon as I saw him."

Weston was feeling sick. His thoughts immediately moved to Amalie and the terror she would undoubtedly experience when she discovered Sorrell's attendance. Even Weston's calm and loving presence couldn't chase away the horrors that would be awakened, reminding her of an act so brutal that it changed the course of her life. But even as Weston's heart hurt for Amalie, he was swept with fury so blinding that the blood suddenly rushed back into his head and his cheeks turned red. All he could think about was vengeance and pure, unadulterated murder. He whirled on his brother.

"Where did you see him?" he demanded.

Sutton knew that tone. He shook his head. "Over on the other side of the field," he said, putting his hands on Weston's chest. "He is surrounded by Billingham knights. I did not tell you that he was here so you could charge over there and get yourself killed. I told you so that you would not be surprised when you saw him. I told you so you could prepare your wife."

He was absolutely right. Weston's jaw was ticking and his hands began to work. He clenched and unclenched his fists and began pacing around as if he needed to go somewhere but couldn't decide which direction to go. He ended up walking in circles, jaw flexing and hands clenching, the low growl of frustration finally erupting into a yell of fury.

The shout was so loud that Amalie popped from the tent with Colton and Aubria in each hand. Her green eyes were wide on her husband as he paced around like a caged animal.

"Weston?" she began to move towards him. "Was that you?"

Weston stopped pacing, looking at his wife as she approached with the children. All he could feel when he looked at her was anguish. Colton broke loose and ran to him. Mechanically, Weston bent down to pick the boy up, his gaze still on Amalie.

Staring at her, he knew he had to tell her. He couldn't keep the information secret and chance her seeing Sorrell or, worse, running in to the man somehow. It wasn't fair to her not to tell her. He handed Colton over to Sutton.

"I must speak with you," he said softly. "Sutton will tend the children."

Aubria and Colton had no problem being handed over to their uncle. They wanted to see the horses and Sutton took them both over to where the horses were being tended. Already, they were screaming to pet the animals. Amalie watched them go before returning her attention to her husband.

"What is it, sweetheart?" she asked, winding her hands into one of his huge gloves. "Why do you look so?"

He took her soft, warm hands and brought them to his lips. The dark blue eyes were intense; he wanted to deliver the news without gloom or doom or fanfare. He didn't want to upset her any more than he had to because he knew, for a fact, that she was going to be devastated. He was devastated, too. He kissed her hands gently.

"I wanted to tell you what Sutton has told me," he said softly. "As you have seen, there are many knights here today. Not all of those men are reputable. In fact, there are several I would classify as unscrupulous and dangerous."

Her brow furrowed slightly. "What is wrong?" she wanted to know, growing outraged. "Is there a knight who has made threats against you?"

He grinned. "Nay, my angel." He kissed her hands again. "At least, there is no one who has been brave enough to threaten me to my face."

"If there was, you would surely tell me so that I might have a word with this man."

He broke down into soft laughter. "You would defend me?"

"I would kill him."

"I believe you."

She laughed softly, watching him kiss her hands. "If that is not the case, then what is it?"

His smile faded once more as his eyes grew sorrowful yet furious at the same time. It was a strange combination.

"Sutton saw Sorrell with the group of knights with Billingham," he said quietly. "I wanted you to know so that you were not surprised. I want you to be prepared."

Amalie stared at him, absorbing his words. At first, they didn't quite register; words she understood but held without impact. Then, the reality of what he was telling her began to sink in and Weston could literally see the transformation come over her.

Weston watched her eyes widen, her face pale, and then her body tense to dramatic proportions. Amalie tried to yank her hands away and he could see the look in her eyes, like a panicked animal. He wouldn't let her pull away – instead, he threw his arms around her and kept her pinned in a crushing embrace. As the panicked gasps began to come, he whispered firmly in her ear.

"He cannot harm you, my angel," he insisted. "The man cannot get near you. I swear upon my oath as your husband that I will kill him before I let him frighten or upset you in any way. Do you believe me?"

She gazed up at him with a terrorized expression, struggling to pull away but realizing his iron grip was unbreakable. Swarmed with fear, she broke down into hot, frightened tears.

"Aye," she wept. "I know… you will not let him harm me, but…"

She trailed off, unable to continue. He readjusted his hold on her to get a better grip and pulled her against his enormous torso. His dark blue eyes blazed at her.

"Easy, my lady, easy," he soothed, trying desperately to calm her before she exploded out of control. "I know you are frightened but you must be strong. He cannot hurt you, I swear it."

She began wiping furiously at her face, struggling to stop the tears. "Oh… Weston," she breathed. "Why is he here?"

He held her as she labored to control her fear. "He came to compete just like any other knight," he said honestly. "He is entitled to compete just as I am."

She shook her head, so hard that her careful hairstyle began to unravel. "Please," she begged. "I want to go. Please, let us go home."

He could only think to pull her into his embrace once more to soothe her hysteria. "Nay," he murmured. "We will not go. There is nothing to fear, for I can tell you for a fact that I intend to kill the man before this day is out."

Her panicked gasps turned into something more, even more horrifying, and she pulled away from him, her hands to his face.

"I did not ask this of you," she sobbed. "I never asked this of you. Why do you say such things?"

He gazed into her frightened face. "For this very reason," he whispered. "I look at you and see the thing most precious in the world to me. I see blind fear on your face and it enrages me like nothing else. The cause of that fear must be eliminated. As a husband, it is my pleasure and my duty. It is the greatest single goal of my life. Do you believe me?"

Wide-eyed, cheeks damp with tears, Amalie nodded slowly but he could tell that she was unbalanced. She had a wild-eyed look about her in spite of the fact that she was calming.

"Good," he kissed her forehead, her wet cheek. Putting his arm around her shoulders, he began to lead her towards the large tent. "Now, I want you to lie down and rest for a while. Esma and my mother can tend the children while you sleep."

Amalie clutched his hands. "Where are you going?" she half-demanded, half-begged. "Please do not leave me. I do not want you to leave me."

He gave her a squeeze as they entered the tent. "There is a meeting at sundown for all competitors," he told her. "I must attend the meeting so…"

"Nay!" she threw her arms around his waist, her face pressed against his cold metal breastplate. "Do not leave me. Please!"

He sighed heavily, very quickly realizing that there would be no way he could argue or compromise his way out of this. She was shaken and terrified, rightfully so, and those emotions were only compounded by the misery of the early pregnancy. He had no choice but to stay. If he were to leave her, she would panic and he had no way of knowing what she would do. He didn't even want to think about it.

He put his arms around her and took her into the tent, leading her over to the bed that had been fashioned out of a traveling mattress stuffed with grass and straw, heavy furs, pillows and linens. It was big and comfortable.

"Lie down, my angel," he said, gently guiding her onto the bed. "I will not leave your side, I promise."

She still clutched his hands even as he sat her on the bed. "Do you swear it?"

"I do."

Amalie obediently lay down, but her eyes were fixed on him. She appeared like she was afraid he was going to go back on his word and run from the tent. She still hadn't let go of his hands. As she lay her head down on the fluffy, silk pillow, she suddenly burst into fresh tears.

"I am sorry, West," she sobbed. "I am ridiculous, I know it. But I cannot help it."

He leaned over her, kissing her head as he managed to remove one hand from her grasp and began to unfasten his plate armor.

"You are nothing of the kind," he murmured. "You have been dealing with a miserable pregnancy, two very small children, and a husband who sorely taxes your patience. I do not know how you find the strength to put up with me."

Her tears were fading as she gazed up at him. "Surely you jest," she sniffled, a smile coming to her pale lips as her hand went to his cheek. "You are my angel. I do not know what I would do without you."

He returned her smile, removing the breastplate and casting it onto the grassy floor as he leaned down and kissed her again. Since she wouldn't let go of his hand, he brought her fingers to his lips, kissing them as he sat down on the bed beside her.

Very shortly, he was lying beside her, his lips feasting on her soft mouth, his hands moving to intimate places. She was dressed in a brilliant green surcoat but he wedged his hands in behind her and unfastened the back of the gown, eventually rolling her over onto her stomach and kissing her exposed skin as he removed the coat.

As he hoped, she began to calm as his gentle hands and tender mouth worked their magic. She was tense, trembling with fear, and his enormous hands massaged her naked shoulders and back. Having been married to the woman for over four years, he knew her fairly well and was usually able to relax her this way. She was a slave to a back massage. But this time, it was different. She was terrified and panicked, and he didn't blame her. As he straddled her slender body and rubbed her shoulders, his mind began to wander to Sorrell.

He would see the man at some point, of that he had no doubt. It was going to be a struggle not to rush at him and snap his neck. Murder would not be condoned but, in this lawless land, vengeance was commonplace. No one would deny a husband his retribution against a man who assaulted his wife. Moreover, he was the Constable of North Yorkshire and the Northern Dales. He *was* the law.

Sorrell, as far as he knew, had no idea that de Royans had married Lady Amalie, which was the first thing Weston intended to tell the man when he saw him. He wanted to see the fear in the man's eyes and take great pleasure in it. After that, Sorrell would know that his hours on this earth were numbered. Weston de Royans was out for blood and no man would survive his wrath. Weston wasn't sure how or when he would accomplish his vengeance yet, but it would happen. At a time of his choosing, Sorrell would pay for every horrible thing he did to Amalie.

As Weston thought on the pain and agony he would bring about, his hands must have tightened on Amalie. She was able to feel his tension and she turned her head slightly to look up at him.

"West?" she murmured, relaxed and limp after her bout with panic. "What is wrong, sweetheart?"

He forced a smile. "Nothing," he whispered, leaning down to kiss her cheek. "Everything is fine."

Before she could press him, he began to kiss her sensually, his mouth moving along her cheek to her ear and onto her naked shoulders. Even though her surcoat was unfastened to the waist, she was still clothed in it and he lay on top of her, his big hands reaching under her skirts to pull her legs apart so he could settle his bulk down between them.

As Amalie groaned softly, his hands snaked up the skirt, finding her pantalets and pulling them down to her knees. Then he tossed her skirts up, nearly covering her head, as he began to nibble on her smooth, round buttocks.

Amalie gasped as he put his hands underneath her pelvis and lifted her up, shoving his face into the junction between her legs. He listened to her pant as he licked her mercilessly, knowing exactly how much she could take before she was ready to climax. He played with her, his fingers in the private grooves of her body as he released his breeches and his great organ burst forth, hard and heated. Pulling her up by the pelvis, he eased into her slick and waiting body from behind.

Amalie groaned at his entry, burying her face in the pillow as he thrust into her. As the gentle afternoon waned outside, Weston made love to his wife, thinking only of the great love he felt for her. He refused to let anything else enter his mind. After they climaxed together, he kissed her and hugged her until she drifted off to sleep.

When Weston heard her deep, heavy breathing, he knew she was not likely to wake up easily, so he carefully climbed from the bed and refastened his breeches. Collecting his breastplate and other pieces of mail that had come off in the heat of passion, he quietly moved out of the tent.

It was quiet and relatively sunny outside with the huge oak tree creating lovely and muted shade across the tents. Weston looked around for his brother. Sutton was nowhere to be found but he spied his children by the base of another oak tree several dozen yards away with his mother and Esma watching over them. He made his way over to them, his armor slung up over one enormous shoulder.

"Do you know where Sutton has gone?" he asked his mother.

Elizabeth looked up from Colton and the small sword he was swinging around. "Nay, Weston," she said. "He left the children with me and said he had business to attend to."

Weston nodded faintly, looking around over the huge field where the competitors were encamped, attempting to locate his brother in the sea of people and tents. As he was looking off to the west, he noticed the standards of Billingham blowing in the breeze about a quarter of a mile away and he could feel himself tense. At least he knew where Sorrell was camped now, which made it easier for him to keep track of the man.

Eyes on the distant banners of crimson and yellow, Weston unslung the armor and mail from his shoulder and was preparing to pull the mail coat over his head when Colton suddenly let out a scream.

The boy was off and running with Esma trying to keep pace. Weston looked to see the sources of his son's excitement; another competitor had brought his children with him and on a vacant area of the encampment, two small children were trying to drive a goat cart. A bald man in pieces of armor was trying to direct them but the children couldn't quite get the two goats going in the same direction.

Esma caught Colton before he could run right into the cart and Colton was loudly unhappy about it. He kept pointing to the cart and crying. Aubria, however, stood quite calmly next to her father, slipping her small hand into his big mitt as she watched her brother throw a fit.

"Dada," she turned her sweet, little face up to him. "Can I please have a goat cart?"

Weston smiled down at her; he wasn't surprised with the request. "Perhaps when we return home," he told her. "We will have to ask your mother."

Aubria wasn't happy with his reply. "But, *Dada*," she insisted. "I love the goats. Can I please have one?"

He just sighed and picked her up, kissing her soft cheek. "You cannot always have everything you want, Aubria," he said softly.

She wrapped her little arms around his neck, looking at him as if she had no idea what he meant. "But I *love* them."

Weston wasn't quite getting through to her and he just kissed her cheek again. "I know you do." He set her down gently and resumed with his mail. "Go over and see them, then. But mind you do not get too close. I do not want them to run you over."

Aubria looked at the goats and cart in the distance. She was sizing up the children driving the rig; her mind tended to work quite cunningly at times in spite of her young age.

"I will go ask them if I can have their goats," she said decisively. "They will want to give them to me."

Weston lifted an eyebrow at her. "They will?"

She nodded firmly. "I will let them be my friend if they give me the goats."

Weston shook his head at her, fighting off a grin. "Angel, those goats belong to those children. They are pets." He bent down so he could look her in the eye. "They love the goats, too. Perhaps they do not want to give them away."

Aubria was undeterred. "They will want to give them to me. I will love them more."

Weston scratched his head in a doubtful gesture, preparing a reply she would hopefully understand, when she abruptly charged off. Aubria lived in a world where everyone did as she wanted and she had no enemies. She was the queen. So Weston gave up trying to talk her out of it, assuming she would learn the disappointment firsthand when the children rejected her demands. As he pulled his mail coat over his head, he caught sight of his mother now standing next to him. He glanced over at her as he straightened out the mail coat, noticing that she was smiling at Aubria.

"She is the exact image of you as a child," Elizabeth said softly, watching her bold granddaughter march right up to the children in the goat cart. "She is brave and intelligent. You must be very proud of her."

Weston looked over at his mother. *She is the exact image of you as a child.* Elizabeth had divulged many deep secrets today, perhaps more than she should have. Weston could have kept the illusion going for her, the illusion that Aubria was his flesh and blood, but somehow, he couldn't seem to do it.

Now that Elizabeth had told him her most personal secrets, he thought, perhaps, he might do the same. He found that he wanted to.

"Since this has been a day of confessions, I also have something to confess." He looked at his mother as he straightened out the neck of his mail coat. "You must never repeat what I tell you, not ever. Is that clear?"

Elizabeth gazed at him seriously. "Of course, Weston. I would never repeat something you told me in confidence."

Weston stopped fussing with his neck, his dark blue gaze moving to the beautiful, blond girl as she spoke with the two children in the goat cart.

"I met Amalie when I was assigned to Hedingham Castle as the garrison commander," he told her quietly. "As you may or may not be aware, her brother is the Duke of Ireland, personal confidant to King Richard. But when Richard fell out of favor with the nobles, they also condemned Amalie's brother. The man fled to Ireland in fear of his life and left his sister behind at the mercy of the nobles."

Elizabeth looked frightened. "Sweet Amalie," she whispered. "The poor child. What became of her?"

Weston sighed, watching now as Esma set Colton to his feet and the little boy toddled over to the goat cart where his sister was.

"She was raped by the first Bolingbroke garrison commander." He looked at his mother then, the pain evident in his face. "When he was removed and I was assigned, my first introduction to Amalie was when she attempted to kill herself. The rape resulted in a pregnancy, the results of which you see in Aubria. Amalie wanted to die rather than live with the shame. I knew she was determined to kill herself and I did not want the responsibility to be mine if she managed to accomplish it, so I spent most of my time with her to prevent her from doing anything foolish. But during the time I spent with her, I came to know a remarkable woman that I fell deeply in love with. So I married her and accepted Aubria as my child. It was the best thing I have ever done."

Elizabeth gazed at him in shock. "My dear God," she breathed. "Poor, sweet Amalie. Did you know she was pregnant when you married her, Weston?"

He nodded. "Aye," he replied. "When I first took command of Hedingham, I knew she had been brutalized by the previous garrison commander but I did not know she had been raped until much later. In the time we spent together during the first few weeks of our acquaintance, I fell in love with the woman and just as I was preparing to declare my intentions, she committed herself to a convent. I spent three months going to the convent every day to see her and ask for her hand, but every day she turned me away. I was finally able to see her and she confessed the pregnancy. But it did not matter; I loved her so much that I was willing to overlook it. It did not matter at all."

Elizabeth's wide-eyed gaze had softened. She smiled faintly at him.

"Is this true?" she whispered. "I knew Weston de Royans to be a pious and controlled knight, not given to whims of compassion or pity. You have built your reputation on such things. Yet you married a woman compromised by another man? I find that astonishing."

He could see she wasn't taunting him. In fact, she looked extremely pleased. He smiled weakly.

"What happened was not her fault," he murmured. "My Amalie is the sweetest, purest woman who has ever walked the face of this earth, and the day I married her was the best day of my life. I have a beautiful, bright daughter and a son that is the envy of all men. I have been extremely blessed and I consider my family a reward for the good life I have lived. I would not change a thing."

Elizabeth's smile broadened. "I am so happy to have lived long enough to see you know such joy," she said softly. "It is something I have prayed for daily since you were born. I am only sorry..."

She trailed off and he looked at her. "Sorry for what?"

Her smile was forced as she tried to nervously cover. "I am sorry for nothing," she said too quickly. "I only meant that I am sorry that... well, that..."

He faced her fully. "Say what you mean, Mother. I shall not become angry, I swear it."

She looked at him, her lips in a tremulous smile. She visibly relaxed. "I… I was going to say that I am sorry Heston did not get to see your happiness. He would have been overjoyed."

Weston's expression tensed slightly. "I will assume that he knew he was my father."

"He did."

Weston pondered that information for a moment. Since all confessions were coming forth, he had one more. "I am sorry I did not have the same conversation with him that I had with you," he admitted softly. "I would have told him… that I never hated him."

Impulsively, Elizabeth reached out and touched his stubbled cheek. "He knew that. You do not need to explain yourself. But he never gave up hope that he would someday reconcile with you."

Weston stared at her, feeling the impact of her words. Having a son himself made him realize what it must have been like for his grandfather, or more correctly, his father in the matters of estrangement. It must have been hell. Weston couldn't imagine how he would feel if Colton stopped speaking to him and, with that awareness, all of the barricades he had kept up against his mother and father seemed to crumble away. He just couldn't keep them up any longer.

With a heavy sigh, he took his mother's hand and kissed it. "Forgive me," he whispered. "For letting a child's clouded memory mold my adult life, please forgive me. Although I do not regret the man I have become or the blessings I have, I do regret my behavior towards you and my father. I hope you will forgive me in time."

Elizabeth's eyes filled with tears. "Oh, Weston," she breathed. "There is nothing to forgive, truly. Heston loved you very much. He was very proud of you."

A scream suddenly distracted them and they both looked over to see Colton as he tried to hijack the goat cart. He had the goats by the head and was pulling them as Aubria tried to pull one of the children out of the cart. Weston let go of his mother and bolted over to the tussle, apologizing to the bald knight as he grasped both of his children and pulled them away from the goats.

Colton was screaming hysterically and Aubria was sobbing as if her heart were broken as Weston stoically brought them back over to the encampment. By the time they arrived, Amalie was emerging from the big tent.

She looked pale and tired as she opened her arms up for Colton. Weston handed over the boy, reaching down to pick up his daughter.

"What happened?" Amalie asked wearily.

Weston had Aubria's head cuddled up against his big face. "The goat cart," he said. "They tried to steal it. I fear I am raising a pair of thieves."

Amalie sighed, rocking Colton gently as the boy rubbed at his eyes. "'Tis your fault," she told her husband.

He lifted his eyebrows at her. "My fault? What did I do?"

She shook her head, exhausted and irritable. "Because you never deny them anything so they do not know any limits." She reached out for Aubria and Weston reluctantly handed the child over. "If you were to deny their wishes once in a while, we would not have this problem. You spoil them too much, Weston."

Weston looked like a kicked dog as he watched his wife pull the children into the tent with her. He could hear their crying and her soft, soothing voice. As he stood there, feeling wounded, he caught movement out of the corner of his eye and saw his mother standing there. She was smiling up at him.

He frowned at her. "Why do you look at me like that? I am not a bad father, you know."

Elizabeth laughed softly. "You are a wonderful father," she said. "I have seen you with your children enough to know that. But you are just the way Heston was."

"How is that?"

"He spoiled you and Sutton rotten."

248

Weston made a face at her, moving away swiftly so she would not see his grin. But Elizabeth saw it, laughing at him as he disappeared into the big tent after his family.

Elizabeth stood there long after Weston disappeared, reflecting on their conversation and feeling more joyful than she had in years. To have Weston's acceptance was like a dream; her first born child who had grown into such a remarkable and powerful man. She knew that Heston would have been thrilled and she was sorry he never knew his son's acceptance and forgiveness.

Glancing up at the sky, she suspected that, wherever he was, he knew anyway.

CHAPTER TWENTY-ONE

THE FOLLOWING MORNING, the tournament of Keighley burst into full spectacle.

The day dawned brilliantly blue with a cold, crisp breeze that snapped the standards all across the tournament field and the competitors' encampment. Weston was snuggled down in the big bed in the main tent with Aubria and Colton sleeping between him and Amalie, waking when his son thrashed around in his sleep and Weston ended up with a baby arm thrown across his face.

It was before dawn and he could hear the birds outside tweeting and dogs barking in the distance. The smell of smoke was heavy as the servants and soldiers began stoking the morning blazes. Weston lay there a moment, gazing at his sleeping wife and children, thinking that, surely, there were no sweeter moments in life than this. He smiled as he listened to Colton's baby snores and watched Aubria wrinkle up her pert little nose. He could have laid there forever and watched them. It was peace and joy like he had never known in his life.

But he had to get up so he forced himself to rise, very carefully, making sure to tuck the blankets back down around his family as he did so. Quietly, he stoked the small, brass furnace with a load of charcoal so it would provide more heat against the chilly morning before quitting the tent.

The camp was already moderately busy at this hour as he made his way over to one of the smaller tents where Sutton, John and Heath were sleeping. Sutton and Heath were already up, dressing for the day, but John was slower to rise so Weston went into the tent and kicked the man in the foot to get him moving. The squires were up, as were the men-at-arms, and the chargers were being groomed and fed as the squires began to arrange the knights' tournament implements for the day ahead. There was excitement in the air as the day began to advance.

At the meeting of all participants the night before, which Weston did not attend, the rules had been reviewed and it was announced that the lots would be drawn in the morning to see who competed against who in the first rounds. Sutton had returned to the encampment that night to report everything back to Weston and, based upon his brother's report, Weston was prepared for the day.

He dressed carefully with help from one of the squires, a young man who had followed him from Bolingbroke. Weston donned his undergarments, mail coat and boots before moving on to the heavier pieces of armor used for the joust. Usually, the melee was the first event of any tournament but, for some reason, the Keighley marshals were switching the schedule. The joust would be today followed by the melee tomorrow.

When Weston finally donned the blue, white and silver tunic that had belonged to Heston, he paused a moment to admire it. Heston wasn't as tall or as broad as he was so the tunic, which was meant to fit loosely, was somewhat snug. Still, Weston didn't mind. He ran his hands over the finely woven tunic and murmured a prayer to Heston as he did so. He felt particularly close to the man at the moment, so very sorry that his stubbornness and sense of righteousness had turned into something of an obsession. He hoped to do his father proud today and glorify the de Royans name.

As he finished dressing, he noticed that Sutton, Heath and John were nearly finished as well. Squires swarmed over the knights, making sure they had everything they needed for the day ahead. There was to be a gathering of all competitors two hours past sunrise where the marshals would announce the matches for the day.

Weston presumed by the angle of the sun that they had about an hour until that occurred so he grabbed his helm and made his way from the smaller tent out into his encampment. It was his intention to rouse his wife, who would take some time given her delicate condition, but he was halfway to the tent when he heard a familiar scream emitting from the large tent.

Colton bolted from the tent, half-dressed, as Esma struggled out after him. Weston made a swipe for the boy, but he missed. Colton continued running, passing by the smaller tent just as Sutton emerged. Sutton grabbed his nephew before the boy could get away. Sutton growled like a bear, holding on to the kid by the ankles as he walked him back in the direction of the main tent. Colton's delighted screams filled the air.

As they approached, Amalie emerged, looking harried until she saw Sutton approaching with her son. Then she looked visibly relieved as she reached out to take the boy from his uncle and hand him back to Esma. She caught sight of her husband and smiled wearily.

"Good morning, sweetheart," she greeted him as he came upon her and wrapped her up in a big hug. "You appear ready to take on the world today."

He kissed her sweetly on both cheeks. "I am." He kissed her soft mouth. "How are you feeling?"

She nodded her head easily. "Surprisingly well."

He looked her over; she was dressed in a spectacular, deep blue damask surcoat that matched his tunic and her blond hair was in a thick braid that was wrapped around her head like a crown. Lovely jeweled butterfly pins were attached to her hair and upon her slender neck she wore a simple gold cross on a chain. It made his heart thump with excitement simply to look at her.

"You look absolutely beautiful," he sighed. "I will be the proudest man on the field today."

She smiled, her green eyes studying his handsome face. Her hands came up, gently holding his cheeks as if to memorize every last feature. She seemed pensive.

"West," she said softly. "Please be careful today. I would have you well and whole in my arms tonight."

He kissed her again. "No worries, my angel," he murmured. "I can joust in my sleep."

She sighed faintly. "You are a powerful and talented baron," she noted as she rubbed his cheeks affectionately. "But you are foremost my husband and the father of our children. You could lose everything and I would still love you just as I do now until I die. But remember that no tournament is worth risking your health or life over. Remember that, at the end of the day, it is my husband and lover I want back in my arms as safe as when he left me. That is the most important thing of all."

He smiled and kissed her deeply, listening to Colton scream. Esma was trying to bundle him up in a sweater as he tried to escape the tent again. Weston started laughing at his howling son, pulling away from his wife to watch Colton throw himself on the ground in a fit. Amalie turned to watch as well, shaking her head in resignation.

"I will not be able to keep him in his seat today," she told him. "He will want to be on the field with you and Sutton."

With a final kiss, Weston let go of his wife and made his way over to his son. He picked the boy up just as Esma managed to button the sweater closed. Colton was thrilled that his father had hold of him and tried to remove his massive helm, but Weston stilled the yanking hands.

"Colton," he said softly, firmly. "If you behave yourself today, I will let you ride my horse when I am finished. That means that you will listen to your mother and not cry. Only babies cry and you are not a baby. You are a big boy now. I expect you to act like one."

Colton nodded but he was still trying to pull off the helm. Weston grabbed both hands and held them snug. "You must be a good boy for your mother, do you understand?" he asked the boy. "Do as she tells you and it will make me very happy."

Colton nodded his head, his blue eyes fixed on his father. Weston smiled at the boy and kissed his cheek loudly, but Colton didn't want a kiss. He wanted the helm. Esma saved the day by bringing forth the little steel sword, which settled down Colton immensely.

Weston handed the boy over to his wife as he told his brother to get the men ready. In short time, the de Royans party was ready to move to the tournament field.

CB

THE LISTS IN the tournament arena were overrun with spectators and the families of the participants. It was noisy, busy and chaotic, but it was also very exciting. Amalie had never been to a tournament before and was unsure what to expect, so her first order of business after her husband's safety was to ensure that she and the children enjoyed the day. On her husband's arm as he proudly led her to the tournament arena, she eagerly absorbed the sights.

Weston, Sutton, John and Heath escorted Amalie, the children and Elizabeth to the lists and settled them into a box section near the center line that had a very good view of the entire arena. But their trip there had not been without hazard. On the walk to the field, they had passed the man with the monkey again and Colton went into fits until he was allowed to pet it. He even fed it a walnut. Aubria petted the monkey also and fed it two walnuts before turning to her father and again asking if she could have the monkey because she loved it.

Weston was well aware of Amalie's "say yes or die" expression as he calmly told his daughter that she could not have the monkey. Aubria burst into tears, which set off Colton, and the only way to distract the pair was to whisk them away to the sweets vendor.

Little custard cakes in a wooden box quieted their tears quickly enough. Amalie also purchased dried apples and pears from a fruit vendor as they made their way to the entrance. But there was a smithy just outside the entry that had all manner of toys on display and Colton wanted to inspect every one of them.

Little carts, a toy horse and knight and other toys were available for Colton's awed attention. Sutton was fairly fascinated with the toys as well and the two of them made quite a gawky pair.

Weston was trying to figure out how he could get away with buying a cart for his son without his wife becoming angry when something more valuable caught his attention; there was a silversmith right next to the man with the toys and he took Amalie to the stall to inspect the man's wares.

As Amalie gleefully inspected the array of brooches, necklaces and bracelets with semi-precious stones, Sutton made his move and purchased his nephew a real working cart and his niece a funny weighted bird that would bob over and pretend to drink water. The children were delighted and so was Sutton.

Amalie caught sight of what was happening but before she could protest, Weston purchased a gorgeous silver cross set with dark blue, rough cut sapphires. He also purchased a slender silver band with a row of small, glittery, blue sapphires and slipped it onto her finger with a kiss. In the four years they had been married, she had never had a wedding band.

It was a sweet and tender moment, and Amalie forgot about her spoiled children and their partner in crime, Sutton, as she and Weston shared a few softly murmured words of love. With Mother soothed, the children and their disobedient uncle were able to keep the toys.

Amalie wore the spectacular sapphire cross into the arena. Following Sutton, Elizabeth and the children, with John and Heath bringing up the rear, Weston settled his family into the box area for the competing nobles, in particular, the box reserved for Baron Cononley since the event was taking place in his baronetcy.

In fact, it was usually expected that the lord and lady of the shire dispense awards to the victors of the competition, but Amalie declined from doing so when the mayor of Keighley approached and introduced himself, asking her if she would dispense the favors. She simply wanted to enjoy her first tournament and keep a low profile.

She was, in fact, enjoying it already with the humorous and pleasant mayor and Weston saw it as his chance to leave her and prepare for the announcement of bouts. Leaving two men-at-arms to watch over the group, one of them being Owyn, he departed with his men. He trusted

Owyn more than most when his wife's safety was at stake and with Sorrell wandering the grounds, he wanted someone he trusted in charge of his wife. Owyn knew Sorrell on sight and would therefore know what to do.

But Amalie hadn't mentioned Sorrell that morning nor had she shown any manner of concern that he might be around. She was swept up with the thrill of her first tournament. The lists were jammed by the time the marshals appeared to announce the morning bouts.

The day was warming up but the breeze was still brisk as it blew dust and leaves across the arena floor. Amalie sat with Colton on her lap as he excitedly pointed out all of the knights and horses while Elizabeth and Aubria sat quietly together and observed the excitement. When the marshals began to announce the rounds, Amalie had to listen closely over her son's excited chatter.

There were apparently more competitors than they had expected. Thirty-six houses had showed up to compete and each house had at least one competitor or, as in the case of Baron Cononley, the Earl of Billingham and several other houses, there were four or more men slated to compete. In all, there were one hundred and five men competing and that was divided into fifty-three individual bouts.

The numbers were staggering and the marshals announced that it would take more than one day to accomplish the joust portion. There would be seventeen rounds in both the morning and afternoon of the current day and then the morning of the next day would see the remaining rounds. The winners of those bouts would compete in the second rounds on the afternoon of the second day and so forth. The marshals estimated it would take at least four days to declare a joust winner.

The crowd wasn't displeased with the length of the tournament. In fact, they were cheering wildly. The marshals began to rattle off the lists of the men who would compete against each other, Baron Cononley being the first man listed.

Weston would be competing against Sir Kenneth Pembury of

Bayhall, an enormous man with black hair and bright blue eyes that already had a buzz about him. When his name was announced, half of the women in the lists collectively sighed and Amalie had no idea why until she saw the man; he was big and beautiful. When all of the morning bouts were announced, which also happened to include Sutton against a bear of a man named Sir James Burton from Somerhill in Essex, the knights slated to compete began to take up their positions.

With Weston up first, Amalie's anxiety began to grow. She was excited but she was naturally worried for his safety. When Weston and his big, blond charger took position at the west end of the tournament arena, in full armor and colors bearing the blue and white of Baron Cononley, Colton began to squeal because he spotted his father.

Amalie held tight to the little boy as he jumped up and pointed, very excited at the sight. But Amalie was more nervous than excited and her stomach began to churn with nerves. She held tightly to Colton as the child squirmed, more than once burying her face in his back as she tried to steady her nerves.

To the east of the field, Pembury took up position bearing the family colors of green and black. He was a very big man astride a very big, black horse and Colton was thrilled at the sight. As the marshals took the field for the first pass, the knights on the opposing sides accepted their joust poles. Amalie watched Weston get a good grip on his pole as John and Heath handed him his equipment and gave the charger a final check. She found herself murmuring prayers for his safety, her palms sweating with nerves, as the field marshal finally dropped the first flag.

The chargers snorted and leaped forward as the crowd let forth a deafening roar. Amalie's first reaction was to close her eyes but she found that she couldn't; her attention was riveted to Weston as he charged towards his opponent at breakneck speed. The twelve-foot-long joust pole bearing the colors of Baron Cononley leveled out and held steady, pointed right at Pembury as the knights rushed each other.

The crowd screamed and Amalie tensed as the men drew near. Suddenly, there was a loud crash followed by the splinting of wood as the joust poles made contact.

Weston's shield absorbed the blow from Pembury, but Pembury took a hard hit to the shoulder from Weston's lance. It was so forceful that the lance shattered and pieces of colored wood went flying, some as far as the lists. The crowd roared their approval as both knights came away virtually unscathed.

Weston made a sweeping run in front of the stands on his way back to his starting position, his helmed head seeking out his wife and children in the lists. He pointed a glove hand at them as he rode past and Colton went wild, clapping and yelling for his father. The baby's excitement caused those around him to laugh at his youthful exuberance.

Amalie held on to her crazed son, smiling at her husband as he thundered past. She was so incredibly proud of the man, of his strength and skill, and so incredibly glad that he was uninjured. She found jousting to be rather exciting as long as no one was hurt. As Weston assumed his starting position again with a new pole, the crowd quieted down in suspense of another exciting pass.

Weston's second pass was uneventful and both knights remained seated. But the third pass saw Pembury lift his pole for Weston's head and Weston had to dodge it at the last moment to avoid having his skull crushed. As he dodged, he had a split second to bring his own pole up and he did so, catching Pembury on the clavicle. It was enough to topple Pembury over backwards and hit the dirt with a broken collarbone.

The crowd went mad as the bout ended in victory for Baron Cononley. Favors and flowers began to fly out from the lists, littering the dirt of the arena as Weston made another sweeping pass along the stands until he came to his wife. Then, he pulled his charger up and flipped open his visor, his dark blue eyes finding Amalie among the chaos. When their eyes met, he held out an enormous gloved hand to her.

Amalie stood up with Colton in her arms and made her way down a few steps towards him at the edge of the lists. When she finally reached him, he grasped her gently by the wrist and brought her hand to his partially-covered mouth for a kiss. Colton began screaming, wanting to go to his father, so Weston took the boy from her and settled him on the front of the saddle.

"You were brilliant, sweetheart," Amalie said. "I am so proud of you."

He grinned. "I am pleased you think so, my lady."

She returned his grin, watching Colton as the boy joyfully banged on the saddle. "He is going to scream like a banshee if I take him from you now," she indicated the little boy. "Will you take him to the edge of the field and I will collect him from you there?"

Weston nodded, putting a big hand around his son's torso and completely swallowing it up with the size of the glove. "He can ride with me and wave to the crowd," he spurred his charger forward, speaking to Colton as he did so. "Wave to the crowd, lad. They are cheering for you."

Colton did as he was told, waving happily to the people who were throwing flowers and favors at him. Amalie watched, a smile on her face, as Weston headed off towards the east side of the arena. Gathering her skirts, she turned to follow.

"Keep Aubria here with you," she told Elizabeth. "I will return shortly."

Elizabeth nodded. "Of course, Amalie. We shall wait right here and watch the spectacle, won't we, Aubria?"

Aubria still had the toy bird in her hand, nodding eagerly to her grandmother's suggestion. Blowing a kiss to her daughter, Amalie lifted her skirts as she took the stairs to the field level below. Owyn and another soldier were at the bottom of the stairs, waiting.

Amalie smiled at Owyn when she reached the bottom of the steps. Though she rarely saw him nowadays, he still had a special place in her heart as the man who had saved her life. She knew that Weston had richly rewarded the young man and that he held a place of honor within

Weston's ranks. Gazing into his face was like looking at an old friend.

"Greetings, Owyn," she said.

He smiled at her. "Lady de Royans," he greeted. "Where may I escort you?"

She threw a casual finger towards the east. "I am heading to the edge of the field to collect my son from his father," she replied. "Colton wants to be a knight so badly. He insisted on riding with his father when the bout was over."

Owyn grinned. "He will make a fine knight, my lady. He already has half of Netherghyll under his submission."

Amalie laughed. "He does, doesn't he?" she shrugged. "He is a bright, healthy boy. I fear he may have half of England under submission by the time he is five years old."

Owyn nodded in agreement. "May I escort you to the edge of the field, my lady?"

She nodded. "You had better. I do not want my husband to become enraged because I walked alone."

Owyn nodded emphatically as they began to walk out onto the boulevard. "There is no knowing what kinds of deviants lurk about at an event such as this," he told her. "You could be molested by any number of characters."

She looked at him, a look of distaste on her features. "What a pleasant thought," she remarked dryly, then she began to look around and notice their surroundings as they proceeded. "Have you been to many tournaments, Owyn?"

He shook his head, his gaze on the big arena to their right. "Only two," he replied. "One when I was just a lad and then another about six or seven years ago. Most young men view them as hunting grounds."

She peered up at him. "Hunting grounds?"

He looked somewhat chagrinned. "Hunting for young ladies, my lady," he said. "Perhaps I should not have told you that."

She laughed. "Lest you forget that I have seen Heath and John in action over the past couple of days." She lifted an eyebrow at him. "I know exactly what they are doing. Speaking of which…"

She trailed off, her focus on something down the avenue, and Owyn turned to see what she was looking at. A small woman with beautiful brown eyes and brown hair was walking towards them in the company of soldiers and servants, her face lighting up when she spied Amalie.

"Lady Amalie!" the woman waved.

Amalie smiled as she went to greet her. "Lady Paget," she took the woman's small hands in her own. "I was hoping we would be able to sit together this morning and watch the games. Are you just arriving?"

Paget nodded, smiling her beautiful, dimpled smile. "My father had an attack of the gout overnight and has decided not to compete," she told her. "But we have two knights who will be competing later this morning. Has your husband already competed?"

"Aye," Amalie responded proudly. "He won against Pembury."

"Wonderful," Paget exclaimed. "Where are you going now? May I accompany you, my lady?"

Amalie nodded and was preparing to reply when a group of men passed by off to her right, men on horseback heading for the eastern edge of the tournament field. Owyn politely took her elbow to move her out of the way of the men and squires and Amalie instinctively glanced up as the group moved through the dusty avenue. It was purely a reflexive move on her part.

Her gaze fell on a few of the men, unconcerned, when her focus came to rest on one man in particular. He was in armor but his head was uncovered and his dirty, light brown hair was evident. There was something oddly familiar about him. He was speaking to one of the squires and his head turned slightly, his gaze inadvertently locking with hers.

It was Sorrell. Amalie suddenly couldn't breathe as their gazes held fast to one another. Sorrell's weathered features appeared shocked for a moment before gradually relaxing into a lascivious smile. Before Amalie could react in any fashion, Sorrell greeted her with feigned gallantry.

"Lady Amalie de Vere," he said loudly. "What a surprise to see you here, my lady. You are far from home but I see that Owyn is with you. I was wondering what became of you and now I see. You must have run off with Owyn after I had my fill of you."

Amalie was so shocked and horrified that she couldn't form a rational answer. Her face, white with the shock of seeing him, suddenly washed bright red with shame. She was suddenly very hot and very nauseous, and the ground was beginning to sway.

Sorrell's loud laughter filled the air as he moved off towards the east with his party as Amalie just stood there in terror. As he faded away, Owyn turned to Amalie with serious concern.

"Are you well, my lady?" He could see the expression of abject horror on her face. "Shall I send for your husband?"

Amalie was stunned, but not so senseless that she could not dig down deep for the last shards of decency and control she possessed. She couldn't fall apart, not yet, though she very much wanted to. Quite calmly, she turned to Lady Paget, who was looking rather confused, and put a soft hand on her wrist.

"My lady," she said, her voice trembling. "I am looking forward to sharing the day with you, but if you will excuse me right now, I am feeling rather ill. I will go and lie down for a while before joining you in the lists."

Paget could see that something had Lady Amalie very rattled. She grasped her with her small, soft hands.

"I will come with you," she insisted. "Let us return to your encampment and I will sit with you while you rest."

Amalie forced a smile but it was all for show. The tears were building and she could not stop them.

"That is very kind but not necessary," she whispered tightly. "Surely you do not want to miss your father's men compete."

Paget wouldn't let go of her hands. "I would rather sit with you," she insisted softly, her brown eyes studying Amalie's distraught face. "Will you please indulge me?"

Amalie couldn't even argue with the woman. She was shattered, desperate to put distance between herself and her horrible nightmare. Owyn knew this; he watched Sorrell ride away, snorting as if he didn't have a care in the world, while Amalie nearly came apart.

Owyn knew what he had to do. Taking charge, he grasped Amalie by the elbow.

"Come along, Lady de Royans," he said firmly. "Let us return to camp and I shall send for your husband."

Amalie just closed her eyes, fat tears rolling down her cheeks, as Owyn and Paget led her off for the competitors' encampment.

CHAPTER TWENTY-TWO

W HEN AMALIE DIDN'T show up at the east end of the arena, Weston wasn't particular concerned. She could get chatty and forget about time so he assumed she was speaking with someone and simply lost track of the time.

Dismounting his charger with Colton in his arms, he told his men he would return as he went in search of Amalie. Sutton's bout was eighth on the card later that morning and Weston was sure he would return in plenty of time. In fact, Sutton, bored with standing around, decided to go with him in search of Amalie.

Carrying Colton in one enormous arm, Weston left the west end of the timber and stone arena and skirted the perimeter back towards the box where his family was seated. He found his mother and daughter sitting where he had left them but no sign of his wife. Elizabeth assured Weston that Amalie had left with a guard, so Weston was unconcerned as he set off in search of her. He passed by the man with the toys and the man with the monkey, which set off Colton again, so they had to pause a few minutes while Colton fed the monkey another walnut.

Leaving the monkey behind, Weston searched the shops along the avenue for any sign of his errant wife. He guessed she might be shopping and inwardly groaned when he wondered how much it was going to cost him. He'd already spent a significant sum on the cross and ring but, in reflection, he didn't much mind spending money on his wife. She was well worth it.

He and Sutton neared the edge of the vendors with still no sign of Amalie. Thinking he might have somehow missed her, he ended back at the east entrance to the arena, watching the crowd of men and animals for her soft blond head. As he stood there and searched, he heard a voice approach from behind.

"De Royans," the man said. "I thought that was you."

Weston turned around, coming face to face with Sorrell. At first, he was shocked almost into numbness; he couldn't seem to speak or move. He thought he might be dreaming but very swiftly realized he wasn't.

Then, the anger bloomed, rising from his toes and exploding into his chest. His first thought was to wrap his hands around the man's neck and snap the bones into dust. But he had Colton in his arms and was in no position to make a provocative move. As the fury swirled in his chest, his second thought was of Amalie. If she had come to the east entrance looking for Weston, then there was a real possibility that she had either seen or run into Sorrell. The fury in his veins turned to molten, liquid lead.

"Sorrell," he greeted, his teeth clenched. "I heard you were here."

Sir John Sorrell bowed gallantly as if flattered by the comment. A man of average height and broad shoulders, he was shaggy and unkempt, having reached his status due to his father's political ties. He was a decent knight, but there were better. Anything he had achieved had been through cunning, deceit, or his father's connections.

"My reputation precedes me," he said arrogantly, eyeing Weston and Colton in a manner that infuriated Weston. "I heard you took over as garrison commander at Hedingham after I left. Is this so?"

Weston took a deep breath; he could already see where this was going. Straight to the subject of Hedingham. Calmly, he handed Colton over to his brother because he was quite sure that the fists and weapons were going to be flying shortly and he didn't want his son in the line of fire.

"It is," he replied evenly.

Sorrell nodded, glancing over at Colton again. The boy seemed to have his attention. "Your son?"

Weston's big body tensed. "He is."

Sorrell nodded, inspecting the boy further. "A fine lad," he looked at Weston. "I had no idea you were married."

"I am," Weston replied, barely able to maintain his control.

Sorrell absorbed the information, either not sensing that Weston was coiled or not caring. He began to tighten up his gauntlets.

"I hope you married well," he commented, his gaze moving off across the arena and the lists. "There are not enough fine women in this country for ambitious men to wed. Look at all of those whores out in the lists, pretending to be fine women yet selling their favors to any man who will look at them."

He snorted ironically as if amused by his own thoughts. Weston just stood there and worked his fists, his dark blue eyes never leaving Sorrell's face. It took every ounce of control he had not to kill the man at that moment. He could just see how careless and disgusting the knight was, and imagining his wife at the mercy of the man nearly drove him out of his mind.

The moment had come; it was here, truth thrust upon him, and he could not back down or look away. He had to face it head-on with as much control as he could possibly muster. For Amalie, he had to do it.

"You remember the Lady Amalie de Vere, do you not?" Weston asked, his voice quivering because he was so tightly wound.

Sorrell looked at him for a moment before breaking down into a lazy smile.

"Of course I do," he replied. "In fact, it is odd that you should ask me, as I just saw her by the arena entrance not a few minutes ago. I was surprised to see her, in fact, because she disappeared from Hedingham shortly after I arrived. I did not know what became of her but it seems she ran away with one of my soldiers. I saw him here as well."

Off to Weston's right, Sutton began to move away with Colton in his arms. He could see where this was leading and was positive there was about to be a blood bath. Looking about frantically, he spied John and Heath several dozen yards away as they supervised some of the squires working on the chargers and Sutton caught John's attention with the wave of a hand.

John grabbed Heath and, soon, both of them appeared at Sutton's side. When they looked at him curiously, all he had to do was point at Weston and Sorrell. No words needed to be spoken, for they all knew the stakes at that moment. Sutton handed Colton off to Heath, who knew the boy better than John did, and Heath took the child away from what would surely be a volatile battle. Only Sutton and John remained, watching, waiting.

Weston, however, wasn't prepared to strike, not just yet. He had lived this moment over and over in his mind, carefully planning out what he intended to say to the man who had so brutally assaulted his wife. He wanted to make sure Sorrell knew the facts before he was struck down. He wanted to make sure there was no mistake. He digested Sorrell's casual statement before replying.

"Did you see where she went?" he asked steadily.

Sorrell shook his head, now fussing with the mail coat around his shoulder. "The last I saw her, she was over by the arena entry," he replied. "Why? Do you know her?"

Weston nodded faintly, taking a step in Sorrell's direction. "You could say that," he said, his voice low. "She did not flee Hedingham as you suspected. She hid from you until you left. I found her when I arrived."

Sorrell looked at him, a bushy eyebrow lifted. "Is that so?" He shrugged, the grin returning to his face. "It is of no matter, I suppose. I had no use for her at the garrison other than to warm my bed. She was a sweet little thing. Delicious."

Weston's heart began to pound as he took another step and ended up very close to Sorrell. His palms were sweating with the need for vengeance. He looked the man in the eye as he spoke.

"Listen to me and listen well," he growled, his voice quaking because he was having so much difficulty reining in his anger. "I married Amalie de Vere. She is my wife. She told me what you did to her, you foul bastard, and I have sworn upon my father's grave every night since that time that when I found you, I would make you pay for every pain and every shame you heaped upon her. You are beyond vile, Sorrell. You are kin and kith to Satan himself and when I wipe you from this earth, every stroke from my blade and every pain you feel will have Amalie's name on it. Is there anything you do not understand so far?"

By this time, Sorrell was looking at Weston with some astonishment. There was no fear in his expression, at least not yet. But there was disbelief.

"You *married* her?" he repeated, shocked. "Why would you do that? She is sister to a perverted madman. She is nothing but a whore."

It was the wrong thing to say and Weston's control snapped. A massive fist lashed out and grabbed Sorrell around the neck while the other fist pounded the man squarely in the face. Sorrell went toppling backwards as Weston pounced on him, using his enormous fists to pummel the man unconscious in a few short blows. But the blows had been so powerful that Sorrell face was destroyed and he was choking on his own blood and broken teeth. It was instantly a bloody, chaotic scene.

Knights and men began jostling to gain a better view of the fight as Weston picked up Sorrell's limp body and hurled the man into the wall of the arena. He swooped upon the unconscious man and began to beat him about the head and chest with his fists, working out years of anger and anguish with every blow. When a few of Billingham's knights saw what was happening, they leaped in to intervene and were stopped by Sutton and John. Soon, a full-scale brawl erupted with Weston, Sutton and John in the middle of it.

The field marshals began to run towards the east end of the arena as the lists erupted in cheers and cries. Everyone could see the massive battle escalating and everyone wanted a good view. This was better entertainment than the tame joust. As the entire area deteriorated and the swords began to come out, all was peaceful and still over in the competitors' encampment as Amalie remained blissfully unaware of the mortal combat being staged in her honor.

CB

"CAN I GET YOU anything, Lady Amalie?" Paget asked softly. "Some wine perhaps?"

Amalie lay upon the big bed she shared with her husband and children, gazing up at Paget's lovely brown eyes. She smiled faintly.

"Nothing, thank you," she sighed. "I am sorry for seeming so silly. I am newly pregnant with my third child and my constitution is not as strong as it normally is. It is very kind of you to sit with me while I rest."

Paget smiled and pulled up a small stool. "It gives us a chance to become better acquainted." She cast Amalie a sidelong glance. "It also gives me the chance to learn more about Sir Sutton."

Amalie's smile grew. "Of course," she said. "What would you like to know?"

Paget shrugged, tucking her silky brown hair behind an ear as she thought on her reply.

"He is devilishly handsome," she admitted, casting Amalie a flirtatious little glance. "Surely he has other women he is interested in. He must have dozens."

Amalie rolled onto her side, sighing as she thought on Sutton. "None that I am aware of," she replied honestly. "You would think that he, indeed, had women following him around. But since I have known the man, I have not seen him with one lady. All he has spoken of is you."

Paget's brown eyes glimmered. "All I have thought of is him," she said softly. "May I beg you to tell me what you know of him? What kind of man is he?"

Amalie's green eyes were warm. "He is kind, thoughtful and considerate," she said. "He loves to laugh. He can be quite happy when he has imbibed too much drink. And he loves my children very much; he spoils them terribly. Like his brother, he will be a wonderful father."

Paget's cheeks pinkened as she averted her gaze, looking to her hands and thinking on handsome Sutton de Royans. "That is good to know," she said shyly. "He… he has led an eventful life in the service of Bolingbroke, has he not?"

Amalie was prepared to reply when the tent flap suddenly slapped back and Heath appeared holding Colton in his arms. The redheaded knight's expression seemed rather anxious and Amalie sat up on the bed, wondering why the man was holding her son. Last she had seen, Weston had hold of Colton. Apprehension began to well in her chest.

"Heath?" She stood up from the bed and went to retrieve Colton. "Where is Weston?"

Heath didn't want to tell her the truth, fearful of her reaction.

"He is over at the arena, Lady de Royans," he said honestly. "He asked me to return his son to camp."

Amalie's apprehension was eased as she took sleepy, fussy Colton in her arms. "Thank you," she replied. "Is it Sutton's turn to compete yet?"

Heath looked edgy. He kept glancing out of the tent in the direction of the arena. "Nay, my lady."

Amalie noticed his behavior and instinctively went to see what he was looking at. Heath couldn't stop her. He couldn't lay his hands on her to physically prevent her from looking, so all he could do was stand back as she stepped from the tent to peer off towards the arena.

Immediately, she could see great clouds of dust and the sounds of men shouting and horses braying. Her brow furrowed.

"What is happening over at the arena?" she asked.

Heath sighed heavily, so very reluctant to tell her. But he had no choice; moreover, he had to return and he didn't want her following him out of curiosity. Perhaps if he told her the truth, she would stay away out of simple fear.

"A scuffle, my lady," he told her hesitantly, then added, "Weston and Sorrell."

Amalie looked at him so swiftly that her neck nearly snapped. Her green eyes were huge in her porcelain face, knowing that whatever was occurring wasn't as simple as a scuffle. Men were fighting and more than likely dying, including Weston. She began to scream.

"Esma!" she cried. "Esma, come and take Colton!"

The tubby servant had been in one of the smaller tents and came bursting forth at the panicked sound of her mistress. Amalie was already running towards her, depositing the fussing boy into Esma's arms before turning on her heel and gathering her skirts. By this time, Paget had emerged from the large tent at the sounds of anxiety, her brown eyes wide with fear.

"Lady Amalie?" she asked, concerned. "What seems to be the...?"

Amalie couldn't even answer her; she was already off running with Heath behind her. Paget, not wanting to be left behind, took off running as well.

Amalie tore across the encampment, her brilliant blue surcoat hiked up around her knees as she raced like the wind towards the east side of the arena. Her heart was in her throat as she approached, terrified that Weston was in trouble. After Weston's declaration yesterday about killing Sorrell, she had little doubt that he meant what he said. She only prayed that, in his assault on Sorrell, the result wasn't a different one than Weston intended.

As she drew close, she could see that a big brawl was taking place with swords and fists. Men she didn't know and had never seen were doing battle as she charged into the maelstrom, ignoring the shouts of Heath as he tried to stop her. All she could think of was finding Weston in this bloody, dusty mess of men and weapons and she slugged through, getting bumped around as she screamed Weston's name.

Dust flew up in her face and she began to shove back as men scuffled around her. One man almost bowled her over and she kicked him squarely in the arse, sending him off balance and away from her. But she spied Sutton in a fistfight with a big knight and she screamed at him, catching his attention and watching as he was clobbered in the mouth. But Sutton came back strong and brained the man, sending him crashing to the ground. Swiftly, he went to Amalie.

He put his big arms around her to protect her. "What are you doing here?" he demanded, blood trickling from his mouth. "We must remove you from this battle."

Amalie dug in her heels. "I am not going anywhere until I find my husband," she declared. "Where is he?"

Sutton truly had no idea. He looked around, a tall man with a good view of the crowd, and spied his brother's cropped blond head in the midst of clashing men over by the arena entry gates.

"He is over by the gates," he told her. "But he will murder me if I do not remove you from this fighting. Please let me …"

She yanked away from him, heading in the direction he had indicated. "If you will not take me to him, I will find him myself."

Sutton caught up with her and surrounded her with his big arms once more. "Nay, Ammy," he summoned the courage to deny her. "For your own safety, you must leave this mess. Weston can handle himself."

Terrified and upset, Amalie thrust a fist into Sutton's neck, causing him to momentarily release his hold on her. Grabbing her now-filthy skirts from all of the dust, she bolted in the direction of the west entrance to the field, screaming Weston's name. It wasn't long before she received a bellowed response.

Amalie thrust herself between a pair of knights and ran headlong into her husband. Weston had been heading in the direction of her cries and nearly ran her down. Horrified, he wrapped his enormous arms around her and held her tightly against him, pulling her away from clashing swords nearby. Amalie wrapped her arms around his neck tightly and he ended up picking her up, keeping her well off the ground and clutched tight against his chest.

"What are you doing here?" he half-demanded, half-pleaded. "Are you well? You are not hurt, are you?"

She shook her head verging on tears. "Nay," she breathed, her head against his. "But Lady Paget and Heath came with me. They are over there, somewhere. We must find Paget…"

She trailed off breathlessly, jabbing a finger off towards the encampment. With his wife still clutched up against his chest, Weston charged off.

"Sutton!" he roared. "To me!"

Sutton was already there. He hadn't been far behind Amalie. "What is…?" he began.

Weston cut him off. "Your Lady Paget is somewhere in this mess," he growled. "Find her before someone hurts her. Find Heath; she may be with him."

Startled, Sutton began throwing men out of the way in his quest to find Paget. More than anything, the fact that she was rumored to be with Heath upset him greatly and his anger was roused. Weston closed in behind him, following the path blazed by his brother with the intention of removing his wife from the fighting.

Because Weston had been one of the original combatants, the field marshals were following him, ordering men to cease fighting in the process. It was mad and chaotic by the time Weston and Amalie reached the edge of the roiling crowd.

When there were no more combatants within close range, Weston carefully set Amalie on her feet. Just as he did so, Heath and Paget approached from several yards away. Paget saw Amalie in her husband's arms and rushed to her.

"My lady?" she grasped Amalie's arm. "Are you well?"

Amalie nodded, clutching Paget's hand. The two of them held on to each other tightly. "I am well," she replied. "But, more importantly, my husband is well."

Paget turned her great brown eyes to Weston and the man could see, in that moment, why she had his brother so smitten. It was the first time he had seen her at close range and she was a beautiful, little thing. But his attention was focused on his wife.

"What madness is this that you would go charging into a group of fighting men?" He was suddenly very angry at his wife now that he had taken her to safety. "Have you lost your mind?"

Instead of bursting into tears, Amalie remained calm in the face of his fury. "I have not lost my mind," she replied steadily. "Where is Sorrell? Did you kill him?"

Weston's fury quickly abated. "He is alive," he said after a moment. "Why did you not come to the entrance to the field as you said you would? Did Sorrell chase you away? He said he saw you."

Amalie let go of Paget and pressed her hands into his big glove. He held her hands, tightly.

"He did not chase me away," she said softly. "But I did see him. It upset me."

Weston was sure that was an understatement and he kissed her gently on the forehead, pulling her into a comforting embrace. At the moment, he could only feel extreme relief that Amalie was safe and that his vengeance against Sorrell, for the moment, was sated. But only for the moment.

"Everything will be well, my angel," he murmured. "Did Colton make it back to camp?"

She nodded, lifting her head to find Heath standing a few feet away. "Heath returned him safely." Her gaze moved to Paget, standing next to her. "And I do not believe you have met the Lady Paget Clifford. She kept me company until Heath and Colton appeared. Lady Paget, this is my husband, Weston."

Paget smiled her dimpled smile at Weston but her gaze was clearly drawn to Sutton, standing to the right of Weston.

"'Tis an honor to meet you, Baron Cononley," she said, her eyes riveted to Sutton. "Sir Sutton, you appear as if you have some injury to your mouth."

Sutton was gazing at her, dreamily, but snapped out of his trance when he realized that something must be amiss on his face. He swiped a finger over his chin and came away with some blood. He smiled weakly.

"It is nothing," he assured her. "But I thank you for your concern."

Paget's pretty smile grew. "I should be happy to tend your wound if needed."

Sutton just stared at her, dumbfounded, as Weston cleared his throat loudly and elbowed his daft brother in the ribs.

"That would be a good idea, Sutton," he said. "Take Lady Paget back to our encampment and let her tend your lip. You have a bout coming up soon, so do not take too long."

Sutton abruptly realized the golden opportunity his brother was suggesting and, with a grin, extended his hand to Paget. She took it happily and he tucked her hand into the crook of his elbow, leading her away towards the competitors' encampment. But he made sure to make a snarling face at Heath as he passed by the man, as if to mark his territory, and Heath looked properly contrite. Pretty though she might be, he knew Lady Paget was out of his league.

Weston and Amalie watched Sutton and Paget walk away with some amusement until two of the field marshals abruptly converged on Weston.

"Baron Cononley," a man with bad skin and yellow teeth spoke. "Were you attacked, my lord? Surely this trouble was caused when you defended yourself."

The smile vanished from Weston's face as he turned to the officials. "I was not attacked," he replied frankly. "I was seeking vengeance against a man who brutally attacked my wife. It is my right and my due. You will not interfere."

The officials looked somewhat taken aback by his response. By now, the brawl was dissipating and men were clearing the area and moving on to the business at hand. Fights like this were not uncommon in great gatherings such as this, especially since feuding factions often appeared at the same event.

As the dust settled and men cleared, the marshals whispered to each other before facing Weston again.

"We will not involve ourselves in personal matters of honor, my lord," the lead marshal said. "But we would like assurance that this will not happen again."

Weston snorted rudely. "I will give you no such assurance."

"Then perhaps you will give it to me."

A big knight in pristine armor approached. He was taller than anyone there, a towering man with brilliant blue eyes and dark hair. Amalie was uncertain and apprehensive of the knight until she glanced up at her husband to see that there was warmth in his expression. Weston, in fact, smiled.

"Le Bec," he rolled the name off his tongue. "It has been ages since I last saw you."

Sir Richmond le Bec returned Weston's smile. He was a very handsome man, rather young, but exuding the agelessness of one with great experience and power. He held out a hand and Weston took it amiably.

"And the last time I saw you, I believe it was in a situation much like this one," le Bec replied, releasing Weston's hand. "Do you never stop fighting, de Royans, or is this a favorite pastime?"

Weston laughed softly. "It is not," he assured him, his smile fading. "This was a matter of honor. I had no choice."

Le Bec held his gaze for a moment before wriggling his eyebrows. "Sorrell is one of my men," he said. "You have put me in an awkward position."

Weston hardened. "I am not sure why," he said quietly. "You do not serve Billingham."

Le Bec shook his head. "I do not, but Henry has stationed me with Billingham for the time being. He has asked me to keep an eye on the border barons with the turmoil currently going on right now."

Weston understood. Both he and le Bec had been commanders for Bolingbroke, serving where Henry sent them as evidenced by Weston going to Hedingham those years ago. Richmond le Bec was a friend of Weston's and a fine knight. But Weston would not back down, not in this matter.

"I am well aware of your position, considering I was stationed at Hedingham for the same purpose," he replied. "However, the business between Sorrell and me is personal and I ask that you respect that."

Above their heads, the peal of horns could be heard as the field was prepared for another joust match. All of the men that had been brawling, for the most part, had returned to their various groups and camps, leaving very few men still standing at the west entrance to the field. Even the lists had filled up again with eager fans, waiting for the next joust between Sir Simon Wellesbourne of Warwickshire and Sir Nicholas de Wolfe of Northwood Castle. As the noise of the games resuming filled the air, Richmond turned his attention to Weston.

"If you ask it, I shall respect it," he said. "But try not to involve half of England in your battles, West."

"Keep Sorrell as far away from me as you can and there will be no more battles."

Richmond nodded faintly, his blue gaze moving between Weston and Amalie, still clutched against her husband's torso, before departing in the direction of the arena.

Amalie and Weston watched him go, realizing he was heading to a group of men clustered near the arena wall by the entrance. It took Amalie a moment to realize that the men were clustered around a limp body that they were trying to lift off the ground. She could see as they raised him to his feet that the injured man was Sorrell.

She gasped when she saw his face; he was covered in blood, barely recognizable. Weston heard her gasp and realized what she was looking at. As he put himself between the bloody vision of Sorrell and his wife with the intention of returning her to the encampment, guttural and loud shouting could be heard behind them. Both Weston and Amalie turned to see Sorrell staggering towards them.

"De Royans!" He was weaving unsteadily, beaten senseless by Weston's big fists. "I will meet you in this arena and gore you with my pole, do you hear me? And when you are rotting in hell, I will send your wife there also. I will take every last pleasure with her first before I…"

Le Bec slapped a hand over Sorrell's bleeding mouth, grabbing the man and turning him away from Weston and his wife.

"Are you truly so stupid, man?" le Bec snarled. "Shut your mouth and live."

Amalie had hold of Weston. She could feel him tense as Sorrell spouted his antagonistic words. She was terrified that Weston was going to charge the man and she held him tightly, knowing he would not move forward if she remained in his path.

"Come with me," she begged steadily. "Let us return to our camp. Please, Weston."

He had his hands on her shoulders, his features set like stone as he listened to Sorrell rant. His fury, his madness, blossomed once again and he was seriously considering charging Sorrell and finishing him off but Amalie's soft voice was breaking through to him, dousing his flame. She was already upset and he was sure that watching him kill a man would do nothing to help her state of mind. All he could do was let her turn him around in the direction of the encampment, unable to resist her and unwilling to put her through more than she had already been through. But he threw one last piece of advice at Sorrell.

"Let us pray we meet in the arena," he told the man. "If we do, know that I will be aiming for your head with every pass. I will kill you and take great pleasure in it, you worthless whoreskin."

"Weston," Amalie hissed, giving him a push towards camp. "Please, let us go."

Heath was helping her, putting himself between Weston and Sorrell to block their view of one another. John, having been with one of the local physics having his bloodied knuckles tended, joined the group and, along with Heath and Amalie, helped push Weston away from the confrontation. But they all knew there would be a time and place for the final battle; there had to be. Weston was bent on blood and now Sorrell was bent on revenge for a bad beating. It would come to a head at some point, some time.

And it would be deadly.

CHAPTER TWENTY-THREE

H E WAS SKULKING.

Beaten, bruised and battered, Sorrell was semi-mobile and, at the moment, he was skulking in the area of de Royans' camp. He had spent the rest of the day struggling with the pain of six broken teeth, a broken jaw and a broken nose, but the agony had only gotten worse. His head felt like it was going to explode and, as the pain increased, so did his twisted sense of hatred and revenge. All he could think of was getting his hands on de Royans and cutting the man's heart out, but he knew that would be impossible. De Royans was too big and too strong to fall victim to something that easy. So Sorrell knew he had to be clever.

He waited until Billingham's camp was silent and sleeping for the most part, slipping free and telling the guards that he was heading into town to find one of the many whores that were open for business that time of night. The guards laughed lewdly and let him go, but Sorrell headed for the opposite side of the encampment where de Royans was housed.

It was very quiet and the night was still as he approached. He could count at least four guards around the de Royans encampment, their movements illuminated by two smoldering bonfires that crackled in the darkness. The various encampments were fairly close so it wasn't a difficult matter for him to creep closer and use other tents to hide his movements.

As he drew near the de Royans encampment, he knew he would have to be swift in order to remain unseen, so he lay in wait by the shadow of a neighboring tent as one of the de Royans guards made his rounds. When the man passed by, Sorrell took the opportunity to slip through the perimeter and hide in the shadows of a small blue and white tent.

He could hear loud snoring coming from inside, correctly assuming that it must house the knights and feeling some fear as he silently crept away. He certainly didn't want to wake any of the de Royans knights, so he slithered on his belly towards the second small tent that was nearer to one of the bonfires. Lifting the edge of the tent, he stuck his head inside.

He could see a woman sleeping on the grass on a pallet and another woman with blond hair sleeping on a more luxurious bed. Seized with fury and an unholy sense of vengeance, he saw the blond hair and thought that perhaps it was de Royans' wife. *Lady Amalie de Vere.* The woman, the whore, who started everything. He should have killed her when he had the chance. Now, he had the chance. Grabbing the blond head, he plunged his dagger deep into the woman's belly.

The woman gasped but did not scream. He slammed his hand over her mouth to ensure that no sound came forth. But when the woman on the grass awoke and saw him, he dropped the dagger and wrapped both hands around her neck, squeezing tightly. The life drained out of her as he watched.

Collecting his dagger, Sorrell slipped from the tent when the de Royans guard made another pass on his rounds. Slipping back into the darkness, he retreated to the safe haven of the Billingham camp, pleased with his work for the night. One by one, he would destroy everything and everyone precious to de Royans.

He would make the man pay.

CB

AMALIE WAS SO distraught that she could not get out of bed. She lay there in the big bed she shared with Weston and the children, sobbing deeply. The children seemed subdued as well because their mother was so upset. They sat on the bed next to her, Colton playing with his little sword and Aubria with her poppet and toy bird. They sat next to their mother silently, sensing the mood of the camp even at their young age. Colton eventually snuggled down next to his mother and just lay there, sucking his thumb.

They could hear Weston outside of the tent as he berated the guards who had the night watch. His voice was bellowing and tense, intermingled with other male voices as the entire encampment went in search of the diabolical murderer who had killed Lady Elizabeth de Royans and a female servant during the night.

The truth was that Weston already knew who had committed the unspeakable crime. Billingham's encampment was in a lockdown and le Bec had arrived to discuss the issue. Amalie could hear her husband shouting at him.

So she lay there and cried, so very devastated at the death of Lady Elizabeth. It didn't seem real. But a panicked guard had awoken them before dawn with a shocking tale of blood and Weston had bolted from their bed to see what the trouble was. He had found his mother dead of a stab wound to her belly and Esma dead of a broken neck. Shocked, sickened, he had roused the entire camp, including his brother, who had rushed to the tent in horror. As Weston stood in the doorway of the small tent, fighting off the urge to vomit, Sutton had taken his mother in his arms and wept.

He was still there, holding his dead mother, praying over her body. Weston had returned to Amalie to tell her what had happened and she had immediately burst into painful tears. Since Weston was Constable of North Yorkshire and the Northern Dales, he was the law in situations such as this but he was having great difficulty composing his thoughts due to the personal nature of the circumstance. Therefore, several field marshals had gathered, as well as the mayor of Keighley and several other ranking knights, to help Weston deal with the situation.

Amalie could hear Weston's agitated voice over the buzz of other male voices outside the tent. He was distraught and struggling to keep himself under control. As Amalie lay there and wept, she began to think that perhaps she was being selfish in her reaction.

Although she had grown to love Lady Elizabeth, the woman was Weston's mother and, by that right, he had the priority to grieve. She thought perhaps she would be of more help to him if she calmed down and tried to comfort the man in his hour of need. This was not the time for her to think only of herself.

So she wiped her tears and got out of bed, fighting off her morning nausea as she used some cold water from the night before and a cake of rose-scented soap to quickly wash her face and body. It was very cold but she struggled through it, drying off quickly and donning a soft white shift and a delicate yellow surcoat. With her hair brushed and braided, hanging long over her right shoulder, she quickly cleaned up the children and made sure they were dressed for the day. She bit back tears when she thought of Esma's passing and how they would all miss her. She was like one of the family. She knew Neilie would be devastated.

Peeking her head from the main tent, she took stock of the scene outside. She could see Weston over by the smaller tent where his mother and Esma were, surrounded by several men including le Bec. She also saw John and Heath, standing a few feet from her husband, their young faces grave. She didn't see Sutton at all. There were at least six soldiers surrounding the main tent and she sent one of them for Heath.

The redheaded knight came to her quickly and she asked him to remain with the children while she attended Weston. Heath entered the tent and Amalie could hear her son squeal happily as he caught sight of the knight. It made her smile, a warm moment in a morning that had been filled with horror. With her skirts swishing softly, she made her way across the grass towards her husband.

Weston was speaking with the group, who turned their attention to Amalie as she approached. Weston, seeing that his audience's attention was diverted, turned to see his wife also. She smiled at him and the careful control he had labored with all morning threatened to come apart. All he wanted to do was collapse in her arms but he steeled himself, reaching out to her as she came upon him. She took his hand tightly and he pulled her up against him, a big arm around her shoulders.

"If you have not yet met my wife, this is the Lady Amalie de Royans," Weston introduced her, then continued on what he had been saying when she had distracted them. "As I was saying, there is no doubt who committed these atrocious acts. You all heard him threaten me and my wife yesterday. It is my intention to take him into custody and have him executed for the murder of my mother. Le Bec himself said that Sorrell left the encampment last night, telling the guards on watch that he was going into town. Instead of doing as he said, he snuck into my encampment and murdered my mother."

Le Bec was standing next to Weston, his big arms folded across his chest as he listened carefully. "And you heard nothing, West?"

Weston shook his head. "Not a sound. Certainly if I had, the situation would be different."

Le Bec wriggled his dark eyebrows. "You have every right to seek justice if what you suspect is true. I am very sorry for you and your family for this tragedy."

"Spare me your sympathies. Give me Sorrell."

He sounded harsh, brutal. Amalie put a hand on his arm to ease him.

"West," she admonished softly, looking to le Bec. "We are thankful for your support, my lord. But knowing the situation as you do, perhaps it would be best to deliver Sorrell to my husband."

Le Bec looked at the beautiful blond woman with the green eyes. "We cannot locate Sorrell this morning, my lady. My men are scouring the area as we speak. When we find him, I intend to interrogate him myself."

Weston's jaw began to tick. "You will turn him over to me, Richmond. It is my right."

Le Bec was trying to stay as neutral, and supportive, as possible. "I have a duty to my men as well as to you, West," he replied steadily. "Let me interrogate Sorrell and see if I can discover the truth of his whereabouts last night. It might not have been him at all. At least give the man a chance to explain himself before you gut him."

Weston exploded. "Give the man his *due*?" his control was vanished as he faced off against le Bec, a substantially taller man. "Did Sorrell give my wife her due when he beat her senseless and raped her to the point of death? Did he give her any consideration at all when he broke her wrist, beat her servants and announced to all who would listen that he had violated Robert de Vere's sister?" He was in le Bec's face, squaring off against him and as angry as anyone had ever seen him. "John Sorrell is the vilest sort of creature that slithers across this earth, a danger to all good men and women in England. I have no doubt he skulked into my camp last night and murdered my mother in her sleep. There would be no one else with the motive or the means to do it. And you ask me to give this beast of a man his due? I will slit his throat before I give him any due consideration and I will kill anyone who stands in the way of my retribution, including you."

Le Bec hadn't moved even though Weston was shouting at him, inches from his face. He remained calm and steadfast, although Weston's words had an impact on him. He swallowed, fighting the sense of sorrow that swept him. He couldn't even look at Lady de Royans.

"All I knew is that you were seeking vengeance because Sorrell attacked your wife," he whispered. "You did not tell me he beat and raped her."

"He did," Weston hissed. "He beat her so badly that she tried to kill herself from the shame of his attack. And you want to give this man his due? He deserves only death and I shall be happy to painfully and resolutely deliver it."

Le Bec couldn't help the anguish in his expression. Now, everything made much more sense. Weston was so wound up that his breathing was coming in harsh, terrible pants and his big body was coiled, prepared to strike out at any moment. He could feel Amalie pulling at him, softly urging him away from le Bec, a man who was his friend and only trying to help.

Weston was beyond rational thought at the moment; he couldn't think for himself. He allowed his wife to pull him back, leading him away from the group of men.

They ended up back in the main tent and Weston made it just inside the flap before throwing his arms around Amalie and collapsing to his knees. She remained on her feet in spite of his substantial burden, her arms wrapped around his head and neck as he buried his face in her belly. The sobs came.

They were heavy and painful. Weston sobbed deeply into his wife's stomach, seeking comfort and absolution and salvation as he held on tightly to her. His grief was being expended and Amalie understood that; she held him tightly, rocking him gently in her arms as he wept. The most powerful man in Northern England was having the weakest moment of his life and she was his rock, his sole source of strength in his desolate darkness.

Amalie stroked his blond head with one hand, feeling his pain to her very bones. Glancing up, she noticed that Heath and the children were over in a corner of the tent, playing with the toys that Sutton had purchased. All three of them looked shocked at what they were witnessing, especially Heath. He had known Weston for years and had never known the man to be anything but completely in control. He looked at Amalie and their eyes met.

"Wine," she whispered to him. "Please, Heath."

The knight bolted from the tent. Meanwhile, Aubria and Colton were watching their father curiously, edging their way over to him as he made strange noises against their mother. Colton got the closest, holding up his little sword against his father's heaving shoulder.

"Surd, Dada?" he said in that hopeful tone that children often use.

"You have it."

Weston heard his little son, turning his head so he could look at the boy. There were tears all over his face, soaking Amalie's surcoat. Colton pushed the sword on his father.

"You have it, Dada," he insisted.

Weston couldn't help but smile at his son, so moved by the little boy who sensed something terrible and was doing what he could to help his father. He was giving him his most prized possession, a gesture that was not lost on Weston. His screaming, spoiled son had a heart and soul, and he was deeply touched.

"Thank you, lad," he said, sniffling. "But you can keep your sword."

Colton stared at him with his big blue eyes, trying to figure out what had his father so upset. Weston put his hand on the boys head and pulled him to his lips for a kiss, but Colton didn't want a kiss. He whined and pulled away, his attention returning to his little sword as he walked away. When he wandered off, Aubria took his place.

"Dada," she said seriously. "We should get the goats. They would make you feel better."

Weston looked into her beautiful little face, a mirror image of her mother, and the tears started to come again. He turned away from her, laying his head on Amalie's belly once more. Amalie stroked his head, his shoulders, soothingly, feeling him tense again.

"What is it, sweetheart?" she whispered.

His eyes were closed, tears streaming down his cheeks. "She is my child," he hissed. "She has always been my child. She is mine."

Amalie sensed what his issue was. She hugged him tightly. "She is absolutely your child," she kissed the top of his head. "There is no part of her that is not yours."

"That foul bastard did not father her. Tell me that is true."

"It is true," Amalie could feel tears sting her eyes. "She is your daughter, body and soul. You are her father."

Without looking, he reached out an enormous hand and grasped Aubria by the arm, pulling her into an embrace against both parents.

Aubria permitted her parents to wrap her up in their arms, although they were both weeping and she didn't know why. The poppet in her hand was more interesting to her as her father kissed her cheek and hugged her gently.

Weston's tears quieted eventually as Amalie cuddled both him and Aubria, her gentle touch soothing his grief-stricken heart. Just as he was calming sufficiently, Sutton entered the tent. His tunic was stained with his mother's blood from where he had held her since early morning, his face pale and his eyes red-rimmed.

One look at his brother on his knees, wrapped up in Amalie's arms, and he knew what had happened. He had heard the shouting while he had been huddled with his mother's body and knew that Weston had lost control. Before he could speak, Colton let out a yell and ran to him, and he picked the boy up, finding comfort with a two year old banging on him with a toy sword. Weston caught sight of his brother and pulled himself away from Amalie's comforting embrace, kissing her hands as he rose stiffly to his feet.

"Where is Mother?" He turned to his brother.

Sutton was trying not to get hit in the head with the sword. "She is still in the tent," he replied. "I summoned a priest."

Weston nodded faintly, feeling emotionally drained. "I will have her prepared for transport back to Netherghyll," he said, running a hand through his cropped blond hair. "There are people I can hire to do that."

"I will do it," Amalie said, struggling against her tears for her husband's sake. "I do not want unfamiliar hands touching her. She should only be touched by those who love her."

Weston and Sutton looked at her. Sutton was less discreet about wiping his tears away. "Thank you, Ammy," Sutton whispered. "She would appreciate that."

Amalie smiled bravely, but it was difficult as both Weston and Sutton wiped at their eyes. She could see how grief stricken they were, powerful knights reduced to weeping little boys at their mother's passing. She wanted to give them what comfort she could.

"Listen to me, both of you," she said softly, moving to Sutton and taking one of his big hands in her own. "Your mother was a lovely woman who loved you both very much. You were extremely lucky to have her in your life. I know this well because my own mother, though alive, has never paid any notice to her only daughter. Elizabeth, in the short time I knew her, was far more of a mother to me than mine ever was. Instead of grieving your loss, which cannot be undone, you must rejoice in the mother you knew and honor her memory. You must rejoice even more because she is now with Heston, someone she loved more than anything else on this earth. Do not grieve for her passing, for she is happy now. She is with her husband."

Sutton kissed her hand and let it go. "She was deeply grieved by his passing," he said softly. "It took something out of her when my father died."

Weston looked curiously at him. "Your father?"

Sutton met his gaze. "Heston was my father. He was yours, also."

Weston's brow furrowed. "How did you know?"

Sutton lifted an eyebrow. "He told me," he replied. "Also, I look just like him. Close resemblance such as that cannot be coincidence."

Weston smiled faintly. "You surprise me, little brother. You are smarter than you look."

"You already knew?"

"I did, but only recently. Mother told me."

"She was very grateful that you two had reconciled."

Weston sighed. "I thank God that I came to my senses when I did."

Sutton nodded, perhaps in reflection, before turning to Amalie. "As for you, my lady, 'tis wise words you speak." He leaned over and kissed her on the forehead. "I shall remember them. Thank you."

Amalie smiled at him, seeing that both men were at least regaining some of their composure and thankful for it. Heath entered the tent at that moment, carrying a big wooden pitcher and several cups.

As he handed the cups over to Weston and Sutton and poured them a measure of wine, Amalie thought the best thing for everyone would be to focus on other things to help them forget their grief, at least for the moment. Especially Weston; he seemed particularly fragile. She watched him down two full cups of wine in short order.

"We have a busy day ahead of us," she said to him. "West, I will need to go into the village and…"

He put up a hand and cut her off. "You are not going anywhere with Sorrell running loose," he informed her. "You and the children will remain by my side every second until he is found."

She nodded patiently. "I understand," she said. "But in order to prepare your mother's body, I will need a few things."

"And you shall have them," he told her. "But not now. I would wait until Sorrell is located first."

Amalie didn't have an argument to that. She simply shrugged and looked to her daughter, who was now standing next to her mother as she played with her poppet. She touched the silky blond head as Sutton, with Colton still in his arms, spoke.

"I hate to bring this up," he said as he looked at his brother, "but you are scheduled for a second round match later this morning. Shall I cancel it?"

"Nay," Amalie said firmly, looking between her husband and brother-in-law. "There is no need. Baron Cononley will compete as scheduled and all will know that not even personal tragedy can prevent my husband from carrying on as he must."

Weston sighed. "I would rather…"

She cut him off. "West, we came to this tournament so that the people of North Yorkshire could see what the new baron is made of. You will win this tournament in tribute to your mother's memory and show everyone your strength of character. Let them see the man I know; let them see and be awed. It is what your mother would want."

Weston gazed into her green eyes, loving the woman so much that he couldn't express it adequately. She was so wise and beautiful. After a moment's hesitation, he reluctantly nodded.

"As you wish," he whispered. "I will compete. But I wanted my mother to witness my victory and be proud of me."

Amalie smiled and went to him, her hands to his rough cheek. "She *was* proud of you," she murmured, kissing his cheek. "You have already made her very proud."

He looked at her, the tears threatening, but he fought them. Clearing his throat loudly, he swallowed the lump in his throat and took a deep, cleansing breath. Leaning down, he kissed her soft lips.

"I would have you remain in the tent for your own safety," he told her. "I will leave Heath and John with you and I'll put another half-dozen soldiers on the perimeter of the tent. Sutton and I must conduct some business now but I will return for you when it is time to take the field."

Amalie nodded, waving him away. "We shall be ready."

With a lingering look to his wife and children, Weston quit the tent with his brother in tow. Sutton handed Colton over to his mother and caught up to his brother outside.

"What will we do now?" he asked Weston.

Weston's gaze was lingering on the group of marshals and knights that were still loitering over by his mother's tent.

"Find Sorrell," he growled. "Find the man and make him pay."

CHAPTER TWENTY-FOUR

B Y EARLY AFTERNOON, Sorrell had still not been located and everyone was coming to think that he had simply fled the town.

Weston should have been satisfied but he was not. He wanted the man in his hands and vowed with every breath he took that he would find him even if it took the rest of his life. How one man, who had no relation or particular association with Weston, could have so badly damaged his life was beyond comprehension. But Sorrell had affected Weston's life in more ways than he could comprehend and Weston wouldn't be satisfied until the man was dead and buried.

Weston was slated to compete in the first round after the nooning hour. He drew Simon Wellesbourne as his competition, a big, blond knight who neatly did away with his opponent yesterday morning after the big brawl. As Weston suited up and prepared for his match, Wellesbourne was doing the same on the east side of the arena.

What Wellesbourne didn't know was that Sorrell was watching him. The man had been hiding in plain sight since his murder spree the night before, losing his armor and weapons in favor of peasant clothing he had stolen off a man he had killed. With dirt smeared on his face and stinking clothes on his body, he had blended in with the crowd of visitors, even when de Royans and Billingham knights turned the town inside-out in their search for him. Sorrell had lain in the gutter, pretending he was drunk, and no one had bothered him. But as the situation began to calm and it was apparent that the joust bouts, including de Royans', were to proceed as normal, Sorrell began to formulate his plan.

By the reaction of Lady Elizabeth de Royans' murder, Sorrell knew that he had struck at the heart of Weston de Royans. He hadn't killed the de Vere bitch but he had gotten very close. He knew that he would never be able to get close to Lady Amalie now that everyone was up in arms; undoubtedly she was well guarded. It would be suicide to try to get near her. With that realization, Sorrell turned his focus to Weston himself.

The man was competing in the first round of the afternoon against Simon Wellesbourne. Sorrell had heard the announcement from the field marshals. With security presence heavy in and around the arena, especially when the Lady Amalie de Royans arrived, Sorrell knew he would have to be very clever. He knew he couldn't simply walk up to de Royans and spear him. But watching Wellesbourne dress for the match over by the edge of the arena gave him an idea.

Sorrell made his way to the eastern edge of the arena, lurking in the shadows of a smithy shack as he watched Wellesbourne put himself together. He knew he had to get Wellesbourne away from his men somehow, and get him alone, but he wasn't quite sure how to accomplish that. Wracking his brain, he was given a gift from the gods when Wellesbourne suddenly broke away from his men and headed to the privy.

Sorrell thanked his good fortune and followed. Caught off guard with a dagger to the back, Simon Wellesbourne's body would be found in the privy pit the next day.

Dressed in Wellesbourne's armor, the helm of which was a bit too big but not enough to make a difference, Sorrell assumed the man's place. With the visor of the helm lowered, Wellesbourne's men unfortunately never knew the difference.

CB

AMALIE SAT IN the lists with her children, Heath and John, watching her husband at the west end of the field take up his station in preparation for making his first pass.

The day was breezy and sunny, perfect game weather, and the lists were filled to capacity with eager fans. The chatter and excitement was at a dull roar as people milled into the arena and found their seats before the games began.

Heath and John had given up their spot in the second round of the joust because Weston did not want to leave his wife without protection, so they sat in the lists with her and eyed the pretty women surrounding them.

Paget eventually joined Amalie even though her father had not wanted her to associate with the de Royans family. Everyone knew a murderer was out for de Royans' blood and Lord Clifford, understandably, did not want his daughter in danger.

Paget was stubborn, however, and joined Amalie anyway. The two of them sat together with the children, surrounded by both de Royans and Clifford knights, and discussing trivial things. Amalie was grateful for the company, a spot of brightness in an otherwise horrendous day.

When Weston moved forward astride his charger to take his position, the crowd went wild and Amalie smiled at the reaction. It made her very proud to hear the reaction for her husband and even though Lady Elizabeth's absence was sorely felt, she knew that Elizabeth would have been overwhelming proud, too. Weston de Royans, the sixth Baron Cononley, was proudly carrying on the family tradition.

Since Weston's previous bout had gone so smoothly, Amalie wasn't feeling any anxiety as the two competitors prepared for their first run. She was looking forward to her husband's victory. But she was distracted from the approaching charge by Aubria, who wasn't particularly interested in watching her father joust. She wanted to go find the man with the monkey. As the marshals took the field and prepared to start the bout, Amalie found herself dealing with a grumpy daughter.

As she pulled her whining daughter onto her lap, the field marshals dropped the flag and the chargers surged forward. Amalie was trying to watch the pass and deal with her daughter at the same time, but Aubria dropped her poppet and began crying. As Amalie bent down to pick up the doll, the crowd suddenly gasped and groaned and a loud smacking sound filled the air.

Amalie's head popped up, startled, but everyone had jumped to their feet so she couldn't see anything. Frightened, she stood up to try and get a better view but all she could see were clouds of dust and debris on the arena floor. She grabbed Heath's arm.

"What happened?" she demanded.

Heath was furious. "Wellesbourne dropped his lance in front of Weston's head," he motioned with his arm across his neck. "'Tis an illegal move meant to break a man's neck. Weston had no choice but to duck out of the way, but he managed to break his lance on Wellesbourne's shield."

Amalie's eyes were wide with shock as she watched her husband circle around the field to resume his starting position for the next round.

"If it is illegal, will the field marshals disqualify him?" she asked.

Heath nodded, watching Wellesbourne and two of the marshals over by the east end. "They should," he replied. "Unless Wellesbourne insists it was an accident, which it was not. It was a deliberate move."

Amalie glanced at Heath, pondering his words, before returning her attention to the field where Wellesbourne was in deep discussion with the marshals. She sighed, picking up Colton when the boy tugged on her and whined.

"Why would he do such a thing?" she wondered aloud.

Heath shook his head, regaining his seat because everyone else was. "I do not know," he said. "Wellesbourne is a man of character. I would not expect dirty tricks from him."

Amalie didn't like the sound of that at all but she regained her seat, holding Colton on her lap. She and Paget exchanged nervous glances before she looked to the west end of the field where Weston and Sutton were in conversation. She could see her husband's helmed head nodding now and again. Paget grasped her arm gently.

"I am sure it was an accident," she said softly. "This pass will be much better."

Amalie smiled weakly. "I hope so," she said, looking at the woman. "Were you able to see Sutton's bout yesterday after the chaos died down?"

Paget grinned, flushing brightly. "I was," she sighed. "He was magnificent."

Amalie's smile grew and she squeezed Paget's hand. "Aye, he is."

Paget's smile faded as she looked off to the west where Sutton was helping Weston with his joust lance. "I… I do not know what to say to him about his mother," she said. "I hardly know him and I do not want him to think me rude or bold by speaking out of turn on a sensitive subject."

Amalie squeezed Paget's hand again. "He would not think you rude or bold to offer your sympathies," she said. "He loved his mother a great deal and will miss her. It would do him good to hear of your concern. It would give him comfort."

Paget's timid smile returned and she nodded in agreement. The crowd roared, distracting them, and they both turned to see that the field marshal had tossed the flag to start the second pass.

Amalie realized that Wellesbourne must have had a good reason for the illegal move, as the second pass had commenced and he had not been disqualified. She watched with apprehension as the chargers drew near one another, the knights leveling their lances along the guide that was built to keep the horses from running in to each other.

Just as they came within striking range, Wellesbourne suddenly lifted his lance. As the crowd watched in horror, he waited until Weston charged past him before swinging the lance backwards with all his might and catching Weston on the back of the head. It all happened so fast that no one had time to react. Unprepared, Weston was knocked off his charger and face first into the dirt of the arena.

The crowd was on its feet at the brutal move. Horrified, Amalie watched as Wellesbourne swiftly swung his charger around and returned to Weston as the man was pushing himself to his knees. Dismounting his charger, Wellesbourne unsheathed the broadsword on his saddle and removed a nasty-looking mace. He was on Weston before the man could get to his feet.

The crowd began screaming and Weston, dazed but not senseless, realized he was in trouble. He could hear Wellesbourne behind him and he rolled to the right, out of the range of the broadsword that crashed down with a powerful stroke on the exact spot he had been laying.

Lashing out a big boot, Weston clipped Wellesbourne in the back of the leg and the man stumbled to his knees, giving Weston time to regain his feet. Something evil and ugly was brewing, and Weston had no idea what was going on.

"Wellesbourne," he barked, breathing heavily. "Have you lost your mind? What goes on?"

With a growl, Wellesbourne swiped his broadsword at Weston, catching the man in the torso with the tip. Weston was heavily padded and armored so the sword didn't do any damage, but the message was clear. Simon Wellesbourne was out for blood.

Turning on his heel, Weston moved as fast as he could for his charger, now lingering several feet away by the field guide. Unsheathing his broadsword and pulling forth his deadly flail, a brutal-looking weapon that was essentially a metal pole with a chain and a spiked ball at the end of the chain, he met Wellesbourne halfway across the arena and delivered a heavy blow that sent Wellesbourne reeling.

In the stands, Amalie was beside herself with panic. She grabbed Heath's arm.

"What is going on?" she demanded. "Why are they fighting like that?"

Heath looked at John and the two of them exchanged concerned glances. They were under orders not to leave Lady de Royans but, clearly, what was happening on the field was not normal. There was something deadly occurring and a glance to the west side of the field showed Sutton moving onto the arena floor.

Sutton, too, sensed something dastardly and, after what had happened to their mother, everything and everyone was suspect. But Sutton refrained from moving any further, watching and waiting like the rest of the crowd. The battle that ensued was truly something to behold.

Weston and Wellesbourne went after each other with a vengeance. It was a brutal battle from the outset; with broadswords in one hand and military weapons in the other, they chopped at, sliced at and tripped each other for several long minutes. Wellesbourne was taking a beating at the hands of Weston, who was clearly superior but taking a fair beating himself. The field marshals tried to intervene but were driven back by Wellesbourne's mace. He wasn't going to let anyone get near Weston or break up the fight. He was mad with bloodlust.

Amalie watched all of it, wide-eyed with terror, until she couldn't take anymore. Weston was in deep trouble before her eyes and she wasn't going to stand back like the rest of them and allow him to be killed. She started to bolt for the field but Heath grabbed her before she could get away. She struggled against him violently.

"Let me go," she snarled. "Let me go or I will kill you!"

Heath held her fast, his big arms wrapped around her body. "Nay, Lady de Royans," he hissed in her ear. "If you go out there, you will distract your husband and enable his opponent to kill him. You must not distract him in any way; no screaming, no crying. Be still and trust him. He needs all of his concentration if he is going to survive this."

Amalie's struggles came to a halt. Heath made perfect sense. So she watched with increasing horror as Weston managed to wrap the chain of his mace around Wellesbourne's leg, giving a good yank and sending the man to his back. As Weston approached with the intention of knocking his opponent unconscious, Wellesbourne suddenly lifted his broadsword and gored Weston in the shoulder.

Amalie screamed and covered her eyes. In fact, the entire crowd screamed in terror as Weston staggered back with an enormous broadsword sticking out of his upper chest. Sutton, without any armor whatsoever, bolted in his brother's direction but Wellesbourne was on his feet, swinging his mace at Sutton's unprotected head.

Sutton provided enough of a distraction that he hoped it would buy his brother time to get away. But instead, Weston fell to his knees, eventually collapsing onto his left side. As Sutton watched in horror, distracted at his brother's collapse, Wellesbourne managed to clip him on the neck with his mace and Sutton was knocked to the ground.

John bolted over the edge of the lists, running for Weston as fast as he could. Amalie was screaming, the children were screaming, as Paget and Heath tried to shield them from what was happening. It was a painful, chaotic scene as John nearly reached Weston, only to be chased off by Wellesbourne. The man picked up Weston's flail where it had fallen onto the ground and swung it at John. Without a shield or a weapon of his own, John was at a disadvantage as he tried to get to Weston. Wellesbourne eventually clipped him on his left shoulder and the flail tore through mail and flesh. John was forced to fall back, bleeding heavily from a nasty wound.

Wellesbourne was rabid with bloodlust, turning for his victim lying in the dirt a few feet away. Weston lay still, the broadsword protruding out of his left shoulder, as Wellesbourne came upon him. The crowd was screaming and other knights were starting to make their way onto the field, in particular, Richmond le Bec.

Richmond was already heading over towards Wellesbourne with a contingent of Billingham knights, instructing the men to spread out and attack Wellesbourne from all sides. Several Clifford knights had also spilled out onto the field, two of them going for Sutton, who was picking himself up out of the dirt with a gushing neck wound.

Wellesbourne, however, would not delay. He would not let them reach Weston in time. He was going to kill the man where he lay and do it gladly. As the crowd roared to titanic proportions, Wellesbourne approach the wounded Weston. He had his mace lifted high, preparing to bash Weston's brains in. Amalie, seeing all of this from her vantage point in the lists in spite of Heath's efforts to shield her, shoved the redheaded knight back by the throat and leaped over the side of the lists.

Amalie hit the ground running. There were a dozen knights out on the field, but no one was making any attempt to help her husband. They were all standing around waiting for him to die. But not Amalie; she couldn't watch her husband's death, not while there was breath left in her body. She was going to save the man or die trying. To hell with staying quiet and inactive; the time had come to act. She would save the man who had once saved her. She would save the man she loved.

She bolted past le Bec, who made a swipe to grab her and barely missed. She ran right into the back of Wellesbourne, who was barely bumped by her insignificant weight. He turned around, furious, to find Amalie throwing fists at him. Reaching out, he grabbed her by the throat.

"You little bitch," he seethed. "You started all of this, you whore. I should have killed you the night I took your innocence but my lust had the better of me. I wanted you again and again, so I allowed you to live. It was my mistake. But I will not make the same mistake now."

Amalie knew that voice; God help her, she knew it all too well. It was the same dark, evil voice that had whispered lewd words to her on the worst night of her life and the hand that held her by the neck had once beaten her senseless. It wasn't Wellesbourne who fought her husband; it was Sorrell.

Amalie opened her mouth and tried to scream but no words would come forth; he was holding her too tightly. His fingers tightened. As the world began to darken, something odd happened.

Sorrell jerked as if he had been struck. His grip on Amalie loosened and he pitched forward, face first. Amalie screamed as she started to fall with him but le Bec grabbed her, pulling her free of the collapsing body. Startled, she looked down to see Sorrell lying in the dirt with a broadsword sticking out of his back. A pair of boots stood at Sorrell's feet and Amalie looked up, fixing on the figure, hardly believing her eyes.

Weston was gazing down at Sorrell's fallen body. He looked pale and in pain, but the big broadsword was no longer sticking out of his left shoulder – it was on the ground and Weston's right hand was pressed over the wound, attempting to stanch the blood flow.

The weapon jutting from Sorrell's back bore the proud insignia of the House of de Royans and Weston kicked the helm from Sorrell's head to get a good look at the man he had just killed. He had come to suspect early in the battle that it was not Wellesbourne he was fighting and made every effort to ensure that Sorrell would pay for his crimes. Now, he finally had.

He stared at the man, absorbing the view, telling himself that it was finally over. He had done what he had set out to do. But he caught a glimpse of his wife out of the corner of his eye and it was all of the enticement he needed to go to her, capturing her against his bloody armor and holding her more tightly than he had ever held her in his life. Amalie threw her arms around his neck and squeezed.

"Are you all right, my angel?" he asked softly, his voice quivering. "Let me see your neck. Let me see what he did to you."

She waved him off, rubbing at her neck. "I am well enough." She was overwhelmed with all that had happened, struggling against the frightened tears. "What happened to Wellesbourne? How did Sorrell come by his armor?"

Weston was weak with blood loss but he held on to his wife as if afraid she were going to slip away. "I do not know," he said grimly, looking up to see Richmond standing a few feet away. "We must search for Wellesbourne."

Le Bec came upon the shaken and wounded pair, and began to wave his men over to begin the cleanup process.

"We will," he replied. "Let us take you back to your encampment and send for a physic. You look as if you need one."

Weston nodded wearily. "Perhaps," was all he would say about needing assistance. "But I am more concerned with my wife. I would have her examined first."

Amalie shook her head vehemently. "Nay," she insisted. "You must be tended immediately. He stuck a sword in you. I thought he had killed you."

She was starting to tear up and Weston hugged her close, kissing her forehead. "Nay, my angel," he whispered. "He could not kill me. But I will admit that it is a decent wound."

He sounded so casual about it, mostly to comfort Amalie so she wouldn't know the wound was worse than he let on. Le Bec watched Lady de Royans as she struggled to compose herself before fixing Weston in the eyes.

"West, I must apologize for this," he said. "I feel as if it is my fault. Had I acted with more speed against Sorrell, perhaps none of this would have happened."

Weston smiled weakly. "It was not your fault," he assured him. "I do not blame you. I am glad you came to my aid. I was starting to wonder if anyone would."

Le Bec wriggled his eyebrows. "We tried," he said. "I would not have let Sorrell bring the mace down upon you; I was prepared to gut him with my sword when your wife tackled him. Then I had to worry about her safety as well, which rather complicated things."

Weston looked at Amalie, exhausted and pale, smeared with his blood. It was the most beautiful sight he had ever seen.

"She was enough of a distraction that I was able to kill him myself," he said quietly, realizing he didn't particularly want to dwell on the event any longer. He smiled at his wife. "You are a very brave woman, Lady de Royans. I am proud of you."

Amalie returned his smile weakly, feeling drained now that the entire event was over. She had been riding on such a terrified high that the cessation of the situation and the fact that her husband was not dead had her rather muddled.

She looked down at Sorrell, face down in the dirt as blood pooled beneath him. It seemed surreal that the man was finally dead, the man who had changed the course of her life on that dark and terrible night. Weston watched her face as she stared at the body.

"What are you thinking, Ammy?" he asked softly.

Her big green eyes were riveted to the corpse. "I am thinking of that night so long ago when I thought he had ruined my life." She looked up at Weston. "But in the same breath, had he not come to Hedingham, I would have never met you. He set off the chain of events that brought you into my life, West, and… and I do not know what I am thinking, only that I thank God for you and every blessed day we share together."

He put his big hand on her head, pulling her towards him until their foreheads touched. It was a sweet, poignant moment as they took comfort in one another. Before Weston could reply, they could hear familiar screaming and they both looked over to see Heath standing at the base of the lists with Paget handing Colton down to him. Heath carefully set Colton onto the ground and as he reached up for Aubria, Colton took off towards his parents.

Weston watched the boy run to them, watching as Amalie reached down to pick the child up. Aubria wasn't far behind, intercepted by her Uncle Sutton who was holding a big bandage against his bloodied neck. It wasn't a bad injury but still a bloody gash, and he was moving well enough that he could take Aubria's hand. Sutton didn't look completely worse for the wear.

"Are you well?" he asked Weston.

Weston nodded wearily. "I will be," he replied. "And you? I did not see you fall."

"You were already on the ground," Sutton told him. "I tried to reach you but, without my armor, it was difficult."

Weston smiled in understanding. "You and my wife make a brave pair, running to my aid in the face of a madman."

"We would die for you, West."

"You almost did."

Sutton grinned, holding on to his neck and letting go of Aubria's hand so she could go to her parents. He happened to glance back at the lists to notice that Heath was helping Paget down to the arena floor. Scowling dramatically, he began looking around frantically.

"Where is that bloody mace?" he demanded.

Weston looked at his brother. "Why do you need it?"

Sutton looked stricken, his blue eyes blazing. "I am going to murder de Lara if he does not have the sense to stay away from Lady Paget." He suddenly spied the mace on the ground and picked it up, shaking it at Heath as the man approached with Paget beside him. "You and I have some business to attend to, de Lara. I told you what would happen if you went near her again."

Heath knew what he meant. He threw up his hands as if to surrender but that wasn't good enough. Sutton, bandaged neck and all, took off running after Heath and the redheaded knight bolted.

Weston and Amalie laughed heartily as Heath leaped over the fence on the east end of the arena and kept going. Sutton, not quite up to par with the neck injury, wasn't able to leap the fence but he did manage to bust through the gate. They could hear Sutton shouting at Heath even at a distance.

By that time, most of the knights in the arena were laughing. Amalie, giggling, fell against her husband, so incredibly grateful for the man's life. The day had brought the pinnacles of both despair and joy, but they had survived and were stronger for it. Amalie had said it best when she had said, *I thank God for you and every blessed day we share together*. Weston did, too.

Torston and Kingston de Royans were born in June of the following year, big healthy boys with their father's good looks. They were three months old when they attended the wedding of their Uncle Sutton to the Lady Paget Clifford, and two years old when they were joined by a sister, Elizabeth, and the first of six cousins when Paget gave birth to Kirkton Clifford de Royans.

Life went on, more children were born, and the love that Weston and Amalie held for each other only deepened. Like a fine wine, it aged beautifully. Amalie sometimes reflected on those days when she had first met Weston and of her repeated attempts to end her life.

Like a guardian angel, Weston never left her side, loving her even when she didn't love herself. It didn't matter to him that to the lady was born a bastard, a child not of his loins. All that mattered to Weston was that he loved Amalie with a passion only dreamed of.

Amalie thought her life had ended on that snowy night all of those years ago. Never had she imagined that the moment Weston de Royans rescued her from the frozen lake was the exact moment she had begun to live.

C3 THE END 80

The House of de Royans includes the novel Unending Love. Weston's descendant, Brighton de Royans, is the antagonist in Unending Love.

Unending Love

Richmond le Bec, the hero from Great Protector, makes his appearance in To the Lady Born.

Great Protector

For more information on other series and family groups, as well as a list of all of Kathryn's novels, please visit her website at www.kathrynleveque. com.

ABOUT KATHRYN LE VEQUE

Medieval Just Got Real.

KATHRYN LE VEQUE is a USA TODAY Bestselling author, an Amazon All-Star author, and a #1 bestselling, award-winning, multi-published author in Medieval Historical Romance and Historical Fiction. She has been featured in the NEW YORK TIMES and on USA TODAY's HEA blog. In March 2015, Kathryn was the featured cover story for the March issue of InD'Tale Magazine, the premier Indie author magazine. She was also a quadruple nominee (a record!) for the prestigious RONE awards for 2015.

Kathryn's Medieval Romance novels have been called 'detailed', 'highly romantic', and 'character-rich'. She crafts great adventures of love, battles, passion, and romance in the High Middle Ages. More than that, she writes for both women AND men – an unusual crossover for a romance author – and Kathryn has many male readers who enjoy her stories because of the male perspective, the action, and the adventure.

On October 29, 2015, Amazon launched Kathryn's Kindle Worlds Fan Fiction site WORLD OF DE WOLFE PACK. Please visit Kindle Worlds for Kathryn Le Veque's World of de Wolfe Pack and find many action-packed adventures written by some of the top authors in their genre using Kathryn's characters from the de Wolfe Pack series. As Kindle World's FIRST Historical Romance fan fiction world, Kathryn Le Veque's World of de Wolfe Pack will contain all of the great story-telling you have come to expect.

Kathryn loves to hear from her readers. Please find Kathryn on Facebook at Kathryn Le Veque, Author, or join her on Twitter @kathrynleveque, and don't forget to visit her website and sign up for her blog at www.kathrynleveque.com.

81280841R00172

Made in the USA
Columbia, SC
19 November 2017